Praise for the Novels of the Dresden Files

"One of the most enjoyable marriages of the fantasy and mystery genres on the shelves." —*Cinescape*

"What's not to like about this series? . . . It takes the best elements of urban fantasy, mixes it with some good old-fashioned noir mystery, tosses in a dash of romance and a lot of high-octane action, shakes, stirs, and serves."
—SF Site

"An invariably entertaining series." —*Locus*

"Harry is as fine and upstanding and dangerous and wounded as any old-time noir detective. . . . Jim Butcher has done nicely in this series, developing and coloring snapshots of Harry Dresden's character."
—*The San Diego Union-Tribune*

"Entertaining. . . . Butcher keeps the writing jocular and lively with generous sprinklings of pop-culture references."
—*The Kansas City Star*

"Dresden investigates with his trademark sardonic flair. Both fans and newcomers will get into the fast-paced action." —*Publishers Weekly*

"Think *Buffy the Vampire Slayer* starring Philip Marlowe . . . a fast and furious adventure with winking nods to Bugs Bunny and John Carpenter."
—*Entertainment Weekly*

continued . . .

"Fans of Laurell K. Hamilton and Tanya Huff will love this series." —*Midwest Book Review*

"Once again, Butcher's urban fantasy features excellent, irreverent humor, the return of favorite characters, and new challenges from unexpected foes . . . a great book to plunge newbies into the dark, magical side of Chicago." —*Library Journal*

"Intricate yet accessible plotting. . . . Butcher smoothly manages a sizable cast of allies and adversaries, doles out needed backstory with crisp efficiency, and sustains just the right balance of hairbreadth tension and comic relief. Encounters with a series of increasingly dangerous 'Billy Goats Gruff' unfold with particular cleverness, and key developments involving Sgt. Karrin Murphy, Harry's reluctant police liaison, will intrigue seasoned fans as well as newcomers attracted by last year's TV adaptation of the series." —*Publishers Weekly*

"It's an edge-of-your-seat thriller enlivened as always by Harry's trademark banter." —*Locus*

"Fans of the Dresden Files will be delighted with this new installment, but fans of urban fantasy generally should grab this one right away. Harry Dresden is perhaps the best-written supernatural detective working today . . . and his adventures only get better." —SFRevu

"Packed with the epic battling characteristic of the Dresden Files, promising something fascinating for the next volume, this is another fine combination of mystery and fantasy, seasoned by Harry's appalling sense of humor."
—*Booklist*

"The tenth addition to Butcher's popular Dresden Files series hints at higher stakes and more personal repercussions in future volumes. . . . This tale of urban sword and sorcery features compelling characters and superb storytelling."
—*Library Journal*

"The body count from the magical melees would do any hard-boiled gumshoe proud. Butcher's believable, likable set of characters goes for the jocular."
—*Publishers Weekly*

"Harry Dresden is a cross between an adult Harry Potter and private eye Jim Rockford from *The Rockford Files*."
—*Madera Tribune*

ALSO BY JIM BUTCHER

THE DRESDEN FILES

Storm Front
Fool Moon
Grave Peril
Summer Knight
Death Masks
Blood Rites
Dead Beat
Proven Guilty
White Night
Small Favor
Turn Coat

"The Warrior" in *Mean Streets*
(with Simon R. Green, Kat Richardson,
and Thomas E. Sniegoski)

THE CODEX ALERA

Furies of Calderon
Academ's Fury
Cursor's Fury
Captain's Fury
Princeps' Fury
First Lord's Fury

JIM BUTCHER

SUMMER KNIGHT

A NOVEL OF THE DRESDEN FILES

A ROC BOOK

ROC
Published by New American Library, a division of
Penguin Group (USA) Inc., 375 Hudson Street,
New York, New York 10014, USA
Penguin Group (Canada), 90 Eglinton Avenue East, Suite 700, Toronto,
Ontario M4P 2Y3, Canada (a division of Pearson Penguin Canada Inc.)
Penguin Books Ltd., 80 Strand, London WC2R 0RL, England
Penguin Ireland, 25 St. Stephen's Green, Dublin 2,
Ireland (a division of Penguin Books Ltd.)
Penguin Group (Australia), 250 Camberwell Road, Camberwell, Victoria 3124,
Australia (a division of Pearson Australia Group Pty. Ltd.)
Penguin Books India Pvt. Ltd., 11 Community Centre, Panchsheel Park,
New Delhi – 110 017, India
Penguin Group (NZ), 67 Apollo Drive, Rosedale, North Shore 0632,
New Zealand (a division of Pearson New Zealand Ltd.)
Penguin Books (South Africa) (Pty.) Ltd., 24 Sturdee Avenue,
Rosebank, Johannesburg 2196, South Africa

Penguin Books Ltd., Registered Offices:
80 Strand, London WC2R 0RL, England

First published by Roc, an imprint of New American Library, a division of
Penguin Group (USA) Inc. Also published in a Roc hardcover edition.

First Printing, September 2002
30 29 28 27 26 25 24 23 22

Copyright © Jim Butcher, 2002
All rights reserved

 REGISTERED TRADEMARK—MARCA REGISTRADA

Printed in the United States of America

Without limiting the rights under copyright reserved above, no part of this
publication may be reproduced, stored in or introduced into a retrieval system,
or transmitted, in any form, or by any means (electronic, mechanical, photo-
copying, recording, or otherwise), without the prior written permission of both
the copyright owner and the above publisher of this book.

PUBLISHER'S NOTE
This is a work of fiction. Names, characters, places, and incidents either are the
product of the author's imagination or are used fictitiously, and any resemblance to actual persons, living or dead, business establishments, events, or
locales is entirely coincidental.
  The publisher does not have any control over and does not assume any
responsibility for author or third-party Web sites or their content.

If you purchased this book without a cover you should be aware that this book
is stolen property. It was reported as "unsold and destroyed" to the publisher
and neither the author nor the publisher has received any payment for this
"stripped book."

The scanning, uploading, and distribution of this book via the Internet or via
any other means without the permission of the publisher is illegal and punishable by law. Please purchase only authorized electronic editions, and do not
participate in or encourage electronic piracy of copyrighted materials. Your
support of the author's rights is appreciated.

This book is for big sisters everywhere who have enough patience not to strangle their little brothers—and particularly for my own sisters, who had more than most. I owe you both so much.

And for Mom, for reasons that are so obvious that they really don't need to be said—but I thought I would make special mention of candy cane cookies and that rocking chair that creaked me to sleep.

Acknowledgments

The author (that's me) wishes to thank all the people who should have been thanked in other books—Ricia and A.J., obviously, and the mighty Jen. Thank you to all the folks who have been so supportive of my work all along, including (but not limited to) Wil and Erin (who fed me great Chicago information and who I missed the first time around), Fred and Chris, Martina and Caroline and Debra and Cam and Jess and Monica and April.

Thank you also to you mighty librarians who have tricked people into reading these books, and to the bookstore personnel (and lurkers) who have gone out of their way to help me get noticed. I admit to being somewhat baffled, but I'm very grateful to you all.

I owe thanks to so many people that I probably am incapable of remembering everyone. If I missed someone, let Shannon know. She will club me on the head with a baseball bat and point out the mistake.

(P.S. Shannon and J.J., as always, thank you. I'd promise to be less of a weirdo, but we all know how long *that* one would last.)

Chapter One

It rained toads the day the White Council came to town.

I got out of the Blue Beetle, my beat-up old Volkswagen bug, and squinted against the midsummer sunlight. Lake Meadow Park lies a bit south of Chicago's Loop, a long sprint from Lake Michigan's shores. Even in heat like we'd had lately, the park would normally be crowded with people. Today it was deserted but for an old lady with a shopping cart and a long coat, tottering around the park. It wasn't yet noon, and my sweats and T-shirt were too hot for the weather.

I squinted around the park for a moment, took a couple of steps onto the grass, and got hit on the head by something damp and squishy.

I flinched and slapped at my hair. Something small fell past my face and onto the ground at my feet. A toad. Not a big one, as toads go—it could easily have sat in the palm of my hand. It wobbled for a few moments upon hitting the ground, then let out a bleary croak and started hopping drunkenly away.

I looked around me and saw other toads on the

ground. A lot of them. The sound of their croaking grew louder as I walked farther into the park. Even as I watched, several more amphibians plopped out of the sky, as though the Almighty had dropped them down a laundry chute. Toads hopped around everywhere. They didn't carpet the ground, but you couldn't possibly miss them. Every moment or so, you would hear the thump of another one landing. Their croaking sounded vaguely like the speech-chatter of a crowded room.

"Weird, huh?" said an eager voice. I looked up to see a short young man with broad shoulders and a confident walk coming toward me. Billy the Werewolf wore sweatpants and a plain dark T-shirt. A year or two ago the outfit would have concealed the forty or fifty extra pounds he'd been carrying. Now they concealed all the muscle he'd traded it in for. He stuck out his hand, smiling. "What did I tell you, Harry?"

"Billy," I responded. He crunched down hard as I shook his hand. Or maybe he was just that much stronger. "How's the werewolf biz?"

"Getting interesting," he said. "We've run into a lot of odd things lately when we've been out patrolling. Like this." He gestured at the park. Another toad fell from the sky several feet away. "That's why we called the wizard."

Patrolling. Holy vigilantes, Batman. "Any of the normals been here?"

"No, except for some meteorological guys from the university. They said that they were having tornadoes in Louisiana or something, that the storms must have thrown the toads here."

I snorted. "You'd think 'it's magic' would be easier to swallow than that."

Billy grinned. "Don't worry. I'm sure someone will come along and declare it a hoax before long."

"Uh-huh." I turned back to the Beetle and popped the hood to rummage in the forward storage compartment. I came out with a nylon backpack and dragged a couple of small cloth sacks out of it. I threw one to Billy. "Grab a couple of toads and pitch them in there for me."

He caught the bag and frowned. "Why?"

"So I can make sure they're real."

Billy lifted his eyebrows. "You think they're not?"

I squinted at him. "Look, Billy, just do it. I haven't slept, I can't remember the last time I ate a hot meal, and I've got a lot to do before tonight."

"But why wouldn't they be real? They look real."

I blew out a breath and tried to keep my temper. It had been short lately. "They could look real and feel real, but it's possible that they're just constructs. Made out of the material of the Nevernever and animated by magic. I hope they are."

"Why?"

"Because all that would mean is that some faerie got bored and played a trick. They do that sometimes."

"Okay. But if they're real?"

"If they're real, then it means something is out of whack."

"What kind of out of whack?"

"The serious kind. Holes in the fabric of reality."

"And that would be bad?"

I eyed him. "Yeah, Billy. That would be bad. It would mean something big was going down."

"But what if—"

My temper flared. "I don't have the time or inclination to teach a class today. Shut the hell up."

He lifted a hand in a pacifying gesture. "Okay, man. Whatever." He fell into step beside me and started picking up toads as we walked across the park. "So, uh, it's good to see you, Harry. Me and the gang were wondering if you wanted to come by this weekend, do some socializing."

I scooped up a toad of my own and eyed him dubiously. "Doing what?"

He grinned at me. "Playing Arcanos, man. The campaign is getting really fun."

Role-playing games. I made a monosyllabic sound. The old lady with the shopping cart wandered past us, the wheels of the cart squeaking and wobbling.

"Seriously, it's great," he insisted. "We're storming the fortress of Lord Malocchio, except we have to do it in disguise in the dead of night, so that the Council of Truth won't know who the vigilantes who brought him down were. There's spells and demons and dragons and everything. Interested?"

"Sounds too much like work."

Billy let out a snort. "Harry, look, I know this whole vampire war thing has you jumpy. And grouchy. But you've been lurking in your basement way too much lately."

"What vampire war?"

Billy rolled his eyes. "Word gets around, Harry. I know that the Red Court of the vampires declared war on the wizards after you burned down Bianca's place last fall. I know that they've tried to kill you a couple of times since then. I even know that the wizards' White Council is coming to town sometime soon to figure out what to do."

I glowered at him. "What White Council?"

He sighed. "It's not a good time for you to be turning into a hermit, Harry. I mean, look at you. When was the last time you shaved? Had a shower? A haircut? Got out to do your laundry?"

I lifted a hand and scratched at the wiry growth of beard on my face. "I've been out. I've been out plenty of times."

Billy snagged another toad. "Like when?"

"I went to that football game with you and the Alphas."

He snorted. "Yeah. In January, Dresden. It's June." Billy glanced up at my face and frowned. "People are worried about you. I mean, I know you've been working on some project or something. But this whole unwashed wild man look just isn't you."

I stooped and grabbed a toad. "You don't know what you're talking about."

"I know better than you think," he said. "It's about Susan, right? Something happened to her last fall. Something you're trying to undo. Maybe something the vampires did. That's why she left town."

I closed my eyes and tried not to crush the toad in my hand. "Drop the subject."

Billy planted his feet and thrust his chin out at me. "No, Harry. Dammit, you vanish from the face of the earth, you're hardly showing up at your office, won't answer your phone, don't often answer your door. We're your friends, and we're worried about you."

"I'm fine," I said.

"You're a lousy liar. Word is that the Reds are bringing more muscle into town. That they're offering their groupies full vampirehood if one of them brings you down."

"Hell's bells," I muttered. My head started to ache.

"It isn't a good time for you to be outside by yourself. Even during daylight."

"I don't need a babysitter, Billy."

"Harry, I know you better than most. I know you can do stuff that other people can't—but that doesn't make you Superman. Everyone needs help sometimes."

"Not me. Not now." I stuffed the toad into my sack and picked up another. "I don't have time for it."

"Oh, that reminds me." Billy drew a folded piece of paper out of the pocket of his sweats and read it. "You've got an appointment with a client at three."

I blinked at him. "What?"

"I dropped by your office and checked your messages. A Ms. Sommerset was trying to reach you, so I called her and set up the appointment for you."

I felt my temper rising again. "You did what?"

His expression turned annoyed. "I checked your mail, too. The landlord for the office dropped off your eviction notice. If you don't have him paid off in a week, he's booting you out."

"What the hell gives you the right to go poking around in my office, Billy? Or calling my clients?"

He took a step in front of me, glaring. I had to focus on his nose to avoid the risk of looking at his eyes. "Get off the high horse, Harry. I'm your freaking friend. You've been spending all your time hiding in your apartment. You should be happy I'm helping you save your business."

"You're damned right it's my business," I spat. The shopping cart lady circled past in my peripheral vision, cart wheels squeaking as she walked behind me. "Mine. As in none of yours."

He thrust out his jaw. "Fine. How about you just crawl back into your cave until they evict you from that, too?" He spread his hands. "Good God, man. I don't need to be a wizard to see when someone's in a downward spiral. You're hurting. You need help."

I jabbed a finger into his chest. "No, Billy. I don't need more *help*. I don't need to be babysitting a bunch of kids who think that because they've learned one trick they're ready to be the Lone Ranger with fangs and a tail. I don't need to be worrying about the vamps targeting the people around me when they can't get to me. I don't need to be second-guessing myself, wondering who *else* is going to get hurt because I dropped the ball." I reached down and snatched up a toad, jerking the cloth bag from Billy's hands on the way back up. "I don't need *you*."

Naturally, the hit went down right then.

It wasn't subtle, as attempted assassinations go. An engine roared and a black compact pickup truck jumped the curb into the park fifty yards away. It jounced and slewed to one side, tires digging up furrows in the sun-baked grass. A pair of men clung to a roll bar in the back of the truck. They were dressed all in black, complete with black sunglasses over black ski masks, and their guns matched—automatic weapons in the mini-Uzi tradition.

"Get back!" I shouted. With my right hand, I grabbed at Billy and shoved him behind me. With my left, I shook out the bracelet on my wrist, hung with a row of tiny, medieval-style shields. I lifted my left hand toward the truck and drew in my will, focusing it with the bracelet into a sudden, transparent, shimmering half-globe that spread out between me and the oncoming truck.

The truck ground to a halt. The two gunmen didn't wait for it to settle. With all the fire discipline of an action-movie extra, they pointed their guns more or less at me and emptied their clips in one roaring burst.

Sparks flew from the shield in front of me, and bullets whined and hissed in every direction as they ricocheted. My bracelet grew uncomfortably warm within a second or two, the energy of the shield taxing the focus to its limit. I tried to angle the shield to deflect the shots up into the air as much as possible. God only knew where all those bullets were going—I just hoped that they wouldn't bounce through a nearby car or some other passerby.

The guns clicked empty. With jerky, unprofessional motions, both gunmen began to reload.

"Harry!" Billy shouted.

"Not now!"

"But—"

I lowered the shield and lifted my right hand—the side that projects energy. The silver ring I wore on my index finger had been enchanted to save a little kinetic energy whenever my arm moved. I hadn't used the ring in months, and it had a whale of a kick to it—one I hardly dared to use on the gunmen. That much force could kill one of them, and that would be basically the same as letting them fill me full of bullets. It would just take a little longer to set in. The White Council did not take kindly to anyone violating the First Law of Magic: Thou Shalt Not Kill. I'd slipped once on a technicality, but it wouldn't happen again.

I gritted my teeth, focused my shot just to one side of the gunmen, and triggered the ring. Raw force, unseen but tangible, lashed through the air and caught the first gunman with a glancing blow across his upper body. His automatic slammed against his chest, and the impact tore the sunglasses off his head and shredded bits of his clothes even as it flung him back and out of the pickup, to land somewhere on the ground on the other side.

The second gunman got less of the blast. What did hit him struck against his shoulder and head. He held on to his gun but lost the sunglasses, and they took the ski mask with them, revealing him to be a plain-looking boy who couldn't have been old enough to vote. He blinked against the sudden light and then resumed his fumbling reload.

"Kids," I snarled, lifting my shield again. "They're sending kids after me. Hell's bells."

And then something made the hairs on the back of my neck try to lift me off the ground. As the kid with the gun started shooting again, I glanced back over my shoulder.

The old lady with her shopping basket had stopped maybe fifteen feet behind me. I saw now that she wasn't as old as I had thought. I caught a flicker of cool, dark eyes beneath age makeup. Her hands were young and smooth. From the depths of the shopping basket she pulled out a sawed-off shotgun, and swung it toward me.

Bullets from the chattering automatic slammed against my shield, and it was all I could do to hold it in place. If I brought any magic to bear against the third attacker, I would lose my concentration and the shield with it—and inexpert or not, the gunman on the truck was spraying around enough lead that sooner or later he wouldn't miss.

On the other hand, if the disguised assassin got a chance to fire that shotgun from five yards away, no one would bother taking me to the hospital. I'd go straight to the morgue.

Bullets hammered into my shield, and I couldn't do anything but watch the third attacker bring the shotgun to bear. I was screwed, and probably Billy was along with me.

Billy moved. He had already gotten out of his T-shirt, and he had enough muscle to ripple—flat, hard muscle, athlete's muscle, not the carefully sculpted build of weight lifters. He dove forward, toward the woman with the shotgun, and stripped out of his sweatpants on the fly. He was naked beneath.

I felt the surge of magic that Billy used then—sharp, precise, focused. There was no sense of ritual in what he did, no slow gathering of power building to release. He blurred as he moved, and between one breath and the next, Billy-the-Naked was gone and Billy-the-Wolf slammed into the assailant, a dark-furred beast the size of a Great Dane, fangs slashing at the hand that gripped the forward stock of the shotgun.

The woman cried out, jerking her hand back, scarlet blood on her fingers, and swept the gun at Billy like a club. He twisted and caught the blow on his shoulders, a snarl exploding from him. He went after the woman's other hand, faster than I could easily see, and the shotgun tumbled to the ground.

The woman screamed again and drew back her hand.

She wasn't human.

Her hands distended, lengthening, as did her shoulders and her jaw. Her nails became ugly, ragged talons, and she raked them down at Billy, striking him across the jaw, this time eliciting a pained yelp mixed with a snarl. He rolled to one side and came up on his feet, circling in order to force the woman-thing's back to me.

The gunman in the truck clicked on empty again. I dropped the shield and hurled myself forward, diving to grip the shotgun. I came up with it and shouted, "Billy, move!"

The wolf darted to one side, and the woman whipped around to face me, her distorted features furious, mouth drooling around tusklike fangs.

I pointed the gun at her belly and pulled the trigger.

The gun roared and bucked, slamming hard against my shoulder. Ten-gauge, maybe, or slug rounds. The woman doubled over, letting out a shriek, and stumbled backward and to the ground. She wasn't down long. She almost bounced back to her feet, scarlet splashed all over her rag of a dress, her face wholly inhuman now. She sprinted past me to the truck and leapt up into the back. The gunman hauled his partner back into the truck with him, and the driver gunned the engine. The truck threw out some turf before it dug in, jounced back onto the street, and whipped away into traffic.

I stared after it for a second, panting. I lowered the shotgun, realizing as I did that I had somehow managed to keep hold of the toad I had picked up in my left hand. It wriggled and struggled in a fashion that suggested I had been close to crushing it, and I tried to ease up on my grip without losing it.

I turned to look for Billy. The wolf paced back over to his discarded sweatpants, shimmered for a second, and became once more the naked young man. There were two long cuts on his face, parallel with his jaw. Blood ran down over his throat in a fine sheet. He carried himself tensely, but it was the only indication he gave of the pain.

"You all right?" I asked him.

He nodded and jerked on his pants, his shirt. "Yeah. What the hell was that?"

"Ghoul," I told him. "Probably one of the LaChaise clan. They're working with the Red Court, and they don't much like me."

"Why don't they like you?"

"I've given them headaches a few times."

Billy lifted a corner of his shirt to hold against the cuts on his face. "I didn't expect the claws."

"They're sneaky that way."

"Ghoul, huh. Is it dead?"

I shook my head. "They're like cockroaches. They recover from just about anything. Can you walk?"

"Yeah."

"Good. Let's get out of here." We headed toward the Beetle. I picked up the cloth sack of toads on the way and started shaking them back out onto the ground. I put the toad I'd nearly squished down with them, then wiped my hand off on the grass.

Billy squinted at me. "Why are you letting them go?"

"Because they're real."

"How do you know?"

"The one I was holding crapped on my hand."

I let Billy into the Blue Beetle and got in the other side. I fetched the first aid kit from under my seat and passed it over to him. Billy pressed a cloth against his face, looking out at the toads. "So that means things are in a bad way?"

"Yeah," I confirmed, "things are in a bad way." I was silent for a minute, then said, "You saved my life."

He shrugged. He didn't look at me.

"So you set up the appointment for three o'clock, right? What was the name? Sommerset?"

He glanced at me and kept the smile from his mouth—but not from his eyes. "Yeah."

I scratched at my beard and nodded. "I've been distracted lately. Maybe I should clean up first."

"Might be good," Billy agreed.

I sighed. "I'm an ass sometimes."

Billy laughed. "Sometimes. You're human like the rest of us."

I started up the Beetle. It wheezed a little, but I coaxed it to life.

Just then something hit my hood with a hard, heavy thump. Then again. Another heavy blow, on the roof.

A feeling of dizziness swept over me, a nausea that came so suddenly and violently that I clutched the steering wheel in a simple effort not to collapse. Distantly, I could hear Billy asking me if I was all right. I wasn't. Power moved and stirred in the air outside—hectic disruption, the forces of magic, usually moving in smooth and quiet patterns, suddenly cast into tumult, disruptive, maddening chaos.

I tried to push the sensations away from me, and labored to open my eyes. Toads were raining down. Not occasionally plopping, but raining down so thick and hard that they darkened the sky. No gentle laundry-chute drop for these poor things, either. They fell like hailstones, splattering on concrete, on the hood of the Beetle. One of them fell hard enough to send a spiderweb of cracks through my windshield, and I dropped into gear and scooted down the street. After a few hundred yards we got away from the otherworldly rain.

Both of us were breathing too fast. Billy had been right. The rain of toads meant something serious was going on, magically speaking. The White Council was coming to town tonight to discuss the war. I had a client to meet, and the vampires had evidently upped the stakes (no pun intended), striking at me more openly than they had dared to before.

I flipped on the windshield wipers. Amphibian blood left scarlet streaks on the cracked glass.

"Good Lord," Billy breathed.

"Yeah," I said. "It never rains—it pours."

Chapter Two

I dropped Billy off at his apartment near campus. I didn't think the ghoul would be filing a police report, but I wiped down the shotgun anyway. Billy wrapped it in a towel I had in the backseat of the Beetle and took it with him, promising to dispose of the weapon. His girlfriend, Georgia, a willowy girl a foot taller than him, waited on the apartment's balcony in dark shorts and a scarlet bikini top, displaying a generous amount of impressively sun-bronzed skin in a manner far more confident and appealing than I would have expected from her a year before. My, how the kids had grown.

The moment Billy got out of the car, Georgia looked up sharply from her book and her nostrils flared. She headed into the house and met him at the door with a first aid kit. She glanced at the car, her expression worried, and nodded to me. I waved back, trying to look friendly. From Georgia's expression, I hadn't managed better than surly. They went into the apartment, and I pulled away before anyone could come out to socialize with me.

After a minute I pulled over, killed the engine, and

squinted up at myself in the rearview mirror of the Beetle.

It came as a shock to me. I know, that sounds stupid, but I don't keep mirrors in my home. Too many things can use mirrors as windows, even doors, and it was a risk I preferred to skip entirely. I hadn't glanced at a mirror in weeks.

I looked like a train wreck.

More so than usual, I mean.

My features are usually kind of long, lean, all sharp angles. I've got almost-black hair to go with the dark eyes. Now I had grey and purplish circles under them. Deep ones. The lines of my face, where they weren't covered by several months of untrimmed beard, looked as sharp as the edges of a business card.

My hair had grown out long and shaggy—not in that sexy-young-rock-star kind of way but in that time-to-take-Rover-to-the-groomer kind of way. It didn't even have the advantage of being symmetrical, since a big chunk had been burned short in one spot when a small incendiary had been smuggled to me in a pizza delivery box, back when I could still afford to order pizza. My skin was pale. Pasty, even. I looked like Death warmed over, provided someone had made Death run the Boston Marathon. I looked tired. Burned out. Used up.

I sat back in my seat.

I hate it when I'm wrong. But it looked like maybe Billy and the werewolves (stars and stones, they sounded like a bad rock band) had a point. I tried to think of the last time I'd gotten a haircut, a shave. I'd had a shower last week. Hadn't I?

I mopped at my face with my shaking hands. The days and nights had been blurring lately. I spent my time in the lab under my apartment, researching 24-7. The lab was in the subbasement, all damp stone and no windows. Circadian rhythms, bah. I'd pretty much dispensed with day and night. There was too much to think about to pay attention to such trivial details.

About nine months before, I'd gotten my girlfriend nearly killed. Maybe more than killed.

Susan Rodriguez had been a reporter for a yellow journal called the *Midwestern Arcane* when we met. She was one of the few people around who were willing to accept the idea of the supernatural as a factual reality. She'd clawed for every detail, every story, every ounce of proof she could dig up so that she could try to raise the public consciousness on the matter. To that end, she'd followed me to a vampire shindig.

And the monsters got her.

Billy had been right about that, too. The vampires, the Red Court, had changed her. Or maybe it would be more accurate to say that they infected her. Though she was still human, technically, she'd been given their macabre thirst. If she ever sated it, she would turn all the way into one of them. Some part of her would die, and she would be one of the monsters, body and soul.

That's why the research. I'd been looking for some way to help her. To create a vaccine, or to purge her body. Something. Anything.

I'd asked her to marry me. She told me no. Then she left town. I read her syndicated column in the *Arcane*. She must have been mailing them in to her editor, so at least I knew she was alive. She'd asked me not to follow her and I hadn't. I wouldn't, until I could figure out a way to get her out of the mess I'd gotten her into. There *had* to be something I could do.

Had to be. There had to be.

I bowed my head, suddenly grimacing so hard that the muscles of my face cramped, ached, and smoldered. My chest felt tight, and my body seemed to burn with useless, impotent flame. I'm a wizard. I should have been able to protect Susan. Should have been able to save her. Should have been able to help her. Should have been smarter, should have been faster, should have been better.

Should have told her you loved her before it was too late. Right, Harry?

I tried not to cry. I willed myself not to with all of my years of training and experience and self-discipline. It would accomplish nothing. It wouldn't put me anywhere closer to finding a cure for Susan.

I was so damned tired.

I left my face in my hands. I didn't want someone walking by to see me bawling.

It took a long time to get myself back under control. I'm not sure how long it was, but the shadows had changed and I was baking in the car, even with the windows down.

It occurred to me that it was stupid to be sitting there on the street for more vampire thugs to come find, plain as day. I was tired and dirty and hungry, but I didn't have the cash to get anything to eat, and by the sun I didn't have the time to go back to the apartment for soup. Not if I was to keep my appointment with Ms. Sommerset.

And I needed that appointment. Billy had been right about that, too. If I didn't start earning my keep again, I would lose the office and the apartment. I wouldn't get much magical research done from a cardboard box in an alley.

Time to get moving, then. I raked my fingers uselessly through my mop of hair and headed for my office. A passing clock told me that I was already a couple of minutes late for the appointment. Between that and my appearance, boy, was I going to wow the client. This day just kept getting better.

My office is in a building in midtown. It isn't much of a building, but it still looked too good for me that day. I got a glare from the aging security guard downstairs and felt lucky that he recognized me from previous encounters. A new guy probably would have given me the bum's rush without blinking. I nodded at the guard and smiled and tried to look businesslike. Heh.

I walked past the elevator on my way to the stairs. There was a sign on it that said it was under repair. The elevator hadn't ever been quite the same since a giant scorpion had torn into one of the cars and someone had thrown the elevator up to the top of its chute with a torrent of wind in order to smash the big bug against the roof. The resulting fall sent the car plummeting all the way back to the ground floor and wreaked havoc with the building in general, raising everyone's rents.

Or that's what I heard, anyway. Don't look at me

like that. It could have been someone else. Okay, maybe not the orthodontist on four, or the psychiatrist on six. Probably not the insurance office on seven, or the accountant on nine either. Maybe not the lawyers on the top floor. Maybe. But it isn't always me when something goes catastrophically wrong.

Anyway, no one can prove anything.

I opened the door to the stairwell and headed up the stairs to my office, on the fifth floor. I went down the hall, past the quiet buzz of the consulting firm that took up most of the space on the floor, to my office door.

The lettering on the frosted glass read HARRY DRESDEN—WIZARD. I reached out to open the door. A spark jumped to my finger when my hand got within an inch or three of the doorknob, popping against my skin with a sharp little snap of discomfort.

I paused. Even with the building's AC laboring and wheezing, it wasn't *that* cool and dry. Call me paranoid, but there's nothing like a murder attempt in broad daylight to make a man cautious. I focused on my bracelet again, drawing on my apprehension to ready a shield should I need it.

With the other hand I pushed open the door to my office.

My office is usually pretty tidy. Or in any case, I didn't remember it being quite as sloppy as it looked now. Given how little I'd been there lately, it seemed unfair that it should have gotten quite that bad. The table by the door, where I kept a bunch of flyers with titles like "Magic for Dummies" and "I'm a Wizard—Ask Me How," sat crookedly against the wall. The flyers were scattered carelessly over its surface and onto the floor. I could smell the faintest stink of long-burnt coffee. I must have left it on. Oops. My desk had a similar fungus coating of loose papers, and several drawers in my filing cabinets stood open, with files stacked on top of the cabinets or thrust sideways into their places, so that they stood up out of the drawers. My ceiling fan whirled woozily, clicking on every rotation.

Someone had evidently tried to straighten things up. My mail sat neatly stacked in three different piles. Both metal trash cans were suspiciously empty. Billy and company, then.

In the ruins of my office stood a woman with the kind of beauty that makes men murder friends and start wars.

She stood by my desk with her arms folded, facing the door, hips cocked to one side, her expression skeptical. She had white hair. Not white-blond, not platinum. White as snow, white as the finest marble, bound up like a captured cloud to bare the lines of her slender throat. I don't know how her skin managed to look pale beside that hair, but it did. Her lips were the color of frozen mulberries, almost shocking in a smooth and lovely face, and her oblique eyes were a deep green that tinted to blue when she tilted her head and looked me over. She wasn't old. Wasn't young. Wasn't anything but stunning.

I tried to keep my jaw from hitting the floor and forced my brain to start doing something by taking stock of her wardrobe. She wore a woman's suit of charcoal grey, the cut immaculate. The skirt showed exactly enough leg to make it hard not to look, and her dark pumps had heels just high enough to give you ideas. She wore a bone-white V-neck beneath her jacket, the neckline dipping just low enough to make me want to be watching if she took a deep breath. Opals set in silver flashed on her ears, at her throat, glittering through an array of colors I wouldn't have expected from opals—too many scarlets and violets and deep blues. Her nails had somehow been lacquered in the same opalescence.

I caught the scent of her perfume, something wild and rich, heavy and sweet, like orchids. My heart sped up, and the testosterone-oriented part of my brain wished that I'd been able to bathe. Or shave. Or at least that I hadn't worn sweatpants.

Her mouth quirked into a smile, and she arched one pale brow, saying nothing, letting me gawk.

One thing was certain—no woman like that would have anything less than money. Lots of money. Money I could use to pay the rent, buy groceries, maybe even splurge a little and get a wheelbarrow to help with cleaning my apartment. I only hesitated for a heartbeat, wondering if it was proper for a full-fledged wizard of the White Council to be that interested in cash. I made up my mind fast.

Phenomenal cosmic powers be damned. I have a lease.

"Uh, Ms. Sommerset, I presume," I managed finally. No one can do suave like me. If I was careful, I should be able to trip over something and complete the image. "I'm Harry Dresden."

"I believe you are late," she replied. Sommerset had a voice like her outfit—rich, suggestive, cultured. Her English had an accent I couldn't place. Maybe European.

Definitely interesting. "Your assistant informed me when to arrive. I don't like to be kept waiting, so I let myself in." She glanced at my desk, then back at me. "I almost wish I hadn't."

"Yeah. I didn't hear you were coming until, uh . . ." I looked around at my office, dismayed, and shut the door behind me. "I know this looks pretty unprofessional."

"Quite correct."

I moved to one of the chairs I keep for clients, facing my desk, and hurriedly cleared it off. "Please, sit down. Would you like a cup of coffee or anything?"

"Sounds less than sanitary. Why should I take the risk?" She sat, her back straight, on the edge of the chair, following me with her eyes as I walked around the desk. They were a cool, noticeable weight on me as I moved, and I sat down at my desk, frowning.

"Are you the kind who takes chances?"

"I like to hedge my bets," she murmured. "You, for example, Mister Dresden. I have come here today to decide whether or not I shall gamble a great deal upon your abilities." She paused and then added, "Thus far, you have made less than a sterling impression."

I rested my elbows on my desk and steepled my fingers. "Yeah. I know that all this probably makes me look like—"

"A desperate man?" she suggested. "Someone who is clearly obsessed with other matters." She nodded toward the stacks of envelopes on my desk. "One who is shortly to lose his place of business if he does not pay his debts. I think you need the work." She began to rise. "And if you lack the ability to take care of such minor matters, I doubt you will be of any use to me."

"Wait," I said, rising. "Please. At least let me hear you out. If it turns out that I think I can help you—"

She lifted her chin and interrupted me effortlessly. "But that isn't the question, is it?" she asked. "The question is whether or not *I* think you can help me. You have shown me nothing to make me think that you could." She paused, sitting back down again. "And yet . . ."

I sat back down across from her. "Yet?"

"I have heard things, Mister Dresden, about people with your abilities. About the ability to look into their eyes."

I tilted my head. "I wouldn't call it an ability. It just happens."

"Yet you are able to see within them? You call it a soulgaze, do you not?"

I nodded warily and started adding together lots of small bits and pieces. "Yes."

"Revealing their true nature? Seeing the truth about the person upon whom you look?"

"And they see me back. Yes."

She smiled, cool and lovely. "Then let us look upon one another, Mister Dresden, you and I. Then I will know if you can be of any use to me. Surely it will cost me nothing."

"I wouldn't be so sure. It's the sort of thing that stays with you." Like an appendectomy scar, or baldness. When you look on someone's soul, you don't forget it. Not ever. I didn't like the direction this was going. "I don't think it would be a good idea."

"But why not?" she pressed. "It won't take long, will it, Mister Dresden?"

"That's really not the issue."

Her mouth firmed into a line. "I see. Then, if you will excuse me—"

This time I interrupted her. "Ms. Sommerset, I think you may have made a mistake in your estimations."

Her eyes glittered, anger showing for a moment, cool and far away. "Oh?"

I nodded. I opened the drawer to my desk and took out a pad of paper. "Yeah. I've had a rough time of things lately."

"You can't possibly know how little that matters to me."

I drew out a pen, took off the lid, and set it down beside the pad. "Uh-huh. Then you come in here. Rich, gorgeous—kind of too good to be true."

"And?" she inquired.

"Too good to be true," I repeated. I drew the .44-caliber revolver from the desk drawer, leveled it at her, and thumbed back the hammer. "Call me crazy, but lately I've been thinking that if something's too good to be true, then it probably isn't. Put your hands on the desk, please."

Her eyebrows arched. Those gorgeous eyes widened enough to show the whites all the way around them. She moved her hands, swallowing as she did, and laid her palms on the desk. "What do you think you are doing?" she demanded.

"I'm testing a theory," I said. I kept the gun and my eyes on her and opened another drawer. "See, lately, I've been getting nasty visitors. So it's made me do some thinking about what kind of trouble to expect. And I think I've got you pegged."

"I don't know what you are talking about, Mister Dresden, but I am certain—"

"Save it." I rummaged in a drawer and found what I needed. A moment later I lifted a plain old nail of simple metal out of the drawer and put it on the desk.

"What's that?" she all but whispered.

"Litmus test," I said.

Then I flicked the nail gently with one finger, and sent it rolling across the surface of my desk and toward her perfectly manicured hands.

She didn't move until a split second before the nail touched her—but then she did, a blur of motion that took her two long strides back from my desk and knocked over the chair she'd been sitting on. The nail rolled off the edge of the desk and fell to the floor with a clink.

"Iron," I said. "Cold iron. Faeries don't like it."

The expression drained from her face. One moment, there had been arrogant conceit, haughty superiority, blithe confidence. But that simply vanished, leaving her features cold and lovely and remote and empty of all emotion, of anything recognizably human.

"The bargain with my godmother has months yet to go," I said. "A year and a day, she had to leave me alone. That was the deal. If she's trying to weasel out of it, I'm going to be upset."

She regarded me in that empty silence for long moments more. It was unsettling to see a face so lovely look so wholly alien, as though something lurked behind those features that had little in common with me and did not care to make the effort to understand. That blank mask made my throat tighten, and I had to work not to let the gun in my hand shake. But then she did something that made her look even more alien, more frightening.

She smiled. A slow smile, cruel as a barbed knife. When she spoke, her voice sounded just as beautiful as it had before. But it was empty, quiet, haunting. She spoke, and it made me want to lean closer to her to hear her more clearly. "Clever," she murmured. "Yes. Not too distracted to think. Just what I need."

A cold shiver danced down my spine. "I don't want any trouble," I said. "Just go, and we can both pretend nothing happened."

"But it has," she murmured. Just the sound of her voice made the room feel colder. "You have seen through this veil. Proven your worth. How did you do it?"

"Static on the doorknob," I said. "It should have been locked. You shouldn't have been able to get in here, so you must have gone through it. And you danced around my questions rather than simply answering them."

Still smiling, she nodded. "Go on."

"You don't have a purse. Not many women go out in a three-thousand-dollar suit and no purse."

"Mmmm," she said. "Yes. You'll do perfectly, Mister Dresden."

"I don't know what you're talking about," I said. "I'm having nothing more to do with faeries."

"I don't like being called that, Mister Dresden."

"You'll get over it. Get out of my office."

"You should know, Mister Dresden, that my kind, from great to small, are bound to speak the truth."

"That hasn't slowed your ability to deceive."

Her eyes glittered, and I saw her pupils change, slipping from round mortal orbs to slow feline lengths. Cat-eyed, she regarded me, unblinking. "Yet have I spoken. I plan to gamble. And I will gamble upon you."

"Uh. What?"

"I require your service. Something precious has been stolen. I wish you to recover it."

"Let me get this straight," I said. "You want me to recover stolen goods for you?"

"Not for me," she murmured. "For the rightful owners. I wish you to discover and catch the thief and to vindicate me."

"Do it yourself," I said.

"In this matter I cannot act wholly alone," she murmured. "That is why I have chosen you to be my emissary. My agent."

I laughed at her. That made something else come into those perfect, pale features—anger. Anger, cold and terrible, flashed in her eyes and all but froze the laugh in my throat. "I don't think so," I said. "I'm not making any more bargains with your folk. I don't even know who you are."

"Dear child," she murmured, a slow edge to her voice. "The bargain has already been made. You gave your life, your fortune, your future, in exchange for power."

"Yeah. With my godmother. And that's still being contested."

"No longer," she said. "Even in this world of mortals, the concept of debt passes from one hand to the next. Selling mortgages, yes?"

My belly went cold. "What are you saying?"

Her teeth showed, sharp and white. It wasn't a smile.

"Your mortgage, mortal child, has been sold. I have purchased it. You are mine. And you *will* assist me in this matter."

I set the gun down on my desk and opened the top drawer. I took out my letter opener, one of the standard machined jobs with a heavy, flat blade and a screw-grip handle. "You're wrong," I said, and the denial in my voice sounded patently obvious, even to me. "My godmother would never do that. For all I know, you're trying to trick me."

She smiled, watching me, her eyes bright. "Then by all means, let me reassure you of the truth."

My left palm slammed down onto the table. I watched, startled, as I gripped the letter opener in my right hand, slasher-movie style. In a panic, I tried to hold back my hand, to drop the opener, but my arms were running on automatic, like they were someone else's.

"Wait!" I shouted.

She regarded me, cold and distant and interested.

I slammed the letter opener down onto the back of my own hand, hard. My desk is a cheap one. The steel bit cleanly through the meat between my thumb and forefinger and sank into the desk, pinning me there. Pain washed up my arm even as blood started oozing out of the wound. I tried to fight it down, but I was panicked, in no condition to exert a lot of control. A whimper slipped out of me. I tried to pull the steel away, to get it *out* of my hand, but my arm simply twisted, wrenching the letter opener counterclockwise.

The pain flattened me. I wasn't even able to get enough breath to scream.

The woman, the faerie, reached down and took my fingers away from the letter opener. She withdrew it with a sharp, decisive gesture and laid it flat on the desk, my blood gleaming all over it. "Wizard, you know as well as I. Were you not bound to me, I would have no such power over you."

At that moment, most of what I knew was that my hand hurt, but some dim part of me realized she was telling the truth. Faeries don't just get to ride in and play puppet master. You have to let them in. I'd let my godmother, Lea, in years before, when I was younger, dumber. I'd given her the slip last year, forced an abeyance of her claim that should have protected me for a year and a day.

But now she'd passed the reins to someone else. Someone who hadn't been in on the second bargain.

I looked up at her, pain and sudden anger making my voice into a low, harsh growl. "Who are you?"

The woman ran an opalescent fingernail through the blood on my desk. She lifted it to her lips and idly touched it to her tongue. She smiled, slower, more sensual, and every bit as alien. "I have many names," she murmured. "But you may call me Mab. Queen of Air and Darkness. Monarch of the Winter Court of the Sidhe."

Chapter

Three

The bottom fell out of my stomach.

A Faerie Queen. A Faerie Queen was standing in my office. I was looking at a Faerie Queen. Talking to a Faerie Queen.

And she had me by the short hairs.

Boy, and I'd thought my life was on the critical list already.

Fear can literally feel like ice water. It can be a cold feeling that you swallow, that rolls down your throat and spreads into your chest. It steals your breath and makes your heart labor when it shouldn't, before expanding into your belly and hips, leaving quivers behind. Then it heads for the thighs, the knees (occasionally with an embarrassing stop on the way), stealing the strength from the long muscles that think you should be using them to run the hell away.

I swallowed a mouthful of fear, my eyes on the poisonously lovely faerie standing on the other side of my desk.

It made Mab smile.

"Yes," she murmured. "Wise enough to be afraid. To

understand, at least in part. How does it feel, to know what you know, child?"

My voice came out unsteady, and more quiet than I would have liked. "Sort of like Tokyo when Godzilla comes up on the beach."

Mab tilted her head, watching me with that same smile. Maybe she didn't get the reference. Or maybe she didn't like being compared to a thirty-story lizard. Or maybe she *did* like it. I mean, how should I know? I have enough trouble figuring out human women.

I didn't meet Mab's eyes. I wasn't worried about a soulgaze any longer. Both parties had to have a soul for that to happen. But plenty of things can get to you if you make eye contact too long. It carries all sorts of emotions and metaphors. I stared at Mab's chin, my hand burning with pain, and said nothing because I was afraid.

I hate being afraid. I hate it more than anything in the whole world. I hate being made to feel helpless. I hate being bullied, too, and Mab might as well have been ramming her fist down my throat and demanding my lunch money.

The Faerie Queens were bad news. Big bad news. Short of calling up some hoary old god or squaring off against the White Council itself, I wasn't likely to run into anything else with as much raw power as Mab. I could have thrown a magical sucker punch at her, could have tried to take her out, but even if we'd been on even footing I doubt I would have ruffled her hair. And she had a bond on me, a magical conduit. She could send just about anything right past my defenses, and there wouldn't be anything I could do about it.

Bullies make me mad—and I've been known to do some foolish things when I'm angry.

"Forget it," I said, my voice hot. "No deal. Get it over with and blast me. Lock the door on your way out."

My response didn't seem to ruffle her. She folded her arms and murmured, "Such anger. Such fire. Yes. I watched you stalemate your godmother the Leanansidhe autumn last. Few mortals ever have done as much. Bold. Impertinent. I admire that kind of strength, wizard. I need that kind of strength."

I fumbled around on my desk until I found the tissue dispenser and started packing the wound with the flimsy fabric. "I don't really care what you need," I told her. "I'm not going to be your emissary or anything else unless you want to force me, and I doubt I'd be much good to you then. So do whatever you're going to do or get out of my office."

"You should care, Mister Dresden," Mab told me. "It concerns you explicitly. I purchased your debt in order to make you an offer. To give you the chance to win free of your obligations."

"Yeah, right. Save it. I'm not interested."

"You may serve, wizard, or you may be served. As a meal. Do you not wish to be free?"

I looked up at her, warily, visions of barbecued me on a table with an apple in my mouth dancing in my head. "What do you mean by 'free'?"

"Free," she said, wrapping those frozen-berry lips around the word so that I couldn't help but notice. "Free of Sidhe influence, of the bonds of your obligation first to the Leanansidhe and now to me."

"The whole thing a wash? We go our separate ways?"

"Precisely."

I looked down at my hurting hand and scowled. "I didn't think you were much into freedom as a concept, Mab."

"You should not presume, wizard. I adore freedom. Anyone who doesn't have it wants it."

I took a deep breath and tried to get my heart rate under control. I couldn't let either fear or anger do my thinking for me. My instincts screamed at me to go for the gun again and give it a shot, but I had to think. It was the only thing that could get you clear of the fae.

Mab was on the level about her offer. I could feel that, sense it in a way so primal, so visceral, that there was no room left for doubt. She would cut me loose if I agreed to her bargain. Of course, her price might be too high. She hadn't gotten to that yet. And the fae have a way of making sure that further bargains only get you in deeper, instead of into the clear. Just like credit card companies, or those student loan people. Now there's evil for you.

I could feel Mab watching me, Sylvester to my Tweetie Bird. That thought kind of cheered me up. Generally speaking, Tweetie kicks Sylvester's ass in the end.

"Okay," I told her. "I'm listening."

"Three tasks," Mab murmured, holding up three fingers by way of visual aid. "From time to time, I will make a request of you. When you have fulfilled three requests, your obligation to me ceases."

Silence lay on the room for a moment, and I blinked. "What. That's *it*?"

Mab nodded.

"Any three tasks? Any three requests?"

Mab nodded.

"Just as simple as that? I mean, you say it like that, and I could pass you the salt three times and that would be that."

Her eyes, green-blue like glacial ice, remained on my face, unblinking. "Do you accept?"

I rubbed at my mouth slowly, mulling it over in my head. It was a simple bargain, as these things went. They could get really complicated, with contracts and everything. Mab had offered me a great package, sweet, neat, and tidy as a Halloween candy.

Which meant that I'd be an idiot not to check for razor blades and cyanide.

"I decide which requests I fulfill and which I don't?"

"Even so."

"And if I refuse a request, there will be no reprisals or punishments from you."

She tilted her head and blinked her eyes, slowly. "Agreed. You, not I, will choose which requests you fulfill."

There was one land mine I'd found, at least. "And no more selling my mortgage, either. Or whistling up the lackeys to chastise or harass me by proxy. This remains between the two of us."

She laughed, and it sounded as merry, clear, and lovely as bells—if someone pressed them against my teeth while they were still ringing. "As your godmother did. Fool me twice, shame on me, wizard? Agreed."

I licked my lips, thinking hard. Had I left her any openings? Could she get to me any other way?

"Well, wizard?" Mab asked. "Have we a bargain?"

I gave myself a second to wish I'd been less tired. Or less in pain. The events of the day and the impending Council meeting this evening hadn't exactly left my head in world-class negotiating condition. But I knew one thing for certain. If I didn't get out from under Mab's bond, I would be dead, or worse than dead, in short order. Better to act and be mistaken than not to act and get casually crushed.

"All right," I said. "We have a bargain." When I said the words, a little frisson prickled over the nape of my neck, down the length of my spine. My wounded hand twitched in an aching, painful pang.

Mab closed her eyes, smiling a feline smile with those dark lips, and inclined her head. "Good. Yes."

You know that look on Wile E. Coyote's face, when he runs at full steam off the cliff and then realizes what he's done? He doesn't look down, but he feels around with one toe, and right then, right before he falls, his face becomes drawn with a primal dread.

That's what I must have looked like. I know it was pretty much what I felt like. But there was no help for it. Maybe if I didn't stop to check for the ground underneath my feet, I'd keep going indefinitely. I looked away from Mab and tried to tend to my hand as best I could. It still throbbed, and disinfecting the wound was going to hurt a lot more. I doubted it would need sutures. A small blessing, I guess.

A manila envelope hit my desk. I looked up to see Mab drawing a pair of gloves onto her hands.

"What's this?" I asked.

"My request," she replied. "Within are the details of a man's death. I wish you to vindicate me of it by discovering the identity of his killer and returning what was stolen from him."

I opened the envelope. Inside was an eight-by-ten glossy black-and-white of a body. An old man lay at the bottom of a flight of stairs, his neck at a sharp angle to his shoulders. He had frizzy white hair, a tweed jacket. Accompanying the picture was an article from the *Tribune*, headlined LOCAL ARTIST DIES IN MIDNIGHT ACCIDENT.

"Ronald Reuel," I said, glancing over the article. "I've heard of him. Has a studio in Bucktown, I think."

Mab nodded. "Hailed as a visionary of the American artistic culture. Though I assume they use the term lightly."

"'Creator of worlds of imagination,' it says. I guess now that he's dead, they'll say all kinds of nice things." I read over the rest of the article. "The police called it an accident."

"It was not," Mab responded.

I looked up at her. "How do you know?"

She smiled.

"And why should you care?" I asked. "It isn't like the cops are after you."

"There are powers of judgment other than mortal law. It is enough for you to know that I wish to see justice done," she said. "Simply that."

"Uh-huh," I said, frowning. "You said something was stolen from him. What?"

"You'll know it."

I put the picture back in the envelope and left it on my desk. "I'll think about it."

Mab assured me, "You will accept this request, Wizard Dresden."

I scowled at her and set my jaw. "I said I'll *think* about it."

Mab's cat-eyes glittered, and I saw a few white, white teeth in her smile. She took a pair of dark sunglasses from the pocket of her jacket. "Is it not polite to show a client to the door?"

I glowered. But I got up out of the chair and walked to the door, the Faerie Queen's heady perfume, the narcotic *scent* of her enough to make me a little dizzy. I fought it away and tried to keep my scowl in place, opening the door for her with a jerky motion.

"Your hand yet pains you?" she asked.

"What do you think?"

Mab placed her gloved hand on my wounded one, and a sudden spike of sheer, vicious cold shot up through the injury like a frozen scalpel before lancing up my arm, straight toward my heart. It took my breath, and I felt my heart skip a beat, two, before it labored into rhythm again. I gasped and swayed, and only leaning against the door kept me from falling down completely.

"Dammit," I muttered, trying to keep my voice down. "We had a deal."

"I agreed not to punish you for refusing me, wizard. I agreed not to punish or harass you by proxy." Mab smiled. "I did that just for spite."

I growled. "That isn't going to make it more likely that I take this case."

"You will take it, emissary," Mab said, her voice confident. "Expect to meet your counterpart this evening."

"What counterpart?"

"As you are Winter's emissary in this matter, Summer, too, has sought out one to represent her interests."

"I got plans tonight," I growled. "And I haven't taken the case."

Mab tilted her dark glasses down, cat eyes on mine. "Wizard. Do you know the story of the Fox and Scorpion?"

I shook my head, looking away.

"Fox and Scorpion came to a brook," Mab murmured, her voice low, sweet. "Wide was the water. Scorpion asked Fox for a ride on his back. Fox said, 'Scorpion, will you not sting me?' Scorpion said, 'If I did, it would mean the death of us both.' Fox agreed, and Scorpion climbed onto his back. Fox swam, but halfway over, Scorpion struck with his deadly sting. Fox gasped, 'Fool, you have doomed us both. Why?' 'I am a scorpion,' said Scorpion. 'It is my nature.' "

"That's the story?" I said. "Don't quit your day job."

Mab laughed, velvet ice, and it sent another shiver through me. "You will accept this case, wizard. It is what you are. It is your nature." Then she turned and walked down the hall, aloof, reserved, cold. I glowered after her for a minute before I shut the door.

Maybe I'd been shut away in my lab too long, but Spenser never mentions that the Faerie Queen has a great ass.

So I notice these things. So sue me.

Chapter Four

I leaned against my door with my eyes closed, trying to think. I was scared. Not in that half-pleasant adrenaline-charged way, but quietly scared. Wait-on-the-results-of-medical-tests scared. It's a rational sort of fear that puts a lawn chair down in the front of your thoughts and brings a cooler of drinks along with it.

I was working for the queen of wicked faeries—well, Queen of Winter, of the Unseelie faeries, at any rate. The Unseelie weren't universally vicious and evil, any more than the Seelie, the Summer fae, were all kind and wise. They were much like the season for which they had been named—cold, beautiful, pitiless, and entirely without remorse. Only a fool would willingly associate with them.

Not that Mab had given me much of a choice, but technically speaking there had been one. I could have turned her down flat and accepted whatever came.

I chewed on my lip. Given the kind of business I was in, I hadn't felt the need to spend too much time hunting for a good retirement plan. Wizards can live a long, long time, but most of the ones that do tend to be the kind that stick at home in their study. Not many tossed their gauntlets into as many faces as I had.

I'd been clever a couple of times, lucky a couple of times, and I'd come out ahead of the game so far—but sooner or later the dice were going to come up snake eyes. It was as simple as that, and I knew it.

Fear. Maybe that was why I'd agreed to Mab's bargain. Susan's life had been twisted horribly, and that was my fault. I wanted to help her before I went down swinging.

But some little voice in the back of my head told me that I was being awfully noble for someone who had flinched when push had come to shove. The little voice told me that I was making excuses. Some part of me that doesn't trust much and believes in even less whispered that I had simply been afraid to say no to a being who could probably make me long for death if I denied her.

Either way, it was too late for questions now. I'd made the bargain, for better or worse. If I didn't want it to end badly, I'd better start figuring out how to get out of it without getting swallowed up in faerie politics. I wouldn't do that by taking the case of Ronald Reuel, I was pretty damn sure. Mab wouldn't have offered it if she hadn't thought it would get me further entangled than I already was. Maybe she had me in a metaphysical armlock, but that didn't mean I was going to jump every time she said "frog." I could figure out something else. And besides, I had other problems on my mind.

There wasn't much time to spare before the Council meeting that evening, so I got my things together and got ready to leave. I paused at the door, with that nagging feeling I get when I'm forgetting something. My eyes settled on my stack of unpaid bills and I remembered.

Money. I'd come here to get a case. To make some cash. To pay my bills. Now I was hip-deep in trouble and heading straight out to sea, and I hadn't gotten a retainer or made one red cent.

I swore at myself and pulled the door shut behind me.

You'd think as long as I was gambling with my soul, I would have thought to get Mab to throw in fifty bucks an hour plus expenses.

I headed out to start taking care of business. Traffic in Chicago can be the usual nightmare of traffic in any large American city, but that afternoon's was particularly bad. Stuck behind a wreck up ahead, the Beetle turned into an oven, and I spent a while sweating and wishing that I wasn't too much of a wizard for a decent modern air conditioner to survive. That was one of the hazards of magical talent. Technology doesn't get along so well when there is a lot of magic flying around. Anything manufactured after World War II or so seemed prone to failure whenever a wizard was nearby. Stuff with microcircuits and electrical components and that kind of paraphernalia seemed to have the most trouble, but even simpler things, like the Beetle's air conditioner, usually couldn't last long.

Running late, I dropped by my apartment and waded through the wreckage looking for my gear for the meeting. I couldn't find everything, and I didn't have time to get a shower. The refrigerator was empty, and all I could find to eat was a half-wrapped candy bar I'd started and never finished. I stuffed it into my pocket, then headed for the meeting of the White Council of Wizardry.

Where I was sure to cut a devastating swath with my couth, hygiene, and natural grace.

I pulled into the parking lot across the street from McCormick Place Complex, one of the largest convention centers in the world. The White Council had rented one of the smaller buildings for the meeting. The sun hung low in the sky, growing larger and redder as it dropped toward the horizon.

I parked the Beetle in the relative cool of the lowest level of the parking garage, got out of the car, and walked around to the front to open the trunk. I was shrugging into my robe when I heard a car coming in, engine rumbling and rattling. A black '37 Ford pickup, complete with rounded fenders and wooden-slat sides on the bed, pulled into the empty space next to mine. There wasn't any rust on the old machine, and it gleamed with fresh wax. A weathered shotgun rode on top of a wooden rack against the rear wall of the passenger compartment, and in the slot beneath it sat a worn old wizard's staff. The Ford crunched to a halt with a kind of dinosaur solidity, and a moment later the engine died.

The driver, a short, stocky man in a white T-shirt and blue denim overalls, opened the door and hopped down from the truck with the brisk motions of a busy man. His head was bald except for a fringe of downy white tufts, and a bristling white beard covered his mouth and jowls. He slammed the door shut with thoughtless strength, grinned, and boomed, "Hoss! Good to see you again."

"Ebenezar," I responded, if without the same ear-ringing volume. I felt myself answer his grin with my own, and stepped over to him to shake his offered hand. I squeezed hard, purely out of self-defense. He had a grip that could crush a can of spinach. "You'd better take the shotgun down. Chicago PD is picky about people with guns."

Ebenezar snorted and said, "I'm too old to go worrying about every fool thing."

"What are you doing out of Missouri, sir? I didn't think you came to Council meetings."

He let out a barking laugh. "The last time I didn't, they saddled me with this useless teenage apprentice. Now I don't hardly dare miss one. They might make him move in again."

I laughed. "I wasn't that bad, was I?"

He snorted. "You burned down my barn, Hoss. And I never did see that cat again. He just lit out and didn't come back after what you did with the laundry."

I grinned. Way back when, I'd been a stupid sixteen-year-old orphan who had killed his former teacher in what amounted to a magical duel. I'd gotten lucky, or it would have been me that had been burned to a briquette instead of old Justin. The Council has Seven Laws of Magic, and the first one is Thou Shalt Not Kill. When you break it, they execute you, no questions asked.

But some of the other wizards had thought I deserved lenience, and there was a precedent for using lethal magic in self-defense against the black arts. I'd been put on a kind of horrible probation instead, with any further infraction against the Laws punishable by immediate summary judgment. But I'd also been sixteen, and legally a minor, which meant I had to go someplace—preferably where the Council could keep an eye on me and where I could learn better control of my powers.

Ebenezar McCoy had lived in Hog Hollow, Missouri, for as long as anyone could remember—a couple of centuries at least. After my trial, the Council packed me off to his farm and put him in charge of the remainder of my education. Education, to Ebenezar, meant a lot of hard work on the farm during the day, studying in the evening, and getting a good night's sleep.

I didn't learn much magic from him, but I'd gotten some more important stuff. I'd learned more about patience. About creating something, making something worthwhile out of my labor. And I'd found as much peace as a teenager could expect. It had been a good place for me then, and he'd given me the kind of respect and distance I'd needed. I would always be grateful.

Ebenezar frowned past me, squinting at the Beetle. I followed his gaze and realized that my car looked like it had been pounded with bloody hailstones. The toad blood had dried to dark caramel brown, except where my windshield wipers had swept it away. Ebenezar looked back at me, lifting his eyebrows.

"Rain of toads," I explained.

"Ah." He rubbed his jaw and squinted at me and then at the cloth wrapped around my hand. "And that?"

"Accident in the office. It's been a long day."

"Uh-huh. You know, you don't look so good, Hoss." He looked up at me, his eyes steady, frowning. I didn't meet the look. We'd traded a soulgaze, years ago, so I wasn't afraid of it happening again. I just didn't want to look at the old man and see disappointment there. "I hear you been getting into some trouble up here."

"Some," I admitted.

"You all right?"

"I'll make it."

"Uh-*huh*. I'm told the senior Council is pretty upset," he said. "Could mean trouble for you, Hoss."

"Yeah. I figured."

He sighed and shook his head, looking me up and down, nose wrinkling. "You don't exactly look like a shining example of young wizardry. And you're not going to make much of an impression wearing that."

I scowled, defensive, and draped the stole of rich blue silk over my head. "Hey, I'm supposed to wear a robe. We all are."

Ebenezar gave me a wry look and turned to the pickup. He dragged a suit carrier out of the back and pulled out a robe of opulent dark fabric, folding it over one arm. "Somehow I don't think a plaid flannel bathrobe is what they had in mind."

I tied the belt of my old bathrobe and tried to make the stole look like it should go with it. "My cat used my good robe as a litter box. Like I said, it's been a long day, sir."

He grunted and took his stumpy old wizard's staff off the gun rack. Then he drew out his scarlet stole and draped it over the robe. "Too hot to wear this damn thing out here. I'll put it on inside." He looked up, pale blue eyes glittering as he swept his gaze around the parking garage.

I frowned at him and tilted my head. "We're late. Shouldn't we be getting to the meeting?"

"In a minute. Some people want to talk before we close the circle." He glanced aside at me and said more quietly, "Senior Council."

I drew in a sharp breath. "Why do they want to talk to us?"

"Not us. You. Because I asked them to, boy. People are scared. If the Senior Council allows things to come to an open vote of the entire Council, it could go badly for you. So I wanted some of them to get a chance to meet you for themselves before they started making choices that could get you hurt."

Ebenezar leaned back against his truck and folded his arms across his belly, bowing his head with his eyes squinted almost completely shut. He said nothing more. Nothing about him betrayed any tension, from the set of his bull neck and solid shoulders to the stillness of his gnarled, work-hardened hands. But I felt it in him, somewhere.

I said quietly, "You're going out on a limb for me, aren't you?"

He shrugged. "Some, maybe."

I felt the anger run hot in my belly, and I tightened the muscles of my jaw. But I made an effort to keep my voice even. Ebenezar had been more than my teacher. He'd been my mentor at a time when I hadn't had anything else left to me. He'd helped me when a lot of other people wanted to kick me while I was down—or, more accurately, decapitate me while I was down. I owed him my life in more than one sense.

It would be wrong for me to lose my temper, no matter how tired or hurt I was. Besides, the old man could probably kick my ass. So I managed to tone my answer down to, "What the hell do you think you're doing, *sir*? I am not your apprentice anymore. I can look out for myself."

He didn't miss the anger. Guess I'm not much of a poker player. He looked up at me and said, "I'm trying to help you, boy."

"I've got all the help I can stand already," I told him. "I've got vampires breathing down my neck, toads falling from the sky, I'm about to get evicted from everywhere, I'm late to the Council meeting, and I am *not* going to stand around out here and suck up to members of the Senior Council to lobby their vote."

Ebenezar thrust out his jaw, rapping his staff against the ground to emphasize his sentences. "Harry, this is not a game. The Wardens and the Merlin are dead set against you. They *will* move. Without support in the Senior Council you're in trouble, Hoss."

I shook my head and thought of Mab's glacial gaze. "It can't be much more than I'm in already."

"The hell it can't. They could make a sacrificial lamb of you."

"They will or they won't. Either way I'm not going to start brownnosing the Council now, Senior or otherwise."

"Harry, I'm not saying you need to get on your knees and beg, but if you would just—"

I rolled my eyes. "What? Offer a couple of favors? Sell my vote to one of the blocs? Fuck that. Pardon my French. I've got enough problems without—" I broke off abruptly, narrowing my eyes. "You're the last one I would expect to be telling me to get involved in Council politics."

Ebenezar scowled at me. "Oh?"

"Yeah. In fact, the last time I checked, you told me the whole swill-spouting pack of lollygagging skunkwallows could transform one another into clams, for all you cared."

"I did not say that."

"Did so."

Ebenezar's face turned red. "Boy, I ought to—"

"Save it," I told him. "Go ahead and punch me or whatever, but threats just aren't hitting me like they used to."

Ebenezar snorted at me and slammed his staff on the concrete once more before turning and stalking several paces away. He stood there for a minute, muttering to himself. Or I thought he was muttering. After a minute, the sound resolved itself into swallowed laughter.

I scowled at his back. "What?" I demanded. "Why are you laughing at me?"

Ebenezar turned out to an open parking space across the row and said, "There. Are you satisfied?"

I never felt a whisper of power, not a breath of magic stirring against me. Whatever veil had been used, it was beyond anything I could have even attempted. I'm not exactly a neurosurgeon when it comes to magic. I've had my moments, but mostly I muddle through by shoving a lot of energy into my spells until it doesn't matter if half of it is slopping out. Magically speaking, I'm a brawny thug, and noisy as hell.

This veil was good, almost perfect, completely silent. Way better than I would be able to do anytime in the next couple of decades. I stared in abrupt shock as it fell and two people I hadn't sensed at all simply flickered into existence in front of me.

The first was a woman better than six feet tall. She wore her grey hair coiled in a net at the base of her neck. She had already put on her robes of office, black silk nearly the same color as her skin, and her purple stole echoed the gems at her throat. Her eyebrows were still dark, and she had one of them arched as she regarded Ebenezar, then me, with a completely unamused expression. When she spoke, her voice was a low, rich alto. "Lollygagging skunkwallows?"

"Matty—" Ebenezar began, laughter still flavoring his words. "You know how I get when I'm talking about Council politics."

"Don't you 'Matty' me, Ebenezar McCoy," she snapped. She looked past my old mentor to focus on me. "Wizard Dresden, I am less than amused with your lack of respect toward the White Council."

I lifted my chin and glared down at the woman without meeting her eyes. It's a tough trick to learn, but if you're motivated enough you can do it. "That's a coincidence. I'm not terribly amused with you spying on me."

The black woman's eyes flashed, but Ebenezar cut in before either of us could gather any more steam. "Harry Dresden," he said drily, "meet Martha Liberty."

She shot him a look and said pointedly, "He's arrogant, Ebenezar. Dangerous."

I snorted. "That's every wizard ever."

Martha continued as if I hadn't spoken. "Bitter. Angry. Obsessive."

Ebenezar frowned. "Seems to me he has good reason to be. You and the rest of the Senior Council saw to that."

Martha shook her head. "You know what he was meant to be. He's too great a risk."

I snapped my fingers twice and hooked a thumb at my own chest. "Hey, lady. He's also right here."

Her eyes flashed at me. "Look at him, Ebenezar. He's a wreck. Look at the destruction he has caused."

Ebenezar took two quick, angry steps toward Martha. "By challenging the Red Court when they were going to kill that young woman? No, Matty. Hoss didn't cause what's happened since. They did. I've read his report. He stood up to them when they damn well needed standing up to."

Martha folded her arms, strong and brown against the front of her robes. "The Merlin says—"

"I know what he says," Ebenezar muttered. "By now I don't even need to hear him say it. And as usual, he's half right, half wrong, and all gutless."

Martha frowned at him for a long and silent moment. Then she looked at me and asked, "Do you remember me, Mister Dresden?"

I shook my head. "They had a hood on me all through the trial, and I missed the meeting Warden Morgan called a couple years back. They were taking a bullet out of my hip."

"I know. I never saw your face before today." She moved then, lifting a slender staff of some dark reddish wood, and walked toward me, the staff clicking with each step. I faced her, bracing myself, but she didn't try to meet my gaze. She studied my features for a long moment and then said, very quietly, "You have your mother's eyes."

An old pain rolled through me. I barely managed more than a whisper in response. "I never knew her."

"No. You didn't." She lifted one wide, heavy hand and passed it through the air on either side of my head, as though smoothing my hair without touching it. Then she raked her eyes over me, staring intently at my bandaged hand. "You hurt. You're in great pain."

"It isn't bad. It should heal in a few days."

"I'm not talking about your hand, boy." She closed her eyes and bowed her head. Her voice came heavily, slowly, as though her lips were reluctant to let the words pass them. "Very well, Ebenezar. I will support you."

She stepped back and away from me, back to the side of the second person who had appeared. I'd almost forgotten about him, and looking at him now I began to see why. He contained a quality of stillness I could all but feel around him—easy to sense but difficult to define. His features, his bearing, everything about him blended into his background, swallowed by that stillness, patient and quiet as a stone beneath moon and sun.

He was of innocuous height, five eight, maybe five nine. His dark hair was plaited in a long braid, despite age that seamed his features like bronzed leather under a scarlet sun, warm and worn. His eyes, beneath silver brows, were dark, inscrutable, intense. Eagle feathers adorned his braid, a necklace of bits of bone circled his throat, and he had a beaded bracelet wrapped around one forearm, which poked out from beneath his black robe. One weathered hand gripped a simple, uncarved staff.

"Hoss," Ebenezar said, "this here is Listens to Wind. But that's always been too much of a mouthful for me, even for a genuine Illinois medicine man. I just call him Injun Joe."

"How—" I began. Maybe some kind of irony could be found in the first part of asking how did he do, but something scratched at my foot and I left off the rest. I let out a yelp and jumped away from a flash of fur near my feet without stopping to see what it was. It had been that kind of day.

I tripped over my own staff and fell down. I scrambled over on my back to put my legs between my face and whatever snarling thing might be coming for me, drawing back one foot to kick.

I needn't have bothered. A raccoon, and a fairly young one at that, stood up on its hind legs and chittered at me in annoyance, soft grey fur bristling wildly as though it had been fit for an animal several sizes larger. The raccoon gave me what I swore was an irritated look, eyes glittering within the dark mask of fur around them, then ran over to Injun Joe's feet and neatly scaled the old man's wooden staff. It swarmed up Injun Joe's arm to perch on his shoulder, still chittering and squeaking.

"Uh," I managed, "how do you do."

The raccoon chirruped again, and Injun Joe tilted his head to one side, then nodded. "Good. But Little Brother is irritated with you. He thinks anyone with that much food should share it."

I frowned; then I remembered the half-eaten stale

candy bar in my pocket. "Oh, right." I pulled it out, broke it in half, and held it out to the raccoon. "Peace?"

Little Brother let out a pleased squeak and darted back down Injun Joe's arm and staff to my hand. He snatched the candy and then retired a few feet away to eat it.

When I looked up, Injun Joe stood over me, offering his hand. "Little Brother thanks you. He likes you, too. How do you do, Wizard Dresden."

I took his hand and got to my feet. "Thanks, uh, Listens to Wind."

Ebenezar interjected, "Injun Joe."

Injun Joe winked one grave eye at me. "The redneck hillbilly doesn't read. Otherwise he'd know that he can't call me that anymore. Now I'm Native American Joe."

I wasn't sure I was supposed to laugh, but I did. Injun Joe nodded, dark eyes sparkling. Then he murmured, "The one you knew as Tera West sends her respects."

I blinked at him.

Injun Joe turned to Ebenezar and nodded, then walked slowly back to Martha's side.

Ebenezar let out a satisfied grunt. "Fine. Now where is the Russian? We haven't got all day."

Martha's expression became remote. Injun Joe's face didn't change, but he moved his eyes to the tall wizard beside him. No one spoke, and the silence grew thick enough to choke on.

Ebenezar's face went very pale, and he suddenly leaned hard on his staff. "Simon," he whispered. "Oh, no."

I stepped up beside Ebenezar. "What happened?"

Martha shook her head. "Simon Pietrovich. Senior Council member. Our vampire expert. He was killed less than two days ago. The whole compound in Archangel, Ebenezar. All of them. I'm sorry."

Ebenezar shook his head slowly. His voice was a pale shadow of its usual self. "I've been to his tower. It was a fortress. How did they do it?"

"The Wardens said that they couldn't be sure, but it looked like someone let the killers in past the defenses. They didn't get away unscathed. There were the remains of half a dozen nobles of the Red Court. Many of their warriors. But they killed Simon and the rest."

"Let them in?" Ebenezar breathed. "Treachery? But even if it was true, it would have to be someone who knew his defenses inside and out."

Martha glanced at me, then back at Ebenezar. Something passed between them in that look, but I couldn't tell what.

"No," Ebenezar said. "That's insane."

"Master to student. You know what the Wardens will say."

"It's buffalo chips. It wouldn't ever get past the Senior Council."

"Eben," Martha said gently, "Joseph and I are only two votes now. Simon is gone."

Ebenezar took a blue bandanna from the pocket of his overalls and rubbed it over his pate. "Damnation," he muttered. "Guts and damnation."

I looked at Ebenezar and then at Martha. "What?" I asked. "What does this mean?"

She said, "It means, Wizard Dresden, that the Merlin and others on the Council are preparing to bring allegations against you accusing you of precipitating the war with the Red Court and placing the responsibility for a number of deaths on your head. And because Joseph and I no longer have the support of Simon on the Senior Council, it means that we cannot block the Merlin from laying it to general vote."

Injun Joe nodded, fingers absently resting on Little Brother's fur. "Many of the Council are frightened, Hoss Dresden. Your enemies will use this opportunity to strike through them. Fear will drive them to vote against you."

I shot Ebenezar a glance. My old mentor traded a long look with me, and I saw his eyes stir with uncertainty.

"Hell's bells," I whispered. "I'm in trouble."

Chapter Five

A heavy silence followed, until Ebenezar flexed the fingers of one hand and his knuckles popped. "Who is up for Simon's place?"

Martha shook her head. "I suspect the Merlin will want one of the Germans."

Ebenezar growled. "I've got fifty years' seniority on every mother's son of them."

"It won't matter," Martha said. "There are too many Americans on the Senior Council already for the Merlin's tastes."

Injun Joe scratched Little Brother's chest and said, "Typical. Only real American on the Senior Council is me. Not like the rest of you Johnny-come-latelies."

Ebenezar gave Injun Joe a tired smile.

Martha said, "The Merlin won't be happy if you decide to press a claim now."

Ebenezar snorted. "Aye. And I can't tell you how that breaks my heart."

Martha frowned, pressing her lips together. "We'd best get inside, Ebenezar. I'll tell them to wait for you."

"Fine," my old teacher said, his words clipped. "Go on in."

Without a further word, Martha and Injun Joe departed, black robes whispering. Ebenezar slipped into his robe and put on his scarlet stole. Then he took up his staff again and strode determinedly toward the convention center. I kept pace silently, and worried.

Ebenezar surprised me by speaking. "How's your Latin coming, Hoss? You need me to translate?"

I coughed. "No. I think I can manage."

"All right. When we get inside, hang on to your temper. You've got a reputation as a hothead for some reason."

I scowled at him. "I do not."

"And for being stubborn and contrary."

"I am not."

Ebenezar's worn smile appeared for a moment, but by then we had reached the building where the Council was to meet. I stopped walking, and Ebenezar paused, looking back at me.

"I don't want to go in with you," I said. "If this goes bad, maybe it's better if you have some distance from me."

Ebenezar frowned at me, and for a second I thought he was going to argue. Then he shook his head and went into the building. I gave him a couple of minutes, and then walked up the steps and went in.

The building had the look of an old-time theater—high, arched ceilings, floors of polished stone laid with strips of carpet, and several sets of double doors leading into the theater itself. The air-conditioning had probably been running full blast earlier, but now there was no sound of fan or vent and the building inside felt warmer than it probably should have. None of the lights were on. You couldn't really expect even basic things like lights and air-conditioning to keep running in a building full of wizards.

All the doors leading into what was apparently an actual theater were closed except for one pair, and two men wearing dark Council robes, scarlet stoles, and the grey cloak of the Wardens stood before them.

I didn't recognize one of the men, but the other was Morgan. Morgan stood nearly as tall as I did, only with maybe another hundred pounds of solid, working-man muscle. He had a short beard, patchy with brown and grey, and he wore his hair in a long ponytail. His face was still narrow, sour, and he had a voice to match it. "Finally," he muttered upon seeing me. "I've been waiting for this, Dresden. Finally, you're going to face justice."

"I see someone had a nice big bowl of Fanatic-Os this morning," I said. "I know you don't like it, Morgan, but I was cleared of all those charges. Thanks to you, actually."

His sour face screwed up even more. "I only reported your actions to the Council. I did not think they would be so"—he spat the word like a curse—"lenient."

I stopped in front of the two Wardens and held out my staff. Morgan's partner lifted a crystal pendant from around his neck and ran the crystal over the staff and then over my head, temples, and down the front of my body. The crystal pulsed with a gentle glow of light as it passed over each chakra point. The second Warden nodded to Morgan, and I started to step past him and into the theater.

He put out one broad hand to stop me. "No," he said. "Not yet. Get the dogs."

The other Warden frowned, but that was all the protest he made. He turned and slipped into the theater, and a moment later emerged, leading a pair of Wardhounds behind him.

In spite of myself, I swallowed and took a half step back from them. "Give me a break, Morgan. I'm not enspelled and I'm not toting in a bomb. I'm not the suicidal type."

"Then you won't mind a quick check," Morgan said. He gave me a humorless smile and stepped forward.

The Wardhounds came with him. They weren't actual dogs. I like dogs. They were statues made of some kind of dark grey-green stone, their shoulders as high as my own belt. They had the gaping mouth and too-big eyes of Chinese temple dogs, complete with curling beards and manes. Though they weren't flesh, they moved with a kind of ponderous liquid grace, stone "muscles" shifting beneath the surface of their skins as if they had been living beings. Morgan touched each on the head and muttered something too vague for me to make out. Upon hearing it, both Wardhounds focused upon me and began to prowl in a circle around me, heads down, the floor quivering beneath their weight.

I knew they'd been enchanted to detect any of countless threats that might attempt to approach a Council meeting. But they weren't thinking beings—only devices programmed with a simple set of responses to predetermined stimuli. Though Wardhounds had saved lives often before, there had also been accidents—and I didn't know if my run-in with Mab would leave a residual signature that might set the Wardhounds off.

The dogs stopped, and one of them let out a growl that sounded soothingly akin to bedrock being ripped apart by a backhoe. I tensed and looked down at the dog standing to my right. Its lips had peeled back from gleaming, dark fangs, and its empty eyes were focused on my left hand—the one Mab had wounded by way of demonstration.

I swallowed and held still and tried to think innocent thoughts.

"They don't like something about you, Dresden," Morgan said. I thought I heard an almost eager undertone to his voice. "Maybe I should turn you away, just to be careful."

The other Warden stepped forward, one hand on a short, heavy rod worn on his belt. He murmured, "Could be the injury, if he's hurt. Wizard blood can be pretty potent. Moody, too. Dog could be reacting to anger or fear, through the blood."

"Maybe," Morgan said testily. "Or it could be contraband he's trying to sneak in. Take off the bandage, Dresden."

"I don't want to start bleeding again," I said.

"Fine. I'm denying you entrance, then, in accordance with—"

"Dammit, Morgan," I muttered. I all but tossed my staff at him. He caught it, and held it while I tore at the makeshift bandages I'd put on my hand. It hurt like hell, but I pulled them off and showed him the swollen and oozing wound.

The Wardhound growled again and then appeared to lose interest, pacing back over to sit down beside its mate, suddenly inanimate again.

I turned my eyes to Morgan and stared at him, hard. "Satisfied?" I asked him.

For a second I thought he would meet my gaze. Then he shoved my staff back at me as he turned away. "You're a disgrace, Dresden. Look at yourself. Because of you, good men and women have died. Today you will be called to answer for it."

I tied the bandage back on as best I could and gritted my teeth to keep from telling Morgan to take a long walk off a short cliff. Then I brushed past the Wardens and stalked into the theater.

Morgan watched me go, then said to his partner, "Close the circle." He followed me into the theater, shutting the door behind him, even as I felt the sudden, silent tension of the Wardens closing the circle around the building, shutting it off from any supernatural access.

I hadn't ever actually seen a meeting of the Council—not like this. The sheer variety of it all was staggering, and I stood staring for several moments, taking it in.

The space was a dinner theater of only moderate size, lit by nothing more than a few candles on each table. The room wouldn't have been crowded for a matinee, but as a gathering place for wizards it was positively swamped. The tables on the floor of the theater were almost completely filled with black-robed wizards, variously sporting stoles of blue, gold, and scarlet. Apprentices in their muddy-brown robes lurked at the fringes of the crowd, standing along the walls or crouching on the floor beside their mentors' chairs.

The variety of humanity represented in the theater was startling. Canted Oriental eyes, dark, rich skins of Africa, pale Europeans, men and women, ancient and young, long and short hair, beards long enough to tuck into belts, beards wispy enough to be stirred by a passing breeze. The theater buzzed in dozens of languages, of which I could identify only a fraction. Wizards laughed and scowled, smiled and stared blankly, sipped from flasks and soda cans and cups or sat with eyes closed in meditation. The scents of spices and perfumes and chemicals all blended together into something pervasive, always changing, and the auras of so many practitioners of the Art seemed to be feeling just as social, reaching out around the room to touch upon other auras, to echo or strike dissonance with their energies, tangible enough to feel without even trying. It was like walking through drifting cobwebs that were constantly brushing against my cheeks and eyelashes—not dangerous but disconcerting, each one wildly unique, utterly different from the next.

The only thing the wizards had in common was that none of them looked as scruffy as me.

A roped-off section at the far right of the hall held the envoys of various organizations of allies and supernatural interests, most of whom I had only a vague idea about. Wardens stood here and there where they could overlook the crowd, grey cloaks conspicuous amid the black and scattered brown ones—but somehow I doubted they were as obtrusive as my own faded blue-and-white flannel. I garnered offended looks from nearly everyone I walked past—mostly white-haired old wizard folk. One or two apprentices nearer my own age covered their mouths as I went past, hiding grins. I looked around for an open chair, but I didn't spot one, until I saw Ebenezar wave at me from a table in the front row of the theater, nearest the stage. He nodded at the seat next to him. It was the only place available, and I joined him.

On the theater stage stood seven podiums, and at six of them stood members of the Senior Council, in dark robes with purple stoles. Injun Joe Listens to Wind and Martha Liberty stood at two.

At the center podium stood the Merlin of the White Council, a tall man, broad of shoulder and blue of eye, with hair falling past his shoulders in shining, pale waves and a flowing silver beard. The Merlin spoke in a rolling basso voice, Latin phrases gliding as smoothly from his mouth as from any Roman senator's.

"*. . . et, quae cum ita sint, censeo iam nos dimittere rees cottidianas et de magna re gravi deliberare—id est, illud bellum contra comitatum rubrum.*" And given the circumstances, I move to dispense with the usual formalities in order to discuss the most pertinent issue before us—the war with the Red Court. "*Consensum habemus?*" All in favor?

There was a general murmur of consent from the wizards in the room. I didn't feel any need to add to it. I tried to slip unnoticed into the seat beside Ebenezar, but the Merlin's bright blue eyes spotted me and grew shades colder.

The Merlin spoke, and though I knew he spoke perfectly intelligible English, he addressed me in Latin, quick and liquid—but his own perfect command of the speech worked against him. He was easy to understand. *"Ahhh, Magus Dresdenus. Prudenter ades nobis dum de bello quod inceperis diceamus. Ex omni parte ratio tua pro hoc comitatu nobis placet."* Ah, Wizard Dresden. How thoughtful of you to join us in discussions of the war you started. It is good to know that you have such respect for this Council.

He delivered that last while giving my battered old bathrobe a pointed look, making sure that anyone in the room who hadn't noticed would now. Jerk. He let silence fall afterward and it was left to me to answer him. Also in Latin. Big fat jerk.

Still, it was my first Council meeting as a full wizard, and he *was* the Merlin, after all. And I *did* look pretty bad. Plus, Ebenezar shot me a warning glance. I swallowed a hot answer and took a stab at diplomacy.

"Uh," I said, *"ego sum miser, Magus Merlinus. Dolor diei longi me tenet. Opus es mihi altera, uh, vestiplicia."* Sorry, Merlin. It's been a very long day. I meant to have my other robe.

Or that's what I *tried* to say. I must have conjugated something wrong, because when I finished, the Merlin blinked at me, expression mild. "Quod est?"

Ebenezar winced and asked me in a whisper, "Hoss? You sure you don't want me to translate for you?"

I waved a hand at him. "I can do it." I scowled as I tried to put together the right words, and spoke again. *"Excusationem vobis pro vestitu meo atque etiam tarditate facio."* Please excuse my lateness and appearance.

The Merlin regarded me with passionless, distant features, evidently well content to let my mouth run. Ebenezar put his hand over his eyes.

"What?" I demanded of him in a fierce whisper.

Ebenezar squinted up at me. "Well. First you said, 'I am a sorry excuse, Merlin, a sad long day held me. I need me a different laundress.' "

I blinked. "What?"

"That's what the Merlin said. Then you said 'Excuses to you for my being dressed and I also make lately.' "

I felt my face heat up. Most of the room was still staring at me as though I was some sort of raving lunatic, and it dawned on me that many of the wizards in the room probably did not speak English. As far as they were concerned, I probably sounded like one.

"Goddamned correspondence course. Maybe you should translate for me," I said.

Ebenezar's eyes sparkled, but he nodded with a grave expression. "Happy to."

I slipped into my seat while Ebenezar stood up and made an apology for me, his Latin terse and precise, his voice carrying easily throughout the hall. I saw the gathered wizards' expressions grow more or less mollified as he spoke.

The Merlin nodded and continued in his textbook-perfect Latin. "Thank you, Wizard McCoy, for your assistance. The first order of business in addressing the crisis before us is to restore the Senior Council to its full membership. As some of you have doubtless learned by now, Senior Council member Pietrovich was killed in an attack by the Red Court two days past."

A gasp and a low murmur ran through the theater.

The Merlin allowed a moment to pass. "Past conflicts with the Red Court have not moved with this kind of alacrity, and this may indicate a shift in their usual strategy. As a result, we need to be able to react quickly to further developments—which will require the leadership provided by a full membership on the Senior Council."

The Merlin continued speaking, but I leaned over to Ebenezar. "Let me guess," I whispered. "He wants to fill the opening on the Senior Council so that he'll be able to control the vote?"

Ebenezar nodded. "He'll have three votes for sure, then, and most times four."

"What are we going to do about it?"

"You aren't going to do anything. Not yet." He looked intently at me. "Keep your temper, Hoss. I mean it. The Merlin will have three plans to take you down."

I shook my head. "What? How do you know that?"

"He always does things that way," Ebenezar muttered. His eyes glittered with something ugly. "A plan, a backup plan, and an ace in the hole. I'll shoot down the first one, and I'll help you with the second. The third is all yours, though."

"What do you mean? What plan?"

"Hush, Hoss. I'm paying attention."

A balding wizard with bristling white eyebrows and a bushy blue beard, his scalp covered in flowing blue tattoos, leaned forward from the far side of the table and glared at me. "Shhhhh."

Ebenezar nodded at the man, and we both turned back to face the stage.

"And it is for this reason," the Merlin continued, "that I now ask Klaus Schneider, as a long-standing senior wizard of impeccable reputation, to take on the responsibility of membership in the Senior Council. All in favor?"

Martha glanced at Ebenezar and murmured, "A moment, honored Merlin. I believe protocol requires that we open the floor to debate."

The Merlin sighed. "Under normal circumstances, Wizard Liberty, of course. But we have little time for the niceties of our usual procedures. Time is of the essence. So, all in—"

Injun Joe interrupted. "Wizard Schneider is a fine enchanter, and he has a reputation for skill and honesty. But he is young for such a responsibility. There are wizards present who are his senior in experience and the Art. They deserve the consideration of the Council."

The Merlin shot Injun Joe a frown. "*Thank* you for your perspective, Wizard Listens to Wind. But though your commentary is welcome, it was not asked for. There is no one present senior to Wizard Schneider who has not already declined a seat upon the Senior Council, and rather than run through meaningless nominations and repeated declinations, I had intended—"

Ebenezar cut in, sotto voce but loud enough for the Merlin to hear him, in English. "You had intended to shove your favorite down everyone's throats while they were too worried to notice."

The Merlin fell abruptly quiet, his eyes falling on Ebenezar in a sudden, pointed silence. He spoke in a low voice, his English carrying a rich British accent. "Go back to your mountain, Ebenezar. Back to your sheep. You are not welcome here, and never have been."

Ebenezar looked up at the Merlin with a toothy smile, Scots creeping back into his vowels. "Aye, Alfred, laddie, I know." He switched back to Latin and raised his voice again. "Every member of the Council has a right to speak his mind on these matters. You all know how important the appointment of one Senior Council member is. How many of you believe this matter too serious to leave to a consensus? Speak now."

The theater rumbled with a general "Aye," to which I added my own voice. Ebenezar looked around the room and then raised an eyebrow at the Merlin.

I could see frustration not quite hidden on the old man's face. I could almost taste his desire to slam his fist down on the podium, but he controlled himself and nodded. "Very well. Then, in accordance with procedure, we will offer the position to the senior-most wizards present." He looked to one side, where a slim-faced, prim-looking wizard sat with a quill, a bottle of ink, and pages and pages of parchment. "Wizard Peabody, will you consult the registry?"

Peabody reached under his table and came out with a bulging satchel. He muttered something to himself and rubbed some ink onto his nose with one finger, then he opened the satchel, which held what looked like a couple of reams of parchment. His eyes glazed over slightly, and he reached into the papers seemingly at random. He drew out a single page, put it on the desk before him, nodded in satisfaction, then read in a reedy voice, "Wizard Montjoy."

"Research trip in the Yucatán," Martha Liberty said.

Peabody nodded. "Wizard Gomez."

"Still sleeping off that potion," provided a grey-cloaked Warden standing by the wall.

Peabody nodded. "Wizard Luciozzi."

"Sabbatical," said the blue-bearded and tattooed wizard behind me. Ebenezar frowned, and one of his cheeks twitched in a nervous tic.

It went on like that for close to a quarter hour. Some of the more interesting reasons for absence included "He got real married," "Living under the polar ice cap," and "Pyramid sitting," whatever that was.

Peabody finally read, with a glance up at the Merlin, "Wizard McCoy." Ebenezar grunted and stood. Peabody read another half-dozen names before stating, "Wizard Schneider."

A small, round-cheeked man with a fringe of gauzy white down over his scalp and a round belly stretching his robes stood up and gave Ebenezar a brief nod. Then he looked up at the Merlin and said, in Latin with a heavy Germanic accent, "While I am grateful for the offer, honored Merlin, I must respectfully decline your nomination, in favor of Wizard McCoy. He will serve the Council more ably than I."

The Merlin looked as though someone had grated slices of lemon against his gums. "Very well," he said. "Do any other senior wizards here wish to present themselves for consideration over Wizard McCoy?"

I was betting no one would, especially given the looks on the faces of the wizards nearby. Ebenezar himself never moved his eyes from the Merlin. He just stood with his feet spread wide apart and planted, his eyes steady, confident. Silence fell over the hall.

The Merlin looked around the hall, his lips pressed tightly together. Finally, he gave his head a very slight shake. "All in favor?"

The room rumbled with a second, more affirmative "Aye."

"Very well," the Merlin said, his upper lip twisting and giving the words an acid edge. "Wizard McCoy, take your place upon the Senior Council."

There was a murmur of what sounded a bit like relief from those in the hall. Ebenezar glanced back and winked at me. "One down. Two to go," he murmured. "Stay sharp." Then he hitched up his robes and stumped onto the stage, to the empty podium between Martha Liberty and Injun Joe. "Less talking, more doing," he said, loudly enough to be heard by the whole hall. "There's a war on."

"Precisely what I was thinking," the Merlin said, and nodded to one side. "Let us address the war. Warden Morgan, would you please stand forward and give the Council the Wardens' tactical assessment of the Red Court?"

An oppressive silence settled over the room, so that I heard every sound of Morgan's boots as he stepped up onto the stage. The Merlin moved aside, and Morgan placed a glittering gem or crystal of some kind upon the podium. Behind that, he set a candle, which he lit with a muttered incantation. Then he framed the candle with his hands and murmured again.

Light streaked from the candle into the crystal in a

glowing stream and sprang up out of the crystal again in a large cone stretching up above the stage, several yards across at the top. Within the cone of light appeared a spinning globe of the Earth, its continents vaguely misshapen, like something drawn from a couple of centuries past.

A murmur ran through the room, and Bluebeard, at my table, muttered in Latin, "Impressive."

"Bah," I said in English. "He stole that from *Return of the Jedi*."

Bluebeard blinked at me, uncomprehending. I briefly debated trying to translate *Star Wars* into Latin and decided against it. See, I can have common sense, too.

Morgan's low voice rumbled out in Latin phrases, rough but understandable. Which meant he spoke it better than me. Jerk. "The flashing red spots on the map are the locations of known attacks of the Red Court and their allies. Most of them resulted in casualties of one form or another." As he spoke, widely scattered motes of red color began to form on the globe like the glowing lights of a Christmas tree. "As you can see, most of the activity has taken place in Western Europe."

A mutter went through the room. The Old World was the domain of the Old School of wizardry—the "maintain secrecy and don't attract attention" way of thinking. I guess they have a point, given the Inquisition and all. I don't belong to the Old School. I have an ad in the Yellow Pages, under "Wizards." Big shocker—I'm the only one there. I have to pay the bills somehow, don't I?

Morgan droned on dispassionately. "We have known for a long time that the main power center of the Red

Court is somewhere in South America. Our sources there are under pressure, and it has become difficult to get any information out of the area. We have had advance warning of several attacks, and the Wardens have managed to intercede with minimal losses of life, with the exception of the attack at Archangel." The globe paused in its spinning, and my eyes fastened on the glowing point of light on the northwest coast of Russia. "Though it is presumed that Wizard Pietrovich's death curse took a heavy toll on his attackers, no one in his household survived the attack. We don't know how they got past his defenses. It would appear that the Red Court may have access to information or aspects of the Art that they have not before had."

The Merlin stepped back to the podium, and Morgan collected his crystal. The globe vanished. "Thank you, Warden," the Merlin said. "As we expected from Council records, our various retreats and Paths through the Nevernever are threatened. Frankly speaking, ladies and gentlemen, the Red Court holds us at a disadvantage within the mortal world. Modern technology so often disagrees with us that it makes travel difficult under the best of circumstances and unreliable in a time of conflict. We vitally need to secure safe Paths through the Nevernever or else risk being engaged and overwhelmed in detail by an opponent who can move more rapidly than we. To that end, we have dispatched missives to both Queens of the Sidhe. Ancient Mai."

My eyes flickered to the podium to the Merlin's left, where stood another of the Senior Council members, apparently the Ancient Mai. She was a tiny woman of Oriental extraction, her skin fine and pale, her granite-colored hair worn in a long braid curled up at the back of her head and held with a pair of jade combs. She had delicate features only lightly touched by the passage of years, though her dark eyes were rheumy. She unfolded a letter written upon parchment and addressed the Council in a creaky but firm voice. "From Summer, we received this answer. 'Queen Titania does not now, nor will she ever choose sides in the disputes of mortal and anthrophage. She bids both Council and Court alike to keep their war well away from the realms of Summer. She will remain neutral.'"

Ebenezar frowned and leaned forward to ask, "And from Winter?"

I twitched.

The Ancient tilted her head and regarded Ebenezar in perfect silence for a moment, somehow implying her annoyance at his interruption. "Our courier did not return. Upon consulting records of former conflicts, we may confidently assume that Queen Mab will involve herself, if at all, in a time and manner of her own choosing."

I twitched more. There was a pitcher of water on the table, along with some glasses. I poured a drink. The pitcher only rattled against the cup a little. I glanced back at Bluebeard and saw him regarding me with a pensive gaze.

Ebenezar scowled. "Now what is that supposed to mean?"

The Merlin stepped in smoothly. "It means that we must continue whatever diplomacy we may with Winter. At all costs, we must secure the cooperation of one of the Sidhe Queens—or at least prevent the Red Court from accomplishing an alliance of its own until this conflict can be resolved."

Martha Liberty lifted both eyebrows. "Resolved?" she said, her tone pointed. "I would have chosen a word like 'finished' myself."

The Merlin shook his head. "Wizard Liberty, there is no need for this dispute to devolve into an even more destructive conflict. If there exists even a small chance that an armistice can be attained—"

The black woman's voice lashed out at the Merlin, harsh and cold. "Ask Simon Pietrovich how interested the vampires are in reaching a peaceable settlement."

"Contain your emotions, Wizard," the Merlin replied, his voice calm. "The loss of Pietrovich strikes each of us deeply, but we cannot allow that loss to blind us to potential solutions."

"Simon knew them, Merlin," Martha said, her tone flat. "He knew them better than any of us, and they killed him. Do you really think that they will be inclined to seek a reasonable peace with us, when they have already destroyed the wizard best able to protect himself against them? Why should they seek a peace, Merlin? They're *winning*."

The Merlin waved a hand. "Your anger clouds your judgment. They will seek a peace because even in victory they would pay too high a cost."

"Don't be a fool," Martha said. "They will never sue for peace."

"In point of fact," said the Merlin, "they already have." He gestured to the second podium on his left. "Wizard LaFortier."

LaFortier was an emaciated man of medium height

and build. His cheekbones stood out grotesquely from his sunken face, and his bulging eyes looked a couple of sizes too large. He had no hair at all, not even eyebrows, and on the whole it gave him a skeletal look. When he spoke, his voice came out in a resonant basso, deep and warm and smooth. "Thank you, Merlin." He held up an envelope in one thin-fingered hand. "I have here a missive from Duke Ortega, the war leader of the Red Court, received this morning. In it he details the Red Court's motivations in this matter and the terms they desire for peace. He also offers, by token of goodwill, a temporary cessation of hostilities in order to give the Council time to consider, effective this morning."

"Bullshit!" The word burst out of my mouth before my brain realized I had said it. A round of snickers, mostly from brown-robed apprentices, echoed through the theater, and I heard fabric rustle as every wizard in the place turned to look at me. I felt my face heat again, and cleared my throat. "Well, it is," I said to the room. Ebenezar translated for me. "I was attacked by a Red Court hit squad only a few hours ago."

LaFortier smiled at me. It stretched his lips out to show his teeth, like the dried face of a thousand-year-old mummy. "Even if you are not lying, Wizard Dresden, I would hardly expect perfect control of all Red Court forces given your role in precipitating this war."

"*Precipitating* it?" I exclaimed. "Do you have any idea what they *did*?"

LaFortier shrugged. "They defended an assault upon their sovereignty, Wizard. You, acting in the role of representative of this Council, attacked a noble of their court, damaged her property, and killed members of said noble's household and her as well. In addition, the records of local newspapers and authorities reveal that during the altercation, several young men and women were also killed—burned up in a fire, I think. Does that sound familiar to you, Wizard Dresden?"

I clenched my jaw, the sudden rush of rage spilling through me in such a torrent that I could scarcely see, much less trust myself to speak. I'd been brought before the Council for the first time when I had been put on trial for violating the First Law of Magic: Thou Shalt Not Kill. I'd burned my old mentor, Justin, to death. When I'd clashed with Bianca, lately of the Red Court, the previous year, I'd called up a firestorm when it looked as if my companions and I were going to buy it anyway. A lot of vampires burned. The bodies of some people had been found afterward, too. There was no way to tell which of them had been victims of the vampires and already dead when the fire got to them and which, if any, had been alive before I came along. I still have nightmares about it. I'm a lot of things, but I'm not a willing murderer.

To my shock, I felt myself gathering in power, getting ready to unleash it at LaFortier, with his skeletal smirk. Ebenezar caught my eye, his own a little wide, and shook his head quickly. I clenched my hands into tight fists instead of blasting anybody with magic and forced myself to sit down again before I spoke. Self-disciplined, that's me. "I have already detailed my recollection of the events in my report to the Council. I stand by them. Anyone who tells you differently than what you read there is lying."

LaFortier rolled his eyes. "How comfortable it must

be to live in such a clear-cut world, Wizard Dresden. But we are not counting the cost of your actions in coins or hours wasted—we are counting it in blood. Wizards are *dying* because of what *you* did while acting in this Council's name." LaFortier swept his gaze to the rest of the theater, his expression stern, controlled. "Frankly, I think it may be wise for the Council to consider that we may indeed stand in the wrong in this matter and that it might be prudent to give careful considerations to the Red Court's terms for peace."

"What do they want?" I snarled at the man, Ebenezar providing the Latin for the rest of the Council. "A pint of blood a month from each of us? Rights to hunt freely wherever they choose? Amulets to shield them from the light of the sun?"

LaFortier smiled at me and folded his hands atop his podium. "Nothing so dramatic, Dresden. They simply want what any of us would want in this situation. They want justice." He leaned toward me, bulging eyes glittering. "They want you."

Chapter Six

Gulp.

"Me?" I said. *Et la*, LaFortier. Feel the bite of my rapier wit.

"Yes. Duke Ortega writes that you, Wizard Dresden, are considered a criminal by the Red Court. In order to end this conflict they wish to extradite you to an area of their designation for trial. A resolution that is, perhaps, distasteful, but may also be only just."

He didn't get the last word out of his mouth before several dozen wizards around the auditorium rose to their feet with outraged shouts. Others stood up to cry out against them, and still more against them. The room descended into a cacophony of shouts, threats, and cussing (among wizards, cursing is a different matter altogether) in dozens of languages.

The Merlin let people shout for a moment before he called out in a ringing voice, "Order!" No one paid him any attention. He tried once more, then lifted his staff and slammed it down hard on the stage beside him.

There was a flash of light, a roar of sound, and a concussion that slopped the water in my glass up over the brim, spilling it on my flannel bathrobe. A couple of the wispier wizards were knocked down by the force of it—but in any case, the shouting ceased.

"Order!" the Merlin demanded again, in exactly the same tone. "I am well aware of the implications of this situation. But lives are at stake. Your lives and my own. We must consider our options with the utmost gravity."

"What options?" Ebenezar demanded. "We are wizards, not a herd of frightened sheep. Will we give one of our own to the vampires now and pretend that none of this has happened?"

LaFortier snapped, "You read Dresden's report. By his own admission, what the Red Court accuses him of is true. They have a just grievance."

"The situation was clearly a manipulation, a scheme to force Dresden to those actions in hopes of killing him."

"Then he should have been smarter," LaFortier said, his tone flat. "Politics is not a game for children. Dresden played and was beaten. It is time for him to pay the price so that the rest of us may live in peace."

Injun Joe put a hand on Ebenezar's arm and spoke quietly. "Peace cannot be bought, Aleron," he murmured to LaFortier. "History teaches that lesson. I learned it. You should have, too."

LaFortier sneered at Injun Joe. "I don't know what you are babbling about, but—"

I rolled my eyes and stood up again. "He's talking about the American tribes losing their land to white settlers, dolt." I figured Ebenezar would leave the insult out of the translation, but there were more stifled snorts from brown robes around the room. "And about Europe's attempts to appease Hitler before the Second World War. Both attempted to purchase peace with compromise, and both got swallowed up bit by bit."

The Merlin glared at me. "I did not recognize you, Wizard Dresden. Until you have the floor, you will refrain from such outbursts or I will have you removed from this meeting."

I clenched my jaw and sat down. "Sorry. Here I was, figuring we had a responsibility to protect people. What was I thinking?"

"We will protect no one, Wizard Dresden, if we are dead," the Merlin snapped. "Be silent or be removed."

Martha Liberty shook her head. "Merlin, it seems clear that we cannot simply hand one of our own over to the Red Court because of their demands. Despite past differences with Council policy, Dresden *is* a fully ranked wizard—and given his performance in recent years, he seems well deserving of the title."

"I do not question his ability with the Art," LaFortier put in. "I question his judgment, his choices. He has played loose and reckless with his status as a wizard since Justin's death." The bald man turned his bulging eyes to the wizards in the theater. "Wizard Harry Dresden. Apprentice to the Wizard Justin DuMorne. Apprentice to the Wizard Simon Pietrovich. I wonder how the Red Court learned enough of Pietrovich's defenses to bypass them so completely, Dresden."

I stared at LaFortier for a second, shocked. Did the man actually believe that I had learned about this Pietrovich's defenses through Justin? Then sold a Senior Council member of the White Council to the vampires? Justin hadn't exactly taken me around much. Before I'd been put on trial, I hadn't even known that there *was* a White Council—or other wizards at all, for that matter. I gave him the only answer I could. I laughed at him. Wheezy, quiet laughter. I shook my head.

LaFortier's expression grew outraged. "You see?" he demanded to the room. "You see in what contempt he holds this Council? His position as a wizard? Dresden has constantly endangered us all with his obtuse indiscretion, his reckless disregard for secrecy and security. Even if it was someone else who betrayed Pietrovich and his students to the Red Court, Dresden is as guilty of their murder as if he himself had cut their throats. Let the consequences of his decisions fall upon him."

I rose and faced LaFortier, but glanced at the Merlin for permission to speak. He gave the floor to me with a grudging nod. "Impossible," I said. "Or at least impractical. I have violated none of the Laws of Magic in this matter, which rules out a summary trial. I am a full wizard. By Council law, I am therefore entitled to an in-depth investigation and trial—neither of which would provide any kind of workable solution anytime soon."

The room rumbled with agreement when Ebenezar finished translating for me. That was hardly a surprise. If the Council jammed a trial down my throat and then threw me to the wolves, it would set a deadly precedent—one that could haunt any wizard in the room, and they knew it.

LaFortier jabbed a forefinger at me and said, "Quite true. Provided that you are, in fact, a full wizard. I move that the Council vote, immediately, to determine whether or not Dresden's status as a wizard is valid. I remind the Council that his appointment to his stole was a de facto decision based upon circumstantial evidence. He has never stood Trial, never been judged worthy by his peers."

"Like hell I haven't," I answered him. "I beat Justin DuMorne in a duel to the death. Is that not Trial enough for you?"

"Wizard DuMorne died, yes," LaFortier said. "Whether he was defeated in an open duel or burned in his sleep is another matter entirely. Merlin, you have heard my motion. Let the Council vote upon the status of this madman. Let us end this foolishness and return to our lives."

Ouch. An angle I hadn't thought of. If I was stripped of my stole, it would be like a medieval noble having his title taken away. I would no longer be a wizard, politically speaking, and according to Council law and to the Accords between the various supernatural factions, the Council would be obligated to turn over a fugitive murderer to the Red Court. Which would mean, if I was fortunate, a horrible death. If I wasn't fortunate, it could be considerably worse.

Given the kind of day I'd been having, my heart started skittering in my chest.

The Merlin frowned and nodded. "Very well, then. We vote upon the issue of the status of one Harry Dresden. Let those who would have him keep his stole vote for, and those who favor that his status be restored to that of apprentice vote against. All those in fav—"

"Wait," Ebenezar interjected. "I invoke my right as a

member of the Senior Council to reduce the vote to the Senior Council alone."

The Merlin glared at Ebenezar. "On what grounds?"

"On the grounds that there exists a great deal of information about this matter of which the Council at large is unaware. It would be impractical to attempt to explain it all."

"Seconded," Injun Joe murmured.

"Accord," Martha Liberty added. "Three votes yea, honored Merlin. Let the Senior Council make this decision."

My heart started beating again. Ebenezar had made the right call. In a room full of frightened men and women, I wouldn't have had a prayer of keeping my stole. With the vote reduced to the Senior Council, maybe I had a fighting chance.

I could almost see the Merlin trying to figure a way out of it, but Council law is pretty clear on that point. The Senior Council members can always take a matter to a closed vote with three supporters.

"Very well," the Merlin said. The room rustled with whispers. "My interests lie in preserving the health and safety of those upon this Council, and of the communities of mankind in general. I vote against Dresden's validity as an initiate wizard of this Council."

LaFortier jumped in, bulging eyes narrowed. "As do I, and for the same reasons."

Ebenezar spoke next. "I've lived with this young man. I know him. He's a wizard. I vote to preserve his status."

Little Brother chittered from his perch on Injun Joe's shoulder, and the old wizard stroked the raccoon's tail with one hand. "My instincts about this man tell me that he comports himself as a wizard should." He gave a very mild glance to LaFortier. "I vote in favor of his status."

"As do I," Martha Liberty added. "This is not a solution. It is merely an action."

Harry three, bad guys two. I turned my eyes to Ancient Mai.

The tiny woman stood with her eyes closed for a moment, her head bowed. Then she murmured, "No wizard should so blatantly misuse his status as a member of this Council. Nor should he be as irresponsible as Harry Dresden has been with his use of the Art. I vote against his retention of wizard status."

Three to three. I licked my lips, and realized at just that moment that I had been too nervous and involved with events to take note of the seventh member of the Senior Council. He was standing at the far left of the stage. Like the other wizards, he wore a black robe, but his dark purple, almost black stole had a deep cowl upon it as well, which covered his face entirely. The candlelit dimness masked in shadow whatever the cowl didn't cover. He was tall. Taller than me. Seven feet, and thin. His arms were folded, hands hidden inside the voluminous sleeves of his robe. Every eye in the place turned to the seventh member of the Council, and a silence deeper than that of the nearby Great Lake enveloped the room.

It lasted for long moments, then the Merlin prompted, quietly, "Gatekeeper. What say you?"

I leaned forward in my chair, my mouth dry. If he

voted against me, I was betting a Warden would zap me unconscious before the sound of his voice died away.

After several of my frantic heartbeats, the Gatekeeper spoke in a resonant, gentle voice. "It rained toads this morning."

A baffled silence followed. It became, a moment later, a baffled mutter.

"Gatekeeper," the Merlin said, his voice more urgent, "how do you vote?"

"With deliberation," the Gatekeeper said. "It rained toads this morning. That bears consideration. And for that, I must hear what word returns with the messenger."

LaFortier eyed the Gatekeeper and said impatiently, "What messenger? What are you talking about?"

The back doors of the theater burst open, hard, and a pair of grey-cloaked Wardens entered the theater. They each had a shoulder under one of the arms of a brown-robed young man. His face was puffy and swollen, and his hands looked like rotten sausages about to burst. Frost clung to his hair in a thick coating, and his robe looked like it had been dipped in water and then dragged behind a sled team from Anchorage to Nome. His lips were blue, and his eyes fluttered and rolled semicoherently. The Wardens dragged him to the foot of the stage, and the Senior Council gathered at its edge, looking down.

"This is my courier to the Winter Queen," Ancient Mai stated.

"He insisted," one of the Wardens said. "We tried to take him for treatment, but he got so worked up about it I was afraid he would hurt himself, so we brought him to you, Ancient."

"Where did you find him?" the Merlin asked.

"Outside. Someone drove up in a car and pushed him out of it. We didn't see who it was."

"You get the license number?" I asked. Both Wardens turned to eye me. Then they both turned back to the Merlin. Neither of them had gotten it. Maybe license plates were too new a concept. They weren't yet a whole century old, after all. "Hell's bells," I muttered. "I would have gotten it."

Ancient Mai carefully descended from the stage and moved to the young man. She touched his forehead and spoke to him gently in what I presumed to be Chinese. The boy opened his eyes and babbled something broken and halting back at her.

Ancient Mai frowned. She asked something else, which the boy struggled to answer, but it was apparently too much for him. He sagged, his eyes rolling back, and went completely limp.

The Ancient touched his hair and said in Latin, "Take him. Care for him."

The Wardens laid the boy on a cloak, and then four of them carried him out, moving quickly.

"What did he say?" Ebenezar asked. He beat me to it.

"He said that Queen Mab bade him tell the Council she will permit them travel through her realm, provided one request is fulfilled."

The Merlin arched a brow, fingers touching his beard thoughtfully. "What does she request?"

Ancient Mai murmured, "She did not tell him. She said only that she had already made her desires known to one of the Council." The Senior Council withdrew together to one side, speaking in low voices.

I didn't pay them any mind. The Ancient's translation of the messenger's words shocked me enough to keep me from so much as breathing, much less speaking. When I could move, I turned back to my table, leaned forward, and banged my head gently on the wooden surface. Several times.

"Dammit," I muttered, in time with the thumps. "Dammit, dammit, dammit."

A hand touched my shoulder, and I looked up to see the shadowed cowl of the Gatekeeper, standing apart from the rest of the Senior Council. His hand was covered by a black leather glove. I couldn't see any skin showing on him, anywhere.

"You know what the rain of toads means," he said, his voice very quiet. His English had a gentle accent, something part British and part something else. Indian? Middle Eastern?

I nodded. "Trouble."

"Trouble." Though I could not see his face, I suspected a very slight smile had colored the word. The cowl turned toward the other Senior Council members, and he whispered, "There isn't much time. Will you answer me one question honestly, Dresden?"

I checked Bluebeard to see if he was listening in. He had leaned way over toward a round-faced grandma-looking wizardess at another table and appeared to be listening intently to her. I nodded to the Gatekeeper.

He waved his hand. No words, no pause to prepare, nothing. He waved his hand, and the sounds of the room suddenly seemed to blur together, robbed of any coherence at all. "I understand you know how to Listen, too. I would rather no one else heard us." The sound of his voice came to me warped, parts pitched high and others low, oddly reverberating.

I gave him a wary nod. "What is the question?"

He reached up to his cowl, black leather against twilight purple, and drew back the hood a little, enough that I could see the gleam of one dark eye and a rough, thin grey beard against bronzed skin. I couldn't see his other eye. His face seemed to ripple and contort in the shadows, and I had an idea that he was disfigured, maybe burned. In the socket of the missing eye, I saw something silver and reflective.

He leaned down closer and whispered near my ear, "Has Mab chosen an Emissary?"

I struggled not to let the surprise show in my face, but I'm not always good at hiding my feelings. I saw comprehension flicker in the Gatekeeper's shadowed eye.

Dammit. Now I understood why Mab had been so confident. She'd known all along that she had set me up for a deal I couldn't refuse. She'd done it without breaking our bargain, either. Mab wanted me to take up her case, and she seemed perfectly happy to meddle in a supernatural war to get what she wanted.

She'd just been toying with me in my office, and I'd fallen for it. I wanted to kick myself. Somewhere out there was a village I'd deprived of its idiot.

In any case, there was no sense lying to the guy whose vote would decide my fate. I nodded to him. "Yes."

He shook his head. "Precarious balance. The Council can afford neither to keep you nor to cast you out."

"I don't understand."

"You will." He drew the cowl back down and murmured, "I cannot prevent your fate, wizard. I can only give you a chance to avoid it on your own."

"What do you mean?"

"Cannot you see what is happening?"

I frowned at him. "A dangerous imbalance of forces. The White Council in town. Mab meddling in our affairs."

"Or perhaps we are meddling in hers. Why has she appointed a mortal Emissary, young wizard?"

"Because someone up there takes a malevolent amusement in my suffering?"

"Balance," the Gatekeeper corrected me. "It is all about balance. Redress the imbalance, young wizard. Resolve the situation. Prove your worth beyond doubt."

"Are you telling me I *should* work for Mab?" My voice sounded hollow, tinny, as though it was trapped in a coffee can.

"What is the date?" the Gatekeeper asked.

"June eighteenth," I said.

"Ah. Of course." The Gatekeeper turned away, and sounds returned to normal. The Gatekeeper joined the rest of the Senior Council, and they trooped back up to their podiums. Podii. Podia. Whatever. Goddamned correspondence course.

"Order," called the Merlin again, and the room grew quiet after a reluctant moment.

"Gatekeeper," the Merlin said, "what is your vote?"

The silent figure of the Gatekeeper silently lifted one hand. "We have set our feet upon a darkling path," he murmured. "A road that will only grow more dangerous. Our first steps are critical. We must make them with caution."

The cowl turned toward Ebenezar, and the Gatekeeper said, "You love the boy, Wizard McCoy. You would fight to defend him. Your own dedication to our cause is not inconsiderable. I respect your choice."

He turned toward LaFortier. "You question Dresden's loyalty and his ability. You imply that only a bad seed can grow from bad soil. Your concerns are understandable—and if correct, then Dresden poses a major threat to the Council."

He turned to Ancient Mai and inclined the cowl forward a few degrees. The Ancient responded with a slight bow of her own. "Ancient Mai," the Gatekeeper said. "You question his ability to use his power wisely. To judge between right and wrong. You fear that DuMorne's teaching may have twisted him in ways even he cannot yet see. Your fears, too, are justified."

He turned to the Merlin. "Honored Merlin. You know that Dresden has drawn death and danger down upon the Council. You believe that if he is removed, so will be that danger. Your fears are understandable, but not reasonable. Regardless of what happens to Dresden, the Red Court has struck a blow against the Council too deep to be ignored. A cessation of current hostilities would only be the calm before the storm."

"Enough, man," Ebenezar demanded. "Vote, for or against."

"I choose to base my vote upon a Trial. A test that will lay to rest the fears of one side of the issue, or prove falsely placed the faith of the other."

"What Trial?" the Merlin asked.

"Mab," the Gatekeeper said. "Let Dresden address Queen Mab's request. Let him secure the assistance of Winter. If he does, that should lay to rest your concerns regarding his ability, LaFortier."

LaFortier frowned, but then nodded at the Gatekeeper.

He turned next to Ancient Mai. "Should he accomplish this, it should show that he is willing to accept responsibility for his mistake and to work against his own best interests for the greater good of the Council. It should satisfy your concerns as to his judgment—to make the mistakes of youth is no crime, but not to learn from them is. Agreed?"

Ancient Mai narrowed her rheumy eyes, but gave the Gatekeeper a precise nod.

"And you, honored Merlin. Such a success may do much to alleviate the pressure of the coming war. If securing routes through the Nevernever places the Red Court at a severe enough disadvantage, it may even enable us to avoid it entirely. Surely it would prove Dresden's dedication to the Council beyond a doubt."

"That's all well and good," Ebenezar said. "But what happens if he fails?"

The Gatekeeper shrugged. "Then perhaps their fears are more justified than your affection, Wizard McCoy. We may indeed conclude that his appointment to full Wizard Initiate may have been premature."

"All or nothing?" Ebenezar demanded. "Is that it? You expect the youngest wizard in the Council to get the best of Queen Mab somehow? *Mab?* That's not a Trial. It's a goddamned execution. How is he even supposed to know what her request was to begin with?"

I stood up, my legs shaking a little. "Ebenezar," I said.

"How the hell is the boy supposed to know what she wants?"

"Ebenezar—"

"I'm not going to stand by while you—" He abruptly blinked and looked at me. So did everyone else.

"I know what Mab wants," I said. "She approached me earlier today, sir. She asked me to investigate something for her. I turned her down."

"Hell's bells," Ebenezar breathed. He took the blue bandanna from his pocket and mopped at his gleaming forehead. "Hoss, this is out of your depth."

"Looks like it's sink or swim, then," I said.

The Gatekeeper murmured to me in English, "Will you accept this, Wizard Dresden?"

I nodded my head. My throat had gone dry. I swallowed and tried to remind myself that there wasn't much choice. If I didn't play with the faeries and come out on top, the Council would serve me up to the vampires on a silver platter. The former might get me really, really killed. The latter would certainly kill me as well—and probably more than that.

As deals went, it blew. But some little part of me that hadn't let me forget all the destruction, maybe even the deaths I'd caused last year, danced gleefully at my apparent comeuppance. Besides, it was the only game in town. I tightened my grip on my staff and spoke as clearly as I could manage.

"Yeah. I accept."

Chapter Seven

The rest of the Council meeting was somewhat anticlimactic—for me, anyway.

The Merlin ordered the wizards to disperse immediately after the meeting via preplanned, secure routes. He also distributed a list to everyone, noting the Wardens near them to call upon if help was needed, and told them to check in with the Wardens every few days, as a safety precaution.

Next, a grizzled old dame Warden went over the theories to a couple of newly developed wards meant to work especially well against vampires. Representatives of the White Council's allies—secret occult brotherhoods, mostly—each gave a brief speech, declaring his or her group's support of the Council in the war.

Toward the end of the meeting, Wardens showed up in force to escort wizards to the beginnings of their routes home. The Senior Council, I presumed, would loiter around for a few days in order to see if I got killed trying to prove that I was one of the good guys. Sometimes I feel like no one appreciates me.

I stood up about three seconds before the Merlin

said, "Meeting adjourned," and headed for the door. Ebenezar tried to catch my eye, but I didn't feel like talking to anyone. I slammed the doors open a little harder than I needed to, stalked out to the Blue Beetle, and drove away with all the raging power the ancient four-cylinder engine could muster. Behold the angry wizard puttputtputting away.

My brain felt like something made out of stale cereal, coffee grounds, and cold pizza. Thoughts trudged around in aimless depression, mostly about how I was going to get myself killed playing private eye for Mab. If things got really bad, I might even drag down a few innocent bystanders with me.

I growled at myself. "Stop whining, Harry," I said in a firm, loud voice. "So what if you're tired? So what if you're hurt? So what if you smell like you're already dead? You're a wizard. You've got a job to do. This war is mostly your own fault, and if you don't stay on the ball, more people are going to get hurt. So stiff upper lip, chin up, whatever. Get your ass in gear."

I nodded at that advice, and glanced toward the envelope Mab had given me, which lay on the passenger seat. I had a name, an address, a crime. I needed to get on the trail of the killer. That meant I would need information—and the people who would have the most information, a couple of days after the fact, would be the Chicago PD.

I drove to Murphy's place.

Lieutenant Karrin Murphy was the head of Chicago PD's Special Investigations team. SI was the city's answer to weirdness in general. They got all of the unusual crimes, the ones that didn't fall neatly into the department's other categories. SI has handled everything from sightings of sewer alligators to grave robbing in one of the city's many cemeteries. What fun. They also got to take care of the genuine supernatural stuff, the things that no one talks about in official reports but that manage to happen anyway. Trolls, vampires, demon-summoning sorcerers—you name it. The city had appointed SI to make sure the paperwork stayed nice and neat, with no mention of preposterous fantasies that could not possibly exist. It was a thankless job, and the directors of SI typically blew it after about a month by refusing to believe that they were dealing with genuine weirdness. Then they got shuffled out of Chicago PD.

Murphy hadn't. She'd lasted. She'd taken things seriously and employed the services of Chicago's only professional wizard (guess who) as a consultant on the tougher jobs. Murphy and I have seen some very upsetting things together. We're friends. She would help.

Murphy lives in a house in Bucktown, near a lot of other cops. It's a tiny place, but she owns it. Grandma Murphy left it to her. The house is surrounded by a neat little lawn.

I pulled up in the Beetle sometime well after summertime dark but before midnight. I knew she'd be home, though I wasn't certain she'd be awake. I made sure that I didn't sound like I was trying to sneak up anywhere. I shut the door of the Beetle hard and walked with firm footsteps to her door, then knocked lightly.

A moment later the curtains on the barred windows beside the door twitched and then fell back into place.

A lock disengaged, then another, then a door chain. I noted, as I waited, that Murphy had a steel-reinforced door just like I did. Though I doubted she'd had as many demons or assassins showing up at it.

Murphy opened the door partway and peered out at me. The woman didn't look like the chief of Chicago PD's monster hunters. Her bright blue eyes were heavy, weary, and underscored with dark bags. She stood five feet nothing in her bare feet. Her golden hair was longer on top than in back, with bangs hanging down to her eyes. She wore a pale peach terry-cloth bathrobe that fell most of the way to her feet.

In her right hand she held her automatic, and a small crucifix dangled on a chain wrapped around her wrist. She looked at me.

"Heya, Murph," I said. I looked at the gun and the holy symbol and kept my voice calm. "Sorry to drop in on you this late. I need your help."

Murphy regarded me in silence for more than a minute. Then she said, "Wait here." She shut the door, returned a minute later, and opened it again, all the way. Then, gun still in hand, she stepped back from the doorway and faced me.

"Uh," I said, "Murph, are you all right?"

She nodded.

"Okay," I said. "Can I come in?"

"We'll know in a minute," Murphy said.

I got it then. Murphy wasn't going to ask me in. There are plenty of monsters running around in the dark that can't violate the threshold of a home if they aren't invited in. One of them had caught up to Murphy last year, nearly killing her, and it had been wearing my face when it did it. No wonder she didn't look exactly overjoyed to see me.

"Murph," I said, "relax. It's me. Hell's bells, there isn't anything that I can think of that would mimic me looking like this. Even demonic fiends from the nether regions of hell have *some* taste."

I stepped across her threshold. Something tugged at me as I did, an intangible, invisible energy. It slowed me down a little, and I had to make an effort to push through it. That's what a threshold is like. One like it surrounds every home, a field of energy that keeps out unwanted magical forces. Some places have more of a threshold than others. My apartment, for example, didn't have much of a threshold—it's a bachelor pad, and whatever domestic energy is responsible for such things doesn't seem to settle down as well in rental spaces and lone dwellings. Murphy's house had a heavy field surrounding it. It had a life of its own; it had history. It was a home, not just a place to live.

I crossed her threshold uninvited, and I left a lot of my power at the door as I did. I would have to really push to make even the simplest of spells work within. I stepped inside and spread my hands. "Do I pass inspection?"

Murphy didn't say anything. She crossed the room and put her gun back into its holster, setting it down on an end table.

Murphy's place was—dare I say it?—*cute*. The room was done in soft yellows and greens. And there were ruffles. The curtains had ruffles, and the couch had more, plus those little knitted things (aren't they called doilies?)

were draped over the arms of the two recliners, the couch, the coffee table, and just about every other surface that seemed capable of supporting lacy bits of froo-fra. They looked old and beautiful and well cared for. I was betting Murphy's grandma had picked them out.

Murphy's own decorating was limited to the gun-cleaning kit sitting on the end table beside the holster for her automatic and a wooden rack over the fireplace that bore a pair of Japanese swords, long and short, one over the other. That was the Murphy I knew and loved. Practical violence ready at hand. Next to the swords was a small row of photographs in holders—maybe her family. A thick picture album with what looked like a real leather cover sat open on the coffee table, next to a prescription bottle and a decanter of some kind of liquor—gin? The decanter was half empty. The glass next to it was completely empty.

I watched her settle down in the corner of the couch in her oversized bathrobe, her expression remote. She didn't look at me. I got more worried by the moment. Murphy wasn't acting like Murphy. She'd never passed up a chance to trade banter with me. I'd never seen her this silent and withdrawn.

Dammit, just when I needed some quick and decisive help. Something was wrong with Murphy, and I hardly had time to play dime-store psychologist, trying to help her. I needed whatever information she could get me. I also needed to help her with whatever it was that had hurt her so badly. I was fairly sure I wouldn't be able to do either if I didn't get her talking.

"Nice place, Murph," I told her. "I haven't seen it before."

She twitched one shoulder in what might have been a shrug.

I frowned. "You know, if conversation is too much for you we could play charades. I'll go first." I held up my hand with my fingers spread. Murphy didn't say anything, so I provided her end of the dialogue. "Five words." I tugged on my ear. "Sounds like . . . What Is Wrong with You?"

She shook her head. I saw her eyes flicker toward the album.

I leaned forward and turned the album toward me. It had been opened on a cluster of wedding pictures. The girl in them must have been Murphy, back when. She had longer, sunnier hair and a kind of adolescent slenderness that showed around her neck and wrists. She wore a white wedding gown, and stood next to a tuxedo-clad man who had to have been ten years older than she was. In other pictures she was shoving cake into his mouth, drinking through linked arms, the usual wedding fare. He had carried her to the getaway car, and the photo-Murphy's face had been caught in a moment of laughter and joy.

"First husband?" I asked.

That got through to her. She glanced up at me for just a second. Then nodded.

"You were a kid in this. Maybe eighteen?"

She shook her head.

"Seventeen?"

She nodded. At least I was getting some kind of response out of her.

"How long were you married to him?"

Silence.

I frowned. "Murph, I'm not like a genius about this stuff or anything. But if you're feeling guilty about something, maybe you're being a little hard on yourself."

Without a word, she leaned forward and picked up the album, moving it aside to reveal a copy of the *Tribune*. It had been folded open to the obituaries page. She picked it up and handed it to me.

I read the first one out loud. "Gregory Taggart, age forty-three, died last night after a long bout with cancer . . ." I paused and looked at the photograph of the deceased and then at Murphy's album. It was the same man, give or take several years of wear and tear. I winced and lowered the paper. "Oh, God, Murph. I'm sorry. I'm so sorry."

She blinked her eyes several times. Her voice came out thready, quiet. "He didn't even tell me that he was sick."

Talk about your nasty surprises. "Murph, look. I'm sure that . . . that things will work out. I know how you're hurting, how you must feel, but—"

"Do you?" she said, still very quiet. "Do you know how I feel? Did you lose your first love?"

I sat quietly for a full minute before I said, "Yeah. I did."

"What was her name?"

It hurt to think the name, much less to say it. But if it helped me get through to Murphy, I couldn't afford to be touchy. "Elaine. We were . . . both of us were orphans. We got adopted by the same man when we were ten."

Murphy blinked and looked up at me. "She was your sister?"

"I don't have any relatives. We were both adopted by the same guy, that's all. We lived together, drove one another nuts, hit puberty together. Do the math."

She nodded. "How long were you together?"

"Oh. Until we were about sixteen."

"What happened? How did she . . ."

I shrugged. "My adoptive father tried to get me into black magic. Human sacrifice."

Murphy frowned. "He was a wizard?"

I nodded. "Strong one. So was she."

"Didn't he try to get Elaine, too?"

"Did get her," I said. "She was helping him."

"What happened?" she asked quietly.

I tried to keep my voice even and calm, but I wasn't sure how well I managed it. "I ran away. He sent a demon after me. I beat it, then went back to save Elaine. She hit me with a binding spell when I wasn't looking, and he tried a spell that would break into my head. Make me do what he wanted. I slipped out of the spell Elaine had on me and took on Justin. I got lucky. He lost. Everything burned."

Murphy swallowed. "What happened to Elaine?"

"Burned," I said quietly, my throat tightening. "She's dead."

"God, Harry." Murphy was quiet for a moment. "Greg left me. We tried to talk a few times, but it always ended in a fight." Her eyes welled up with tears. "Dammit, I should have at least gotten to tell him good-bye."

I put the paper back on the table and closed the

album, studiously not looking at Murphy. I knew she wouldn't want me to see her crying. She inhaled sharply. "I'm sorry, Harry," she said. "I'm flaking out on you here. I shouldn't. I don't know why this is getting to me so hard."

I glanced at the booze and the pills on the table. "It's okay. Everyone has an off day sometimes."

"I can't afford it." She drew the bathrobe a little closer around herself and said, "Sorry, Harry. About the gun." Her words sounded heavy, maybe a little slurred. "I had to be sure it was really you."

"I understand," I said.

She looked at me and something like gratitude touched her eyes. She got up from the couch abruptly and walked down a hallway, out of the living room, and said over her shoulder, "Let me put something else on."

"Sure, okay," I said after her, frowning. I leaned over to the table and picked up the prescription bottle behind the booze, next to the empty tumbler. A medium-sized dose of Valium. No wonder Murphy had been slurring her words. Valium and gin. Hell's bells.

I was still holding the pills when she came back in, wearing baggy shorts and a T-shirt. She'd raked a brush through her hair and splashed water on her face, so that I could barely tell that she'd been crying. She stopped short and looked at me. I didn't say anything. She chewed on her lip.

"Murph," I said, finally, "are you okay? Is there . . . I mean, do you need—"

"Relax, Dresden," she said, folding her arms. "I'm not suicidal."

"Funny you say that. Mixing drinks with drugs is a great way to get it done."

She walked over to me, jerked the pill bottle out of my hands, and picked up the bottle of booze. "It isn't any of your business," she said. She walked into the kitchen, dropped things off, and came back out again. "I'm fine. I'll be fine."

"Murph, I've never seen you with a drink in your life. And Valium? It makes me worry about you."

"Dresden, if you came over here to lecture me, you can leave right now."

I shoved my fingers through my shaggy hair. "Karrin, I swear I'm not lecturing. I'm just trying to understand."

She looked away from me for a minute, one foot rubbing at the opposite calf. It hit me how small she looked. How frail. Her eyes were not only weary, I saw now. They were haunted. I walked over to her and put a hand on her shoulder. Her skin was warm underneath the cotton of her T-shirt. "Talk to me, Murph. Please."

She pulled her shoulder out from under my hand. "It isn't a big deal. It's the only way I can get any sleep."

"What do you mean?"

She took a deep breath. "I mean, I can't sleep without help. The drinks didn't help. The drugs didn't, either. I have to use both or I won't get any rest."

"I still don't get it. Why can't you sleep? Is it because of Greg?"

Murphy shook her head, then moved over to the couch, away from me, and curled up in the corner of it, clasping her hands over her knees. "I've been having nightmares. Night terrors, the doctors say. They say it's different from just bad dreams."

I felt my cheek twitch with tension. "And you can't stay asleep?"

She shook her head. "I wake myself up screaming." I saw her clench her fists. "Goddammit, Dresden. There's no reason for it. I shouldn't get rattled by a few bad dreams. I shouldn't fall to pieces hearing about a man I haven't spoken to in years. I don't know what the fuck is wrong with me."

I closed my eyes. "You're dreaming about last year, aren't you? About what Kravos did to you."

She shivered at the mention of the name and nodded. "I couldn't stop thinking about it for a long time. Trying to figure out what I did wrong. Why he was able to get to me."

I ached inside. "Murph, there wasn't anything you could have done."

"Don't you think I know that?" she said, her voice quiet. "I couldn't have known that it wasn't you. I couldn't have stopped him even if I had. I couldn't have done anything to defend myself. To stop wh-what he did to me, once he was inside my head." Her eyes clouded with tears, but she blinked them away, her jaw setting. "There wasn't anything I could have done. That's what scares me, Harry. That's why I'm afraid."

"Murph, he's dead. He's dead and gone. We watched them put him in the ground."

Murphy snarled, "I *know* that. I know it, Harry. I know he's gone, I know he can't hurt me anymore, I know he's never going to hurt anyone again." She looked up at me for a moment, chancing a look at my eyes. Hers were clouded with tears. "But I still have the dreams. I know it, but it doesn't make any difference."

God. Poor Murphy. She'd taken a spiritual mauling before I'd shown up to save her. The thing that attacked her had been a spirit being, and it had torn her apart on the inside without leaving a mark on her skin. In a way, she'd been raped. All of her power had been taken away, and she'd been used for the amusement of another. No wonder it had left her with scars. Adding an unpleasant shock of bad news had been like tossing a spark onto a pile of tinder soaked in jet fuel.

"Harry," she continued, her voice quiet, soft, "you know me. God, I'm not a whiner. I hate that. But what that thing did to me. The things it made me see. Made me feel." She looked up at me, pain in the lines at the corners of her eyes, which threatened tears. "It won't go away. I try to leave it behind me, but it won't go. And it's eating up every part of my life."

She turned away, grabbing irritably at a box of tissues. I walked over to the fireplace and studied the swords on the mantel, so she wouldn't feel my eyes on her.

After a moment she spoke, her tone changing, growing more focused. "What are you doing here so late?"

I turned back to face her. "I need a favor. Information." I passed over the envelope Mab had given me. Murphy opened it, looked at the pair of pictures, and frowned.

"These are shots from the report of Ronald Reuel's death. How did you get them?"

"I didn't," I said. "A client gave them to me. I don't know where she got them."

She rubbed her eyes and asked, "What did she want from you?"

"She wants me to find the person who killed him."

Murphy shook her head. "I thought this was an accidental death."

"I hear it isn't."

"Where'd you hear that?"

I sighed. "A magic faerie told me."

That got me a suspicious glare, which dissolved into a frown. "God, you're being literal, aren't you?"

"Yeah."

Murphy shook her head, a tired smile at the corners of her mouth. "How can I help?"

"I'd like to look at the file on Ronald Reuel's death. I can't look at the scene, but maybe CPD caught something they didn't know was a clue. It would give me a place to start, at least."

Murphy nodded without looking at me. "All right. One condition."

"Sure. What?"

"If this is a murder, you bring me in on it."

"Murph," I protested, "come on. I don't want to pull you into anything that—"

"Dammit, Harry," Murphy snapped, "if someone's killing people in Chicago, I'm going to deal with them. It's my job. What's been happening to me doesn't change that."

"It's your job to stop the bad guys," I said. "But this might not be a guy. Maybe not even human. I just think you'd be safer if—"

"Fuck safe," Murphy muttered. "My job, Harry. If you turn up a killing, you will bring me in."

I hesitated, trying not to let my frustration show. I didn't want Murphy involved with Mab and company. Murphy had earned too many scars already. The faeries had a way of insinuating themselves into your life. I didn't want Murphy exposed to that, especially as vulnerable as she was.

But at the same time, I couldn't lie to her. I owed her a lot more than that.

Bottom line, Murphy had been hurt. She was afraid, and if she didn't force herself to face that fear, it might swallow her whole. She knew it. As terrified as she was, she knew that she had to keep going or she would never recover.

As much as I wanted to keep her safe, especially now, it wouldn't help her. Not in the long run. In a sense, her life was at stake.

"Deal," I said quietly.

She nodded and rose. "Stay out here. I need to get on the computer, see what I can pull up for you."

"I can wait if it's better."

She shook her head. "I've already taken the Valium. If I wait any longer I'll be too zonked to think straight. Just sit down. Have a drink. Try not to blow up anything." She padded out of the room on silent feet.

I sat down in one of the armchairs, stretched out my legs, let my head fall forward, and dropped into a light doze. It had been a long day, and it looked like it was just going to get longer. I woke up when Murphy came back into the room, her eyes heavy. She had a manila folder with her. "Okay," she said, "this is everything I could print out. The pictures aren't as clear as they could be, but they aren't horrible."

I sat up, took the folder from her and opened it. Murphy sat down in an armchair, facing me, her legs tucked beneath her. I started going over the details in the folder, though my brain felt like some kind of gelatin dessert topped with mush.

"What happened to your hand?" she asked.

"Magic faerie," I said. "Magic faerie with a letter opener."

"It doesn't look good. The dressing isn't right either. You have anyone look at it?"

I shook my head. "No time."

"Harry, you idiot." She got up, disappeared into the kitchen, and came back out with a first aid kit. I decided not to argue with her. She pulled up a chair from the kitchen next to mine, and rested my arm in her lap.

"I'm trying to read here, Murph."

"You're still bleeding. Puncture wounds will ooze forever if you don't keep them covered."

"Yeah, I tried to explain that, but they made me take the bandage off anyway."

"Who did?"

"Long story. So the security guard on the building didn't see anyone come in?"

She peeled off the bandage with brisk motions. It hurt. She fished out some disinfectant. "Cameras didn't pick up anything, either, and there aren't any bursts of static to indicate someone using magic. I checked."

I whistled. "Not bad, Murph."

"Yeah, sometimes I use my head instead of my gun. This will hurt."

She sprayed disinfectant liberally on my hand. It stung.

"Ow!"

"Wimp."

"Any other ways in and out of the building?"

"Not unless they could fly and walk through walls. The other doors are all fire exits, with alarms that would trip if someone opened them."

I kept paging through the file. " 'Broken neck due to fall,' it says. They found him at the bottom of the stairs."

"Right." Murphy used a wipe to clean both sides of my hand, and then she put more disinfectant on. It hurt a bit less. "He had contusions consistent with a fall, and he was an old man. No one seen entering or leaving an apartment building with a high-security system, so naturally—"

"—no one looked for a killer," I finished. "Or reported anything that might have indicated one. Or, wait, did they? Says here that the first officer on the scene found 'slippery goo' on the landing above where Reuel fell."

"But none of the detectives on the scene later found any such thing," Murphy said. She pressed a gauze pad against the wound from either side and began wrapping medical tape around to hold the pads on. "The first officer was a rookie. They figured he was seeing a killing where there wasn't one so he could get in on a murder investigation."

I frowned, turning the printouts of the photographs

around. "See here? The sleeves of Reuel's coat are wet. You can see the discoloration."

She looked and admitted, "Maybe. There's no mention of it, though."

"Slippery goo. It could have been ectoplasm."

"Is that too tight? Ecto-what?"

I flexed my fingers a little, testing the bandage. "It's fine. Ectoplasm. Matter from the Nevernever."

"That's the spirit world, right? Faerieland?"

"Among other things."

"And stuff from there is goo?"

"It turns into goo when there's not any magic animating it. As long as the magic is there, it's as good as real. Like when Kravos made a body that looked like mine and came gunning for you."

Murphy shivered and started putting things back into her kit. "So when whatever it is that has made this ecto goo into matter has gone, it turns back into . . . ?"

"Slime," I said. "It's clear and slippery, and it evaporates in a few minutes."

"So something from the Nevernever could have killed Reuel," Murphy said.

"Yeah," I said. "Or someone could have opened up a portal into the apartment building. There's usually some gunk left when you open a portal. Dust drifting out from the Nevernever. So they could have opened a portal, then gotten out the same way."

"Whoa! Hold it. I thought Faerieland was monsters only. People can go into the Nevernever?"

"If you know the right magic, yeah. It's full of things

that are fairly dangerous, though. You don't just cruise through on a Sunday stroll."

"Jesus Christ," Murphy muttered. "So someone—"

"Or something," I interjected.

"—or something could have gotten into the building and out again. Just like that. Past all the locks and guards and cameras. How scary is that?"

"Could have, yeah. Stepped in, pitched grampa down the stairs, stepped out again."

"God. That poor old man."

"I don't think he was helpless, Murph. Reuel was mixed up with the faeries. I kind of doubt his hands were squeaky clean."

She nodded. "Okay. Had he made any supernatural enemies?"

I held up the picture of the body. "Looks like it."

Murphy shook her head. She swayed a little bit, and then sat down next to me, leaning her head against the corner of the couch. "So what's the next step?"

"I go digging. Pound the proverbial pavement."

"You don't look so good. Get some rest first. A shower. Some food. Maybe a haircut."

I rubbed my eyes with my good hand. "Yeah," I said.

"And you tell me, when you know something."

"Murph, if this was something from the Nevernever, it's going to be out of your"—I almost said "league"—"jurisdiction."

She shrugged. "If it came into my town and hurt someone I'm responsible for protecting, I want to make it answer for that." She closed her eyes. "Same as you. Besides. You promised."

Well, she had me there. "Yeah. Okay, Murph. When I find something out, I'll call."

"All right," she said. She curled up in the corner of the couch again, heavy eyes closing. She leaned her head back, baring the lines of her throat. After a moment, she asked, "Have you heard from Susan?"

I shook my head. "No."

"But her articles are still coming into the *Arcane*. She's all right."

I nodded. "I guess so."

"Have you found anything that will help her yet?"

I sighed and shook my head. "No, not yet. It's like pounding my head against a wall."

She halfway smiled. "With your head, the wall breaks first. You're the most stubborn man I've ever met."

"You say the sweetest things."

Murphy nodded. "You're a good man, Harry. If anyone can help her, it's you."

I looked down so she wouldn't see the tears that made my eyes swim a little, and started putting the file back together. "Thanks, Murph. That means a lot to me."

She didn't answer. I looked up and saw that her mouth had fallen slightly open and her body was totally relaxed, a cheek resting on the arm of the couch.

"Murph?" I asked. She didn't stir. I got up and left the file on the chair. I found a blanket and draped it lightly over her, tucking it in around her. She made a soft sound in the back of her throat and nuzzled her cheek closer to the couch.

"Sleep well, Murph," I said. Then I headed for the door. I locked what I could behind me, made my way back to the Beetle, and drove toward home.

I ached everywhere. Not from sore muscles, but from simple exhaustion. My wounded hand felt like a big throbbing knot of cramping muscle, doused in gasoline and set on fire.

I hurt even more on the inside. Poor Murph had been torn up badly. She was terrified of the things she might have to face, but that made her no less determined to face them. That was courage, and more than I had. I at least was sure that I could hit back if one of the monsters came after me. Murphy didn't have any such certainty.

Murphy was my friend. She'd saved my life before. We'd fought side by side. She needed my help again. She had to face her fear. I understood that. She needed me to help make it happen, but I didn't have to like it. In her condition, she would be extra vulnerable to any kind of attack like the one by Kravos the year before. And if she got hit again before she had a chance to piece herself back together, it might not simply wound her—it might break her entirely.

I wasn't sure I could live with myself if that happened.

"Dammit," I muttered. "So help me, Murph, I'm going to make sure you come out of this okay."

I shoved my worries about Murphy to the back of my mind. The best way to protect her would be to focus on this case, to get cracking. But my brain felt like something had crawled into it and died. The only cracking it was going to be doing was the kind that would land me in a rubber room and a sleeveless coat.

I wanted food. Sleep. A shower. If I didn't take some time to put myself back together, I might walk right into something that would kill me and not notice it until it was too late.

I drove back to my apartment, which is the basement of a rooming house more than a century old. I parked the Beetle outside and got my rod and staff out of the car to take with me. It wasn't much of a walk between my apartment and the car, but I'd been accosted before. Vampires can be really inconsiderate that way.

I thumped down the stairs to my apartment, unlocked the door, and murmured the phrase that would disarm my wards long enough to let me get inside. I slipped in, and my instincts screamed at me that I was not alone.

I lifted the blasting rod, gathering my power and sending it humming through the focus so that the tip burst into brilliant crimson light that flooded my apartment.

And then there she was, a slender woman standing by my cold fireplace, all graceful curves and poised reserve. She wore a pair of blue jeans over long, coltish legs, with a simple scarlet cotton T-shirt. A silver pentacle hung outside the shirt, resting on the curve of modest breasts, and it gleamed in the light from my readied blasting rod. Her skin was pale, like the inner bark of an oak, the living part of the tree, her hair the brown-gold of ripe wheat, her eyes the grey of storm clouds. Her fine mouth twitched, first into a smile and then into a frown, and she lifted elegant, long-fingered hands to show me empty palms.

"I let myself in," she murmured. "I hope you don't mind. You should change your wards more often."

I lowered the blasting rod, too stunned to speak, my heart lurching in my chest. She lowered her hands and closed the distance between us. She lifted herself onto her toes, but she was tall enough that it wasn't much of an effort for her to kiss my cheek. She smelled like wildflowers and sun-drenched summer afternoons. She drew back enough to focus on my face and my eyes, her own expression gentle and concerned. "Hello, Harry."

And I said, in a bare whisper, fighting through the shock, "Hello, Elaine."

Chapter Eight

Elaine walked past me, making a circuit around my apartment. It wasn't much of a tour. The place consists of a living room and a tiny bedroom. The kitchen is pretty much just an alcove with a sink and a fridge. The floor is smooth grey stone, but I'd covered a lot of it with a few dozen rugs. My furniture is all secondhand and comfortable. It doesn't even come close to matching. Bookshelves fill up most of the wall space, and where they don't, I have several tapestries, plus a *Star Wars* movie poster Billy gave me for Christmas. It's the old poster, the one with Princess Leia clinging to Luke's leg.

Anyway, that was my apartment on a normal day. Lately it had suffered from disrepair. It didn't smell so great, and pizza boxes and empty Coke cans had overflowed the trash can and spilled over a significant portion of the kitchen floor. You could barely walk without stepping on clothing that needed to be washed. My furniture was covered with scribbled-on papers and discarded pens and pencils.

Elaine walked through it all like a Red Cross worker through a war zone and shook her head. "I know you weren't expecting me, Harry, but I didn't think I'd be overdressed. You live in this?"

"Elaine," I choked out. "You're alive."

"A little less of a compliment than I would have hoped for, but I guess it could have been worse." She regarded me from near the kitchen. "I'm alive, Harry." Her face flickered with a trace of apprehension. "How are you feeling?"

I lowered myself onto the couch, papers crunching beneath me. I released the power held ready to strike, and the glowing tip of the blasting rod went out, leaving the apartment in darkness. I kept staring at her afterimage on my vision. "Shocked," I said finally. "This isn't happening. Hell's bells, this has got to be some sort of trick."

"No. It's me. If I was something out of the Nevernever, could I have crossed your threshold uninvited? Do you know anyone else who knows how you set up your wards?"

"Anyone could figure it out eventually," I said.

"All right. Does anyone else know that you failed your driver's test five times in one week? Or that you sprained your shoulder trying to impress me going out for football our freshman year? That we soulgazed on our first night together? I think I can still remember our locker combination, if you like."

"My God, Elaine." I shook my head. Elaine, alive. My brain could not wrap itself around the idea. "Why didn't you contact me?"

I saw her, dimly, lean against the wall. She was quiet for a while, as though she had to shape her words carefully. "At first because I didn't even know if you had survived. And after that . . ." She shook her head. "I wasn't sure I wanted to. Wasn't sure you'd want me to. So much happened."

My shock and disbelief faded before a sudden aching pain, and an old, old anger. "That's putting it mildly," I said. "You tried to destroy me."

"No," she said. "God, no, Harry. You don't understand. I never wanted that."

My voice gained a hard edge. "Which is why you hit me with that binding. Why you held me down while Justin tried to destroy me."

"He never wanted you dead—"

"No, he just wanted to break into my head. Wanted to control me. Make me into some kind of . . . of . . ." Words failed me in the face of my frustration.

"Thrall," Elaine said quietly. "He'd have wrapped you in enough spells to guarantee your loyalty. To make you his thrall."

"And that's worse than dead. And you *helped* him."

Her voice crackled with anger of its own. "Yes, Harry. I helped him. That's what thralls *do*."

My rising ire abruptly quieted. "What . . . what are you saying?"

I saw her dim shape bow its head. "Justin caught me about two weeks before he sent that demon to capture you. That day I stayed home sick, remember? By the time you got home from school, he had me. I tried to fight him, but I was a child. I didn't have enough experience to resist him. And after he had enthralled me, I didn't see why I should fight anymore."

I stared at her for a long minute. "So you're telling me that you didn't have any choice," I breathed. "He forced you to do it. He made you help him."

"Yes."

"Why the hell should I believe you?"

"I don't expect you to."

I rose and paced back and forth restlessly. "I can't believe you're trying to tell me that the devil made you do it. Do you have any idea how lame that excuse sounds?"

Elaine watched me carefully, her grey eyes pensive and sad. "It wasn't an excuse, Harry. Nothing can excuse the kind of pain I put you through."

I stopped and frowned at her. "Then why are you telling me?"

"Because it needs to be said," she murmured. "Because that's what happened. You deserve to know that."

It was quiet for a long time; then I asked, "He really had enthralled you?"

Elaine shivered and nodded.

"What was it like?"

She fretted at her lower lip. "I didn't know it was happening. Not at the time. I didn't have the ability to think clearly. Justin told me that you just needed to be shown what to do and that if I would hold you still long enough to let him explain things to you it would all work out. I believed him. Trusted him." She shook her head. "I never wanted to hurt you, Harry. Never. I'm sorry."

I sat down and rubbed my face with my hands, my emotions running high and out of control again. Without the anger to support me, all that was left inside was pain. I thought I had gotten over Elaine's loss, her betrayal. I thought I had forgotten it and moved on. I was wrong. The wounds burst open again, as painful as they had ever been. Maybe more so. I had to fight to control my breathing, my tone.

I had loved her. I wanted very badly to believe her.

"I . . . I looked for you," I said quietly. "In fire and water. I had spirits combing the Earth for any trace of you. Hoping that you'd survived."

She pushed away from the wall and walked to the fireplace. I heard her putting in wood, and then she murmured something soft and low. Flame licked up over the logs easily, smoothly, low and blue, then settled into a dark golden light. I watched her profile as she stared down at the fire. "I got out of the house before you and Justin were finished," she said finally. "His spells had begun to unravel, and I was struggling against them. Confused, terrified. I must have run. I don't even remember doing it."

"But where have you been?" I asked. "Elaine, I looked for you for years. Years."

"Where you couldn't have found me, Harry. You or anyone else. I found sanctuary. A place to hide. But there was a price, and that's why I'm here." She looked up at me, and though her features were calm and smooth, I could see the fear in her eyes, hear it coloring her voice. "I'm in trouble."

My answer came out at once. For me, chivalry isn't dead; it's an involuntary reflex. It could have been any woman asking for help, and I'd have said the same thing. It might have taken me a second or two longer, but I would have. For Elaine, there was no need to think about it for even that long. "I'll help."

Her shoulders sagged and she nodded, pressing her lips together and bowing her head. "Thank you. Thank you, Harry. I hate doing this, I hate bringing this to you after all this time. But I don't know where else to turn."

"No," I said, "it's all right. Really. What's going on? Why do you think you're in trouble? What do you mean, you're paying a price?"

"It's complicated," she said. "But the short version is that I was granted asylum by the Summer Court of the Sidhe."

My stomach dropped about twenty feet.

"I built up a debt to Titania, the Summer Queen, in exchange for her protection. And now it's time to pay it off." She took a deep breath. "There's been a murder within the realms of the Sidhe."

I rubbed at my eyes. "And Titania wants you to be her Emissary. She wants you to find the killer and prove that the Winter Court is to blame. She told you that you would be contacted tonight by Mab's Emissary, but she didn't tell you who it was going to be."

Elaine's eyes widened in shock, and she fell silent. We stared at each other for a long moment before she whispered, "Stars and stones." She pushed her hair back from her face with one hand, in what I knew to be a nervous gesture, even if it didn't look it. "Harry, if I don't succeed, if I don't fulfill my debt to her, I'm . . . it's going to be very bad for me."

"Hooboy," I muttered, "tell me about it. Mab's more or less got me over the same barrel."

Elaine swore quietly. "What are we going to do?"

"Uh," I said.

She looked at me expectantly.

I scowled. "I'm thinking, I'm thinking. Uh."

She rose and took a few long-legged strides across the living room and back, agitated. "There must be something . . . some way out of this. God, sometimes their sense of humor makes me sick. Mab and Titania are laughing right now."

If I'd had the energy, I'd have been pacing, too. I closed my eyes and tried to think. If I didn't succeed on Mab's behalf, she wouldn't grant rights of passage to the Council. The Council would judge that I had failed my trial, and they'd wrap me up and deliver me to the vampires. I didn't know the specifics of Elaine's situation, but I doubted she had a deal that was any less fatal. My head hurt.

Elaine continued pacing, exasperated. "Come on, Harry. What are you thinking?"

"I'm thinking that if this dilemma grows any more horns I'm going to shoot it and put it up on the wall."

"I know this will never sink into your head, but this isn't a time for jokes. We need to come up with something."

"Okay. I've got it," I said. "Get your stuff and come with me."

Elaine reached back to the shadows beside the fireplace and withdrew a slender staff of pale wood, carved with swirling, abstract shapes. "Where are we going?"

I pushed myself up. "To talk to the Council and get their help."

Elaine lifted her eyebrows. "Don't take this the wrong way, Harry, but are you crazy?"

"Hear me out."

She pressed her lips together, but gave me a quick nod.

"It's simple. We're in way over our heads. We need help. You've got to come out to the Council in any case."

"Says who?"

"Oh, come on. You're human, Elaine, and a wizard. That's what is really important to them. They'll side with us against the faeries, help us figure a way out of this mess."

Elaine twitched at my use of the word, flicking a look around her as if by reflex. "That doesn't sound like the Council I've heard of."

"Could be that you've heard a skewed point of view," I said.

Elaine nodded. "Could be. The Council I've heard of nearly executed you for defending yourself against Justin."

"Well, yeah, but—"

"They put you on probation under threat of summary execution, and you all but had to kill yourself to get cleared."

"Well, I was all but killing myself anyway. I mean, I didn't do it so that the Council would—"

She shook her head. "God, Harry. You just can't see it, can you? The Council doesn't *care* about you. They don't want to protect you. They will only put up with you as long as you toe the line and don't become an inconvenience."

"I'm already inconvenient."

"A liability, then," Elaine said.

"Look, some of the Council have their heads up their rear ends, sure. But there are good people there, too."

Elaine folded her arms and shook her head. "And how many of those good people don't want a thing to do with the Council?"

"Elaine—"

"No, Harry. I mean it. I don't want anything to do with them. I've lived this long without the Council's so-called protection. I think I can muddle through a little longer."

"Elaine, when they find out about you, it needs to be from you. If you come forward, it's going to cut down on any uneasiness or suspicion they might feel."

"Suspicion?" Elaine exclaimed. "Harry, I am not a criminal."

"You're just asking for trouble, Elaine."

"And how are they going to find out about me? Hmmm? Were you planning on running off to tattle?"

"Of course not," I said. But I was thinking how much trouble I was going to be in if one of the Wardens heard I was associating with someone who might be a violator of the First Law, and one of Justin DuMorne's apprentices at that. With the cloud of disfavor I was already under, adding that kind of suspicion to it might be enough to sink me, regardless of how the investigation turned out. Do I have a great life or what?

"I won't say anything," I said finally. "It has to be your choice, Elaine. But please believe me. Trust me. I have friends in the Council, too. They'll help."

Elaine's expression softened and became less certain. "You're sure?"

"Yeah," I said. "Cross my heart."

She leaned on her oddly carved staff and frowned. She was opening her mouth to speak when my reinforced door rattled under the rapping of a heavy fist.

"Dresden," Morgan growled from the other side of the door. "Open up, traitor. There are questions I need you to answer."

Chapter Nine

Elaine shot me a wide-eyed look and mouthed the word, "Council?"

I nodded and pointed to my staff, in the corner along with my sword cane. Elaine picked it up without a word and tossed it to me. Then she moved silently through the door of my darkened bedroom and vanished inside.

The door rattled again. "Dresden," Morgan growled, "I know you're in there. Open the door."

I swung it open before he could go on. "Or you'll huff and you'll puff and so on?"

Morgan glowered at me, tall, sour, and dour as ever. He'd traded his robes and cloak for dark slacks, a grey silk shirt, and a sport coat. He carried a golf bag on one shoulder, and most people wouldn't have noticed the hilt of a sword nestled among the golf clubs. He leaned forward, cool eyes looking past me and into my apartment. "Dresden. Am I interrupting anything?"

"Well, I was going to settle down with a porn video and a bottle of baby oil, but I really don't have enough for two."

Morgan's expression twisted in revulsion, and I felt an

absurd little burst of vindictive satisfaction. "You disgust me, Dresden."

"Yeah, I'm bad. I'm a bad, bad, bad man. I'm glad we got that settled. Good-bye, Morgan."

I started to shut my door in his face. He slammed his palm against it. Morgan was a lot stronger than me. The door stayed open.

"I'm not finished, Dresden."

"I am. It's been one hell of a day. If you've got something to say, say it."

Morgan's mouth set in a hard smile. "Normally I appreciate that kind of directness. Not with you."

"Gee, you don't appreciate me. I'll cry myself to sleep."

Morgan stroked his thumb over the strap to the golf bag. "I want to know how it is, Dresden, that Mab just happened to come to you about this problem. The one thing that can preserve your status with the Council, and it just happened to fall to you."

"Clean living," I said. "Plus my mondo wheels and killer bachelor pad."

Morgan looked at me with flat eyes. "You think you're funny."

"Oh, I *know* I'm funny. Unappreciated, but funny."

Morgan shook his head. "Do you know what I think, Dresden?"

"You think?" Morgan didn't smile. Like I said, unappreciated.

"I think that you've planned all of this. I think you are in with the vampires and the Winter Court. I think this is part of a deeper scheme."

I just stared at him. I tried not to laugh. I really did. Well. Maybe I didn't try all that hard.

The laughter must have gotten to Morgan. He balled up his fist and slammed a stiff jab into my belly that took the wind out of my sails and half dropped me to my knees.

"No," he said. "You aren't going to laugh this off, traitor." He stepped into my apartment. The threshold didn't make him blink. The wards I had up caught him six inches later, but they weren't designed to be too much of an impediment to human beings. Morgan grunted, spoke a harsh word in a guttural tongue, maybe Old German, and slashed his hand in front of him. The air hissed and popped with static electricity, sparks flashing from his fingertips. He shook his fingers briefly, then walked in.

He looked around the place and shook his head again. "Dresden, you might not be a bad person, all in all. But I think that you're compromised. If you aren't working with the Red Court, then I am certain that they are using you. Either way, the threat to the Council is the same. And it's best removed by removing you."

I tried to suck in a breath and finally managed to say, "What the hell are you talking about?"

"Susan Rodriguez," Morgan said. "Your lover, the vampire."

Anger made bright lights flash behind my eyes. "She's *not* a vampire," I snarled.

"They turned her, Dresden. No one goes back. That's all there is to it."

"They haven't. She's not."

Morgan shrugged. "That's what you would say if

she'd addicted you to the venom. You'd say or do just about anything for them by now."

I looked up at him, teeth bared. "Get the fuck out of my house."

He walked over to the fireplace and picked up a dust-covered gift card I'd left sitting on the mantel. He read it and snorted. Then he picked up a picture I had of Susan. "Pretty," he said. "But that's easy to come by. Odds are she was their pawn from the first day she met you."

I clenched my hands into fists. "You shut your mouth," I said. "You just shut your mouth about her. That's not how it was."

"You're a fool, Dresden. A young fool. Do you really think that a normal mortal woman would want anything to do with you or your life? You can't accept that she was just a tool. One of their whores."

I spun to the corner, letting go of my staff, and picked up my sword cane. I drew the blade free with a steely rasp and turned toward Morgan. He saw it coming and had already drawn the bright silver blade of the Wardens from the golf bag.

Every tired, aching, angry bone in my body wanted to lunge at him. I'm not heavy with muscle, but I'm not slow, and I've got arms and legs miles long. My lunge is quick, and I can do it from a long way back. Morgan was a seasoned soldier, but in such close quarters it would be a question of reflexes. Advantage to the guy with the sword weighed in ounces instead of stones.

In that moment, I was sure that I could have killed him. He might have taken me with him, but I could have done it. And I wanted to, badly. Not in any sort of intellectual sense, but in the part of the brain that does all of its thinking after the fact. My temper had frayed to bloody tatters, and I wanted to vent it on Morgan.

But a thought snuck in past the testosterone and spoiled my rage. I stopped myself. Shaking, and with my knuckles white on my sword cane, I drew myself up straight. And I said, very quietly, "That's number three."

Morgan's brow furrowed, and he stared at me, his own weapon steadily extended toward me. "What are you talking about, Dresden?"

"The third plan. The Merlin's ace in the hole. He sent you here to pick a fight with me. With my door still standing open. There's another Warden outside, listening, isn't there? A witness, so that you have a clean kill. Hand the body over to the vampires. End of problem, right?"

Morgan's eyes widened. He stammered over the first word. "I don't know what you're talking about."

I picked up the sheath half of the sword cane and slipped the blade back into it. "Sure, you don't. Get out, Morgan. Unless you'd prefer to stab an unarmed man who isn't offering you violence."

Morgan stared at me for a moment more. Then he shoved the sword back into the golf bag, swung it onto his shoulder, and headed for the door.

He was almost out when there was a clunk from my bedroom. I shot a look at the doorway.

Morgan stopped. He looked at me and then at my bedroom. Something ugly sparkled in his gaze. "Who is in the bedroom, Dresden? The vampire girl, perhaps?"

"No one," I said. "Get out."

"We'll see," Morgan said. He turned and walked to my bedroom door, one hand still on the sword. "You and those who consort with your like will be brought to task very soon. I'm looking forward to it."

My heart started pounding again. If Morgan found Elaine, there were about a million things that might happen, and none of them were good. There seemed little I could do, though. I couldn't warn her, and I couldn't think of a way to get Morgan out of my apartment any faster.

Morgan peered through the doorway and looked around, then abruptly let out a hoarse cry and jumped back. At the same time, there was a harsh feline yowl, and Mister, my bobtailed grey cat, came zooming out of the bedroom. He darted between Morgan's legs and then streaked past him, out of the apartment and up the stairs into the summer evening.

"Gosh, Morgan," I said, "my cat might be a dangerous subversive. Maybe you'd better interrogate him."

Morgan straightened, his face slightly red. He coughed and then stalked to the door. "The Senior Council members wish me to tell you that they will be nearby but that they will not interfere in this Trial or aid you in any way." He took a business card out of his shirt pocket and let it fall to the floor. "That's the contact number for the Senior Council. Use it when you have failed the Trial."

"Don't let the door hit you on the brain on the way out," I responded.

Morgan glared at me as he left. He slammed the door behind him and stomped up the stairs.

I started trembling maybe half a minute after he left—reaction to the stress. At least I hadn't done it in front of him. I turned around, leaned back against the door with my eyes closed, and folded my arms over my chest. It was easier not to feel myself shaking that way.

Another minute or two passed before I heard Elaine move quietly out of my bedroom. The fire popped and crackled.

"Are they gone?" Elaine asked. Her voice was very carefully steady.

"Yeah. Though I wouldn't put it past them to watch my place."

I felt her fingers touch my shoulder. "You're shaking, Harry."

"I'll be all right."

"You could have killed him," Elaine said. "When you first drew."

"Yeah."

"Was he really setting you up like you said?"

I looked at her. Her expression was worried. "Yeah," I said.

"God, Harry." She shook her head. "That's way past paranoia. And you want me to give myself to those people?"

I covered her hand with mine. "Not to them," I said. "Not everyone on the Council is like that."

She looked at my eyes for a moment. Then, carefully, she drew her hand out from under mine. "No. I'm not going to make myself vulnerable to men like that. Not again."

"Elaine," I protested.

She shook her head. "I'm leaving, Harry." She brushed her hair back from her face. "Are you going to tell them?"

I took a deep breath. If the Wardens found out that Elaine was still alive and avoiding them, there would be a literal witch hunt. The Wardens weren't exactly known for their tolerance and understanding. Morgan was walking, talking proof of that. Anyone who helped shield her from the Wardens would get the same treatment. Didn't I already have enough problems?

"No," I said. "Of course not."

Elaine gave me a strained smile. "Thank you, Harry." She lifted her staff closer to her, holding it with both hands. "Can you get the door for me?"

"They're going to be out there watching."

"I'll veil. They won't see me."

"They're good."

She shrugged and said without emphasis, "I'm better. I've had practice."

I shook my head. "What are we going to do about the faeries?"

"I don't know," she said. "I'll be in touch."

"How can I contact you?"

She nodded toward the door. I opened it. She stepped up beside me and kissed my cheek again, her lips warm. "You're the one with the office and the answering service. I'll contact you." Then she stepped to the door, murmuring quietly under her breath. There was a glitter of sudden silver light around her that made me blink. When I opened my eyes again, she was gone.

I left the door open for a moment, and it was just

as well that I did. Mister came padding back down the stairs a moment later and looked up at me with a plaintive meow. He prowled back into the apartment, curling around my legs and purring like a diesel engine. Mister is thirty pounds or so of tomcat. I figure one of his parents must have been a saber-toothed tiger. "Good timing, by the way," I told him, and shut the door, locking it.

I stood in the dim, warm firelight of the room. My cheek still tingled where Elaine had kissed it. I could smell her lingering perfume, and it brought with it a pang of almost tangible memories, a flood of things I thought I had forgotten. It made me feel old, and tired, and very alone.

I walked to the mantel and straightened the card Susan had sent me the previous Christmas. I looked at her picture, next to the card. She'd been in a park that weekend, wearing a blue tank top and cutoff shorts. Her teeth were impossibly white against her darkly tanned skin and coal-black hair. I'd taken the picture while she was laughing, and her dark eyes shone.

I shook my head. "I am tired, Mister," I said. "I am ridiculously tired."

Mister meowed at me.

"Well, resting would be the sane thing to do, but who am I to throw stones, right? I mean, I'm talking to my cat." I scratched at my beard and nodded to myself. "Just a minute on the couch. Then to work."

I remember sitting down on the couch, and after that everything went blissfully black.

Which was just as well. The next day things got complicated.

Chapter Ten

I wasn't too tired to dream. Evidently, my subconscious—we've met, and he's kind of a jerk—had something on his mind, because the dream was a variation on the theme that had taken up most of my sleeping hours since I'd last seen Susan.

The dream began with a kiss.

Susan has a gorgeous mouth. Not too thin and not too full. Always soft, always warm. When she kissed me, it was like the world went away. Nothing mattered but the touch of her lips on mine. I kissed the dream-Susan, and she melted against me with a soft sound, the length of her body pliant, eager. Her fingers reached up and trailed over my chest, nails lightly raking.

I leaned back from the kiss after a long moment, and my eyes felt almost too heavy to open. My lips quivered and tingled with sensation, a feeling that begged for more kisses to make it cease. She looked up at me, dark eyes smoldering. Her hair had been pulled back into a long, silken tail that fell between her shoulder blades. It had grown longer, in the dreams. Her lovely aquiline face tilted up toward mine.

"Are you all right?" I asked her. I always did. And, as always, she gave me a small, sad smile and did not answer. I bit my lip. "I'm still looking. I haven't given up."

She shook her head and drew back from me. I had the presence of mind to look around. A dark alley this time, with the heavy, pounding music of a dance club making the nearest wall vibrate. Susan wore dark tights and a sleeveless blouse, and my black-leather duster had been draped over her shoulders and fell to brush her feet. She looked at me intently and then turned toward the entrance to the club.

"Wait," I said.

She walked to the door and turned back to me, extending her hand. The door opened, and dim, reddish light flooded out over her, doing odd things to the shadows over her face. Her dark eyes grew larger.

No, that wasn't right. The black of her pupils simply expanded, until the whites were gone, until there was nothing but darkness where her eyes should have been. They were vampire eyes, huge and inhuman.

"I can't," I said. "We can't go in there, Susan."

Her features grew frustrated, angry. She extended her hand to me again, more forcefully.

Hands came out of the darkness in the doorway, slim, pale, androgynous. They slipped over Susan, slowly, caressingly. Tugging at her clothing, her hair. Her eyes fluttered closed for a moment, her body growing stiff, before her weight shifted slowly toward the doorway.

Longing shot through me, sudden, mindless, and sharp as a scalpel's blade. Hunger, a simple and nearly violent need to touch, to be touched, followed it into me, and I suddenly could not think. "Don't," I said, and stepped toward her.

I felt her hand take mine. I felt her press herself to me with another moan, and her lips, her mouth, devoured mine with ravenous kisses, kisses I answered with my own, harder and more demanding as my doubts faded. I felt it when her kiss turned poisonous, when the sudden narcotic numbness swept through my mouth and began to spread through my body. It didn't make any difference. I kissed her, tore at her clothes, and she tore at mine. The hands helped, but I didn't pay any attention to them anymore. They were an unimportant background sensation in comparison to Susan's mouth, her hands, her skin velvet and warm beneath my fingers.

There was no romance, nothing but need, animal, carnal. I pushed her against a wall in the dim scarlet light, and she wrapped herself around me, frantic, her body urging me on. I pressed into her, sudden sensation of silk and honey, and had to fight for control, throwing my head back.

She quivered then, and as always, she struck. Her mouth closed on my throat, a flash of heat and agony that melted into a narcotic bliss like that of her kiss—but more complete. Languid delight spread through me, and I felt my body reacting, all traces of control gone, thrusting against her, into her. The motion slowly died as sheer, shivering ecstasy spread through me. I began to lose control of my limbs, muscles turning to gelatin. I sank slowly to the floor. Susan rode me down, her mouth hot and eager on my throat, her body, her hips moving now, taking over the rhythm.

The pleasure of the venom melted my thoughts, and they slid free of my flesh, floating over the ground. I looked down on my body, beneath Susan, pale and still on the floor, eyes empty. I saw the change take her. I saw her body twist and buck, saw her skin split and rip open. I saw something dark and horrible tear its way out, all gaping dark eyes and slippery black hide. Blood, my blood, smeared its mouth.

The creature froze in shock, staring down at my corpse. And as I began to drift away, the creature threw back its head, its body rubbery and sinuous as a snake's, and let out an inhuman, screeching yowl full of rage, pain, and need.

I bolted up out of sleep with a short cry, my skin sheathed in a cold sweat, my muscles aching and stiff.

I panted for a moment, looking around my apartment. My lips tingled with remembered kisses, my skin with dreamed caresses.

I forced myself to my feet with a groan and staggered toward my shower. There were times when it was just as well that I had disconnected the water heater to head off magically inspired mishaps. It made bathing sheer torture in the winter, but sometimes there's no substitute for a cold shower.

I stripped and stood under chilly water for a while, shaking. Not necessarily from cold, either. I shook with a lot of things. First with raw and mindless lust. The shower took the edge off of that in a few moments. Don't get me wrong. I didn't have any particular death-sex fixation. But I had been used to a certain amount of friendly tension relieving with Susan. Her absence had killed that for me, completely—except for rare moments during the damned dreams when my hormones came raging back to the front of my thoughts again as though making up for lost time.

Second, I trembled with fear. My nightmares might be one part lusty dream, but they were also a warning. Susan's curse could kill me and destroy her. I couldn't forget that.

And finally, I shook with guilt. If I hadn't let her down, maybe she wouldn't be in this mess. She was gone, and I didn't have the vaguest idea where she was. I should have been doing more.

I stuck my head in the water, and shoved those thoughts away, washing myself off with a ton of soap and the last shampoo in the bottle. I scrubbed at my beard and finally reached out and got my straight razor, then spent a few minutes and a lot of care removing it. Dark, wiry black hair fell in clumps to the shower floor, and my face tingled as it breathed its first air for a couple of months. But it felt good, and as I went through the routine of grooming, my thoughts cleared.

I dug some clean clothes out of my closet, padded out into the living room, and pulled back the rug that covered the trapdoor leading to the subbasement. I swung the door open, lit a candle, and descended the stepladder staircase into my lab.

My lab, in contrast to the havoc upstairs, looked like something run by a particularly anal-retentive military clerk. A long table ran down the middle of the room, between a pair of other tables, one on either wall, leaving only narrow walkways. White steel wire shelves on the walls held the host of magical components I used in research. They resided in a variety of jars, bottles, boxes, and plastic containers, most with labels listing the contents, how much was left, and when I had acquired the item. The tables were clean except for stacks of notes, a jar of pens and pencils, and myriad candles. I lit a few of them and walked down to the other end of the lab, checking the copper summoning circle set into the floor and making sure that nothing lay across it. You never knew when a magic circle would come in handy.

One area of the lab had retained the casual chaos that had been its major theme before I'd taken up nearly full-time residence last year. One shelf, still battered old wood, hadn't been changed or updated. Candleholders, covered in multiple shades of melted wax that had spilled down over them, sat at either end of the shelf. Between them was a scattering of various articles—a number of battered paperback romances, several Victoria's Secret catalogs, a scarlet scrap of a silk ribbon that had been tied into a bow on a naked young woman named Justine, one bracelet from a broken set of handcuffs, and a bleached old human skull.

"Bob, wake up," I said, lighting candles. "I need to pick your brain."

Lights, orange and nebulous, kindled deep in the shadows of the skull's eye sockets. The skull quivered a little bit on its shelf and then stretched its toothy mouth open in an approximation of a yawn. "So was the kid right? Was there some portent-type action going on?"

"Rain of toads," I said.

"Real ones?"

"Yeah."

"Ouch," said Bob the Skull. Bob wasn't really a skull. The skull was just a vessel for the spirit of intellect that resided inside and helped me keep track of the constantly evolving metaphysical laws that govern the use of magic. But "Bob the Skull" is a lot easier to say than "Bob the Spirit of Intellect and Lab Assistant."

I nodded, breaking out my Bunsen burners and beakers. "Tell me about it. Look, Bob, I've got kind of a difficult situation here and—"

"Harry, you aren't going to be able to do this. There *is* no cure for vampirism. I like Susan too, but it can't be done. You think people haven't looked for a cure before now?"

"*I* haven't looked for one before now," I said. "And I've had a couple of ideas I want to look at."

"Aye, Cap'n Ahab, arr har har har! We'll get that white devil, sir!"

"Damn right we will. But we've got something else to do first."

Bob's eyelights brightened. "You mean something other than hopeless, pointless vampire research? I'm already interested. Does it have to do with the rain of toads?"

I frowned, got out a pad of paper and a pencil, and started scratching things down. Sometimes that helped me sort things out. "Maybe. It's a murder investigation."

"Gotcha. Who's the corpse?"

"Artist. Ronald Reuel."

Bob's eyelights burned down to twin points. "Ah. Who is asking you to find the killer?"

"We don't know he was killed. Cops say it was an accident."

"But you think differently."

I shook my head. "I don't know a thing about it, but Mab says he was killed. She wants me to find the killer and prove that it wasn't her."

Bob fell into a shocked silence nearly a minute long. My pen scratched on the paper until Bob blurted, "Mab? *The* Mab, Harry?"

"Yeah."

"Queen of Air and Darkness? *That* Mab?"

"Yeah," I said, impatient.

"And she's your *client*?"

"Yes, Bob."

"Here's where I ask why don't you spend your time doing something safer and more boring. Like maybe administering suppositories to rabid gorillas."

"I live for challenge," I said.

"Or you *don't*, as the case may be," Bob said brightly. "Harry, if I've told you once, I've told you a thousand times. You don't get tangled up with the Sidhe. It's always more complicated than you thought it would be."

"Thanks for the advice, skull boy. It wasn't like I had a choice. Lea sold her my debt."

"Then you should have traded her something for your freedom," Bob said. "You know, stolen an extra baby or something and given it to her—"

"Stolen a *baby*? I'm in enough trouble already."

"Well, if you weren't such a Goody Two-shoes all the time . . ."

I pushed at the bridge of my nose with my thumb.

This was going to be one of those conversations that gave me a headache, I could tell already. "Look, Bob, can we stick to the subject, please? Time is important, so let's get to work. I need to know why Reuel would have been knocked off."

"Gee whiz, Harry," Bob said. "Maybe because he was the Summer Knight?"

My pencil fell out of my fingers and rolled on the table. "Whoa," I said. "Are you sure?"

"What do you think?" Bob replied, somehow putting a sneer into the words.

"Uh," I said. "This means trouble. It means . . ."

"It means that things with the Sidhe are more complicated than you thought. Gee, if only someone had warned you at some point not to be an idiot and go making deals."

I gave the skull a sour look and recovered my pencil. "How much trouble am I in?"

"A lot," Bob said. "The Knights are entrusted with power by the Sidhe Courts. They're tough."

"I don't know much about them," I confessed. "They're some kind of representative of the faeries, right?"

"Don't call them that to their faces, Harry. They don't like it any more than you'd like being called an ape."

"Just tell me what I'm dealing with."

Bob's eyelights narrowed until they almost went out, then brightened again after a moment, as the skull began to speak. "A Sidhe Knight is mortal," Bob said. "A champion of one of the Sidhe Courts. He gets powers in line with his Court, and he's the only one who is allowed to act in affairs not directly related to the Sidhe."

"Meaning?"

"Meaning that if one of the Queens wants an outsider dead, her Knight is the trigger man."

I frowned. "Hang on a minute. You mean that the Queens can't personally gun down anyone who isn't in their Court?"

"Not unless the target does something stupid like make an open-ended bargain without even trying to trade a baby for—"

"Off topic, Bob. Do I or don't I have to worry about getting killed this time around?"

"Of course you do," Bob said in a cheerful tone. "It just means that the Queen isn't allowed to actually, personally end your life. They could, however, trick you into walking into quicksand and watch you drown, turn you into a stag and set the hounds after you, bind you into an enchanted sleep for a few hundred years, that kind of thing."

"I guess it was too good to be true. But my point is that if Reuel was the Summer Knight, Mab couldn't have killed him. Right? So why should she be under suspicion?"

"Because she could have done it indirectly. And Harry, odds are the Sidhe don't really care about Reuel's murder. Knights come and go like paper cups. I'd guess that they were upset about something else. The only thing they really care about."

"Power," I guessed.

"See, you can use your brain when you want to."

I shook my head. "Mab said something had been taken, and that I'd know what it was," I muttered. "I guess that's it. How much power are we talking about?"

"A Knight of the Sidhe is no pushover, Harry," Bob said, his tone earnest.

"So we're talking about a lot of magic going AWOL. Grand theft mojo." I drummed my pen on the table. "Where does the power come from originally?"

"The Queens."

I frowned. "Tell me if I'm off track here. If it comes from the Queens, it's a part of them, right? If a Knight dies, the power should snap back to the Queen like it was on a rubber band."

"Exactly."

"But this time it didn't. So the Summer Queen is missing a load of power. She's been weakened."

"If everything you've told me is true, yes," Bob said.

"There's no more balance between Summer and Winter. Hell, that could explain the toads. That's a serious play of forces, isn't it?"

Bob rolled his eyelights. "The turning of the seasons? Duh, Harry. The Sidhe are closer to the mortal world than any other beings of the Nevernever. Summer's had a slight edge for a while now, but it looks like they've lost it."

"And here I thought global warming was due to cow farts." I shook my head. "So, Titania loses a bunch of juice, and naturally suspicion falls on her archenemy, Mab."

"Yeah. It *is* kind of an archenemy-ish thing to do, you have to admit."

"I guess." I frowned down at my notes. "Bob, what happens if this imbalance between the Courts continues?"

"Bad things," Bob said. "It will mess around with

weather patterns, cause aberrant behavior in plants and animals, and sooner or later the Sidhe Courts will go to war with one another."

"Why?"

"Because, Harry. When the balance is destroyed, the only thing the Queens can do is to blow everything to flinders and let it settle out into a natural distribution again."

"What does that mean to me?" I asked.

"Depends on who has the edge when everything is settled," Bob said. "A war could start the next ice age, or set off an era of rampant growth."

"That last one doesn't sound so bad."

"No. Not if you're an Ebola virus. You'll have lots of friends."

"Oh. Bad, then."

"Yeah," Bob said. "Keep in mind that this is theory, though. I've never seen it happen. I haven't existed that long. But it's something the Queens will want to avoid if they can."

"Which explains Mab's interest in this, if she didn't do it."

"Even if she did," Bob corrected me. "Did she ever actually tell you she was innocent?"

I mulled it over for a moment. "No," I said finally. "She twisted things around a lot."

"So it's possible that she *did* do it. Or had it done, at any rate."

"Right," I said. "So to find out if it was one of the Queens, we'd need to find her hitter. How tough would it be to kill one of these Knights?"

"A flight of stairs wouldn't do it. A couple of flights of stairs wouldn't do it. Maybe if he went on an elevator ride with you—"

"Very funny." I frowned, drumming my pen on the table. "So it would have taken that little something extra to take out Reuel. Who could manage it?"

"Regular folks could do it. But they wouldn't be able to do it without burning buildings and smoking craters and so on. To kill him so that it looked like an accident? Maybe another Knight could. Among the Sidhe, it was either the Winter Knight or one of the Queens."

"Could a wizard do it?"

"That goes without saying. But you'd have to be a pretty brawny wizard, have plenty of preparation and a good channel to him. Even then, smoking craters would be easier than an accident."

"The wizards have all been in duck-and-cover mode lately. And there are too many of them to make a practical suspect pool. Let's assume that it was probably internal faerie stuff. That cuts it down to three suspects."

"Three?"

"The three people who could have managed it. Summer Queen, Winter Queen, Winter Knight. One, two, three."

"Harry, I said it could have been one of the Queens."

I blinked up at the skull. "There are more than two?"

"Yeah, technically there are three."

"Three?"

"In each Court."

"Three Queens in each *Court*? *Six*? That's just silly."

"Not if you think about it. Each Court has three Queens: The Queen Who Was, the Queen Who Is, and the Queen Who Is to Come."

"Great. Which one does the Knight work for?"

"All of them. It's kind of a group thing. He has different duties to each Queen."

I felt the headache start at the base of my neck and creep toward the crown of my head. "Okay, Bob. I need to know about these Queens."

"Which ones? The ones Who Are, Who Were, or Who Are to Come?"

I stared at the skull for a second, while the headache settled comfortably in. "There's got to be a simpler parlance than that."

"That's so typical You won't steal a baby, but you're too lazy to conjugate."

"Hey," I said, "my sex life has nothing to do with—"

"Conjugate, Harry. Conju— Oh, why do I even bother? The Queen is just the Queen. Queen Titania, Queen Mab. The Queen Who Was is called the Mother. The Queen Who Is to Come is known as the Lady. Right now, the Winter Lady is Maeve. The Summer Lady is Aurora."

"Lady, Queen, Mother, gotcha." I got a pencil and wrote it down, just to help me keep it straight, including the names. "So six people who might have managed it?"

"Plus the Winter Knight," Bob said. "In theory."

"Right," I said. "Seven." I wrote down the titles and then tapped the notebook thoughtfully and said, "Eight."

"Eight?" Bob asked.

I took a deep breath and said, "Elaine's alive. She's on the investigation for Summer."

"Wow," Bob said. "Wow. And I told you so."

"I know, I know."

"You think she might have gacked Reuel?"

"No," I said. "But I never saw it coming when she and Justin came after me, either. I only need to think about if she had the means to do it. I mean, if you think it would have been tough for me, maybe she wasn't capable of taking down Reuel. I was always a lot stronger than her."

"Yeah," Bob said, "but she was better than you. She had a lot going for her that you didn't. Grace. Style. Elegance. Breasts."

I rolled my eyes. "So she's on the list, until I find some reason she shouldn't be."

"How jaded and logical of you, Harry. I'm almost proud."

I turned to the folder Mab had given me and went through the newspaper clippings inside. "Any idea who the Winter Knight is?"

"Nope. Sorry," Bob said. "My contacts on the Winter side are kinda sketchy."

"Okay, then," I sighed and picked up the notebook. "I know what I need to do."

"This should be good," Bob said drily.

"Bite me. I have to find out more about Reuel. Who was close to him. Maybe someone saw something. If the police assumed an accident, I doubt there was an investigation."

Bob nodded, somehow managing to look thoughtful. "So are you going to take out an ad in the paper or what?"

I went around the lab and started snuffing candles. "I thought I'd try a little breaking and entering. Then I'll go to his funeral, see who shows."

"Gosh. Can I do fun things like you when I grow up?"

I snorted and turned to the stepladder, taking my last lit candle with me.

"Harry?" Bob said, just before I left.

I stopped and looked back at him.

"For what it's worth, be careful." If I hadn't known any better, I'd have said Bob the Skull was almost shaking. "You're an idiot about women. And you have no idea what Mab is capable of."

I looked at him for a moment, his orange eyes the only light in the dimness of my frenetically neat lab. It sent a little shiver through me.

Then I clomped back up the stepladder and went out to borrow trouble.

Chapter Eleven

I made a couple of phone calls, slapped a few things into a nylon backpack, and sallied forth to break into Ronald Reuel's apartment.

Reuel had lived at the south edge of the Loop, in a building that looked like it had once been a theater. The lobby yawned up to a high ceiling and was spacious and pretty enough, but it left me looking for the velvet ropes and listening for the disorganized squawking of an orchestra warming up its instruments.

I walked in wearing a hat with an FTD logo and carrying a long white flower box under one arm. I nodded to an aging security guard at a desk and went on past him to the stairs, my steps purposeful. You'd be surprised how far a hat, a box, and a confident stride can get you.

I took the stairs up to Reuel's apartment, on the third floor. I went up them slowly, my wizard's senses open, on the lookout for any energies that might yet be lingering around the site of the old man's death. I paused for a moment, over the spot where Reuel's body had been found, to be sure, but there was nothing. If a lot of magic had been put to use in Reuel's murder, someone had covered its tracks impressively.

I went the rest of the way up to the third floor, but it wasn't until I opened the door to the third-floor hallway that my instincts warned me I was not alone. I froze with the door from the stairway only half open, and Listened.

Listening isn't particularly hard. I'm not even sure it's all that magical. I can't explain it well, other than to say that I'm able to block out everything but what I hear and to pick up things I would normally miss. It's a skill that not many people have these days, and one that has been useful to me more than once.

This time, I was able to Listen to a half-whispered basso curse and the rustle of papers from somewhere down the hall.

I opened the flower box and drew out my blasting rod, then checked my shield bracelet. All in all, in close quarters like this, I would have preferred a gun to my blasting rod, but I'd have a hell of a time explaining it to security or the police if they caught me snooping around a dead man's apartment. I tightened my grip on the rod and slid quietly down the hall, hoping I wouldn't need to use it. Believe it or not, my first instinct isn't always to set things on fire.

The door to Reuel's apartment stood half open, and its pale wood glared where it had been freshly splintered. My heart sped up. It looked like someone had beaten me to Reuel's place. It meant that I must have been on the right track.

It also meant that whoever it was would probably not be thrilled to see me.

I crept to the door and peered inside.

What I could see of the apartment could have been imported from 429-B Baker Street. Dark woods, fancy scrollwork, and patterns of cloth busier than the makeup girl at a Kiss concert filled every available inch of space with Victorian splendor. Or rather, it once had. Now the place looked wrecked. A sideboard stood denuded of its drawers, which lay upturned on the floor. An old steamer chest lay on its side, its lid torn off, its contents scattered onto the carpet. An open door showed me that the bedroom hadn't been spared the rough stuff either. Clothes and broken bits of finery lay strewn about everywhere.

The man inside Reuel's apartment looked like a catalog model for Thugs-R-Us. He stood a hand taller than me, and I couldn't tell where his shoulders left off and his neck began. He wore old frayed breeches, a sweater with worn elbows, and a hat that looked like an import from the Depression-era Bowery, a round bowler decorated with a dark grey band. He carried a worn leather satchel in one meat-slab hand, and with the other he scooped up pieces of paper, maybe index cards, from a shoe box on an old writing desk, depositing them in the bag. The satchel bulged, but he kept adding more to it with rapid, sharp motions. He muttered something else, emitted a low rumble, and snatched up a Rolodex from the desk, cramming it into the satchel.

I drew back from the door and put my back against the wall. There wasn't any time to waste, but I had to figure out what to do. If someone had shown up at

Reuel's place to start swiping papers, it meant that Reuel had been hiding evidence of one kind or another. Therefore, I needed to see whatever it was Kong had in that satchel.

Somehow, I doubted he would show me if I asked him pretty please, but I didn't like my other option, either. In such tight quarters, and with other residents nearby, I didn't dare resort to any of my kaboom magic. Kaboom magic, or evocation, is difficult to master, and I'm not very good at it. Even with my blasting rod as a focus, I had accidentally dealt out structural damage to a number of buildings. So far, I'd been lucky enough not to kill myself. I didn't want to push it if I didn't have to.

Of course, I could always just jump the thug and try to take his bag away. I had a feeling I'd be introduced to whole new realms of physical discomfort, but I could try it.

I took another peek at the thug. With one hand, he casually lifted a sofa that had to weigh a couple of hundred pounds and peered under it. I drew back from the door again. Fisticuffs, bad idea. Definitely a bad idea.

I chewed on my lip a moment more. Then I slipped the blasting rod back into the flower box, squared up my FTD hat, stepped around the corner, and knocked on the half-open door.

The thug's head snapped around toward me, along with most of his shoulders. He bared his teeth, anger in his eyes.

"FTD," I said, trying to keep my voice bland. "I got a delivery here for a Mr. Reuel. You want to sign for it?"

The thug glowered at me from beneath the shelter of his overhanging brow. "Flowers?" he rumbled a minute later.

"Yeah, buddy," I said. "Flowers." I came into the apartment and thrust the clipboard at him, idly wishing I had some gum to chomp. "Sign there at the bottom."

He glowered at me for a moment longer before accepting the clipboard. "Reuel ain't here."

"Like I care." I pushed a pen at him with the other hand. "Just sign it and I'll get going."

This time he glared at the pen, then at me. Then he set the satchel on the coffee table. "Whatever."

"Great." I stepped past him and put the flower box down on the table. He clutched the pen in his fist and scrawled on the bottom of the paper. I reached down with one hand as he did, plucked a piece of paper a little bigger than a playing card from the satchel, and palmed it. I got my hand back to my side just before he finished, growled, and shoved the clipboard at me.

"Now," he said, "leave."

"You bet," I told him. "Thanks."

I turned to go, but his hand shot out and his fingers clamped on to my arm like a steel band. I looked back. He narrowed his eyes, nostrils flared, and then growled, "I don't smell flowers."

The bottom fell out of my stomach, but I tried to keep the bluff going. "What are you talking about, Mr., uh"—I glanced down at the clipboard—"Grum."

Mr. Grum?

He leaned down closer to me, and his nostrils flared

again, this time with a low snuffling sound. "I smell magic. Smell wizard."

My smile must have turned green to go with my face. "Uh."

Grum took my throat in one hand and lifted me straight up off the ground with a strength no human could duplicate. My vision reduced itself to a hazy tunnel, and the clipboard fell from my fingers. I struggled against him uselessly. His eyes narrowed, and he bared more teeth in a slow smile. "Should have minded your own business. Whoever you are." His fingers started tightening, and I thought I heard something crackle and pop. I had to hope it was his knuckles instead of my trachea. "Whoever you were."

It was too late by far to use my shield bracelet, and my blasting rod lay out of reach on the coffee table. I fumbled in my pocket, as my vision started to go black, for the only weapon I had left. I had to pray that I was right in my guess.

I found the old iron nail, gripped it as best I could, and shoved it hard at Grum's beefy forearm. The nail bit into his flesh.

He screamed, a throaty, basso bellow that shook the walls. He flinched and spun, hurling me away from him. I hit the door to Reuel's bedroom, slamming it all the way open, and got lucky. I landed on the bed rather than on one of the wooden pillars at its corners. If I'd hit one of those, I'd have broken my back. Instead, I hit the bed, bounced, fetched up hard against the wall, then tumbled back to the bed again.

I glanced up to see that Grum looked very different than he had a moment before.

Rather than the film noir tough-guy getup, he wore a loincloth of some kind of pale leather—and nothing more. His skin was a dark russet, layered with muscle and curling dark hair. His ears stood out from the sides of his head like satellite dishes, and his features had flattened, becoming more bestial, nearly like those of a gorilla. He was also better than twelve feet tall. He had to hunch over to stand, and even so his shoulders pressed against the ten-foot ceiling.

With another roar, Grum tore the nail from his arm and flung it to one side. It went completely through the wall, leaving a hole the size of my thumb. Then he spun back to me, baring teeth now huge and jagged, and took a stalking step toward me, the floor creaking beneath his feet.

"Ogre," I wheezed. "Crap!" I extended my hand toward the blasting rod and focused my will. *"Ventas servitas!"*

A sharp and sudden torrent of air caught up the flower box and hurled it straight toward me. It hit me in the chest hard enough to hurt, but I snatched it, brought out my blasting rod, and trained it on Grum as he closed on me. I slammed more will through the rod, its tip bursting into scarlet incandescence.

"Fuego!" I barked as I released the energy. Fire in a column the size of my clenched fist flashed out at Grum and splashed against his chest.

It didn't slow him down, not by a second. His skin

didn't burn—his hair didn't even singe. The fire of my magic spilled over him and did absolutely nothing.

Grum shouldered his way through the bedroom door, cracking the frame as he did, and raised his fist. He slammed it down at the bed, but I didn't wait around to meet it. I flopped over to the far side of the bed and tumbled down to the space between the bed and the wall. He reached for me, but I rolled underneath the bed, bumped against his feet, and scrambled toward the door.

I almost made it. But something heavy and hard slammed against my legs, taking them out from under me and knocking me down. I only had time to realize, dimly, that Grum had picked up an antique Victorian chair that resembled, more than anything else, a throne, and hurled it at me.

The pain kicked in a second later, but I crawled toward the door. The ogre's feet pounded in rapid succession, and the floor shook as he grew closer and closer to me.

From the hall, a querulous female voice demanded, "What's all that racket? I have already called the police, I have! You fruits get out of our hall, or they'll lock you away!"

Grum stopped. I saw frustration and rage flicker over his apelike features. Then he snarled, stepped over me, and picked up the satchel. When he headed for the door, I rolled out of his way. He was big enough to simply crush my chest if he stepped on me, and I didn't want to make it easy for him.

"You got lucky," the ogre growled. "But this is not over." Then his form blurred and shifted, growing smaller, until he wore the same appearance he had a few moments before. He settled his bowler with one hand, then stalked out the door, aiming a kick at me in passing. I cringed away from it, and he was gone.

"Well?" demanded that same voice. "What's it going to be, you fruit? Get out!"

Police sirens wailed somewhere outside. I got up, wobbled for a moment, and put my hand against the wall to help myself stay up. I turned the other hand over to look at the piece of paper I'd stolen from Grum's satchel.

It wasn't paper. It was a photograph. Nothing fancy—just an instant-camera shot. It showed old white-haired Reuel, standing in front of the Magic Castle at one of the Disney parks.

Several young people stood beside him and around him, smiling, sunburned, and apparently happy. One was a tall, bull-necked young woman in faded jeans, with her hair dyed a shade of muddy green. She had a wide smile and a blunt, ugly face. Standing beside her was a girl who should have been in a lingerie catalog, all curves and long limbs in her brief shorts and bikini top, her hair also green, but the color of summer grass rather than that of pond scum. On the other side of Reuel was a pair of young men. One of them, a short, stocky fellow with a goatee and sunglasses, had his fingers lifted into a V behind the head of his companion, a small, slender man with his skin sunburned to the color of copper and his blond hair bleached out to nearly white.

Who were they? Why had Reuel been with them? And why had Grum seemed so intent on removing their picture from Reuel's apartment?

The sirens grew closer, and if I didn't want to get locked up by some well-meaning member of Chicago's finest, I needed to leave. I rubbed at my aching throat, winced at the wrenching, cramping pain in my back, wondered about the photograph, and stumbled out of the building.

Chapter Twelve

I got out of the old apartment building and back to the Blue Beetle without being mugged by any attackers, inhuman or otherwise. As I pulled out, a patrol car rolled up, blue bubbles flashing. I drove away at a sedate pace and tried to keep my shaking hands from making the car bob or swerve. No one pulled me over, so I must have done all right. Score one for the good guys.

I had time to think, though I wasn't sure I wanted to. I'd gone to Reuel's apartment on a simple snoop, not really expecting to find much, if anything. But I'd gotten lucky. Not only had I shown up at the right place, I'd done it at the right time. Someone obviously wanted to hide something there—either more pictures like the one I'd found or other papers from somewhere in the place. What I needed to determine now was what Grum had been trying to collect or—nearly as good—why he was trying to make some kind of evidence vanish. Failing that, knowing who he was working for would do almost as well—ogres aren't exactly known for their independent initiative. And given what was going on, it would be ludicrous to assume that one of the heavyweight thugs of the lands of Faerie just happened to be doing an independent contract in the home of the recently deceased.

Ogres were wyldfae—they could work for either Winter or Summer, and they could have a range of personalities and temperaments running the gamut from jovially violent to maliciously violent. Grum hadn't seemed to be on the cheerful end of that particular scale, but he *had* been both decisive and restrained. The average walking mountain of muscle from Faerie wouldn't have held back from beating me to a pulp, regardless of what the neighbors shouted. That meant that Grum had more savvy than the average bear, that he was dangerous—even if I didn't take into account how easily he had ignored the spells I'd hurled at him.

All ogres have an innate capacity for neutralizing magical forces to one degree or another. Grum had grounded out my spells like I'd been scuffing my feet on the carpet to give him a little static electricity zap. That meant that he was an old faerie, and a strong one. The quick and thorough shapeshifting supported that assessment as well. Your average club-swinging thewmonger couldn't have taken human form, complete with clothing, so ably.

Smart plus strong plus quick equals badass. Most likely he was a trusted personal guard or a highly placed enforcer.

But for whom?

At a stop light I stared at the photograph I'd taken from Grum.

"Damn," I muttered, "who are these people?"

I added it to the list of questions still growing like fungus in a locker room.

Ronald Reuel's funeral had already begun by the time I arrived. Flannery's Funeral Home in the River North area had been a family-run business until a few years before. It was an old place, but had always been well kept. Now the carefully landscaped shrubbery had been replaced with big rocks, which were no doubt easier to maintain. The parking lot had a lot of cracks in it, and only about half of the outdoor lights were burning. The sign, an illuminated glass-and-plastic number that read QUIET ACRES FUNERAL HOME, glared in garish green and blue above the front door.

I parked the Beetle, tucked the photo into my pocket, and got out of the car. I couldn't casually take my staff or my blasting rod into the funeral home. People who don't believe in magic look at you oddly when you walk in toting a big stick covered with carvings of runes and sigils. The people who know what I am would react in much the same way as if I had walked in draped in belts of ammo and carrying a heavy-caliber machine gun in each hand, John Wayne–style. There could be plenty of each sort inside, so I carried only the low-profile stuff: my ring, mostly depleted, my shield bracelet, and my mother's silver pentacle amulet. My reflection in the glass door reminded me that I had underdressed for the evening, but I wasn't there to make the social column. I slipped into the building and headed for the room where they'd laid out Ronald Reuel.

The old man had been dressed up in a grey silk suit with a metallic sheen to it. It was a younger man's suit, and it looked too big for him. He would have looked more comfortable in tweed. The mortician had done only a so-so job of fixing Reuel up. His cheeks were too red and his lips too blue. You could see the dimples on his lips where thin lines of thread had been stitched through them to hold his mouth closed. No one would have mistaken this for an old man in the midst of his nap—it was a corpse, plain and simple. The room was about half full, people standing in little knots talking and passing back and forth in front of the casket.

No one was standing in the shadows smoking a cigarette or looking about with a shifty-eyed gaze. I couldn't see anyone quickly hiding a bloody knife behind his back or twirling a moustache, either. That ruled out the Dudley Do-Right approach to finding the killer. Maybe he, she, or they weren't here.

Of course, I supposed it would be possible for faeries to throw a veil or a glamour over themselves before they came in, but even experienced faeries have trouble passing for mortal. Mab had looked good, sure, but she hadn't really looked *normal*. Grum had been much the same. I mean, he'd looked human, sure, but also like an extra on the set of *The Untouchables*. Faeries can do a lot of things really well, but blending in with a crowd generally isn't one of them.

In any case, the crowd struck me as mostly relatives and business associates. No one matched the pictures, no one seemed to be a faerie in a bad mortal costume, and either my instincts had the night off or no one was using any kind of veil or glamour. Bad guys one, Harry zero.

I slipped out of the viewing room and back into the

hallway in time to hear a low whisper somewhere down the hall. That grabbed my attention. I made the effort to move quietly and crept a bit closer, Listening as I went.

"I don't *know*," hissed a male voice. "I looked for her all day. She's never been gone this long."

"Just my point," growled a female voice. "She doesn't stay gone this long. You know how she gets by herself."

"God," said a third voice, the light tenor of a young man. "He did it. He really did it this time."

"We don't know that," the first man said. "Maybe she finally used her head and got out of town."

The woman's voice sounded tired. "No, Ace. She wouldn't just leave. Not on her own. We have to do something."

"What can we do?" the second male said.

"Something," the woman said. "Anything."

"Wow, that's specific," the first male, apparently Ace, said with his voice dry and edgy. "Whatever you're going to do, you'd better do it fast. The wizard is here."

I felt the muscles in my neck grow tense. There was a short, perhaps shocked silence in the room down the hall.

"Here?" the second male echoed in a panicky tone. "Now? Why didn't you tell us?"

"I just did, dimwit," Ace said.

"What do we do?" the second male asked. "What do we do, what do we do?"

"Shut up," snapped the female voice. "Shut *up*, Fix."

"He's in Mab's pocket," said Ace. "You know he is. She crossed over from Faerie today."

"No way," said the second voice, presumably Fix. "He's supposed to be a decent sort, right?"

"Depends on who you hear it from," said Ace. "People who get in his way have had a habit of getting real dead."

"God," said Fix, panting. "Oh God, oh God."

"Look," said the woman, "if he's here, we shouldn't be. Not until we know what it means." Furniture, maybe a wooden chair, creaked. "Come on."

I slipped back down the hall and around the corner into the lobby as I heard footsteps leaving the small side room. They didn't come toward me. Instead, they moved farther down the hall, away from the lobby. They had to be heading for a back door. I chewed on my lip and weighed my options. Three very apprehensive folks, maybe human, maybe not, heading down a darkened hall toward a back door that doubtless led into an equally dark alley. It sounded like a recipe for more trouble.

But I didn't think I had any options. I counted to five and then followed the footsteps.

I saw only a retreating shadow at the far end of the hall. I looked into the room the three had been in as I went past it and found a small lounge with several upholstered chairs. I hesitated for a moment at the corner and heard the soft click of a metal door opening, then closing again. As I rounded the corner, I saw a door with a faded sticker spelling EXIT.

I went to the door and opened it as quietly as I could, then poked my head out into the alley it opened into and rubbernecked around.

They were standing not five feet away—three of the young people from Reuel's photo. The small, skinny man with the blond-white hair and dark tan was facing me. He was dressed in what looked like a secondhand brown suit and a yellow polyester clip-on tie. His eyes widened almost comically, and his mouth dropped open in shock. He squeaked, and it was enough to let me identify him as Fix.

Beside him was the other young man, Ace. He was the one with the dark curly hair and goatee, wearing a grey sport coat with a white shirt and dark slacks. He still had his sunglasses on when he turned to look at me, and he clawed at the pocket of his jacket upon seeing me.

The third was the brawny, homely young woman with the muddy green hair and heavy brow. She had on a pair of jeans tight enough to show the muscles in her thighs and a khaki blouse. She didn't hesitate. She didn't even look. She just turned, her arm sweeping out as she did, and fetched me a blow to my cheek with the back of one shovel-size hand. I managed to move with it a bit at the last second, but even so the impact threw me out of the doorway and into the alley. Stars and cartoon birdies danced in my vision, and I rolled, trying to get clear before she could hit me again.

Ace pulled a small-caliber semiautomatic from his jacket pocket, but the woman growled at him, "Don't be stupid! They'd kill us all."

"Hebbity bedda," I said, by way of attempting a greeting. My mouth had gone rather numb, and my tongue felt like a lead weight. "Jussa hangonna sayke hee."

Fix jumped up and down, pointing at me, his voice shrill. "He's casting on us!"

The woman kicked me in the ribs hard enough to knock the wind out of me. Then she picked me up by the back of my pants, grunting with the effort, and threw me into the air. I came down ten feet away in an open Dumpster and crunched down amid cardboard boxes and stinking refuse.

"Go," the woman barked. "Go, go, go!"

I lay in the garbage for a minute, trying to catch my breath. The sound of three sets of running feet receded down the alley.

I had just sat up when a head popped into view over me, vague in the shadows. I flinched and threw up my left arm, willing power through the shield bracelet. I accidentally made the shield too big, and sparks kicked up where the shield intersected the metal of the Dumpster, but by their light I saw whose head it was.

"Harry?" Billy the Werewolf asked. "What are you doing in there?"

I let the shield drop and extended a hand to him. "Looking for suspects."

He frowned and hauled me out of the trash. I wobbled for a second or two, until my head stopped spinning quite so quickly. Billy steadied me with one hand. "You find any?"

"I'd say so, yeah."

Billy nodded and peered up at me. "Did you decide that before or after they hit you in the face and threw you in the garbage?"

I brushed coffee grounds off my jeans. "Do I tell you how to do your job?"

"Actually, yeah. All the time."

"Okay, okay," I muttered. "Did you bring the pizza?"

"Yeah," Billy said. "Got it back in the car. Why?"

I brushed at my shaggy hair. What I hoped were more coffee grounds fell out. I started walking down the alley toward the front of the building. "Because I need to make a few bribes," I said, looking back over my shoulder at Billy. "Do you believe in faeries?"

Chapter

Thirteen

Billy held the pizza while I drew the chalk circle on the ground, back in the alley. "Harry," he said, "how is this supposed to work exactly?"

"Hang on," I said. I didn't quite complete the circle, but took the pizza box from him. I opened it, took out one piece, and put it down in the middle of the circle on a napkin. Then I dabbed a bit of blood from the corner of my mouth where the girl had slugged me onto the bottom of the piece of pizza, stepped back, and completed the circle without willing it closed.

"Pretty simple," I said. "I'll call the faerie in close to the pizza there. He'll smell it, jump on it, eat it. When he does, he'll get the bit of my blood, and it will be enough energy to close the circle around him."

"Uh-huh," Billy said, his expression skeptical. He took out a second piece and started to take a bite. "And then you beat the information out of him?"

I took the piece out of his hand, put it back in the box, and closed it. "And then I bribe the information out of him. Save the pizza."

Billy scowled at me, but he left the pizza alone. "So what do I do?"

"Sit tight and make sure no one else tries to pop me while I'm talking to Toot-toot."

"Toot-toot?" Billy asked, lifting an eyebrow.

"Hell's bells, Billy, I didn't pick the name. Just be quiet. If he thinks there are mortals around he'll get nervous and leave before I can snare him."

"If you say so," Billy said. "I was just hoping to do more good than to deliver pizza."

I raked my fingers through my hair. "I don't know what you could do yet."

"I could track those three in the picture you showed me."

I shook my head. "Odds are they just got into a car and left."

"Yeah," he said, some forced patience in his voice. "But if I get their scent now, it might help me find them later on."

"Oh," I said, feeling a bit stupid. Okay, so I hadn't considered the whole shapeshifting angle. "Fine, if you want to. Just be careful, all right? I don't know what all might be prowling around."

"Okay, Mom," Billy said. He set the pizza box on top of a closed trash can, fell back down the alley, and vanished.

I waited until Billy had gone to find a nice patch of shadows to step into. Then I closed my eyes for a moment, drawing up my concentration, and began to whisper the faerie's Name.

Every intelligent being has a Name, a specific series of

spoken sounds linked to its very being. If a practitioner knows the Name of something, knows it in every nuance and detail of pronunciation, then he can use that Name to open a magical conduit to that being. That's how demons get summoned to the mortal world. Call something's Name and you make contact with it—and if you're a wizard, that means that you can then exercise power over it, no matter where in the world it is.

Controlling an inhuman being via its Name is a shady area of magic, only one step removed from taking over the will of another mortal. According to the White Council's Seven Laws of Magic, that's a capital crime—and they make zero-tolerance policies look positively lenient.

Given how much the Council loves me, I'm a tad paranoid about breaking any of the Laws of Magic, so while I was calling the faerie's Name, I put only the tiniest trickle of compulsion into it, just enough to attract his unconscious attention, to make him curious about what might be down this particular alley. I whispered the faerie's Name and stood in the shadows, waiting.

Maybe ten minutes later, something made from a hummingbird and a falling star spiraled down from overhead, a flickering ball of blue-white light. It alighted on the ground, the light dimming to a luminous sheen over the form of a tiny faerie, Toot-toot.

Toot stood about six inches tall. He had a mane of dandelion-fluff hair the color of lilacs and a pair of translucent dragonfly wings rising from his shoulders. Otherwise he looked almost human, his beauty a distant echo of the lords of Faerie, the Sidhe. On his head he wore what looked like a plastic Coke bottle cap. It was tied into place with a piece of string that ran under his chin, and his lilac hair squeezed out from beneath it all the way around, all but hiding his eyes. In one hand he carried a spear fashioned from a battered old yellow number 2 pencil, some twine, and what must have been a straight pin, and he wore a little blue plastic cocktail sword through another piece of twine on his belt.

Toot landed in a cautious crouch near the pizza, as though streaking in like an errant shot from a Roman candle might not have alerted anyone watching to his presence. He tiptoed in a big circle around the piece of pizza, and made a show of looking all around, one hand lifted to shade his eyes. Then he raised his arm into the air, balled up a tiny fist, and pumped it up and down a few times.

Immediately, half a dozen similar streaks of glowing color darted down out of the air, each one a different color, each one containing a tiny faerie at its center. They alighted more or less together, and every one of them was armed with a weapon that might have been cobbled together from the contents of a child's school box.

"Caption!" Toot-toot piped in a shrill voice. "Report!"

A green-lit faerie beside Toot snapped to attention and slapped herself on the forehead with one hand, then turned sharply to her left and barked, "Loo Tender, report!"

A purple-hued faerie came to attention as well and smacked himself in the head with one hand, then turned to the next faerie beside him and snapped, "Star Jump, report!"

And so it went down the line, through the "Corpse Oral," the "First Class Privy," and finally to the "Second Class Privy," who marched up to Toot-toot and said, "Everyone's here, Generous, and we're hungry!"

"All right," Toot-toot barked. "Everyone fall apart for messy!"

And with that, the faeries let out shrill hoots of glee, tossed aside their weapons and armaments, and threw themselves upon the piece of pizza.

As soon as the little faeries started eating, the magic circle snapped closed around them with a hardly audible *pop* as it sprang into place. The effect was immediate. The faeries let out half a dozen piercing shrieks of alarm and buzzed into the air, smacking into the invisible wall of the circle here and there, sending out puffs of glowing dust motes when they did. They fell into a panicked spiral around the inside of the circle, until Toot-toot landed on the ground, looked up at the other faeries, and started shouting, "Ten Huts! Ten Huts!"

The other faeries abruptly came to a complete stop in the air, standing rigidly straight. Evidently, they couldn't do that and keep their little wings going at the same time, because they promptly fell to the alley floor, landing with a half-dozen separate "ouches" and as many puffs of glowing faerie dust.

Toot-toot recovered his pencil spear and stood at the very edge of the closed circle, peering out at the alley. "Harry Dresden? Is that you?"

I stepped out from my hiding spot and nodded. "It's me. How you doing, Toot?"

I expected a torrent of outraged but empty threats. That was Toot-toot's usual procedure. Instead, he let out a hiss and crouched down in the circle, spear at the ready. The other tiny faeries took up their own weapons and rushed to Toot-toot's side. "You can't make us," Toot said. "We haven't been Called and until we are, we belong to ourselves."

I blinked down at them. "Called? Toot, what are you talking about?"

"We're not stupid, Emissary," Toot-toot said. "I know what you are. I can smell the Cold Queen all over you."

I wondered if they made a deodorant for that. I lifted my hand in a placating gesture. "Toot, I'm working for Mab right now, but it's just another client, okay? I'm not here to take you anywhere or make you do anything."

Toot planted the eraser end of his spear on the ground, scowling suspiciously up at me. "Really?" he demanded.

"Really," I said.

"Promise?"

"Promise."

"Super duper double dog promise spit swear?"

I nodded. "Super duper double dog promise spit swear," I repeated gravely.

"Spit!" Toot demanded.

I spat on the ground.

"Oh. Well, then," Toot said. He dropped his spear and darted over to the pizza, much to the consternation of the other little faeries, who let out piping shrills of protest and then followed him. The piece of pizza didn't last long. It was like watching one of those nature shows, where the piranha devour some luckless thing that falls in the water—except here there were glittering wings and motes and puffs of glowing, colorful dust everywhere.

I watched, frowning, until Toot-toot flopped onto his back, his tummy slightly distended. He let out a contented sigh, and the other faeries followed suit.

"So, Harry," Toot said, "who do you think is going to win the war?"

"The White Council," I said. "The Red Court's got no depth on the bench and nothing in the bullpen."

Toot snorted and flipped his plastic bottle-cap helm off his head. His hair waved around in the breeze. "Just because they don't have any cows doesn't mean that they won't win. But I don't mean *that* war."

I frowned. "You mean between the Courts."

Toot nodded. "Yeah."

"Okay. What's with the armor and weapons, Toot?"

The faerie beamed. "Neat, huh?"

"Highly scary," I said gravely. "But why do you have them?"

Toot folded his arms and said, with all the gravity that six inches of fluff and pixie dust can muster, "Trouble's coming."

"Uh-huh. I hear the Courts are upset."

"More than just upset, Harry Dresden. The drawing of the wyldfae is beginning. I saw some dryads walking with a Sidhe Knight from Summer, and a canal nereid climbed up out of the water a couple of blocks over and went into a Winter building."

"Drawing of the wyldfae. Like you guys?"

Toot nodded and propped his feet up on the legs of the Star Jump, who let out a surprisingly basso belch. "Not everyone plays with the Courts. We mostly just do our jobs and don't pay much attention. But when there's a war on, the wyldfae get Called to one side or another."

"Who picks which way you go?"

Toot shrugged. "Mostly the nice wyldfae go to the Warm Queen and the mean ones go to Cold. I think it's got something to do with what you've been doing."

"Uh-huh. So have you been doing Warm or Cold things?"

Toot let out a sparkling laugh. "How should I remember all those things?" He patted his stomach and then rose to his feet again, eyes calculating. "Is that a pizza box you have there, Harry?"

I held the box out and opened it, showing the rest of the pizza. There was a collective "Ooooo" from the faeries, and they all pressed to the very edge of the circle, until it flattened their little noses, staring at the pizza in fascinated lust.

"You've sure given us a lot of pizza the past couple of years, Harry," Toot said, with a swallow. He didn't look away from the box in my hands.

"Hey, you gave me a hand when I needed it," I said. "It's only fair, right?"

"Only fair?" Toot spat, outraged. "It's . . . it's . . . it's *pizza*, Harry."

"I'm wanting some more work done," I said. "I need information."

"And you're paying in pizza?" Toot asked, his tone hopeful.

"Yes," I said.

"Wah-hoo!" Toot shouted and buzzed into the air in an excited spiral. The other faeries followed him with similar carols of happiness, and the blur of colors was dizzying.

"Give us the pizza!" Toot shouted.

"Pizza, pizza, pizza!" the other faeries shrilled.

"First," I said, "I want some questions answered."

"Right, right, right!" Toot screamed. "Ask already!"

"I need to talk to the Winter Lady," I said. "Where can I find her, Toot?"

Toot tore at his lavender hair. "Is *that* all you need to know? Down in the city! Down where the shops are underground, and the sidewalks."

I frowned. "In the commuter tunnels?"

"Yes, yes, yes. Back in the part the mortals can't see, you can find your way into Undertown. The Cold Lady came to Undertown. Her court is in Undertown."

"What?" I sputtered. "Since when?"

Toot whirled around in impatient loops in the air. "Since the last autumn!"

I scratched at my hair. It made sense, I supposed. Last autumn, a vengeful vampire and her allies had stirred up all sorts of supernatural mischief, creating turbulence in the border between the real world and the Nevernever, the world of spirit. Shortly after, the war between the wizards and the vampires had begun.

Those events had probably attracted the attention of all sorts of things.

I shook my head. "And what about the Summer Lady? Is she in town?"

Toot put his fists on his hips. "Well, *obviously*, Harry. If Winter came here, Summer had to come too, didn't it?"

"Obviously," I said, feeling a little slow on the uptake. Man, was I off my game. "Where can I find her?"

"She's on top of one of those big buildings."

I sighed. "Toot, this is Chicago. There are a lot of big buildings."

Toot blinked at me, then frowned for a minute before brightening. "It's the one with the pizza shop right by it."

My head hurt some more. "Tell you what. How about you guide me to it?"

Toot thrust out his little chin and scowled. "And miss pizza? No way."

I gritted my teeth. "Then get me someone else to guide me. You've got to know someone."

Toot scrunched up his face. He tugged at one earlobe, but it evidently didn't help him remember, because he had to rub one foot against the opposite calf and spin around in vacant circles for ten whole seconds before he whirled back to face me, the nimbus of light around him brightening. "Aha!" he sang. "Yes! I can give you a guide!" He jabbed a finger at me. "But only if that's all the questions, Harry. Pizza, pizza, pizza!"

"Guide first," I insisted. "Then pizza."

Toot shook his arms and legs as though he would fly apart. "Yes, yes, yes!"

"Done," I said. I opened the pizza box and set it on top of a discarded crate nearby. Then I stepped over to the circle, leaned down, and with a smudge of my hand and an effort of will broke it, freeing the energies inside.

The faeries chorused several pitches and variants of "Yahoo!" and streaked past me so quickly that they left a cone of wild air behind them, tossing my unruly hair and scattering lighter pieces of garbage around the alley. They tore into the pizza with much the same gusto they'd used on the one piece earlier, but there was enough of it now to keep them from mangling it in mere seconds.

Toot zipped over to hover in front of my face and held out his little palm. A moment later, something that looked like an errant spark from a campfire whirled down and lighted on his palm. Toot said something in a language I couldn't understand, and the tiny light pulsed and flickered as though in response.

"Right," Toot said, nodding to the light. I peered more closely at it, and could just barely make out a tiny, tiny form inside, no larger than an ant. Another faerie. The light pulsed and flickered, and Toot nodded to it before turning to me.

"Harry Dresden," Toot-toot said, holding out his palm, "this is Elidee. She's going to pay me back a favor and guide you to the Winter Lady and then to the Summer Lady. Good enough?"

I frowned at the tiny faerie. "Does she understand me?"

I barely saw Elidee stamp a tiny foot. The scarlet light around her flickered sharply, twice.

"Yes," Toot-toot translated. "Two lights for yes, and one light for no."

"Two for yes, one for no," I muttered.

Toot frowned. "Or is that one for yes and two for no? I can never keep it straight." And with that, the little faerie blurred and zipped past me and away to join the swarm of softly flashing lights demolishing the pizza.

Elidee, for her part, recovered from the miniature cyclone that Toot-toot left in his wake, whirled around dizzily for a few moments, then spiraled down to me and settled on the bridge of my nose. My eyes crossed trying to look at her. "Hey," I said, "do I look like a couch to you?"

Two flashes.

I sighed. "Okay, Elidee. Do you want any pizza before we go?"

Two flashes again, brighter. The tiny faerie leapt up into the air again and zoomed over to the cloud around the pizza.

Footsteps came down the alley, then Billy stepped out of the shadows, pulling his sweatshirt down over his muscular stomach. I felt a brief and irrational surge of jealousy. I don't have a muscular stomach. I'm not overlapping my belt or anything, but I don't have abs of steel. I don't even have abs of bronze. Maybe abs of plastic.

Billy blinked at the pizza for a moment and said, "Wow. That's sort of pretty. In a *Jaws* kind of way."

"Yeah," I said. "Don't look at it for too long. Faerie lights can be disorienting to mortals."

"Gotcha," Billy said. He glanced back at me. "How'd it go? You get what you needed?"

"Yeah," I said. "You?"

He shrugged. "Alley isn't the best place to pick up scents, but I should be able to recognize them again if I'm in my other suit. They didn't smell quite normal."

"Gee, what are the odds."

Billy's teeth showed in the dark. "Heh. So what are we waiting for?"

Elidee picked just then to glide back over to me and settle once more on the bridge of my nose. Billy blinked at her and said, "What the hell?"

"This is our guide," I said. "Elidee, this is Billy."

Elidee flashed twice.

Billy blinked again. "Uh, charmed." He shook his head. "So? What's the plan?"

"We go confront the Winter Lady in her underground lair. I do the talking. You stay alert and watch my back."

He nodded. "Okay. You got it."

I looked over to see the last piece of pizza lifted up into the air by greedy faerie hands. They clustered around it, tearing and ripping, and it was gone in seconds. With that, the faeries swarmed away like a squadron of potbellied comets and vanished from view.

Elidee fluttered off my nose and started drifting down the alley in the other direction. I followed her.

"Harry?" Billy asked, his voice a touch hopeful. "Are you expecting trouble?"

I sighed and rubbed at the space between my eyebrows.

Definitely getting a headache. It was going to be a long night.

Chapter

Fourteen

Elidee led Billy and me through alleys, up a fire escape to the roof of a building and then down on the other side, and through a junk-cluttered abandoned lot on the way to the Pedway. It took us better than half an hour of scrambling after the tiny faerie through the muggy heat, and by the end of it I wished I'd told Toot-toot that we wanted someone who could read a street map and guide us there in a car.

Chicago's commuter tunnels are fairly recent construction, compared to much of the rest of the city. The tunnels are a maze if you don't know them—long stretches of identical overhead lights, drab, clean walls dotted with advertising posters, and intersections bearing plain and not always helpful directional signs. The tunnels closed after the workday and wouldn't open up again until around six the next morning, but Elidee led us to an unfinished building at Randolph and Wabash. She flitted around in front of a service access door that proved to be unlocked and that led down to a similar door that opened onto a darkened section of the Pedway that looked as though it had been under construction but was abandoned when the building had shut down.

It was completely dark, so I slipped the silver pentacle off my neck, lifting it in my hand and focusing a quiet effort of will upon it. The five-pointed star has been a symbol of magic for centuries, representing the four elements and the power of spirit bound within the circle of will—primal power under the control of human thought. I held the pentacle before me, and as I concentrated it began to glow with a gentle blue light, illuminating enough of our surroundings that we could navigate through the dark, silent tunnels. The little faerie drifted in front of us down the tunnel, and we followed her without speaking. She took us to the intersection with the main tunnels of the Pedway and on a brief walk down another tunnel, to a section shut behind a rusting metal gate with a sign that read, DANGER KEEP OUT. The gate proved to be unlocked, and we went down the tunnel, into a damper section of tunnels, rife with the smell of mold, that was clearly not a part of the Pedway proper.

After another fifty or sixty feet we reached a place where the walls became rough and uneven and shadows lay thick and heavy, despite the glow of my wizard's light.

Elidee drifted over to an especially dark section of wall and flew in a little circle in front of it.

"Okay," I said. "I guess this is where we get in."

"What is where we get in?" Billy asked, his voice skeptical. "Get into where?"

"Undertown," I said. I ran my hands over the wall.

To the casual touch it appeared to be bare, unfinished concrete, but I felt a slight unsteadiness when I pressed against it. It couldn't have been solid stone. "Must be a panel here somewhere. Trigger of some kind."

"What do you mean, 'Undertown'? I've never heard of it before."

"I was probably working here for five or six years before I did," I said. "You have to understand the history of Chicago. How they did things here."

Billy folded his arms. "I'm listening."

"The city is a swamp," I said, still searching for a means of opening the door with my fingertips. "We're darn near level with Lake Michigan. When they first built the place, the town kept sinking into the muck. I mean, every year it sank lower. They used to build streets, then build a latticework of wood over them, and then *another* street on top of that, planning on them slowly sinking. They planned houses the same way. Built the front door on the second floor and called it a 'Chicago entry,' so when the house sank, the front door would be at ground level."

"What about when the street sank?"

"Built another one on top of it. So you wound up with a whole city existing under the street level. They used to have a huge problem with rats and criminals holing up under the streets."

"But not anymore?" Billy asked.

"The rats and thugs mostly got crowded out by other things. Became a whole miniature civilization down here. And it was out of sight of the sun, which made it friendly space for all the night-crawling critters around."

"Hence, Undertown," Billy said.

I nodded. "Undertown. There are a lot of tunnels around Chicago. The Manhattan Project was housed in them for a while during World War Two. Did all that atomic bomb research."

"That's cheerful. You come down here a lot?"

I shook my head. "Hell, no. All kinds of nastiness lives down here."

Billy frowned at me. "Like what?"

"Lots of things. Stuff you don't often see on the surface. Things even wizards know almost nothing about. Goblins, spirits of the earth, wyrms, things that have no name. Plus the usual riffraff. Vampires sometimes find lairs down here during the day. Trolls can hide here too. Molds and fungi you don't get in most of the natural world. You name it."

Billy pursed his lips thoughtfully. "So you're taking us into a maze of lightless, rotting, precarious tunnels full of evil faeries and monsters."

I nodded. "Maybe leftover radiation, too."

"God, you're a fun guy, Harry."

"You're the one who wanted in on the action." My fingers found a tiny groove in the wall, and when I pressed against it a small, flat section of stone clicked and retracted. The switch had to have triggered some kind of release, because the section of wall pivoted in the center, turning outward, and forming a door that led into still more dank darkness. "Hah," I said with some satisfaction. "There we go."

Billy pressed forward and tried to step through the door, but I put a hand on his shoulder and stopped him. "Hang on. There are some things you need to know."

Billy frowned, but he stopped, listening.

"These are faeries. We'll probably run into a lot of the Sidhe, their nobles, hanging out with the Winter Lady. That means that they're going to be dangerous and will probably try to entrap you."

"What do you mean, entrap me?" Billy said.

"Bargains," I said. "Deals. They'll try to offer you things, get you to trade one thing for another."

"Why?"

I shook my head. "I don't know. It's in their nature. The concept of debt and obligation is a huge factor in how they behave."

Billy lifted his eyebrows. "That's why that little guy worked for you, right? Because he owed you for the pizza and he had a debt to you."

"Right," I said. "But it can work both ways. If you owe *them* something, they have a conduit to you and can use magic against you. The basic rule is not to accept any gifts from them—and for God's sake, don't *offer* them any gifts. They find anything other than an equal exchange to be either enticing or insulting. It isn't a big deal with little guys like Toot, but if you get into it with a Sidhe Lord you might not live through it."

Billy shrugged. "Okay. No gifts. Dangerous faeries. Got it."

"I'm not finished. They aren't going to be offering you wrapped packages, man. These are the Sidhe. They're some of the most beautiful creatures there are. And they'll try to put you off balance and tempt you."

"Tempt me? Like with sex, is that what you're saying?"

"Like any kind of sensual indulgence. Sex, food, beauty, music, perfume. When they offer, don't accept it, or you'll be opening yourself up to a world of hurt."

Billy nodded. "Okay, got it. Let's go already."

I eyed the younger man, and he gave me an impatient look. I shook my head. I don't think I could have adequately conveyed the kind of danger we might be walking into with mere words in any case. I took a deep breath and then nodded to Elidee. "All right, Tinkerbell. Let's go."

The tiny scarlet light gave an irritated bob and then darted through the concealed doorway and into the darkness beyond. Billy narrowed his eyes and followed it, and I went after him. We found ourselves in a tunnel where one wall seemed to be made of ancient, moldering brick and the other of a mixture of rotting wooden beams, loose earth, and winding roots. The tunnel ran on out of the circle of light from my amulet. Our guide drifted forward, and we set out to follow her, walking close together.

The tunnel gave way to a sort of low-roofed cavern, supported here and there by pillars, mounds of collapsed earth, and beams that looked like they'd been added in afterward by the dwellers in Undertown. Elidee circled in place a bit uncertainly, then started floating to the right.

I hadn't been following the little faerie for five seconds before the skin on the back of my neck tried to crawl up over my head and hide in my mouth. I drew up short, and I must have made some kind of noise, because Billy shot a look back at me and asked, "Harry? What is it?"

I lifted a hand to silence him and peered at the darkness around me. "Keep your eyes open," I said. "I don't think we are alone."

From the shadows outside the light came a low hissing sound. The rest of my skin erupted in gooseflesh, and I shook my shield bracelet clear. I lifted my voice and said clearly, "I am the Wizard Dresden, Emissary of the Winter Court, bound to pay a call upon the Winter Lady. I've no time or desire for a fight. Stand clear and let me pass."

A voice—a voice that sounded like a tortured cat might, if some demented being gave it the gift of speech—mewled out of the shadows, grating on my ears. "We know who you are, wizard," the voice said. Its inflections were all wrong, and the tone seemed to come from not far above the ground, somewhere off to my right. Elidee let out a high-pitched shriek of terror and zipped back to me, diving into my hair. I felt the warmth of the light around the tiny faerie like a patch of sunlight on my scalp.

I traded a look with Billy and turned toward the source of the voice. "Who are you?"

"A servant of the Winter Lady," the voice replied from directly behind me. "Sent here to guide you safely through this realm and to her court."

I turned in the other direction and peered more closely toward the sound of the voice. The werelight from my amulet suddenly gleamed off a pair of animal eyes, twenty feet away and a few inches from the floor. I looked back at Billy. He'd already noted the eyes and turned to put his back to mine, watching the darkness behind us.

I turned back to the speaker and said, "I ask again. Who are you?"

The eyes shifted in place, the voice letting out an angry, growling sound. "Many names am I called, and many paths have I trod. Hunter I have been, and watcher, and guide. My Lady sent me to bring you thither, safe and whole and well."

"Don't get mad at me, Charlie," I snapped. "You know the drill as well as I do. Thrice I ask and done. Who are you?"

The voice came out harsh and sullen, barely intelligible. "Grimalkin am I called by the Cold Lady, who bids me guide her mother's Emissary with safe conduct to her court and her throne."

I let out a breath. "All right," I said. "So lead us."

The eyes bobbed in place, as though in a small bow, and Grimalkin mewled again. There was a faint motion in the shadows outside my light, and then a dull greenish glow appeared upon the ground. I stepped toward it and found a faint, luminous footprint upon the ground, a vague paw, feline but too spread out and too thin to be an actual cat's. Just as I reached it, another light appeared on the floor several feet away.

"Make haste, wizard," mewled Grimalkin's voice. "Make haste. The Lady waits. The season passes. Time is short."

I moved toward the second footprint, and as I reached it a third appeared before us, in the dark, and so on.

"What was that all about?" Billy murmured. "Asking it the same thing three times, I mean."

"It's a binding," I murmured in reply. "Faeries aren't allowed to speak a lie, and if a faerie says something three times, it has to make sure that it is true. It's bound to fulfill a promise spoken thrice."

"Ah," Billy said. "So even if this thing hadn't actually been sent to guide us safely, you making him say so three times would mean that he'd be obligated to do it. Got it."

I shook my head. "I wanted to make sure Grimalkin was on the level. But they hate being bound like that."

From ahead of us, the faintly glowing eyes appeared briefly, accompanied by another mewling growl that sent a chill down my spine.

"Oh," Billy said. He didn't look any too calm himself. His face had gone a little pale, and he walked with his hands clenched into fists. "So if Grimalkin had good intentions to begin with, wouldn't that make him angry that you needlessly bound him?"

I shrugged. "I'm not here to make friends, Billy. I'm here to find a killer."

"You've never even heard of diplomacy, have you?"

We followed the trail of footprints on the ground for another twenty minutes or so, through damp tunnels, sometimes only a few feet high. More sections of the tunnel showed evidence of recent construction—if you could call swirling layers of stone that seemed to have been smoothed into place like soft-serve ice cream "construction." We passed several tunnels that seemed entirely new. Whatever beings lived down here, they didn't seem too shy about expanding. "How much further?" I asked.

Grimalkin let out a *mrowl*ing sound from somewhere nearby—not in the direction of the next footprint, either. "Very near, noble Emissary. Very near now."

The unseen faerie guide was good to its word. At the next glowing footprint, no other appeared. Instead, we came to a large, elaborately carved double doorway. Made of some black wood I could not identify, the doors were eight or nine feet high, and carved in rich bas-relief. At first I thought the carvings were of a garden theme—leaves, vines, flowers, fruit, that kind of thing. But as I walked closer to the door, I could see more detail in the light of my glowing amulet. The forms of people lay among the vines. Some sprawled amorously together, while others were nothing more than skeletons wrapped in creeping roses or corpses staring with sightless eyes from within a bed of poppies. Here and there in the garden one could see evidence of the Sidhe—a pair of eyes, a veiled figure, and their hangers-on, little faeries like Toot-toot, leaf-clad dryads, pipe-wielding satyrs, and many, many others hiding from the mortals' views, dancing.

"Nice digs," Billy commented. "Is this the place?"

I glanced around for our guide, but I didn't see any more footprints or any feline eyes. "I guess it must be."

"They aren't exactly subtle, are they?"

"Summer's better at it than Winter. But they all can be when it suits them."

"Uh-huh. You know what bothers me, Harry?"

"What?"

"Grimalkin never said he'd guide us out again."

I glanced back at Billy. Quiet, hissing laughter came

out of the darkness, directionless. I took a deep breath. Steady, Harry. Don't let the kid see you get nervous. Then I turned to the door and struck it solidly with my fist, three times.

The blows rang out, hollow and booming. Silence fell on the tunnels for a long moment, until the doors split down the middle, and let out from behind them a flood of light and sound and color.

I don't know what I'd expected from the Winter Court, but it wasn't big band music. A large brass section blared from somewhere behind the doors, and drums rattled and pounded with the rough, genuine sound of actual skins. The lights were colored and muted, as if the whole place was lit by Christmas strands, and I could see shadows whirling and moving inside—dancers.

"Careful," I muttered. "Don't let the music get to you." I stepped up to the great doors and passed through them.

The room could have come from a Roaring Twenties hotel. Hell, it might have been, if the hotel had sunk into the earth, turned slightly upon its side, and been decorated by things with no concept of human values. Whatever it had once been, it had always been meant for dancing. The dance floor was made of blocks of rose-colored marble, and even though the floor was tilted, the blocks had been slipped to the level, here and there, creating something that looked almost like a flight of low, shallow stairs. Over the treacherous blocks danced the Winter Sidhe.

Beautiful didn't come close. It didn't start to come close. Men and women danced together, dressed in regalia of the 1940s. Stockings, knee-length skirts, dress uniforms of both the army and the navy that looked authentic to the month and year. The hairstyles in evidence corresponded as well, though the color didn't always match the setting. One Sidhe girl I saw wore hers dyed sapphire-blue, and others wore braids of silver and gold, or of other colors. Here and there, light gleamed from metal or gems set into ears, brows, or lips, and the riot of subtle colors gathered around each and every dancer in its own distinct, fascinating nimbus, a corona of energy, of power manifesting itself as the Sidhe danced.

Even without the whirling auras, the way they moved was something hypnotic in itself, and I had to force my eyes away from it after only a few seconds of lovely legs being displayed as a woman spun, body arched back underneath a strong man's hands, throats bared and breasts offered out, as hair caught the gleam of the colored lights and threw it back in waves of color. I couldn't look anywhere on the dance floor without seeing someone who should have been making fun of people on the covers of magazines for being too ugly.

Billy hadn't been as paranoid as me, and he stood staring at the dance floor, his eyes wide. I nudged him with my hip, hard enough to make his teeth clack together, and he jerked and gave me a guilty look.

I forced my eyes away from the dancers, maybe twenty couples all told, to check out the rest of the ballroom.

To one side of the room stood a bandstand, and the musicians on it all wore tuxes. They were mortals, human. They looked normal, which was to say almost deformed in comparison to the dancers they performed for. Both men and women played, and none of them looked well rested or well fed. Their tuxes were stained with sweat, their hair hung lank and unwashed, and a closer look showed a silver manacle bound around the ankle of each of them, attached to a chain that ran through the bandstand, winding back and forth among them. They didn't look upset, though—far from it. Every one of them was bent to the music, faces locked in intensity and concentration. And they were *good*, playing with the unity of tone and timing that you only see from bands who have really honed their art.

That didn't change the fact that they were prisoners of the fae. But they evidently had no particular problems with the notion. The music rattled the great stone room, shaking dust from the ceiling hidden in the darkness overhead while the Sidhe danced.

Opposite the bandstand, the dance floor descended directly into a pool of water—or what I presumed was water, at any rate. It looked black and unnaturally still. Even as I watched, the waters stirred, moved by something out of sight beneath the surface. Color rolled and rippled over the dark surface, and I got the distinct impression that the pool wasn't water. Or not just water. I fought down another shiver.

Beyond the dance floor, on the side of the room opposite me, stood raised tiers of platforms, each one set with a separate little table, one that could sit three or four at the most, each one with its own dim, green-shaded lamp. The tables all stood at different relative heights to one another, staggered back and forth—until the tiers reached a pinnacle, a single chair made out of what looked like silver, its flaring back carved into a sigil, a snowflake the size of a dinner table. The great chair stood empty.

The drummer on the bandstand went into a brief solo, and then the instruments cut off altogether—but for one. The other band members sagged into their seats, a couple of them simply collapsing onto the floor, but the lead trumpet stayed standing, belting out a solo while the Winter Lords danced. He was a middle-aged man, a little overweight, and his face flushed scarlet, then purple as his trumpet rang out through the solo.

Then, all at once, the Sidhe stopped dancing. Dozens of beautiful faces turned to watch the soloist, eyes glittering in the muted light.

The man continued to play, but I could see that something was wrong. The flush of his face deepened even more, and veins began to throb in his forehead and throat. His eyes widened and began to bulge, and he started shaking. A moment later the music began to falter. The man tore his face away from the trumpet, and I could see him gasping for breath. He couldn't get it. A second later he jerked, then stiffened, and his eyes rolled up in his head. The trumpet slipped from his fingers, and he fell, first to his knees and then limply over onto his side, to the floor of the bandstand. He hit with finality, his eyes open but not focused. He twitched once more, and then his throat rattled and he was still.

A murmur went through the Sidhe, and I looked back to see them parting, stepping aside with deep bows and curtseys for someone emerging from their midst. A tall girl walked slowly toward the fallen musician. Her features were pale, radiant, perfect—and looked like an adolescent copy of Mab's. That was where the resemblance ended.

She looked young. Young enough to make a man feel guilty for thinking the wrong thoughts, but old enough to make it difficult not to. Her hair had been bound into long dreadlocks, each of them dyed a different shade, ranging from a deep lavender to pale blues and greens to pure white, so that it almost seemed that her hair had been formed from glacial ice. She wore leather pants of dark, dark blue, laced and open up the outside seams from calf to hip. Her boots matched the pants. She wore a white T-shirt tight enough to show the tips of her breasts straining against the fabric, framing the words OFF WITH HIS HEAD. She had hacked the shirt off at the top of her rib cage, leaving pale flesh exposed, along with a glitter of silver flashing at her navel.

She moved to the downed musician with a liquid grace, a thoughtless, casual sensuality that made a quiver of arousal slip down my spine. She settled down over him, throwing a leg over his hips, straddling him, and idly raked long, opalescent fingernails over his chest. He didn't move. Didn't breathe.

The girl licked her lips, her mouth spreading into a lazy smile, before she leaned down and kissed the corpse's dead lips. I saw her shiver with what was unmistakably pleasure. "There," she murmured. "There, you see? Never let it be said the Lady Maeve does not fulfill her promises. You said you'd die to play that well, poor creature. And now you have."

A collective sigh went up from the assembled Sidhe, and then they began applauding enthusiastically. Maeve looked back over her shoulder at them all with a lifted chin and a lazy smile before she stood up and bowed, left and right, to the sound of applause. The applause died off when Maeve stalked away from the corpse and to the rising tiers of dinner seats, stepping lithely up them until she reached the great silver throne at the top. She dropped into it, turned sideways, and idly threw her legs over one arm, arching her back and stretching with that same lazy smile. "My lords and ladies, let us give our poor musical brutes a little time to recover their strength. We have a visitor."

The Sidhe began drifting toward the tables on the tiers, stepping into place one by one. I stood where I was and said nothing, though as they settled down I became increasingly conscious of their attention, of the glittering intensity of immortal eyes upon me.

Once they were all settled in, I stepped forward and walked across the dance floor until I stood at the foot of the tier. I looked up at Maeve and inclined my head to her. "Lady Winter, I presume."

Maeve smiled at me, showing a dimple, and gave one foot a girlish bounce. "Indeed."

"You know in what capacity I am here, Lady?"

"Naturally."

I nodded. Nothing like a frontal assault, then. "Did you arrange the murder of the Summer Knight?"

Silence fell on the room. The regard of the Winter Sidhe grew more intent, more uncomfortable.

Maeve's mouth spread into a slow smile, which in turn became a quiet, rolling laugh. She let her head fall back with it, and the Sidhe joined in with her. They sat there laughing at me for a good thirty seconds, and I felt my face begin to heat up with irrational embarrassment before Meave waved one hand in a negligent gesture and the laughter obediently died away.

"Stars," she murmured, "I adore mortals."

I clenched my jaw. "That's swell," I said. "Did you arrange the murder of the Summer Knight?"

"If I had, do you really think I would tell you?"

"You're evading," I growled. "Answer the question."

Maeve lifted a fingertip to her lips as though she needed it to hold in more laughter. Then she smiled and said, "I can't just give you that kind of information, Wizard Dresden. It's too powerful."

"What is that supposed to mean?"

She sat up, crossing her legs with a squeak of leather, and settled back on the throne. "It means that if you want me to answer that question, you're going to have to pay for it. What is the answer worth to you?"

I folded my arms. "I assume you have something in mind. That's why you sent someone to give us safe passage here."

"Quick," she murmured. "I like that. Yes, I do, wizard." She extended a hand to me and gestured to an open seat at the table to the right and a little beneath the level of her throne. "Please sit down," she said. Her teeth shone white. "Let's make a deal."

Chapter Fifteen

"You want me to cut another deal with the Sidhe," I said. I didn't bother to hide my disbelief. "When I burst out laughing at you, do you think you'll be offended?"

"And why should you find the notion amusing?"

I rolled my eyes. "Christ, lady, that's what got me into this crap to begin with."

Maeve's lips slithered into a quiet smile, and she left her hand extended, toward the seat beside her. "Remember, wizard, that you came to seek something from me. Surely it would not harm you to listen to my offer."

"I've heard that before. Usually right before I get screwed."

Maeve touched the tip of her tongue to her lips. "One thing at a time, Mister Dresden."

I snorted. "Suppose I don't want to listen."

Something in her eyes suddenly made her face cold and unpleasant. "I think it might be wise for you to indulge me. I simply go mad when someone ruins a good party mood."

"Harry," Billy muttered, "these people are giving me

the creeps. If she's playing games with you, maybe we should go."

I grimaced. "Yeah, that would be the smart thing. But it wouldn't get me any answers. Come on."

I stepped forward and started climbing up to the table Maeve had indicated. Billy followed closely. Maeve watched me the whole time, her eyes sparkling.

"There," she said, once I'd been seated. "Not so untamable as he claimed."

I felt my jaw get a little tighter as Billy took a seat beside me. A trio of brightly colored lights zipped in, bearing a silver tray holding a crystalline ewer of water and two glasses. "As who said?"

Maeve waved a hand airily. "No matter."

I glared at her, but she didn't seem bothered. "All right, lady," I said. "Talk."

Maeve idly stretched out a hand. A goblet of some golden liquid appeared in her fingers and rimed over with frost as I watched. She took a sip of the drink, whatever it was, and then said, "First, I will name my price."

"There'd better be a blue light special. I don't have much to trade, all things considered."

"True. I cannot ask for a claim over you, because Queen Mab has that already. But let me see." She tapped a fingernail to her lips again and then said, "Your issue."

"Eh?" I said, glibly.

"Your issue, wizard," she said, toying with a violet dreadlock. "Your offspring. Your firstborn. And in exchange I will give you the knowledge you seek."

"News flash, Coldilocks. I don't have any children."

Maeve laughed. "Naturally not. But the details could be arranged."

Evidently that was a cue. The dark pool of maybe-water stirred, drawing my eye. Ripples whispered as they lapped at the edges of the pool.

"What's that?" Billy whispered to me.

The waters parted, and a Sidhe girl rose out of the pool. She was tall, slender, water sliding down over pale, naked, supple curves. Her hair was a deep shade of emerald green, and as she kept on coming up out of the water, walking up what were apparently submerged stairs, I could tell that it wasn't dyed. Her face was sweetly angelic, sort of girl-next-door pretty. Her hair clung to her head, her throat, her shoulders, as did beads of water that glistened and threw back the fae-lights in dozens of colors. She extended her arms, and immediately half a dozen little lights, pixies, zipped out of nowhere, bearing a swath of emerald silk. They draped it over her extended arms, but the cloth served to emphasize, rather than conceal, her nakedness. She looked up at the tables with her feline fae-eyes and inclined her head to Maeve. Then she focused upon me.

There was an abrupt pulling sensation, something as simple and as difficult to resist as gravity. I felt a sudden urge to get up and go down to her, to remove the silk cloth and to carry her into the water. I wanted to see her hair fan out beneath the surface, feel her naked limbs sliding around me. I wanted to feel that slender waist beneath my hands, twist and writhe with her in the warm, weightless darkness of the pool.

Beside me, Billy gulped. "Is it just me, or is it getting a little warm in here?"

"She's pushing it on you," I said quietly. My lips felt a little numb. "It's glamour. It isn't real."

"Okay," Billy said without conviction. "It isn't real."

He reached for a glass and the ewer of water, but I grabbed his hand. "No. No food. No drink. It's dangerous."

Billy cleared his throat and settled back in his seat. "Oh. Right. Sorry."

The girl glided up the tiers of tables, glittering pixies in darting attendance around her, gathering her hair back with ornate combs, fastening gleaming jewels to her ears, lacing more about her throat, wrist, ankle. I couldn't help but follow the motion of the lights, which took my eyes on a thorough tour of her body. The urge to go to her became even stronger as she neared, as I smelled her perfume, a scent like that of the mist hovering over a still lake beneath a harvest moon.

The green-haired woman smiled, lips closed, then drew up in a deep curtsey to Maeve, and murmured, "My Lady."

Maeve reached out and took her hand, warmly. "Jen," she murmured. "Are you acquainted with the infamous Harry Dresden?"

Jen smiled, and her teeth gleamed between her lips. They were as green as seaweed, spinach, and fresh-steamed broccoli. "Only by reputation." She turned to me and extended her hand, arching one verdant brow.

I gave Billy a self-conscious glance and rose to take the

Sidhe-lady's hand. I nudged Billy's foot with mine, and he stood up too.

I bowed politely over Jen's hand. Her fingers were cool, damp. I got the impression that her flawless skin should have been prune-wrinkled, but it wasn't. I had to fight an urge to kiss the back of her hand, to taste her cool flesh. I managed to keep a neutral tone to my voice and said, "Good evening."

The Sidhe-lady smiled at me, showing her green teeth again, and said, "Something of a gentleman. I wouldn't have expected it." She withdrew her hand and said, "And tall." Her eyes roamed over me in idle speculation. "I like tall men."

I felt my cheeks flush and grow warmer. Other parts suffered from similar inflammation.

Maeve asked, "Is she lovely enough to suit you, wizard? You've no idea how many mortal men have longed for her. And how few have known her embrace."

Jen let out a quiet laugh. "For more than about three minutes, at any rate."

Maeve drew Jen down until the nearly nude Sidhe lady knelt beside the throne. Maeve toyed with a strand of her curling, leaf-green hair with one hand. "Why not agree to my offer, wizard? Spend a night in the company of my maiden. Is it not a pleasant price?"

My voice came out more quietly than I'd intended. "You want me to get a child on her. A child you would keep."

Maeve's eyes glittered. She leaned toward me and said, very quietly, "Do not let that concern you. I can feel your hunger, mortal man. The needs in you. Hot as a fever. Let go for a time. No mortal could sate you as she will."

I felt my eyes drawn to the Sidhe woman, trailing down the length of pale flesh left bared between the idle drapes of emerald silk, following the length of her legs. That hunger rose again in me, a raw and unthinking need. Scent flooded over me—a perfume of wind and mist, of heated flesh. Scent evoked more phantom sensations of the silken caress of delicate fae-hands, sweetly hot rake of nails, winding strength of limbs tangled with mine.

Maeve's eyes brightened. "Perhaps she is not enough for you? Perhaps you would wish another. Even myself." As I watched, Jen leaned her cheek against Maeve's thigh and placed a soft kiss upon the tight leather. Maeve shifted, a slow, sensual motion of her hips and back, and murmured, "Mmmm. Or more, if your thirst runs deep enough. Drive a hard bargain, wizard. All of us would enjoy that."

The longing, an aching force of naked need, redoubled. The two faeries were lovely. More than lovely. Sensuous. Willing. Perfectly unrestrained, perfectly passionate. I could feel that in them, radiating from them. If I made the bargain, they *would* make the evening one of nothing but indulgence, sensation, satiation, delight. Maeve and her handmaiden would do things to me that you only read about in magazines.

"Dear *Penthouse*," I muttered, "I never thought something like this would happen to me . . ."

"Wizard," Maeve murmured, "I see you weighing the consequences in your eyes. You think too much. It weakens you. Stop thinking. Come down into the earth with us."

Some mathematical and uncaring part of my brain way the hell in the back of my head reminded me that I *did* need that information. A simple statement from Maeve would tell me if she was the killer or not. *Go ahead*, it told me. *It isn't as though it's going to be painful for you to pay her price. Don't you deserve to have something pleasant happen to you for a change? Make the bargain. Get the information. Get wasted on kisses and pleasure and soft skin. Live a little—before that borrowed time you're on runs out.*

I reached out with a shaking hand to the crystal ewer on the table. I clenched it. It clinked and rattled against the glass as I poured cool, sparkling water into it.

Maeve's smile grew sharper.

"Harry," Billy said, his voice uncertain. "Didn't you just say something bad about—you know, taking food or drink from fa—uh, from these people?"

I put the pitcher down and picked up the glass of water.

Jen rubbed her cheek against Maeve's thigh and murmured, "They never really change, do they?"

"No," Maeve said. "The males all fall to the same thing. Isn't it delicious?"

I unbuttoned the fly in my jeans, undid the zipper a little, and dumped the cold water directly down my pants.

Some shocks of sensation are pleasant. This one wasn't. The water was so cold that tiny chips of ice had formed in it, as though it was trying to freeze itself from the inside out. That cold went right down where I had intended it to go, and everything in my jeans tried to contract into my abdomen in sheer, hypothermic horror. I let out a little yelp, and my skin promptly crawled with gooseflesh.

The gesture had its intended effect. That overwhelming, almost feral hunger withered and vanished. I was able to take my eyes off the Winter Lady and her handmaiden, to clear my thoughts into something resembling a sane line of reason. I shook my head a bit to be sure and then looked up at Maeve. Anger surged through me, and my jaw clenched tight, but I made an effort to keep my words at least marginally polite. "Sorry, sweetie, but I have a couple problems with that offer."

Maeve's lips tightened. "And those would be?"

"One. I'm not handing over a child to you. Not mine, not anyone's, not now, and not ever. If you had a brain in your head, you'd have known that."

Maeve's already pale face blanched even more, and she sat bolt upright on her throne. "You *dare*—"

"Shut up," I snarled, and it came out loud enough to ring off the walls of the ballroom. "I'm not finished."

Maeve jerked as though I'd slapped her. Her mouth dropped open, and she blinked at me.

"I came here under your invitation and protection. I am your *guest*. But in spite of that you've thrown glamour at me anyway." I stood up, my hands spread on the table, leaning toward her for emphasis. "I don't have time for this crap. You don't scare me, lady," I said. "I only came here for answers—but if you keep pushing me, I'm going to push back. Hard."

Maeve's evident anger evaporated. She leaned back on her throne, lips pursed, her expression placid and enigmatic. "Well, well, well. Not so easily captured, it would seem."

A new voice, a relaxed, masculine drawl, slid into the silence. "I told you, Maeve. You should have been polite. Anyone who declares war on the Red Court isn't going to be the sort to take kindly to pressure." The speaker stepped into the ballroom through the double doors and walked casually to the banquet tables and toward Maeve's throne.

It was a man, maybe in his early thirties, medium build, maybe half an inch shy of six feet tall. He wore dark jeans, a white T-shirt, and a leather jacket. Droplets of dark reddish brown stained the shirt and one side of his face. His scalp was bald but for a stubble of dark hair.

As he approached, I picked out more details. He had a brand on his throat. A snowflake made of white scar tissue stood out sharply against his skin. The skin on one side of his face was red and a little swollen, and he was missing half of the eyebrow and a crescent of the stubble on his scalp on that side—he'd been burned, and recently. He reached the throne and dropped to one knee before it, somehow conveying a certain relaxed insolence with the gesture, and extended a box to Maeve.

"It is done?" Maeve asked, an almost childlike eagerness in her voice. "What took you so long?"

"It wasn't as easy as you said it would be. But I did it."

The Winter Lady all but snatched the carved box from his hands, avarice lighting her eyes. "Wizard, this is my Knight, Lloyd of the family Slate."

Slate nodded to me. "How are you?"

"Impatient," I responded, but I nodded back to him warily. "You're the Winter Knight?"

"So far, yeah. I guess you're the Winter Emissary. Asking questions and investigating and so on."

"Yep. Did you kill Ronald Reuel?"

Slate burst out laughing. "Christ, Dresden. You don't waste time, do you?"

"I've filled my insincere courtesy quota for the day," I said. "Did you kill him?"

Slate shrugged and said, "No. To be honest with you, I'm not sure I *could* have killed him. He's been at this a lot longer than me."

"He was an old man," I said.

"So are a lot of wizards," Slate pointed out. "I could have bench-pressed him, sure. Killing him is something else altogether."

Maeve let out a sudden hiss of anger, the sound eerily loud. She lifted her foot and kicked Slate in the shoulder. Something popped when she did, and the force of the kick drove the Winter Knight down a tier, into the table and the Sidhe seated there. The table toppled, and Sidhe, chairs, and Knight went sprawling.

Maeve rose to her feet, sending the green-toothed Jen scooting away from her. She drew what looked like a military-issue combat knife from the carved box. It was crusted with some kind of black gelatinous substance, like burned barbecue sauce. "You stupid animal," she snarled. "Useless. This is useless to me."

She hurled the knife at Slate. The handle hit him in the biceps of his left arm just as he sat up again. His face twisted in sudden fury. He took up the knife, rose to his feet, and stalked toward Maeve with murder in his eye.

Maeve drew herself up, her face shining with a sudden terrible beauty. She lifted her right hand, ring finger and thumb both bent, and murmured something in a liquid, alien tongue. Sudden blue light gathered around her fingers, and the temperature in the room dropped by about forty degrees. She spoke again, and flicked her wrist, sending glowing motes of azure flickering toward Slate.

The snowflake brand flared into sudden light, and Slate's advance halted, his body going rigid. The skin around the brand turned blue, then purple, then black, spreading like a stop-motion enhanced film of gangrene. A quiet snarl slipped from Slate's lips, and I could see his body trembling with the effort to continue toward Maeve. He shuddered and took another step forward.

Maeve lifted her other hand, her index finger extended while the others curled, and a sudden wind whipped past me, cold enough that it stole the breath from my lungs. The wind whipped madly around Slate, making his leather coat flap. Bits of white frost started forming on his eyelashes and eyebrows. His expression, now anguished as well as full of rage, faltered, and his advance halted again.

"Calm him," Maeve murmured.

Jen slipped behind Slate, wrapping her arms around his neck, leaning her mouth down close to his ear. Slate's eyes flickered with hot, violent hate for a moment, and then began to grow heavier. Jen ran her hand slowly down the sleeve of his jacket, fingers caressing his wrist. His arm lowered as I watched. A moment later, Jen slid the jacket from his shoulders. The T-shirt was sleeveless, and Slate's arms were hard with muscle—and tracked with needle marks. Jen held out a hand, and another darting pixie handed her a hypodermic needle. Jen slipped it into the bend of his arm, still whispering to him, sliding the plunger slowly down.

Slate's eyes rolled back in his head, and he sank to his knees. Jen went down with him, wrapped around him like kelp on a swimmer, her mouth next to his ear.

Maeve lowered her hands, and the wind and the cold died away. She lifted a shaking hand to her face and stepped back to the throne, settling stiffly onto it, narrowed eyes locked on Slate's increasingly malleable form. Her cheekbones stood out more sharply than before, her eyes looked more sunken. She gripped the arms of the throne, her fingers twitching.

"What the hell was that?" Billy whispered.

"Probably what passes for a polite disagreement," I muttered. "Get up. We're leaving."

I stood up. Maeve's eyes darted to me. Her voice came out dry, harsh. "Our bargain is not complete, wizard."

"This talk is."

"But I have not answered your question."

"Keep your answer. I don't need it anymore."

"You don't?" Maeve asked.

"We don't?" Billy said.

I nodded toward Slate and Jen. "You had to push yourself to make him stand still. Look at you. You're just about out of gas right now from going up against your own Knight." I started down the tiers, Billy coming with me.

"Besides that, you're sloppy, sweetheart. Reckless. A clean killing like Reuel's takes a plan, and that isn't you."

I could feel her eyes pressing against my back like frozen thorns. I ignored her.

"I did not give you leave to go, wizard," she said, her voice chilly.

"I didn't ask."

"I won't forget this insolence."

"I probably will," I said. "It's nothing special. Come on, Billy."

I walked to the double doors and out. As soon as we were both outside, the doors swung shut with a huge, hollow boom that made me jump. Darkness fell, sudden and complete, and I fumbled for my amulet as my heart lurched in panic.

The spectral light from my amulet showed me Billy's strained face first, and then the area immediately around us. The double doors were gone. Only a blank stone wall remained where they had been.

"Gulp," Billy said. He shook his head for a moment, dazed. "Where did they go?"

I rested my fingers against the stone wall, reaching out for it with my wizard's senses. Nothing. It was rock, not illusion. "Beats the hell out of me. The doors here must have been a way to some other location."

"Like some kind of teleport?"

"More like a temporary entrance into the Nevernever," I said. "Or a shortcut through the Nevernever to another place on Earth."

"Kind of intense in there. When she made it get all cold. I've never seen anything like that before."

"Sloppy," I said. "She was laying a binding on Slate. Her power was sloshing over into changing the temperature. A child could do better."

Billy let out a short, quiet laugh. "After what we just saw, anyone else would still be shaking. You're giving her the rating from the Russian judge."

"So sue me." I shrugged. "She's strong. Strong isn't everything."

Billy glanced up at me. "Could you do what she did?"

"I'd probably use fire."

His eyebrows went up, his expression impressed. "Do you really think Maeve's not the killer?"

"I do," I said. "This murder was clean enough to look like an accident. Maeve's obviously got impulse-control issues. Doesn't make for much of a methodical murderer."

"What about Slate?"

I shook my head, my brow tightening. "Not sure about him. He's mortal. There's nothing that says he couldn't lie to us. But I got what I was looking for, and I found out a couple of things on top of that."

"So why are you frowning?"

"Because all I got was more questions. Everyone's been telling me to hurry. Faeries don't do that. They're practically immortal and they're not in a rush. But Mab and Grimalkin both have tried to rush me now. Maeve went for the high-pressure sales tactic too, like she didn't have time for anything more subtle."

"Why would they do that?"

I sighed. "Something's in motion. If I don't run

down the killer, the Courts could go to war with one another."

"That would explain the whole World War Two dress motif back there."

"Yeah, but not why time would be so pressing." I shook my head. "If we could have stayed longer, I might have been able to work out more, but it was getting too nervous in there."

"Discretion, valor," Billy said by way of agreement. "We leave now, right?"

"Elidee?" I asked. I felt a stirring in my hair, and then the tiny pixie popped out to hover in the air in front of me. "Can you lead us back to my car?"

The pixie flashed in the affirmative and zipped away. I lifted my amulet and followed.

Billy and I didn't speak until our guide had led us out of the underground complex not far from where I'd parked the Blue Beetle. We cut through an alley.

About halfway down it, Billy grabbed my arm and jerked me bodily behind him, snapping, "Harry, get back!"

In the same motion he swung out one foot and kicked a metal trash can. It went flying, crashing into something I hadn't seen behind it. Someone let out a short, harsh gasp of pain. Billy stepped forward and picked up the metal lid that had fallen to the ground. He swung it down at the shape. It struck with a noisy crash.

I took a couple of steps back to make sure I was clear of the action, and reached for my amulet again. "Billy," I said, "what the hell?"

I felt the sudden presence at my back half a second

too late to get out of the way. A hand the size of a dinner plate closed on the back of my neck like a vise and lifted. I felt my heels rise until my toes were just barely touching the ground.

A voice, a feminine contralto, growled, "Let go of the amulet and call him off, wizard. Call him off before I break your neck."

Chapter Sixteen

Being held up by your neck hurts. Trust me on this one. I lifted my hands by way of attempting to convey compliance and said, "Billy, get off him."

Billy took a step back from the pale-haired young man he'd knocked down. Fix whimpered and scuttled away on his hands and butt. His borrowed brown suit was soiled and torn, and his yellow polyester tie hung from his collar by only one of its clips. He put his back against the alley wall, eyes wide beneath his shock of white dandelion hair.

Billy's eyes flicked from my assailant to Fix and back. He squinted at her for a moment, then set his jaw in an expression of casual determination. "Harry? You want me to take her?"

"Wait a minute," I managed to say. "Okay, he's off. Put me down."

The grip on the back of my neck relaxed, and as I touched ground again I took a step toward Billy, turning to face the woman who had held me.

As I expected, it was the tall, muscular young woman from the funeral home, her muddy green hair hanging lankly over her eyes and one cheek. She folded her arms and shifted her weight from one foot to the other. "Fix? Are you okay?"

The smaller man panted, "My lip is cut. It isn't bad."

The woman nodded and faced me again.

"All right," I said. "Who the hell are you?"

"My name's Meryl," she said. Her voice was surprisingly quiet, contrasting with her size. "I wanted to apologize to you, Mr. Dresden. For hitting you and throwing you into the Dumpster."

I raised my eyebrows. "Are you sure you got the right guy, Meryl? No one ever apologizes to me for anything."

She pushed at her hair with one hand. It fell right back over her face. "I'm sorry. I was scared earlier, and I acted without thinking."

I traded a glance with Billy. "Uh, okay. I'm pretty sure lurking in a dark alley to mug me with your apology isn't the usual way to go about saying you're sorry. But I didn't read that Mars-Venus book, so who knows."

Her mouth twitched, and she relaxed her stance by a tiny degree. "I didn't know how else to find you, so I was just waiting near your car."

"Okay," I said. My neck still throbbed where her fingers had clamped on. Five to one I would have wonderful stripy bruises the next day. I nodded and turned away. "Apology accepted. Now if you'll excuse me, I have things I need to do."

A note of panic crept into her voice. "Wait. Please."

I stopped and looked back at her.

"I need to talk to you. Just for a minute." She took a deep breath. "I need your help."

Of course she did.

"It's very important."

Of course it was.

The headache started coming back. "Look, Meryl, I've got a lot on my plate already."

"I know," she said. "Investigating Ron's death. I think I can help you."

I pursed my lips. "You were close to Reuel?"

She nodded. "Me. Fix. Ace. And Lily."

I flashed back on the photo of Reuel and the four young people. "Green-haired girl? Very cute?"

"Yes."

"Where's Ace?"

"He had to go to work right after the funeral. But Lily's why I need to talk to you. She's missing. I think she's in trouble."

I started filling in context on the conversation I'd overheard between them. "Who are you?"

"I told you. My name is Meryl."

"Okay, fine. *What* are you, Meryl?"

She flinched at the question. "Oh. I'm sorry, I didn't know what you meant." She raked at her hair again. "I'm a changeling. We all are."

"A what?" Billy asked.

I nodded, getting it. "Changeling," I said to Billy. "She's half mortal and half fae."

"Aha," Billy said. "Which means what?"

I shrugged. "It means that she has to choose whether to remain a mortal or become wholly fae."

"Yes," she said. "And until then I'm under the rule of the Court of my fae father. Winter. The others too. That's why the four of us stuck together. It was safer."

Billy nodded. "Oh."

"Meryl," I said, "what makes you think your friend is in trouble?"

"She's not very independent, Mister Dresden. We share an apartment. She doesn't have a very good idea of how to take care of herself, and she gets nervous if she's out of the apartment for too long."

"And what do you think happened to her?"

"The Winter Knight."

Billy frowned. "Why would he hurt people in his own Court?"

Meryl let out a brief, hard laugh. "Because he can. He had a thing for Lily. He would hurt her, frighten her. He got off on it. He was furious when Maeve told him to back off. And once Ron was gone . . ." Her voice trailed off and she turned her head to one side.

"How does Reuel fit into this?" I asked.

"He was protecting us. Maeve had been torturing us for fun, and we didn't know where to turn. Ron took us in. He put us under his protection, and no one in Winter was willing to cross him."

"What about your fae dad?" Billy asked. "Didn't he do anything to look out for you?"

Meryl gave Billy a flat look. "My mother was raped by a troll. Even if he'd been strong enough to do anything about Maeve hurting us, he wouldn't have. He thinks he's already done enough by not devouring my mom on the spot."

"Oh," Billy said. "Sorry."

I frowned. "And with the Summer Knight gone, you think Slate grabbed the girl."

Meryl said, "Someone broke into the apartment. It looked like there had been a struggle."

I let out a sigh. "Have you contacted the police?"

She eyed me. "Oh, yeah, of course. I called them and told them that a mortal champion of the fae came and spirited away a half-mortal, half-nixie professional nude model to Faerieland. They were all over it."

I had to admire the well-placed sarcasm. "It doesn't take a supernatural studmuffin to cause something very bad to happen to a cute girl in this town. Your plain old mortal kidnappers and murderers can manage just fine."

She shook her head. "Either way, she's still in trouble."

I lifted a hand. "What do you want from me?"

"Help me find her. Please, Mister Dresden."

I closed my eyes. I didn't have time, energy, or brainpower to spare for this. The smart thing would be to blow her off entirely, or to promise her I'd do it and promptly forget about it. "This just isn't a good time." I felt like crap the second I said it. I didn't look at the changeling's face. I couldn't. "There's too much trouble already, and I don't even know if I can help myself, much less your friend. I'm sorry."

I turned to go, but Meryl stepped in front of me. "Wait."

"I told you," I said. "There's nothing I can—"

"I'll pay you," Meryl said.

Oh, right. Money.

I was about to lose the office and the apartment, and

this faerie work only paid in misery. I needed to pay some bills. Go to the grocery store. My mouth didn't actually water, but it was close.

I shook my head again. "Look, Meryl, I wish I could—"

"Double your fee," she said, her voice urgent.

Double. My. Fee. I hesitated some more.

"Triple," she said. She reached for her back pocket and produced an envelope. "Plus one thousand cash, up front, right now."

I looked back at Fix, still trembling and leaning against the alley wall, a handkerchief pressed to his mouth. Meryl continued to rock from one foot to the other, her eyes on the ground, waiting.

I tried to look at things objectively. A thousand bucks wouldn't spend if I got myself killed while distracted by the additional workload. On the other hand, if I lived through this thing the money would be necessary. My stomach growled, and a sharp pang of hunger made me clench the muscles of my belly.

I needed the work—but more to the point, I needed to be able to live with myself. I wasn't sure I was comfortable with the idea of looking back on this particular patch of memory and seeing myself leave some helpless girl, changeling or not, to the metaphoric wolves. People don't ask me for help if they're anything less than desperate. The changelings had been terrified of me only a few hours before. If they had turned to me for help now, it was because they were out of options.

And they also had money.

"Dammit, dammit, dammit," I muttered. I snatched

the envelope. "All right. I'll look into it and do what I can—but I can't make you any promises."

Meryl let out a shuddering breath. "Thank you. Thank you, Mr. Dresden."

"Yeah," I sighed. I reached into my pocket and pulled out a slightly crumpled business card. "Here's my office number. Call and leave a message to let me know how I can reach you."

She took the card and nodded. "I don't know if I can pay your fees all at once. But I'll be good for it, even if it takes a while."

"We can worry about that later, when we're all safe and sound," I said. I nodded to her, then to Fix, and started walking down the alley again. Billy kept an eye on the pair of them and followed me.

We reached the parking lot of the funeral home a few minutes later. The lights were all out, and the Blue Beetle was the only car left in the lot. No one had bothered to steal it. What a shock.

"So what's next?" Billy asked.

"I'll call Murphy. See what she can tell me about Lloyd Slate."

Billy nodded. "Anything I can do to help?"

"Actually, yeah," I said. "Get out the phone book and call the hospitals. See if the morgues have a green-haired Jane Doe."

"You think she's dead, then?"

"I think it would be a lot simpler if she was."

He grimaced. "Calling morgues? There must be about a million of them in Chicagoland. Isn't there anything else I could do?"

"Welcome to the glamorous world of private investigation. You want to help or not?"

"Okay, okay," Billy said. "My car's a block over. I'll get back to you as soon as I'm done making calls."

"All right. I'll probably be at my place, but if not you know the drill."

Billy nodded. "Be careful." Then he walked quickly down the street without looking back.

I fumbled my keys out and walked to the Beetle.

I didn't smell the blood until I was close enough to touch the car. Through the window I saw a form, more or less human-shaped, curled up on my passenger seat. I circled cautiously to the other side of the car, then abruptly opened the door.

Elaine fell out of the car onto the pavement of the parking lot. She was drenched in blood that had soaked through her T-shirt, matted her golden-brown hair on one side, and run down her flanks to saturate her jeans to mid thigh. Her silver pentacle shone with liquid scarlet. The bare skin of her forearms was covered with long slashes and blood, and her face looked white. Dead.

My heart hammered in my chest, and I leaned down to her, fumbling at her throat. She still had a very slow pulse, but her skin felt cool and waxy. She started shuddering and whispered, "Harry?"

"I'm here. I'm here, Elaine."

"Please," she whispered. "Oh, God, please help me."

Chapter Seventeen

I laid Elaine out, first thing, and tried to determine the extent of her injuries. Her forearms had been laced open in several places, but the worst injury was on her back, just inside of her left clavicle—a nasty puncture wound. The edges of it had puckered closed, but it hadn't stopped the bleeding completely, and if she was bleeding internally she could be done for.

I would need both hands to put pressure on the wound. No help was on the way. There was little I could do for her, so I picked her up and put her back into the Beetle, then jumped in myself and started the ignition.

"Hang in there, Elaine," I said. "I'm getting you to a hospital. You're going to be all right."

She shook her head. "No. No, too dangerous."

"You're hurt too badly for me to take care of it," I said. "Relax. I'll be with you."

She opened her eyes and said with sudden, surprising insistence, "No hospitals. They'll find me there."

I started up the car. "Dammit, Elaine. What else am I supposed to do?"

She closed her eyes again. Her voice grew fainter by

the word. "Aurora. Summer. Rothchild Hotel. There's an elevator in back. She'll help."

"The Summer Lady?" I demanded. "You're joking, right?"

She didn't answer me. I looked over at her, and my heart all but stopped as I saw her head lolling, her body slumped. I jammed the Beetle into gear and jounced out onto the road.

"Rothchild Hotel," I muttered. "More faeries. Keen."

I got us to the hotel, one of the nice places along the shores of Lake Michigan. I skipped the huge valet-littered front drive and zipped the Beetle into the back parking lot, looking for some kind of service drive, or freight elevator, or maybe just a door with a sign on it that said, SUMMER COURT OF THE FAERIES THIS WAY.

I felt a slight warmth on my ear, and then Elidee zoomed out in front of my face and bumped up against the window. I rolled the window down a bit, and the tiny faerie streaked out ahead of my car, guiding me to the back of the lot. She stopped, circling an unobtrusive, unlit breezeway. Then she sped away, her task evidently completed.

I quickly parked the car and set the brake. Elaine may have been slender, but she had too much muscle to be light. She'd always had the build of a long-distance runner, long and lean and strong. She was only just conscious enough to make it a little easier for me to carry her, wrapping her arms around my neck and leaning her head on my shoulder. She trembled and felt cold.

Doubt gnawed at me as I took her down the breezeway. Maybe I should have ignored her and gone to the hospital.

I kept going until it became too dark to see, and I started to put Elaine down so that I could take out my amulet to make some light. Just as I did, a pair of elevator doors swept open, spilling light and canned music onto the breezeway.

A girl stood in the doors. She was five nothing, a hundred and nothing, her sunny hair pulled back into a braid. She wore a blue T-shirt with white painter's overalls, and she was liberally splattered with flecks of what looked like clay. Her rosy mouth opened in dismay as she saw me standing there with Elaine.

"Oh, no!" she exclaimed. She beckoned me urgently. "Come on, get her inside. The Lady can see to her."

My arms and shoulders had begun to burn with the effort of supporting Elaine, so I didn't waste time talking. I shuffled forward into the elevator and leaned against the back wall with a wheeze. The girl closed the elevator doors, took a key from her overalls pocket, and inserted it into a solitary keyhole where you would expect a bunch of buttons to be. The elevator gave a little lurch and started up.

"What happened to Ela?" the girl asked me. She looked from me to Elaine and chewed on one lip.

Ela? "Beats me. I found her like this in my car. She told me to bring her here."

"Oh. Oh, God," the girl said. She looked at me again. "You're with Winter, aren't you?"

I frowned. "How did you know?"

She shrugged. "It shows."

"I'm with Winter for now. But it's a one-shot deal. Think of me as a free agent."

"Perhaps. But an agent of Winter all the same. Are you sure you want to be here?"

"No," I said. "But I'm sure I'm not leaving Elaine until I'm convinced she's in good hands."

The girl frowned. "Oh."

"Can't this thing go any faster?" My shoulders burned, my back ached, my bruises were complaining, and I could feel Elaine's breathing growing weaker. I had to fight not to scream in sheer frustration. I wished there had been a bank of buttons to push, just so that I could have slammed the right button a bunch of times in a senseless effort to speed up the elevator.

The doors opened a geological epoch later, onto a scene as incongruous as a gorilla in a garter belt.

The elevator had taken us to what could only have been the roof of the hotel, assuming the roof opened up onto a section of rain forest in Borneo. Trees and greenery grew so thick that I couldn't see the edge of the roof, and though I could hear the nighttime noises of Chicago, the sounds were vague in the distance and could almost not be heard over the buzz of locusts and the chittering of some kind of animal I did not recognize. Wind rustled the forest around me, and silver moonlight, brighter than I would have thought possible, gave everything an eerie, surreal beauty.

"I'm so glad I was going out for more clay just then. This way," the girl said, and started off on a trail through the forest. I followed as quickly as I could, puffing hard to keep holding Elaine. It wasn't a long walk. The trail wound back and forth and then opened onto a grassy glade.

I stopped and looked around. No, not a glade. More like a garden. A pool rested at its center, still water reflecting the moon overhead. Benches and stones of a good size for sitting on were strewn around the landscape. Statuary, most of it marble and of human subjects, stood here and there, often framed by flowers or placed between young trees. On the far side of the pool stood what at first glance I took to be a gnarled tree. It wasn't. It was a throne, a throne of living wood, its trunk grown into the correct shape, branches and leaves spreading above it in stately elegance, roots spreading and anchoring it in the earth.

People stood here and there. A paint-spattered young man worked furiously on some sort of portrait, his face set in concentration. A tall man, his ageless beauty and pale hair marking him as one of the Sidhe, stood in the posture of a teacher beside a slender girl, who was drawing back a bow, aiming at a target of bundled branches. On the far side of the glade, smoke rose from stones piled into the shape of an oven or a forge, and a broad-chested man, shirtless, bearded, heavy-browed and fierce-looking, stood on the other side of it, wielding a smith's hammer in regular rhythm. He stepped away from the forge, a glowing-hot blade gripped in a set of tongs, and dunked it into a trough of silvery water.

When I got a better look at him, I understood what

he was. Steam rose in a cloud over his heavy, equine forelegs, then over his human belly and broad chest, and the centaur stamped a rear hoof impatiently, muttering under his breath, while colored lights played back and forth in the water of the trough. Haunting pipe music, sad and lovely, drifted through the glade from a young woman, mortal, sitting with a set of reed pipes, playing with her eyes closed.

"Where is she?" I demanded. "Where is the Lady?"

The centaur's head snapped around, and he snarled in a sudden, harsh basso. He took up his hammer again, whipped it in a quick circle, and started toward me at a slow canter, Clydesdale-sized hooves striking the ground with dull thumps. "Winterbound? Here? It cannot be borne."

I tensed, holding Elaine a little closer, and my heart lurched into a higher gear. The centaur was huge and looked ready to kill. "Whoa, there, big fella. I'm not looking for trouble."

The centaur bared his teeth at me and spoke, his deep voice filled with outrage. "There you stand with our Emissary's blood on your hands and expect us to believe you?"

The tall Sidhe man barked, "Korrick, hold."

The centaur drew up short, rearing onto his hind legs and kicking at the air with heavy hooves. "My lord Talos," he growled in frustration. "This arrogance cannot be tolerated."

"Peace," the Sidhe lord said.

"But, my *lord*—"

The Sidhe lord stepped between me and the centaur, his back to me. He wore close-fit trousers of dark green and a loose shirt of white linen. The Sidhe lord said nothing, and I couldn't see his expression, but the centaur's face reddened, then blanched. He bowed his head, a stiff gesture, and then walked back over to his forge, hooves striking the ground in sharp, angry motions.

The Sidhe—Talos, I presumed—turned back to me and regarded me with calm, feline eyes the color of a summer sky. He had the pale hair of the Sidhe, hanging in a straight, fine sheet to brush his shoulders. There was a quality of quiet confidence in his features, of relaxed strength, and the sense of him was somehow less alien than that of most of the Sidhe I had encountered. "I hope you will not judge Korrick too harshly, sir. You are, I take it, Harry Dresden?"

"If I'm not, he's going to be upset with me when he catches me running around in his underpants."

Talos smiled. The expression came easily to his features. "Then I grant you passport and license in agreement with the Accords. I am Talos, Lord Marshal of the Summer Court."

"Yeah, that's great, nice to meet you," I said. "Hey, do you think you could help me save this woman's *life* now?"

The Sidhe's smile faded. "I will do what I can." He glanced to the side and gestured with a roll of his wrist.

The garden flew into activity. A cloud of pixies darted through the air, bearing stalks of green plants and broad, soft leaves. They piled them into a soft-looking mound near the side of the pool. Talos looked at me for permission and then gently took Elaine's weight into his arms. My shoulders and biceps all but screamed in relief. The Sidhe lord carried Elaine to the bed of leaves and laid her down upon it. He touched her throat and then her brow with one hand, his eyes closing.

"Weak," he said quietly. "And cold. But she has strength left in her. She will be all right for a little while."

"No offense, but your people have some odd notions about time. Go get your Lady. She needs to see to Elaine now."

Talos regarded me with that same quiet, opaque expression. "She will be here when she will be here. I cannot hurry the sunrise, nor the Lady."

I started to tell him where he could stick his sunrise, but I bit back the words and tried to take out some frustration by clenching my fists. My knuckles popped.

A hand touched my arm, and the girl, the sculptor from the elevator, said, "Please, sir. Let me get you something to drink, or some food. Mortal food, I mean. I wouldn't offer the other kind."

"Like hell," I said. "Not until Elaine is taken care of."

From where he knelt beside Elaine, Talos lifted both eyebrows, but he shrugged his shoulders. "As you wish." He rested his fingertips lightly on either side of her face and bowed his head. "My skills are rather limited. I can at least assure that she loses no ground."

There was a quiet surge of energy, something as gentle and strong as the weight of a wave lifting you off your feet. Elaine suddenly took a deep breath, and color came back into her cheeks. She blinked her eyes open for a moment, then sighed and closed them again.

"Talos can sustain her for a time," the girl said. "Until the Lady decides. He has been Ela's guardian and friend for several years." She tugged at my arm. "Please, take something to eat. You'll make us poor hosts if you do not."

My stomach growled again, and my throat started to complain after all the hard breathing I'd been doing. I exhaled through my nose and nodded to the girl, who led me to one of the benches not far away and pulled a plastic Coleman cooler from underneath it. She rummaged inside, then tossed me a cold can of Coke, a small bag of potato chips, and a long hoagie. None of them held any of the subtle, quivering lure of faerie fare.

"Best I can do for now," she said. "Turkey sub sound all right?"

"Marry me," I responded, tore into the food with fervor, and spent a couple of minutes indulging in one of the purest primal pleasures. Eating. Food never tastes so good as when you are starving, and Talos had granted me safe passport under the Accords, so I wasn't worried about any drugs in it.

While I ate, the girl drew a short stand over to her, on which was a clay bust of a young woman, parts of it still rough, still marked with the tracks of her fingers. She dipped them into a bowl of water attached to the stand and started working on the bust.

"What happened to her?" she asked.

"Hell if I know," I said between bites. "She was in my car like that. Wanted me to bring her here."

"Why did you?" She flushed. "I mean, you're working for Summer's enemies. Right?"

"Yeah. But it doesn't mean I'm friendly with them." I shook my head, washed down a half-chewed bite with a long drink of Coke. Heaven. I ate for a moment more and then frowned at the bust she was working on. The face seemed familiar. I studied it a bit, then asked, "Is that Lily?"

The girl blinked at me. "You know her?"

"Of her," I said. "She's a changeling, isn't she?"

The girl nodded. "Winter, but she hasn't chosen to go over to them. She was under Ronald's protection, and she models for us sometimes." She gestured vaguely toward the young man who was painting intently. "See, there are a few other pieces she modeled for around here."

I looked around the garden and picked out a pair of statues among all the rest. Both were nudes of white marble. One of them depicted the girl in a tiptoe stretch, arms over her head, body arched prettily. The other showed her kneeling, looking at something cupped in her hands, her expression one of quiet sadness. "Seems like she's well liked."

The girl nodded. "She's very gentle, very sweet."

"Very missing," I said.

She frowned. "Missing?"

"Yeah. Her roommate asked me to see if I could find her. Have you seen her in the past couple of days?"

"She hasn't been here to model, and I've never seen her anywhere but here. I'm sorry."

"Worth a shot," I said.

"Why are you looking for her?"

"I told you. Her roommate asked for my help. I gave it." Which was mostly true. Technically, I suppose, I'd sold it. I got the uneasy feeling that I might start feeling too guilty over the cash Meryl had given me to spend it. "I'm a tad busy this week, but I'll do what I can."

The girl's brow furrowed as she worked at the bust. "You're not like anyone else I've ever met who was working for Winter. Mab usually likes her agents . . . colder, I think. Hungrier. More cruel."

I shrugged. "She wanted someone to find a killer. I've had some experience."

She nodded. "Still, you seem like a decent enough person. It makes me sad to think that you've gotten entangled in Winter's snares."

I stopped chewing and looked up at her, hard. "Oh, Hell's bells."

She looked at me and lifted an eyebrow. "Hmm?"

I put the sandwich down and said, "You're her. You're the Summer Lady."

The shadow of a smile touched the girl's lips, and she bowed her head toward me. Her blond hair cleared out to Sidhe white, her fingers and limbs suddenly seemed slightly longer, and her features became almost identical to Maeve's, eyes vertically slitted and almost violently green. She still wore the coveralls and blue T-shirt, and was still liberally covered in flecks of clay, though. They stood out in sharp contrast to her fair skin and pale hair.

"Call me Aurora," she said. "It's a little easier for everyone."

"Uh, right," I said. I finished the bite I was on and said, "So are you going to stop playing games with me and help Elaine, Aurora?"

She glanced over at Elaine, lying on the ground, and her expression grew troubled. "That depends."

My teeth clenched, and I said in a falsely pleasant voice, "On what?"

She turned her calm, inhuman eyes to me. "On you."

"Don't go getting specific on me, now," I said. "I wouldn't know how to handle it."

"Do you think this is a joke, Mister Dresden? A game?"

"I know damn well it isn't a game."

She shook her head. "And that is where you are wrong. It is a game, but unlike the ones you know. You aren't allowed to know the rules to this game, and it was never intended to be fair. Do you know why Mab chose *you*, wizard?"

I glared at her. "No."

"Neither do I," she said. "And that is my part of the game. Why choose you? It must be because she expects something of you that she would get from no one else. Perhaps bringing Ela here is what she expected."

"What's the difference?" I demanded. "Elaine is hurt. Your Emissary has been wounded in the line of duty. Don't you think you should get her moving again?"

"But if that is what Winter expects, it could be used

against me. I am the least Queen of Summer, but even so I must be cautious in the use of my power."

I snorted. "Maeve sure as hell doesn't think that way."

"Of course not," she said. "She's Winter. She's violent, vicious, merciless."

"And your centaur is just the soul of gentleness and understanding."

Aurora sighed and lowered her clay-crusted fingers. "I hope you will forgive Korrick's temper. He is usually a merrier sort. Everyone's been edgy because of matters here."

"Uh-huh," I said. "Just so we're clear, that was really mortal food, wasn't it?"

"Yes," she said. "I have no desire to threaten your freedom, Mister Dresden, or to bind you in any way."

"Good." I knew she couldn't lie to me, so I took another bite of the sandwich and some more chips. "Look, I'm not here to try to undermine your power or sabotage Summer, Aurora. I just want you to help Elaine."

"I know," she said. "I believe you. But I don't trust you."

"What reason do you have not to trust me?"

"I've watched you," she responded. "You're a mercenary. You work for hire."

"Yeah. To pay the bills and—"

She lifted a hand. "You've made bargains with demons."

"Nickel-and-dime stuff, nothing huge or—"

"You traded yourself to the Leanansidhe for power."

"When I was younger, and a hell of a lot stupider, and in trouble—"

Her inhuman eyes met mine, penetrating. "You've *killed*."

I looked away from her. There wasn't much to say to that. My stomach turned, and I pushed the food a bit away from me.

Aurora nodded, slowly. "From the beginning, you have been meant to be a destroyer. A killer. Do you know the original purpose of a godparent, Mister Dresden?"

"Yeah," I said. I felt tired. "A godparent was chosen to ensure that a child had religious and moral guidance and teaching."

"Indeed," she said. "And your godmother, your teacher and guide, is the most vicious creature of Mab's Court, more than Maeve's equal, second in strength only to Mab herself."

I let out a harsh laugh. "Teacher? Guide? Is that what you think Lea is to me?"

"Isn't she?"

"Lea barely noticed me except when she thought she could get something from me," I spat. "The rest of the time she couldn't care less. The only thing she taught me was that if I didn't want to get walked on I had to be smarter than her, stronger than her, and willing to do something about it."

Aurora turned her lovely face fully toward me and regarded me with deep, quiet eyes. "Yes." Unease gnawed at my belly as she continued. "The strong conquer and the weak are conquered. That is Winter. That is what you have learned." She leaned closer and said, quietly emphatic, "That is what makes you dangerous. Do you see?"

I stood up and walked a few paces away. Aurora didn't say anything. I heard drips of water as she washed her hands in the little bowl.

"If you aren't going to help Elaine, tell me. I'll take her to the hospital."

"Do you think I should help her?"

"I don't give a damn if you do or not," I said. "But one way or another I'm going to make sure she's taken care of. Make up your mind."

"I already have. What remains is for you to make up yours."

I took a wary breath before asking, "Meaning?"

"Of the two people who entered this garden, Mister Dresden, Elaine is not the most grievously wounded. You are."

"Like hell. I've just got some cuts and bruises."

She rose and walked toward me. "Those aren't the wounds I mean." She reached out and laid a slender hand over my heart. Her skin was warm, even through my shirt, and the simple fact of her touch brought me a small but noticeable sense of comfort. Susan had been gone for months, and with the exception of the occasional assault, no one had actually touched me.

She looked up at me and nodded. "You see. You've been badly wounded, Mister Dresden, and you have found neither rest nor respite from your pains."

"I'll live."

"True," she said. "But this is where it always begins. Monsters are born of pain and grief and loss and anger. Your heart is full of them."

I shrugged. "And?"

"And it makes you vulnerable. Vulnerable to Mab's influence, to temptations that would normally be unthinkable."

"I'm handling temptation pretty damned well, thank you."

"But for how long? You need to *heal*, wizard. Let me help you."

I frowned at her, and at her hand. "How?"

Aurora gave me a small, sad smile. "I'll show you. Here."

Her palm pressed a bit closer to me, and somewhere inside me a dam broke open. Emotions welled up like a riotous rainbow. Scarlet rage, indigo fear, pale blue sadness, aching yellow loneliness, putrid green guilt. The tide flooded through me, coursed over me like a bolt of lightning, searing and painful and beautiful all at once.

And after the tide receded, a deep, quiet stillness followed. A sensation of warmth suffused me, gently easing away my aches and bruises. It spread over my skin, like sunlight on a lazy afternoon outside, and with the warmth my cares began to evaporate. My fear vanished, and I began to relax muscles I hadn't realized were stretched tight as the warmth spread. I floated in warmth for a time, the release from pain an ecstasy in itself.

When I came back to my senses, I was lying on my back on the grass, staring up at leaves and silver-starred sky. My head lay in Aurora's lap. She knelt behind me, and her hands rested lightly, warm and soft, along the sides of my face. The pain began to return to my body, thoughts, and heart, like some quiet and odious tide washing in garbage from a polluted sea. I heard myself make a small sound of protest.

Aurora looked down at me, her eyes concerned. "Worse even than I suspected. You didn't even realize how much pain you were in, did you?"

My chest heaved and I let out a quiet sob. The warmth faded entirely, and the sheer weight of the difficulties I had to face pressed down on me, suffocating me.

Aurora said, "Please, let me help you. We'll make it a bargain, Mister Dresden. Desist. Relax your efforts to help Winter. Stay here for a time and let me grant you a measure of peace."

Real tears formed, making my vision blur. I mopped at my face with my hands, struggling to think clearly. If I took the deal, it would probably mean my ass. Backing off from Mab's offer would mean that I didn't get a good outcome for the White Council, which meant that they would buy peace with the Red Court of Vampires for the low, low price of one Harry Dresden, slightly damaged.

"Forget it," I said, my voice weak. "I've got a job to do."

Aurora closed her eyes for a moment and nodded. "At least you are true to your word, Mister Dresden. Your honor is admirable. Even if it is misguided."

I forced myself to sit up, away from Aurora. "Go on," I said. "Help Elaine."

"I will," she assured me. "But she is in no danger for the moment, and it will take me some time. There is something I wish to say to you first."

"Okay. Talk."

"How much did Mab tell you about Ronald's death?"

I shook my head. "That he was dead. That the mantle of power he wore went missing. That the killer had to be found."

"Did she tell you why?"

I frowned. "Not exactly."

Aurora nodded and folded her hands in her lap. "Summer readies to go to war against Winter."

I frowned. "You mean it's not just a theoretical possibility anymore. It's real."

"I know no other kind of war. The loss of the Summer Knight has forced Summer's hand."

"I'm not sure I follow."

Her pale brow knit into a soft frown. "The power of our Knights is considerable. It carries a sort of weight that only a free mortal can possess. That power, that influence, is a critical element of the balance between our Courts."

"Except now yours is gone."

"Exactly."

"Which makes Summer weaker."

"Yes."

I nodded. "Then why the hell are you planning an attack?"

"The seasons are changing," Aurora said. "In two

days' time, Midsummer will be upon us. The height of Summer's strength."

She said nothing more, letting me do the math. "You think Winter has taken away your Knight," I said. "And if you wait, you're only going to grow more and more weak, while Winter gets stronger. Right?"

"Correct. If we are to have any chance of victory, we must strike at the peak of our strength. It will be the only time when our Court might be near equal to Winter's strength. Otherwise, the seasons will change, and at Midwinter Mab and her creatures will come for us. And they *will* destroy us, and with us the balances of the mortal world." She lifted her green eyes from her hands to my face. "Winter, Mister Dresden. Endless Winter. Unending and vicious cycles of predator and prey. Such a world would not be kind to mortals."

I shook my head. "Why would Winter pull this now? I mean, if they had waited another couple of days, they could have held all the cards. Why leave you enough space to wriggle out?"

"I cannot even pretend to know the mind of Winter," Aurora said. "But I know that they must not be allowed to destroy us. For your sake as well as ours."

"Boy, everybody's looking out for my best interests."

"Wizard, please. Promise me that you will do what you can to stop them."

"I'm finished making promises." I stood up and started for the path that led back to the elevator and out, but part of me wanted to do nothing but return to the comfort Aurora had offered. I paused and squeezed my eyes shut, focusing my resolve. "But I will say this. I'm going to find the killer and straighten this out, and I'm going to do it before Midsummer."

I didn't bother to add, "Because I'm as good as dead if I don't."

No need to belabor the obvious.

Chapter

Eighteen

I got the hell away from the Rothchild and found a pay phone. Murphy picked up on the first ring. "Dresden?"

"Yeah."

"Finally. You all right?"

"I need to talk to you."

There was a short pause, then her voice softened. "Where?"

I rubbed at my head with the heel of one hand, trying to nudge my brain into gear. My thoughts stumbled around sluggishly and in no particular order. "Dunno. Someplace public, bunch of people, quiet enough to talk."

"In Chicago. At this time of night."

"Yeah."

"Okay," Murph said. "I guess I know a place." She told me. We agreed to meet in twenty minutes and hung up.

As I pulled into the parking lot, I reflected that odds were that not a lot of clandestine meetings involving mystical assassination, theft of arcane power, and the balance of power in the realms of the supernatural had taken place in a Wal-Mart Super Center. But then again, maybe they had. Hell, for all I knew, the Mole Men used the changing rooms as a place to discuss plans for world domination with the Psychic Jellyfish from Planet X and the Disembodied Brains-in-a-Jar from the Klaatuu Nebula. I know I wouldn't have looked for them there.

After midnight the Wal-Mart wasn't crowded, but it wasn't the usual deserted parking lot you'd expect after hours around Wrigleyville, either. The store was open all night, and there were plenty of people in a town like Chicago who would do their shopping late. I had to park about halfway down a row and walk through the cool of the evening before stepping into the refrigerator-cold of the enormous store, whose massive air conditioners had too much momentum to slow down for a few paltry hours of darkness.

A greeter nodded sleepily to me as I came in, and I passed up his offer of a shopping cart. Before I'd gotten all the way into the store, Murphy fell into step beside me. She was wearing a Cubs jacket, jeans, and sneakers, and she had her blond hair tucked up underneath an undecorated black ball cap. She walked with her hands in her pockets, and her expression, one of belligerent annoyance, didn't seem to fit on someone that short. Wordlessly, we walked past all the little hole-in-the-wall franchise businesses, closed and locked up behind their grills, and settled down at the generic cafe near the deli section of the grocery store.

Murphy chose a booth where she could watch the door, and I sat across from her, where I could watch her back. She picked up a couple of cups of coffee, bless her noble heart. I dumped sugar and creamer into mine until bits floated on the surface, stirred it up, and took a slow sip that nearly scalded my tongue.

"You don't look so good," Murphy said.

I nodded.

"You want to talk about it?"

To my own surprise, I did. I set the coffee down and said without preamble, "I'm furious, Murph. I can't think straight, I'm so mad."

"Why?"

"Because I'm screwed. That's why. No matter what I do, I'm going to take it up the ass."

Lines appeared between her eyebrows. "What do you mean?"

"It's this job," I said. "Investigating Reuel's death. There's a lot of resistance and I don't know if I can beat it. And if I don't beat it before tomorrow night, things are really going to go to hell."

"The client isn't being helpful?"

I let out a bitter laugh. "Hell, for all I know the client is doing this to me just so I can get myself horribly killed."

"You don't trust them, then."

"Not as far as I could kick her. And the people who are supposed to be working with me are driving me nuts." I shook my head. "I feel like some guy in a magician's box, just before he starts pushing all those swords through it. Only it's not a trick, and the swords are real, and they're going to start skewering me any second. The bad guys are doing their best to get me wiped out or screwed up.

The good guys think I'm some kind of ticking psycho, just waiting to go off, and it's like pulling teeth to try to get a straight answer out of any of them."

"You think you're in danger."

"I know it," I said. "And it's just too damned big." I fell quiet for a moment, and sipped my coffee.

"So," Murph said. "Why did you want to see me?"

"Because the people who should be backing me up are about to throw me to the wolves. And because the only person actually helping me is green enough to get himself killed without a babysitter." I set the empty cup down. "And because when I asked myself who I could trust, I came up with a damned short list. You're it."

She settled back in her seat with a slow, long exhalation. "You're going to tell me what's going on?"

"If you're willing," I said. "I know I've kept things from you. But I've done it because I thought it was how I could protect you best. Because I didn't want you to get hurt."

"Yeah," she said. "I know. It's annoying as hell."

I tried to smile. "In this case, ignorance is bliss. If I tell you this stuff, it's going to be serious. Just knowing it could be dangerous for you. And you aren't going to be able to get away from it, Murph. Not ever."

She regarded me soberly. "Then why tell me now?"

"Because you deserve to know, long since. Because you've risked your life for me, and to protect people from all the supernatural crud that's out there. Because being around me has bought you trouble, and knowing more about it might help you if it comes your way again." My cheeks flushed, and I admitted, "And because I need your help. This is a bad one. I'm afraid."

"I'm not going anywhere, Harry."

I gave her a tired smile. "One last thing. If you come in on this, you have to understand something. You have to promise me that you won't haul SI and the rest of the police in on everything. You can dig up information, use them discreetly, but you can't round up a posse and go gunning for demons."

Her eyes narrowed. "Why the hell not?"

"Because bringing mortal authorities into a conflict is the nuclear assault of the supernatural world. No one wants to see it happen, and if they thought you might do it, they'd kill you. Or they'd pull strings higher up and get you fired, or framed for something. They would never allow it to pass. You'd get yourself ruined or hurt or killed and it's likely a lot of people would go down with you." I paused to let the words sink in, then asked, "Still want me to tell you?"

She closed her eyes for a moment and then nodded, once. "Hit me."

"You're sure?"

"Yeah."

"All right," I said. And I told Murphy all of it. It took a while. I told her about Justin and about Elaine. I told her about the supernatural forces and politics at play in and around the city. I told her about the war I'd started because of what the Red Court had done to Susan. I told her about the faeries and Reuel's murder.

And most of all, I told her about the White Council.

"Those spineless, arrogant, egomaniacal sons of bitches," Murphy growled. "Who the hell do they think they are, selling out their own people like that?"

Some silent, delighted part of me let out a mental cheer at her reaction.

She made a disgusted noise and shook her head. "So let me get this straight," she said. "You started a war between the Council and the Red Court. The Council needs the support of the faeries in order to have a chance at victory. But they can't get that support unless you find this killer and restore the stolen magical power thingie—"

"Mantle," I interjected.

"Whatever," Murphy said. "And if you don't get the magic whatsit, the Council fixes you up in a carryout box for the vampires."

"Yeah," I said.

"And if you don't find the killer before Midsummer, the faeries slug it out with each other."

"Which could be bad no matter who won. It would make El Niño look as mild as an early spring thaw."

"And you want my help."

"You've worked homicide before. You're better at it than me."

"That goes without saying," she said, a trace of a smile on her mouth. "Look, Harry. If you want to find out who did the killing, the best way to start is to figure out why."

"Why what?"

"Why the murder. Why Reuel got bumped off."

"Oh, right," I said.

"And why would someone try to take you out in the park yesterday?"

"It could have been almost anyone," I said. "It wasn't like it was a brilliant attempt, as far as they go."

"Wrong," Murphy said. "Not neat, but not stupid either. After you called earlier tonight, I snooped around."

I frowned at her. "You found something?"

"Yeah. Turns out that there have been two armed robberies in the past three days: first outside of Cleveland and then at a gas station just this side of Indianapolis, coming toward Chicago."

"That doesn't sound out of the ordinary."

"No," Murphy said. "Not unless you throw in that in both cases, someone was grabbed at the scene and abducted, and both times the video security broke down just as the robbery started. Eyewitnesses in Indiana identified the perpetrator as a woman."

I whistled. "Sounds like our ghoul, then."

Murph nodded, her lips pressed together. "Any chance those people she grabbed are alive?"

I shook my head. "Not likely. She probably ate them. A ghoul can go through forty or fifty pounds of meat a day. She'll put whatever's left someplace where animals can get to it, cover her tracks."

She nodded. "I figured. The pattern matches several incidents over the past twenty years. It took me a while to piece it together, but something similar has happened three times in connection with the operations of a contract killer who calls herself the Tigress. A friend at the FBI told me that they suspect her of a number of killings in the New Orleans area and that Interpol thinks she's pulled jobs in Europe and Africa, too."

"Hired gun," I said. "So who did the hiring?"

"From what you've said, my money's on the vampires. They're the ones who benefit most from you being dead. If they punch your ticket, the Council will probably sue for peace, right?"

"Maybe," I said, but I doubted it. "If that's what they had in mind, it's stupid timing. They Pearl-Harbored a bunch of wizards somewhere in Russia two nights ago, and the Council was pretty angry about it."

"Okay. So maybe they figure that if your investigation finds Reuel's killer and gets the Council brownie points with the faeries, they're in for a real fight. Killing you before that happens makes sense."

"Except that when it went down, I wasn't involved in the investigation yet."

Murphy shook her head. "I wish we could get you together with a sketch artist, describe her."

"Doubt it would help much. She was in makeup at first, and I didn't give her a second look. By the time I was paying attention, she mostly looked like something out of a Japanese horror cartoon."

She glanced down at her now cold coffee. "Not much we can do but wait, then. I've got a couple of sources trying to turn up more, but I wouldn't bet anything on them. I'll let you know."

I nodded. "Even if we find her, it might not help with the faerie stuff."

"Right," she said. "Mind if I ask you a few questions? Maybe I'll see something you don't."

"Okay."

"This dreadlock chick. Maeve, you said her name was?"

"Yeah."

"How sure are you in your instinct about her? That she couldn't have done the murder, I mean."

"Pretty close to certain."

"But not completely."

I frowned thoughtfully. "No. Faeries are tricky that way. Not completely."

Murphy nodded. "What about Mab?"

I rubbed at my chin, feeling the beginnings of stubble. "She never out and out denied responsibility for Reuel's death, but I don't think she's the killer."

"What makes you say that?"

"I don't know."

"I do. She could have picked anyone she wanted to represent her interests, and she chose you. If she wanted to cover her tracks, it would make more sense for her to choose someone less capable and with less experience. She wouldn't have picked someone as stupidly stubborn as you."

I scowled. "Not stupidly," I said. "I just don't like to leave things undone."

Murphy snorted. "You don't know the meaning of 'give up,' dolt. You see my point."

"Yeah. I guess it's reasonable."

"So what about this Summer girl?"

I blew out a breath. "It doesn't seem to hang on her

very well. She was kinder than any faerie I ever met. She could have been pretty darned unpleasant to me, but she wasn't."

"How about the other mortal, then? The Winter Knight."

"He's a violent, vicious heroin addict. I could see him tossing Reuel down those stairs, sure. But I'm not sure he's savvy enough to have worked enough magic to steal the mantle. He was more of a plunder-now-and-think-later sort of guy." I shook my head. "I've got three more faeries to talk to, though."

"Summer Queen and both Mothers," Murphy nodded. "When will you see them?"

"As soon as I can work out how. The Ladies are the closest to the mortal world. They aren't hard to find. The Queens and the Mothers, though, will live in Faerie proper. I'll have to go there to find a guide."

Murphy lifted her eyebrows. "A guide?"

I grimaced. "Yeah. I don't want to, but it's looking like I'm going to have to pay my godmother a visit."

Murphy quirked an eyebrow. "Seriously? You have a faerie godmother?"

"Long story," I said. "Okay, I want to get moving. If you could—"

The store lights went out, all at once.

My heart all but stopped. A second later, battery-powered emergency lights came up and revealed a roiling cloud of silver-grey mist spreading into the store from the doors. The mist rolled over a startled cashier, and the woman slumped, her mouth slightly open and her eyes unfocused, staring.

"Good Lord," Murphy said softly. "Harry, what's happening?"

I had already gotten out of the booth and grabbed the salt shaker from our table, and the one next to it. "Trouble. Come with me."

Chapter Nineteen

At first I tried to circle around to the exit doors, but the mist proved to be flowing through them as well. "Curse it! We can't get out that way."

Murphy's face went more pale as a young man flung himself at the exit doors. The moment he hit the mist, his running steps faltered. He came to a halt, a puzzled expression on his face, and stared around him blankly, as his shoulders slumped.

"Dear God," she whispered. "Harry, what is that?"

"Come on, to the back of the store," I said, and started running that way. "I think it's a mind fog."

"You *think*?"

I scowled over my shoulder at Murphy. "I've never seen one before, just heard about them. They shut down your head, flatline your ability to remember things, scramble your thoughts. They're illegal."

"Illegal?" Murphy yelled. "Says who?"

"Says the Laws of Magic," I muttered.

"You didn't say anything about any Laws of Magic," Murphy said.

"If we get out of here alive, I'll explain it to you sometime." We ran down a long aisle toward the back of the store, passing housewares, then seasonal goods on our left, while grocery aisles stretched out on our right. Murphy stopped abruptly, broke open the covering over a fire alarm, and jerked it down.

I looked around hopefully, but nothing happened.

"Damn," Murphy muttered.

"Worth a try. Look, the people in the fog should be all right once it's gone, and whoever this is, they won't have any reason to hurt them once we're not around. We'll get out the back door and get away from here."

"Where are we going to go?"

"I don't know," I confessed, as I started moving again. "But anywhere is better than where the bad guys chose to attack and have their pick of a hundred hostages, right?"

"Okay," Murphy said. "Getting out of here is good."

"I bet the bad guys are counting on that, trying to flush us out into a dark alley. You carrying?"

Murphy was already drawing her gun from under her jacket, a well-used military-issue Colt 1911. "Are you kidding?"

I noticed that her hands were shaking. "New gun?"

"Old reliable," she said. "You told me magic can jam a flaky gun."

"Revolver would be even better."

"Why don't I just throw rocks and sharp sticks while I'm at it, Tex?"

"Auto bigot." I spotted an EMPLOYEES ONLY sign. "There," I said, and went that way. "Out the back."

We headed for the swinging doors under the sign. I

hit them first, shoving them open. A grey wall of mist lay in front of me and I leaned back, trying to stumble to a halt. If I let myself touch the mist, I might not have enough of my wits left to regret it. I stumbled a foot short of it and almost fell forward, but Murphy grabbed my shirt and jerked me sharply back.

We both backed away, into the store. "Can't get out that way," Murphy said. "Maybe they don't want to herd you anywhere. Maybe they just want to gas you and kill you while you're down."

I swept my gaze around the store. Cold grey mist rolled forward, slow and steady, in every direction. "Looks like," I said. I nodded down a tall, narrow aisle containing auto parts. "Down there, quick."

"What's down here?" Murphy asked.

"Cover. I have to get us a defense against that mist." We reached the open space at the end of the aisle, and I nodded to Murphy. "Here—stop here and stand close to me."

She did it, but I could still see her shaking as she asked, "Why?"

I looked up. The mist had reached the far end of the aisle and was gliding slowly down it. "I'm going to put up a circle that should keep it off us. Don't step out of it or let any part of you cross outside."

Murphy's voice took on a higher, more tense pitch. "Harry, it's coming."

I twisted open both salt shakers and started pouring them out in a circle around us, maybe three feet across. As I finished the circle, I invested it with the slightest effort of will, of intent, and it closed with a sudden snap of silent, invisible energies. I stood up again, holding my breath, until the mist touched it a moment later.

It roiled up against the circle and stopped, as though a cylinder of Plexiglas stood between it and us. Murphy and I both let out our breath in slow exhalations. "Wow," she said quietly. "Is that like a force field or something?"

"Only against magical energies," I said, squinting around us. "If someone comes along with a gun, we're in trouble."

"What do we do?"

"I think I can protect myself if I'm ready to do it," I said. "But I need to set up a charm on you."

"A what?"

"Charm, short-term magic." I fumbled at my shirt until I found a frayed thread and started pulling it out. "I need a hair."

Murphy gave me a suspicious frown, but she reached under her hat and unceremoniously jerked out several dark gold hairs. I plucked them up and twisted them together with the strand of thread. "Give me your left hand."

She did. Her fingers shook so hard that I could feel it when I put my own around them. "Murph," I said. She kept looking up and down the aisle, her eyes a little wild. "Karrin."

She looked up at me. She looked very young, somehow.

"Remember what I said yesterday," I said. "You're hurt. But you'll get through it. You'll be okay."

She closed her eyes tightly. "I'm scared. So scared I'm sick."

"You'll get through it."

"What if I don't?"

I squeezed her fingers. "Then I will personally make fun of you every day for the rest of your life," I said. "I will call you a sissy girl in front of everyone you know, tie frilly aprons on your car, and lurk in the parking lot at CPD and whistle and tell you to shake it, baby. Every. Single. Day."

Murphy's breath escaped in something like a hiccup. She opened her eyes, a mix of anger and wary amusement easing into them in place of the fear. "You do realize I'm holding a gun, right?"

"You're fine. Hold your hand still." Though her fingers still trembled a little, the wild, panicked spasms had ceased. I wrapped the twist of hair and thread around her finger.

Murphy kept on peering through the mist, her gun steady. "What are you doing?"

"Enchantment like that mist is invasive," I said. "It touches you, gets inside you. So I'm setting you up with a defense. Left side is the side that takes in energy. I'm going to block that mist's spell from going into you. Tie a string around your finger so you won't forget."

I tied the string in an almost complete knot, so that it would need only a single tug to finish. Then I fumbled my penknife out of my pocket and pricked the pad of my right thumb. I looked up at Murphy, trying to clear my thoughts for the spell.

She regarded me, her face pale and uncertain. "I've never really seen you, you know. Do it. Before."

"It's okay," I told her. I met her eyes for a dangerous second. "I won't hurt you. I know what I'm doing."

She lifted the corner of her mouth in a quick smile that made her eyes sparkle. She nodded and returned to peering out through the mist.

I closed my eyes for a moment and then began gathering my focus for the spell. We were already within a circle, so it happened fast. The air tightened on my skin, and I felt the hairs along my arms rise as the power grew. *"Memoratum,"* I murmured. I tied off the improvised string and touched the bead of blood on my thumb to the knot. *"Defendre memorarius."*

The energy rushed out of me and into the spell, wrapping tight around the string and pressing against Murphy. A wave of goose bumps rippled up her arm, and she drew in a sudden sharp breath. "Whoa."

I looked at her sharply. "Murph? You okay?"

She blinked down at her hand, and then up at me. "Wow. Yeah."

I nodded, and took my pentacle out of my shirt. I wrapped it around my left hand, leaving the five-pointed star lying against my knuckles. "Okay, we're pushing our luck enough. Let's hope this works and get the hell out of here."

"Wait, you don't know if it will work?"

"It should work. It ought to. In theory."

"Great. Would it be better to stay here?"

"Heh, that's a joke, right?"

Murphy nodded. "Okay. How will we know if it works?"

"We step outside the circle and if we don't drift into la-la land," I said, "we'll know it worked."

She braced her charmed hand on the butt of her gun. "That's what I love about working with you, Dresden. The certainty."

I broke the circle with a shuffle of my foot and an effort of will. It scattered with a pressured sigh, and the grey mist slid forward and over us.

It glided over my skin like a cold and greasy oil, something foul and cloying and vaguely familiar that made me want to start brushing it off. It writhed up over my arms, prickles of distraction and disorientation crawling over my limbs. I focused on the pentacle on my left hand, the solid, cool weight of it, the years of discipline and practice that it represented. I pushed the clinging mist away from my sensations, deliberately excluded it from my perception by sheer determination. A ripple of azure static flickered along the chain of my amulet, flashed around the pentacle, then faded, taking with it the distraction of the mind fog.

Murphy glanced back at me and said, voice low, "You okay? You looked shaky for a second."

I nodded. "I got it now. You okay?"

"Yeah. Doesn't feel like anything."

Damn, I'm good—sometimes. "Go. Out through the garden center."

Murphy had the gun—she walked in front. I kept my eyes open on our flanks as she headed down an aisle. We passed a customer and an employee, down a side aisle, pressed against a wall where they'd apparently tried to avoid the mist. Now they stood with faintly puzzled expressions on their faces, eyes not focused. Another shopper, an old man, stood in an aisle, swaying precariously on his feet. I stopped beside him and said quietly, "Sir, here, sit down for a minute," and helped him sit down before he fell.

We went past another slackly staring employee, her blue smock marked with dirt stains and smelling of fertilizer, and headed for the doors leading out to the garden center.

My memory screamed a sudden alarm at me, and I lurched forward, diving past Murphy and out into the mist-shrouded evening within the chain-link boundaries of the garden center. A hard, sudden weight hit me, driving my thighs and hips down to the floor. My head whiplashed against it a moment later, complete with a burst of phantom light and very real pain.

I rolled, as the employee we'd just passed reversed her grip on a wickedly sharp set of pruners and stabbed them down at me. I oozed to one side in a sluggish dodge. The steel tips of the tool tore through my shirt and some of my skin before biting into the concrete. I kept rolling and kicked at the woman's ankles. She avoided me with a kind of liquid agility, and I looked up into the human face of the ghoul assassin from the rain of toads. The Tigress.

She didn't look particularly pretty, or particularly exotic, or particularly anything. She looked like no one in particular—medium height, medium build, no flattering curves, no outrageous flaws, no nothing. Medium-brown hair, of unremarkable cut and length. She wore jeans, a polo top, the Wal-Mart smock, all very normal.

The gun she started drawing from under the smock commanded attention, though—a revolver, snub-nosed, but it moved with the kind of weight that made me think high-caliber. I started trying to pull a shield together, but the defense I'd been holding against the mist and the blow to my head tangled up the process, slowed me down—not much, but enough to get me really dead.

Murphy saved me. As the Tigress brought the gun to bear on me, Murphy closed with her, trapping the ghoul's gun arm with her own and doing something with her left hand as she twisted her body at the hips, her strong legs spread wide.

Murphy was a faithful practitioner of aikido, and she knew about grappling. The Tigress let out a shriek. Not a girly wow-does-that-hurt shriek, but the kind of furious, almost whistling sound you expect from a bird of prey. There was a snapping, popping sound, then a clap of thunder, the roar of a discharged gun at close quarters, the sudden sharp smell of burnt powder, and the revolver went skittering free.

The ghoul stabbed the pruners at Murphy, but she was already on the way out, grunting with effort, her entire attack one circle that sent the Tigress stumbling away into a stand of large potted ferns.

Murphy spun to face the ghoul. She took a shooting stance and snarled, "Get on your face on the floor. You are under arrest. You have the right to remain silent."

The ghoul changed. Skin tore at the corners of her mouth as it dropped open and gaped nightmarishly wide, canines lengthening as her lips peeled away from her teeth. Her shoulders jerked and twisted, hunching up and growing wider at the same time, her clothes stretching out while her body grew more hunched. Her fingers lengthened, talons extending from the tips until her hands were spread as wide as the lawn rakes on a display behind her, and a fetid smell of decay and worse flooded out.

Murphy's face went bloodless as she stared at the transformation. If she'd been dealing with an armed thug, I think she would have been fine. But the ghoul wasn't and she wasn't. I saw the fear come surging up through her, winding its way into her through the scars a maddened ghost had left on her spirit the year before. Panic hit her, and her breath came in strangled gasps as a demon from a madman's nightmare clawed its way free of the bushes, spread its talons, and let out a rasping, quivering hiss. Murphy's gun started quivering, the barrel jerking erratically left and right. I struggled to get on my feet and back into the game, but my ears still rang and the constant pressure of the mist slowed me down.

The Tigress must have seen the terror that held Murphy. "A cop, eh?" the ghoul rasped, drool foaming between its teeth, dribbling down its chin. It started slowly toward Murphy, claw tips dragging along the floor. "Aren't you going to tell me that I have the right to an attorney?"

Murphy let out a small, terrified sound, frozen in place, her eyes wide.

It laughed at her. "Such a big gun for a sweet girl. You smell sweet. It makes me hungry." It continued forward, laughter still kissing every word, its distorted, inhuman voice continuing in a steady murmur. "Maybe I should let you arrest me. Wait until we're in the car. If you smell that good, I wonder how good you taste."

I guess the ghoul shouldn't have laughed. Murphy's eyes cleared and hardened. The gun steadied, and she said, "Taste this, bitch."

Murphy started shooting.

The ghoul let out another shriek, this one full of surprise and pain. The bullets didn't drive her back. That's for comic books and TV. Real bullets just rip through you like lead weights through cheesecloth. No gaping, bloody holes appeared in the ghoul's chest, but sudden flowers of scarlet sprayed out from her back, covering the potted ferns with bloody dewdrops.

The ghoul threw her arms up and recoiled, turning, screaming, and threw herself at the ferns.

Murphy kept shooting.

The ghoul stumbled and dropped down amid the ferns, still kicking and struggling wildly, knocking pots over, breaking others, scattering vegetable matter and dirt all over the floor.

Murphy kept shooting.

The gun clicked empty, and the ghoul half-rolled onto her ruined back, the stolen blue smock now ripped with huge holes and soaked through with blood. The ghoul choked and gagged, scarlet trickling out of her mouth. She let out another hiss, this one bubbling, and held up her hands in supplication. "Wait," she rasped. "Wait, please. You win, I give up."

Murphy ejected the clip, put in a fresh one, and worked the slide on the gun. Then she took a shooting stance again and sighted down the barrel, her blue eyes calculating, passionless, merciless.

She didn't see the sudden shadow against the mist to her right, huge and hulking, backlit by emergency lights at the other end of the garden center. I did, and finally shoved my dazed self back to my feet. "Murph!" I shouted. "To your right!"

Murphy's head snapped around, and she darted to her left, even as a garden hoe swept down and shattered against the concrete where she'd been standing. The ghoul scrambled back through the ferns and vanished into the mist, leaving blood smeared everywhere. Murphy backpedaled and shot at the form in the mist, then ducked as another arm swept a shovel in a scything arc that just missed her head.

Grum the Ogre rolled forward out of the mist, in his scarlet-skinned, twelve-foot-tall hulking form, a shovel clenched in one fist. Without slowing a step, he scooped up a twenty-gallon ceramic pot and threw it at Murphy like a snowball. She scooted behind a stack of empty loading palettes, and the pot exploded against them.

Magic would be useless against the ogre. I looked wildly around me, then seized a jumbo-sized plastic bag of round, tinted-glass potting marbles. "Hey!" I shouted. "Tall, red, and ugly!"

Grum's head spun around farther than I would have thought possible with a neck that thick, and his already beady eyes narrowed even more. He let out a bellowing roar and turned toward me, his huge feet slamming down on the concrete.

I tore open the bag and dumped it out toward him. Blue-green marbles spread over the floor in a wave. Grum's foot slammed down on several as he advanced, and I hoped for the best. Grum continued toward me unslowed, and when his great foot lifted, I saw small circles of powdered glass on the ground.

I snarled a curse and ran deeper into the garden center, Grum's footsteps heavy behind me. I heard Murphy shoot again, a pair of shots, and tried to keep a mental count of her rounds. Four, in the new clip? Did she have another reload? And how many rounds did that Colt hold anyway?

A sharper, more piercing report cracked through the area—rifle fire. Murphy's Colt barked twice more, and she called, "Harry, someone's covering the exit with gunfire!"

"Kinda busy here, Murph!" I shouted.

"What the hell is that thing?"

"Faerie!" I shouted. Grum was already trying to kill me, so there was no point in being diplomatic. "It's a big, ugly faerie!" I started swiping things off of shelves to crash in the aisle behind me. I'd gained some distance on Grum, but it could be that he just needed time to gather momentum. I heard him snarl again, and he took a swing with the shovel in his hand. He was short of me, but it whooshed loudly enough to make me flinch.

I looked wildly for something made of steel to throw at the ogre or to defend myself with. The mist kept me from seeing more than a couple of yards ahead of me, and from what I could see, I was just heading deeper and deeper into the plant-vending area. The smell of summer-heated greenery, of fertilizer and mild rot, filled my nose and mouth. I rounded the end of the aisle and ducked through a narrow gate and out from under the canopy top that gave shade to this part of the garden center, into a roofless area bounded by a high chain-link fence and filled with young trees and greenery standing in silent rows.

I looked around wildly for a way out into the parking lot at large, and checked how close the ogre was, flicking a glance back over my shoulder.

Grum stopped at the gate to the fenced area and, with a small smile on his lips, swung the gate shut. As I watched, he covered his hand with a plastic trash bag, and bent the latch like soft clay. Metal squealed and the gate fastened shut with no more effort than I would need to close a twist-tie.

My heart fell down through my stomach, and I looked around me.

The chain-link fence was at least nine feet high, with a strand of barbed wire at the top, meant to stop incursions of baby-tree nappers, I guessed. A second gate, much bigger, stood closed—and the latch had been twisted exactly like the other, warped closed. It was a neat little trap, and I'd been chased right into it.

"Dammit," I said.

Grum let out a grating laugh, though I could barely see anything but his outline, several yards away in the mist. "You lose, wizard."

"Why are you doing this?" I demanded. "Who the hell are you working for?"

"You got no guess?" Grum said. There was a note

of casual arrogance to his voice. "Gee. That's too bad. Guess you go to your grave not knowing."

"If I had a nickel for every time I'd heard that," I muttered, looking around me. I had a few options. None of them were good. I could open a way into the Nevernever and try to find my way through the spirit realm and back into the real world somewhere else—but if I did that, not only might I run into something even worse than I already had in front of me, but if I got unlucky I might hit a patch of slower time and not emerge back into my Chicago for hours, even days. I might also be able to melt myself a hole in the fence with conjured flame, providing I didn't burn myself to a cinder doing it. I didn't have my blasting rod with me, and without it my control could be shaky enough to manage just that.

I could probably pile a bunch of baby trees, loading palettes, sacks of potting soil, and so on against the outer wall of chain-link fence and climb out. I might get cut up on the barbed wire, but hell, that would be better than staying here. Either way, there was no time to waste standing around deciding. I turned toward the nearest set of young trees, picked up a couple, and tossed them against the fence. "Murphy! I'm stuck, but I think I can get clear! Get out of here now!"

Murphy's voice floated to me, directionless in the fog. "Where are you?"

"Hell's bells, Murph! Get out!"

Her gun barked twice more. "Not without you!"

I threw more stuff on the pile. "I'm a big boy! I can

take care of myself!" I took a long step up onto the pile, and tested my grip. It was enough to let me reach the top. I figured I could pull myself up and worry about the barbed wire when I got there. I started climbing out.

I was looking at a faceful of barbed wire and pushing at the fence with my toes when I felt something wrap around my ankles. I looked down and saw a branch wrapped around my legs. I kicked at it irritably.

And then as I watched, another branch lifted from the pile and joined the first. Then a third. And a fourth. The branches beneath my feet heaved and I suddenly found myself hauled up into the air, swinging upside down from my heels.

It was an awkward vantage point, but I watched as the trees and plants and soil I'd thrown into a pile surged and writhed together. The young trees tangled their limbs together, growing before my eyes as they did, lengthening and growing thicker to become part of a larger whole. Other bits of greenery, clumps of dirt, and writhing vines and leaves joined the trees, whipping through the air apparently of their own volition and adding to the mass of the thing that held me.

It took shape and stood up, an enormous creature of vaguely human shape made all of earth and root and bough, twin points of brilliant emerald-green light burning in its vine-writhing, leaf-strewn head. It had to have been nine or ten feet tall, and nearly that far across. Its legs were thicker than me, and branches spread out above its head like vast horns against the background of luminous mind fog. The creature lifted its head and screamed, a sound of tortured wood and creaking limb and howling wind.

"Stars and stones, Harry," I muttered, my heart pounding, "when will you learn to keep your mouth shut?"

Chapter Twenty

"**M**urphy!" I screamed. "Get clear!"

The plant monster— No, wait. I couldn't possibly refer to that thing as a "plant monster." I'd be a laughingstock. It's hard to give a monster a cool name on the spur of the moment, but I used a name I'd heard Bob throw out before.

The chlorofiend lifted me up and shook me like a set of maracas. I focused on my shield bracelet, running my will, bolstered by sudden fear, through the focus. My skin tingled as the shield formed around me, and I shaped it into a full sphere. I was barely in time. The chlorofiend threw me at a post in the chain-link fence. Without the shield, it would have broken my back. I slammed into it, feeling the energy of the shield tighten around me, spreading the impact over the whole of my body instead of solely at the point of impact. The shield transferred a portion of the kinetic energy of impact into heat and light, while the rest came through as an abrupt pressure. The result was like a sudden suit of oven-warmed elastic closing on me, and it felt about three sizes too small. It knocked the wind out of my lungs. Azure and argent light flashed in a vague sphere around me.

I didn't bounce much, just fell to the concrete. The shield gave out a more feeble flash when I hit. I got up off the ground and dodged away from the chlorofiend, but it followed me, slapping aside a stand of wooden tomato stakes with one leafy arm. Its glowing green eyes blazed as it came. I ran up against the fence at the back end of the lot, and the chlorofiend's huge fist smashed down at me again.

I lifted my shield bracelet against it, but the blow tossed me a dozen feet, down the length of fence and into a set of huge steel partitioned shelves holding hundreds of fifty-pound bags of mulch, potting soil, and fertilizer. I lay there dazed for a second, staring at an empty aisle display proclaiming in huge scarlet letters WEED-B-GONE ONLY 2.99!!! I clutched at the display and got to my feet again in time to duck under the chlorofiend's fist as it punched at my head.

It hit one of the metal shelves instead of me, and there was a shriek of warping metal, a creaking yowl of pain from the fiend, and a burst of sizzling smoke. The creature drew its smoking fist back and screeched again, eyes blazing even brighter, angrier.

"Steel," I muttered. "So you're a faerie something or other too." I looked up at the enormous shelves as I ran down the length of them, and a second later I heard the chlorofiend turn and begin pacing after me. I started gathering in my will as I ran, and I allowed the physical shield to fall, leaving me only enough defense to keep the mist from blitzing my head. I would need every bit of strength I could muster to pull off my sudden and desperate plan—and if it didn't work, my shield wouldn't protect me for long in any case. Sooner or later, the chlorofiend would batter its way through my defenses and pound me into plant food.

I pulled ahead of it, but it started gaining momentum, catching up to me. As I reached the end of the row, the end of the steel shelves, I turned to face it.

Hell's bells, that thing was big. Bigger than Grum. I could see through it in places, where twists of branches and leaves were not too closely clumped with earth, but that didn't make it seem any less massive or dangerous.

If this didn't work, I wasn't going to last long enough to regret it.

Most magic is pretty time-consuming, what with drawing circles and gathering energies and aligning forces. Quick and dirty magic, evocation, is drawn directly from a wizard's will and turned loose without benefit of guide or limit. It's difficult and it's dangerous. I suck at evocation. I only knew a couple that I could do reliably, and even they required a focus, such as my shield bracelet or blasting rod, to be properly controlled.

But for doing big dumb things that require a lot of energy and not much finesse, I'm usually fine.

I lifted my arms, and the mist was stirred by a sudden rush of moving air. The chlorofiend pounded closer, and I closed my eyes, pouring more energy out, reaching for the wind. *"Vento,"* I muttered, feeling more power stir. The chlorofiend bellowed again, sending a jolt of fear through me, and the winds rose even more. *"Vento! Vento, ventas servitas!"*

Power, magic, coursed through my outstretched arms and lashed out at the night. The wind rose in a sudden roar, a screaming cyclone that whirled into being just in front of me and then whirled out toward the heavy metal shelving.

The chlorofiend screamed again, nearly drowned out by the windstorm I'd called, only a few yards away.

The enormous, heavy shelves, loaded with tons of materials, let out a groan of protest and then fell, toppled over onto the chlorofiend with a deafening din that ripped at my ears and shook the concrete floor.

The chlorofiend was strong, but it wasn't that strong. It went down like a bush under a bulldozer, shrieking again as the steel shelves crushed it and burned into its substance. A foul greyish smoke rose from the wreckage, and the chlorofiend continued to scream and thrash, the shelves jerking and moving.

Exhaustion swept over me with the effort of the spell, and I glowered down at the fallen shelves. "Down," I panted, "but not out. Dammit." I watched the shelves for a moment and decided that the chlorofiend probably wouldn't shrug it off for a few minutes. I shook my head and headed for the gate into the enclosure. Hopefully, Grum hadn't twisted things up so badly that I couldn't get out.

He had. The metal latch on the gate had been pinched into a mess by his talons. They had scored the metal in sharp notches, like an industrial cutter. Note to self: Don't think steel can stop Grum's fingernails. I checked above and decided to risk climbing the fence and getting through the barbed wire.

I had gotten maybe halfway up the chain-link fence when Murphy limped out of the mist on the other side, her gun pointed right at me.

"Whoa, whoa, Murph," I said. I showed her my hands and promptly fell off the fence. "It's me."

She lowered the gun and let out her breath. "Christ, Harry. What are you doing?"

"Texas cage match. I won." From behind me, the chlorofiend let out another shriek and the shelving groaned as it shifted. I gulped and looked back. "Rematch doesn't look promising, though. Where have you been?"

She rolled her eyes. "Shopping."

"Where's Grum and the ghoul?"

"Don't know. The ghoul's blood trail went out, but someone shot at me when I followed it. Haven't seen the ogre." She blinked at the gate's latch. "Damn. Guess he shut you in here, huh?"

"Pretty much. You get shot?"

"No, why?"

"You're limping."

Murphy grimaced. "Yeah. One of those bastards must have thrown a bunch of marbles on the floor. I slipped on one. It's my knee."

"Oh," I said. "Uh."

Murphy blinked at me. "*You* did that?"

"Well, it was a plan at the time."

"Harry, that's not a plan, it's a Looney Tune."

"Kill me later. Help me out of here now." I squinted up at the barbed wire. "Maybe if you get a rake, you can push it up for me so that I can slide between it and the fence."

"We're twenty feet from the hardware department, genius," Murphy said. She limped back into the mist, and returned half a minute later carrying a pair of bolt cutters. She cut a slit in the chain-link fence and I squeezed through it while the chlorofiend thrashed, still pinned.

"I could kiss you," I said.

Murphy grinned. "You smell like manure, Harry." The smile faded. "What now?"

The trapped monster's thrashing sent several smaller shelves toppling over, and I rubbernecked nervously. "Getting out is still first priority. That thing is down, but it'll be coming before long."

"What is it?"

"Chlorofiend," I said.

"A what?"

"Plant monster."

"Oh, right."

"We need to get out."

Murphy shook her head. "Whoever was covering the exit out front can probably see the other doors too. A silhouette in a doorway is a great target. It's just like a shooting range."

"How the blazes did they see you through the mist?"

"Is that really important right now? They can, and it means we can't go out the front."

"Yeah," I said. "You're right. The main exits are covered, that thing is in the garden center, and ten to one Ogre Grum is watching the back."

"Ogre, check. What's his deal?"

"Bullets bounce off him, and he shakes off magic like

a duck does water. He's strong and pretty quick and smarter than he looks."

Murphy let out a soft curse. "You can't blast him like you did the loup-garou?"

I shook my head. "I gave him a hard shot once already. I may as well have been spitting on him."

"Doesn't look like we have much choice for getting out."

"And even if we do, Grum or that plant thing could run us down, so we'll need wheels."

"We have to go through one of them."

"I know," I said, and headed back into the store.

"Where are you going?" Murphy demanded.

"I have a plan."

She limped after me. "Better than the Looney Tune one, I hope."

I grunted in reply. No need to agree with her.

We both realized that if this plan wasn't better than the last one, then, as Porky Pig would say, That's all, folks.

Chapter
Twenty-one

Three minutes later Murphy and I went out the back door, and Grum was waiting for us.

He rose up out of the shadows by the large trash bins with a bull elephant's bellow and stomped toward us. Murphy, dragging a leg and wrapped somewhat desperately in a plaid auto blanket, let out a shrill cry and turned to run, but tripped and fell to the ground before the ogre.

I kept my left hand behind my back and lifted my right. Flame danced up from my cupped fingers, and I thundered, "Grum!"

The ogre's beady eyes turned to me, glittering. He let out another rumbling snarl.

"Stand thee from my path!" I called in that same overdramatic voice, "lest I grow weary of thee and bereft thee of thy life!"

The ogre focused wholly on me now, striding forward, past the whimpering form of Murphy. "I do not fear thy power, mortal," he snarled.

I lifted my chin and waved my fire-holding hand around a bit. "This is thy last warning, faerie dog!"

Grum's beady eyes grew angrier. He let out a harsh laugh and did not slow down. "Feeble mortal trickster. Thy spellfire means nothing to me. Do thy worst."

Behind Grum, Murphy threw the auto blanket off of her shoulders, and with one rip of the starting cord fired up her shiny new Coleman chain saw. She engaged the blade with a hissing whirr of air and without preamble swung it in an arc that ended precisely at the back of Grum's thick, hairy knee. The steel blade chewed through the ogre's hide as if it was made of Styrofoam. Blood and bits of meat flew up in a gruesome cloud.

The ogre screamed, his body contorting in agony. The scarlet skin around the injury immediately swelled, darkening to black, and tendrils of infectious-looking darkness spread from the wound up over the ogre's leg and hip within the space of a breath. He swept one huge fist at Murphy, but she was already getting out of his reach. The ogre's weight came down on the injured leg, and Grum fell to earth with a heavy thud.

I started forward to help, but everything was happening fast, and my movements felt nightmarishly slow. The ogre rolled to his belly at once, maddened at the touch of the iron in the chain saw's blade, and started dragging himself toward Murphy faster than I would have believed with just his arms, talons gouging into the concrete. She hurried away from him, limping, but Grum slammed one fist down on the concrete so hard that half a dozen feet away, she was jarred off balance and fell.

Grum got hold of Murphy's foot and started dragging her back toward him. She let out a hollow gasp, then twisted and wriggled. She slipped out of her sneaker and hauled herself away from the ogre, her face gone white and drawn.

I ran up behind Grum, pulling my left hand out from behind my back, the fingers of my right hand still curled around the flickering flame I'd shown the ogre. A large yellow-and-green pump-pressure water gun sloshed a little in my left fist. I lowered it and squeezed the trigger. A stream of gasoline sprayed out all over Grum's back, soaking the ogre's skin. Grum whirled toward me halfway through, and I shot the gasoline into his eyes and nose, eliciting another scream. He bared his fangs and glared at me through eyes swollen almost shut.

"Wizard," he said, hardly understandable through the fangs and the drool, "your spellflame will not stop me."

I turned my right hand slowly, and showed Grum the burning can of Sterno I'd been palming. "Good thing I've got this plain old vanilla fire, then, huh?"

And I tossed the lit can of Sterno onto the gasoline-soaked ogre.

Hamstrung and blazing like a birthday candle, Grum screamed and thrashed. I skipped back and around him, helping Murphy up to her feet as the ogre slammed himself against the ground and then against the back wall of the Wal-Mart. He did that in a frenzy for maybe twenty seconds, before uttering an odd, ululating cry and hurling himself at a deep shadow behind a trash bin—and vanished, the light from the flames simply disappearing.

Murphy got up only with my help, her face pale with pain. She could put no weight at all on her wounded leg. "What happened?"

"We whipped him," I said. "He packed up and headed back to Faerie."

"For good?"

I shook my head. "For now. How's your leg?"

"Hurts. Think I broke something. I can hop on the other one."

"Lean on me," I said. We went a few paces, and she swayed dangerously. I caught her before she toppled. "Murph?"

"Sorry, sorry," she gasped. "Hopping, bad idea."

I helped her back down to the ground. "Look, stay here, against the wall. I'll get the Beetle and pull it around here to you."

Murphy was in enough pain to keep her from arguing. She did draw her gun, switch the safety on, and offer it to me. I shook my head. "Keep it. You might need it."

"Dresden," Murphy said, "my gun has been about as useful as fabric softener in a steel mill tonight. But someone out there has a rifle. If they're using one, it's because they're a human, and you don't have most of your magic stuff with you. Take the gun."

She was right, but I argued anyway. "I can't leave you defenseless, Murph."

Murphy hauled up the leg of her jeans and pulled a tiny automatic from an ankle holster. She worked the slide, checked the safety, and said, "I'm covered."

I took the Colt, checked the chamber and the safety, more or less by reflex. "That's a *cute* little gun there, Murph."

She scowled at me. "I have small ankles. It's the only one I can hide there."

I chanted, teasing, "Murphy's got a girl gun, Murphy's got a girl gun."

Murphy glowered at me and hauled the chain saw to within easy reach. "Come a little closer and say that."

I snorted at her. "Give me a couple minutes," I said. "I'll tell you it's me. Some of these bad guys can play dress up—so if you aren't sure who it is . . ."

Murphy nodded, pale and resolved, and rested her hand on the gun.

I drew a deep breath and walked through the mist around the side of the building and toward the front parking lot. I kept close to the wall and moved as quietly as I could, Listening as I went. I gathered up energy for the shield bracelet and held my left hand ready. I held the gun in my right. Holding a pair of defenses focused around my left hand, I would have to do all my shooting with my right. I'm not a very good shot even when I can use both hands, so I just had to hope that no sharpshooting would be required.

I got to the front of the building before I heard something click in the fenced area of the garden center. I swallowed and pointed the Colt at it, noting that I wasn't sure how many rounds the gun had left.

As I came closer, through the mist, I saw the chain fence around the ruined area where I'd been trapped with the chlorofiend. It had been torn down in a swath ten feet wide, and from what I could see of the inside, the tree-thing wasn't there anymore. Great. I took a few steps closer to the break in the fence to stare at the ruined chain link. I'd expected bent and stretched wire, still hot enough to burn where it had torn. Instead, I found edges cut off as neatly as with a set of clippers and coated with frost.

I checked around on the ground and found sections of wire, none of them longer than two or three inches. Steam curled up from them, and the cold in the air near the fence made me shiver. The fence had been frozen, chilled until the steel had become brittle and then shattered.

"Winter," I muttered. "I guess that wasn't much of a stretch."

I swept my eyes around through the mist, left my ears open, and paced as quietly as I could toward the dim, flickering lights that lay somewhere ahead in the parking lot. I'd parked the Beetle in an aisle almost even with the front doors, but I didn't have a reference point through the mist. I just headed out, picked the first row of cars, and started prowling silently along them, looking for the Beetle.

My car wasn't in the first row, but a thin stream of some kind of yellowish fluid was. I traced it to the next row, and found the Beetle sitting there in its motley colors. Another leak. They weren't exactly unheard of in a wizard's car, but this would be a hell of a time for the Beetle to get hospitalized.

I got in and set the gun down long enough to shove my keys in the ignition. My trusty steed wheezed and groaned a few times, but the engine turned over with an apologetic cough and the car rattled to life. I put it in gear, pulled through the empty space in front of me, and headed for the back of the building to get Murphy.

I had just passed the garden center with its ruined

fence when my windows abruptly frosted over. It happened in the space of a breath, ice crystals forming and growing like plants on a stop-motion film until my view was completely cut off. The temperature dropped maybe fifty degrees, and the car sputtered. If I hadn't given it a bunch of gas, it would have stalled. The Beetle lurched forward, and I rolled down the window, sticking my head out the side in an effort to see what was going on.

The chlorofiend loomed up out of the mist and brought one huge, knobby fist down on the Beetle like an organic wrecking ball. The force of it crumpled the hood like tin foil and drove the shocks down so that the frame smushed up against the tires. The impact threw me forward against the steering wheel and drove the breath out of me with a shock of pain.

The impact would have rolled any car with an engine under the hood. Most of the mass of the car would have been driven down, the lighter rear end would have flipped up, and me without my seat belt would have been bounced around like a piece of popcorn.

The old Volkswagens, though, have their engine in the back. Most of the weight of the car got bounced up a little in the air, then came back down to the ground with a jolt.

I slammed my foot on the gas harder, and the Beetle's engine sputtered gamely in response. As big and strong as the chlorofiend might be, it wasn't solid and it wasn't as heavy as a living mass of the same size. The Beetle bounced up from the blow that had crumpled the empty storage compartment under the hood and slammed into the chlorofiend without losing much of its momentum.

The beast let out a shriek of what might have been surprise, and was definitely pain. My car hammered into it with a flickering of scarlet static and a cloud of smoke from the substance of the faerie creature, swept under its legs, and drove the chlorofiend atop its hood.

I kept my foot on the gas, held the wheel as steadily as I could with one hand, and stuck my head out the window so I could see. The chlorofiend screamed again, the magic around it gathering in a cloud that made the hairs on my neck stand up, but the Beetle rattled through the attempt to hex it down, carrying the chlorofiend the length of the Wal-Mart garden center and to the back of the building.

"Think of it as payback for all those telephone poles," I muttered to the Beetle, and slammed on the brakes.

The chlorofiend rolled off of my car, skidded on the asphalt, and slammed into the side of a metal trash bin with a yowl of pain and an exploding cloud of dirt clods. Only one of my headlights appeared to have survived the attack, and even it flickered woozily through the mist and the cloud of dust and dirt rising from the chlorofiend.

I slammed the car into reverse, backed up a few more feet, then put it back into neutral. I raced the engine, then popped the clutch and sent the Beetle hurtling at the monster. I braced myself for the impact this time, and pulled my head in before I hit. The impact felt violent, shockingly loud, and viscerally satisfying. The chlorofiend let out a broken-sounding creak, but until I backed the car up and whipped the wheel around so that I could see out the side window, I couldn't tell what had happened.

I'd torn the thing in half at about the middle, pinching it between the battered, frost-coated Beetle and the metal trash bin. Thank the stars it hadn't been a fiberglass job. The legs lay against the trash bin, now only a pile of twisted saplings and earth, while the arms flailed toward me, a dozen long paces away, uselessly pounding the asphalt.

I spat out my window, put the car into gear again, and went to get Murphy.

I jumped out of the car and had to wrench the passenger door hard to get it to open. Murphy pushed herself up, using the wall for support, and stared at the frost-covered Beetle with wide eyes. "What the hell happened?"

"The plant monster."

"A plant monster and Frosty the Snowman?"

I got on her wounded side to support her. "I took care of it. Let's go."

Murphy let out another small sound of pain, but she didn't let it stop her from hobbling along toward the car. I was just about to help her in when she shouted, "Harry!" and threw her weight against me.

The chlorofiend, the upper half, had somehow clawed its way out of the mist, and one long, viny limb was reaching for me. I fell back, away from it, and tried to shield Murphy with my body.

It got me. I felt fingers the size of young tree trunks wrap around my throat and jerk me away from Murphy like I was a puppy. More branch-fingers got one of my thighs, and I felt myself suspended in the air and pulled slowly apart.

"Meddler," hissed an alien voice from somewhere near the chlorofiend's glowing green eyes. "You should never have involved yourself in these affairs. You have no concept of what is at stake. Die for your arrogance."

I tried for a witty riposte, but my vision blacked out and my head felt like it was trapped in a slowly tightening vise. I tried gathering forces, attempting to push them through my shield bracelet, but the moment I did there was a rustle of wood and leaves, and the bracelet snapped off of my wrist, broken. I tried to gather another spell—and realized as I did that my concentration had wavered too much and that my defense against the insidious enchantment of the mist had begun to fail. My thoughts broke apart into irregular pieces, and I struggled to reach for them and put them together again as the pressure on my body increased, became a red-hot agony.

I only dimly heard the chain saw start up again, and Murphy's scream of challenge. The charm she wore wasn't relying on my concentration. It wouldn't last long, but it would keep the mist away from her for a few more minutes. The chlorofiend let out a shriek, and I heard the saw biting into wood, felt wood chips hitting my face.

I tumbled free, sapling branches tangled all around my head and shoulders, leaves and dirt scratching my face. My leg was still in the chlorofiend's grip, but I could breathe again.

The mist pressed close to me, giving me a sense of detachment and disinterest. It was hard to make any sense of what happened next. Murphy hopped closer, her weight on the one leg, and swept the chain saw through the chlorofiend's other arm. I fell to the ground, more inert tree parts around me.

The chlorofiend waved its arms at Murphy, but they didn't have the crippling force I'd seen it use before. They merely jostled her and knocked her down. Murphy snarled, crawling on her hands and knees, dragging the chain saw with her. She lifted it again and drove it at the creature's head, engine racing, blade singing through the air. The chlorofiend screamed in protest and frustration, lifting the stumps (hah hah, get it, stumps?) of its arms in feeble defense. Murphy tore through them with the chain saw, snicker-snack, and then drove the blade directly between the chlorofiend's glowing green eyes.

The monster shrieked again, writhing, but its arms never managed to do more than shove Murphy around a bit. Then it let out a final groan, and the eyes winked out. Murphy suddenly sat atop a mound of dirt and leaves and gnarled branches.

I lay there, staring stupidly at her, then heard a gunshot, the sharp, cracking report of a rifle. Murphy threw herself down and rolled toward me. A second shot rang out, and a puff of leaves a foot to Murphy's right leapt into the air.

Another sound cut through the night—police sirens, getting closer. Murphy dragged me and herself over the ground toward the car. I heard a harsh curse somewhere in the mist, and then a pair of footsteps retreating. A moment later, I thought the mist was starting to thin out.

"Harry," Murphy said, shaking me. I blinked at her, and the relief showed in her worried expression. "Harry, can you hear me?"

I nodded. My mouth felt dry and my body ached. I fought to clear my head.

"Get us in the car," she said, enunciating the words. "Get us in the car and get us out of here."

The car. Right. I hauled Murphy into the Beetle, got in myself, and stared at the frosted windshield. The heat of the summer night was already melting the frost away, and I could see through it in spots.

"Harry," Murphy said, exasperated, her voice thin and shaky. "Drive!"

Oh, right. Drive. Get out. I put the Beetle in gear, more or less, and we lurched out of the parking lot and out of the mist.

Chapter Twenty-two

"**You're *kidding*,**" Billy said, his voice touched with disbelief. "A chain saw? Where did you get the gasoline?"

Murphy looked up from her wounded leg and the willowy Georgia, who had cut her jeans away and was cleaning out the long gashes she'd acquired from ankle to mid calf. "Gas generator, backup power supply for all the food freezers. They had a ten-gallon plastic jug of it."

Billy's apartment was not a large one, and with a dozen people in it, even with the air-conditioning running full blast, it was too hot and too crowded. The Alphas, Billy's werewolf accomplices, were out in force. We'd been challenged by a tall, thin young man in the parking lot and shadowed to the door by a pair of wolves who kept just far enough away to make it difficult to see them in the shadows.

When I'd first seen them, the Alphas had been a collection of misfits with bad hair, acne, and wannabe tough guy leather outfits. In the year and a half since, they'd changed. None of them had that pale look anymore, none of them looked wheezy, and like Billy, the kids who'd been carrying baby fat had swapped it for lean, fit muscle. They hadn't become a gang of Hollywood soap opera stars or anything, but they looked more relaxed, more confident, more happy—and I saw some scars, some of them quite vicious, showing on bare limbs. Most of the kids wore sweats, or those pullover knit dresses, garments that could be gotten out of in a hurry.

Pizza boxes were stacked three-deep on the table, and a cooler of soft drinks sat on the floor nearby. I piled a plate with half-warm pizza, picked up a Coke, and found a comparatively empty stretch of wall to lean against.

Billy shook his head and said, "Look, Harry, some of this doesn't make sense. I mean, if they could really run around doing this mind fog thing, shouldn't we have heard about it by now?"

I snorted and said around a mouthful of pizza, "It's pretty rare, even in my circles. No one who got hit with it will remember it. Check the paper tomorrow. Ten to one, emergency services showed up after we left, put out the fires, pulled a bunch of confused people out of the building, and the official explanation is a leaky gas line."

Billy snorted. "That doesn't make any sense. There's not going to be evidence of an exploding line, no leak is going to show up at the gas company, no continuing fire of leaking gas—"

I kept eating. "Get real, Billy," I said. "You think people are going to be taken seriously by City Hall if they tell them, 'We really don't know what messed up all these people, we don't know what caused all the damage, we don't know why no one heard or saw anything, and we don't know what the reports of gunshots at the scene were about?' Hell, no. People would be accused of incompetence, publicly embarrassed, fired. No one wants that. So, gas leak."

"But it's stupid!"

"It's life. The last thing the twenty-first century wants to admit is that it might not know everything." I popped open the Coke and guzzled some. "How's the leg, Murph?"

"It hurts," Murphy reported, considerately leaving out the implied "you idiot."

Georgia stood up from attending Murphy's leg and shook her head. She was nearly a foot taller than Billy, and had bound her blond hair back into a tight braid. It emphasized the gauntness of her features. "The cuts and bruises are nothing major, but your knee could be seriously damaged. You should have it checked out by a real doctor, Lieutenant Murphy."

"Karrin," Murphy said. "Anyone who mops up my blood can call me Karrin." I tossed Murphy a Coke. She caught it and said, "Except you, Dresden. Any diet?"

I put several slices of pizza on a paper plate and passed them over. "Live a little."

"All right, Karrin," Georgia said, folding her arms. "If you don't want a twenty-five-thousand-dollar surgery along with seven or eight months of rehab, we need to get you to the hospital."

Murphy frowned, then nodded and said, "Let me eat something first. I'm starving."

"I'll get the car," Georgia said. She turned to Billy. "Make sure she doesn't put any weight on her leg when you bring her down. Keep it straight if you can."

"Got it," Billy said. "Phil, Greg. Get that blanket. We'll make a litter out of it."

"I'm not an infant," Murphy said.

I put my hand on her shoulder. "Easy," I said in a quiet voice. "They can handle themselves."

"So can I."

"You're hurt, Murph," I said. "If you were one of your people, you'd be telling you to shut up and stop being part of the problem."

Murphy shot me a glower, but its edge was blunted by the big mouthful of pizza she took. "Yeah. I know. I just hate being sidelined."

I grunted.

"What are you going to do?" she asked.

I shook my head. "Finish this Coke. I haven't planned much past that."

She sighed. "All right, Harry. Look, I'll be home in a few hours. I'll keep digging, see if I can turn up anything about Lloyd Slate. If you need information on anything else, get in touch."

"You should rest," I told her.

She grimaced at her leg. Her knee was swollen to a couple of times its normal size. "Looks like I'm going to have plenty of time for that."

I grunted again and looked away.

"Hey, Harry," Murphy said. When I didn't look at her, she continued, "What happened to me wasn't your fault. I knew the risks and I took them."

"You shouldn't have had to."

"No one should. We live in an imperfect world, Dresden. In case that hasn't yet become obvious enough for you." She nudged my leg with her elbow. "Besides. You were lucky I was there. The way I count it, I'm the one who put on the boots."

A smile threatened my expression. "You did what?"

"Put on the boots," Murphy said. "I put on the boots and kicked some monster ass. I dropped the ghoul, and I'm the one who rammed a chain saw through the head of that plant monster thing. Crippled the ogre, too. What did you do? You threw a can of Sterno at him. That's barely an assist."

"Yeah, but I soaked him in gasoline first."

She snorted at me, around more pizza. "Shutout."

"Whatever."

"Murphy three, Dresden zero."

"You didn't do all of it."

"I put on the boots."

I raised my hands. "Okay, okay. You've . . . got boots, Murph."

She sniffed and took an almost dainty sip of Coke. "Lucky I was there."

I squeezed her shoulder and said, with no particular inflection, "Yes. Thank you."

Murphy smiled up at me. From the window, one of the Alphas reported, "Car's ready."

Billy and a couple more laid out a blanket and then carefully lifted Murphy onto it. She tolerated them with a roll of her eyes, but hissed with discomfort even at the gentle motion.

"Call," she said.

"Will."

"Watch your back, Harry." Then they carried her out.

I picked up some more pizza, exchanged some more or less polite chitchat with some of the Alphas, and made my escape from the crowded living room of the apartment to the balcony. I shut the sliding glass door behind me. Only one light in the parking lot provided any illumination, so the balcony was mostly covered in sheltering shadows. The night was a close one, humidity cooking along at a lazy summer broil, but even so it felt less claustrophobic than the crowded apartment.

I watched Billy and the Alphas load Murphy into a minivan and drive off. Then there was as much silence as you ever get in Chicago. The hiss of tires on asphalt was a constant, liquid background, punctuated with occasional sirens, horns, mechanical squeaks and squeals, and the buzzing of one lost locust that must have been perched on a building nearby.

I put my paper plate on the wooden balcony railing, closed my eyes, and took a deep breath, trying to clear my head.

"Penny for your thoughts," said a quiet female voice.

I nearly jumped off the balcony in sheer reaction. My hand brushed the paper plate, and the pizza fell to the parking lot below. I whirled around and found Meryl sitting in a chair at the other side of the balcony, deep in shadows, her large form nothing more than a more solid piece of darkness—but her eyes gleamed in the half-light, reflecting traces of red. She watched the plate fall and then said, "Sorry."

"S'okay," I said. "Just a little nervous tonight."

She nodded. "I was listening."

I nodded back to her and returned to looking at nothing, listening to night sounds. After a while, she asked me, "Does it hurt?"

I waved my bandaged hand idly. "Sort of."

"Not that," she said. "I meant watching your friend get hurt."

Some of my racing thoughts coalesced into irritated anger. "What kind of question is that?"

"A simple one."

I took an angry hit from my can of Coke. "Of course it hurts."

"You're different than I thought you'd be."

I squinted over my shoulder at her.

"They tell stories about you, Mister Dresden."

"It's all a lie."

Her teeth gleamed. "Not all of them are bad."

"Mostly good or mostly bad?"

"Depends on who's talking. The Sidhe crowd thinks you're an interesting mortal pet of Mab's. The vampire wannabe crowd thinks you're some kind of psychotic vigilante with a penchant for vengeance and mayhem. Sort of a one-man Spanish Inquisition. Most of the magical crowd thinks you're distant, dangerous, but smart and honorable. Crooks think you're a hit man for the outfit, or maybe one of the families back East. Straights think you're a fraud trying to bilk people out of their hard-won cash, except for Larry Fowler, who probably wants you on the show again."

I regarded her, frowning. "And what do you think?"

"I think you need a haircut." She lifted a can to her mouth and I caught a whiff of beer. "Bill called all the morgues and hospitals. No Jane Doe with green hair."

"Didn't figure there would be. I talked to Aurora. She seemed concerned."

"She would. She's everyone's big sister. Thinks she needs to take care of the whole world."

"She didn't know anything."

Meryl shook her head and was quiet for a while before she asked, "What's it like being a wizard?"

I shrugged. "Mostly it's like being a watch fob repairman. It's both difficult and not in demand. The rest of the time . . ."

More emotion rose in me, threatening my self-control. Meryl waited.

"The rest of the time," I picked up, "it's scary as hell. You start learning the kinds of things that go bump in the night and you figure out that 'ignorance is bliss' is more than just a quotable quote. And it's—" I clenched my hands. "It's so damned *frustrating*. You see people getting hurt. Innocents. Friends. I try to make a difference, but I usually don't know what the hell is going on until someone is already dead. Doesn't matter what kind of job I do—I can't help those folks."

"Sounds hard," Meryl said.

I shrugged. "I guess it isn't any different than what anyone else goes through. The names just get changed." I finished off the Coke and stomped the dead soldier flat. "What about you? What's it like being a changeling?"

Meryl rolled the beer can between her broad hands. "About like anyone, until you hit puberty. Then you start feeling things."

"What kinds of things?"

"Different, depending on your Sidhe half. For me it

was anger, hunger. I gained a lot of weight. I kept losing my temper over the most idiotic things." She took a drink. "And strength. I grew up on a farm. My older brother rolled a tractor and it pinned him, broke his hip, and caught on fire. I picked it up and threw it off him, then dragged him back to the house. More than a mile. I was twelve. My hair had turned this color by the next morning."

"Troll," I said quietly.

She nodded. "Yeah. I don't know the details about what happened, but yeah. And every time I let those feelings get loose, the more I lost my temper and used my strength, the bigger and stronger I got. And the worse I felt about what I did." She shook her head. "Sometimes I think it would be easier to just choose the Sidhe half. To stop being human, stop hurting. If it wasn't for the others needing me . . ."

"It would turn you into a monster."

"But a happy monster." She finished her beer. "I should go check on Fix—he's sleeping now—and try to call Ace. What are you going to do?"

"Try to add up some facts. Meet some contacts. Interview more Queens. Maybe get a haircut."

Her teeth showed again in a smile, and she rose. "Good luck." She went back into the noisy apartment and shut the door.

I closed my eyes and tried to think. Whoever had sent the Tigress, Grum, the chlorofiend, and the lone gunman after me had been trying to kill me. It was a reasonable assumption, then, that I was on the right track. Generally speaking, the bad guys don't try to bump off an investigator unless they're worried he's actually about to find something.

But if that was true, then why had the Tigress taken a shot at me the day before I'd gotten the case? She could have been working for the Red Court and taken a new contract that just happened to be me, but it didn't sound likely. If the ghoul had been on the same contract, it meant that I'd been judged a threat to the killer's plans from day one, if not sooner.

The frost on my car's windows had probably been the doing of someone from Winter. I mean, a wizard could do the same thing, but as devastating spells go, that one seemed to be kinda limited. The ghoul, presumably, would work for anyone who paid. The chlorofiend, though . . . I hadn't expected it to talk, or to be intelligent.

The more I thought about the plant monster, the more things didn't add up. It had picked a spot and had its allies herd me to it. That wasn't the behavior of your average thug, even of the magical variety. It had a sense of personal conflict about it, as if the chlorofiend had a particular bone to pick with me.

And how the hell had Murphy killed it? It was stronger than your average bulldozer, for crying out loud. It had socked me once when I had my full shield going, and it still hurt. It had clipped me a couple of times and nearly broken bones.

The chlorofiend should have flattened Murphy into a puddle of slurry. It had hit her at least a dozen times, yet it seemed like it had only tapped her, as though unable to risk doing more damage. Then a lightbulb flashed on somewhere in my musty brain. The chlorofiend hadn't been a being, as such. It had been a construct—a magical vessel for an outside awareness. An awareness both intelligent and commanding, but one who could not, for some reason, kill Murphy when she attacked it. Why?

"Because, Harry, you idiot, Murphy isn't attached to either of the Faerie Courts," I told myself. Out loud.

"What's that got to do with it?" I asked myself. Again out loud. And people think I'm crazy.

"Remember. The Queens can't kill anyone who isn't attached to the Courts through birthright or bargain. She couldn't kill Murphy. Neither could the construct she was guiding."

"Damn," I muttered. "You're right."

A Queen seemed reasonable, then—probably from Winter. Or, more realistically, the frosted windshield could have been a decoy. Either way, I couldn't figure who would have had a reason to come after me with something as elaborate as a mind fog and a veritable army of assassins.

Which reminded me. The mind fog had to have come from somewhere. I wasn't sure if the Queens could have managed something like that outside of Faerie. If they couldn't, it meant that the killer had a hired gun, someone who could pull off a delicate and dangerous spell like that.

I started running down that line of thought, but only a moment later the wind picked up into a stiff, whistling breeze that roared through the air and swept down through the city. I frowned at the sudden shift in the weather and looked around.

I didn't find anything obvious, but when I glanced up, I saw the lights going out. A vast cloud bank was racing north, fast enough that I could see it eating the stars. A second wall of clouds was sailing south, toward the first bank. They met in only moments, and as they did, light flashed from cloud to cloud, brighter than daylight, and thunder shook the balcony beneath my feet. Not long after that, a drop of freezing-cold water landed on my head, quickly followed by a mounting torrent of chilly rain. The still-rising wind whipped it into a miserable downpour.

I turned and pulled open the door into the apartment with a frown. The Alphas were peering out windows, speaking quietly with one another. Across the room, Billy finished messing around with a television, and a rather rumpled-looking weatherman appeared, the image flickering with interference lines and bursts of snow.

"Guys, guys," Billy said. "Hush, let me listen." He turned up the volume.

". . . a truly unprecedented event, an enormous Arctic blast that came charging like a freight train through Canada and across Lake Michigan to Chicagoland. And if that wasn't enough, a tropical front, settled quietly in the Gulf of Mexico, has responded in kind, rushing up the Mississippi River in a sudden heat wave. They've met right over Lake Michigan, and we have received several reports of rain and bursts of hail. Thunderstorm warnings have been issued all through the Lake Michigan area, and a tornado watch is in progress for the next hour in Cook County. National Weather Service has also issued a flash flood warning and a travel advisory for the eastern half of

Illinois. This is some beautiful but very violent weather, ladies and gentlemen, and we urge you to remain in shelter until this storm has time to . . ."

Billy turned the volume down. I looked around the room and found nearly a dozen sets of eyes focused on me, patient and trusting. Bah.

"Harry," Billy said at last, "that isn't a natural storm, is it?"

I shook my head, got another Coke out of the cooler, and headed tiredly for the door. "Side effect. Like the toads."

"What does it mean?"

I opened the door and said, without looking back, "It means we're running out of time."

Chapter

Twenty-three

I took the Beetle a ways north of town, keeping to the lake shore. Rain sheeted down, and lightning made the clouds dance with shadow and flame. Maybe ten miles from the center of town, the downpour eased up, and the air became noticeably colder—enough so that in jeans and a T-shirt, I was shivering. I pulled the car off Sheridan Road a couple miles north of Northwestern University, out toward Winnetka, set the parking brake and locked it up, and trudged toward the shore of the lake.

It was a dark night, but I called no lights to guide me, and I didn't carry a flashlight. It took my eyes a while, but I finally managed to start making out shapes in the darkness and found my way through the light woods around this part of the lake shore to a long, naked promontory of rock thrusting itself a dozen yards into the water. I walked to the end of the stone and stood there for a moment, listening to the thunder rolling over the lake, the wind stirring the water into waves nearly like those of the sea. The air itself felt restless, charged with violence, and the light rain that still fell was uncomfortably cold.

I closed my eyes, pulling together energy from the elements around me, where water met stone, air met water, stone met air, and drawing as well from my own determination. The power coursed into me, dancing and seething with a quivering life of its own. I focused it with my thoughts, shaped it, and then opened my eyes and lifted my arms, wrists out so that the old pale round scars on either side of the big blue veins there felt the rain falling on them.

I pushed out the power I'd gathered and called into the thunder and rain, "Godmother! *Vente*, Leanansidhe!"

A sudden presence appeared beside me, and a woman's voice said, "Honestly, child, it isn't as though I'm far away. There's no reason to shout."

I jerked in surprise and nearly fell into the lake. I turned to my left to face my faerie godmother, who stood calmly upon the surface of the water, bobbing up and down a bit as waves passed under her feet.

Lea stood nearly my own height, but instead of dark contrasts and harsh angles, she was a creature of gliding curves and gentle shades. Hair the color of flame coursed in curls and ringlets to below her hips, and tonight she wore with it a gown of flowing emerald silk, laced through with veins of ochre and aquamarine. A belt made from a twisted braid of silken threads of gold wound around her waist, and a dark-handled knife rested on a slant at her hip through a loop in the belt.

She was one of the high Sidhe, and her beauty went without saying. The perfection of her form was complemented by features of feminine loveliness, a full mouth, skin like cream, and oblong, feline eyes of gold, cat-slitted like those of most fae. She took in my surprise with a certain reserved mirth, her mouth set with a tiny smile.

"Good evening, Godmother," I said, trying for a proper degree of politeness. "You look lovely as the stars tonight."

She let out a pleased sigh. "Such a flatterer. I'm already enjoying this conversation so much more than the last."

"I'm not dying this time," I said.

The smile faded. "That is a matter of opinion," she responded. "You are in great danger, child."

"Thinking about it, I realize I generally have been whenever you were around."

She clucked reprovingly. "Nonsense. I've never had anything but your best interests at heart."

I barked out a harsh laugh. "My best interests. That's rich."

Lea arched a brow. "What reason have you to think otherwise?"

"For starters, because you tricked me out of a big evil-slaying magic sword and sold me to Mab."

"Tut," Lea said. "The sword was just business, child. And as for selling your debt to Mab . . . I had no choice in the matter."

"Yeah, right."

She arched her brows. "You should know better, dear godchild. You know I cannot speak what is untrue. During our last encounter I returned to Faerie with great power and upset vital balances. Those balances had to be redressed, and your debt was the mechanism that the Queen chose to employ."

I frowned at her for a minute. "Returned with great power." My eyes fell to the knife at her waist. "That thing the vampires gave you?"

She rested her fingers lightly on the knife's hilt. "Don't cheapen it. This athame was no creation of theirs. And it was less a gift than a trade."

"*Amoracchius* and that thing are in the same league? Is that what you're saying?" Gulp. My faerie godmother was dangerous enough without a big-time artifact of magic. "What is it?"

"Not what, but whose," Lea corrected me. "And in any case, you may be assured that surrendering my claim on you to Mab was in no way an attempt to do you harm. I have never meant you lasting ill."

I scowled at her. "You tried to turn me into one of your hounds and keep me in a kennel, Godmother."

"You'd have been perfectly safe there," she pointed out. "And very happy. I only wanted what was best for you because I care for you, child."

My stomach did a neat little rollover, and I swallowed. "Yeah. Uh. It's very . . . you. I guess. In a demented, insane way, I can understand that."

Lea smiled. "I knew you would. To business, then. Why have you called to me this night?"

I took a deep breath and braced myself a little. "Look, I know we haven't gotten along really well lately. Or ever. And I don't have a lot to trade with, but I had hoped you'd be willing to work out a bargain with me."

She arched a red-gold brow. "To what ends?"

"I need to speak to them," I said. "To Mab and Titania."

Her expression grew distant, pensive. "You must understand that I cannot protect you from them, should they strike at you. My power has grown, poppet, but not to those heights."

"I understand. But if I don't get to the bottom of this and find the killer, I'm as good as dead."

"So I have heard," my godmother said. She lifted her right hand and extended it to me. "Then give me your hand."

"I *need* my hand, Godmother. Both of them."

She let out a peal of laughter. "No, silly child. Simply put your hand in mine. I will convey you."

I gave her a sidelong look and asked warily, "At what price?"

"None."

"*None?* You never do anything without a price."

She rolled her eyes and clarified, "None to you, child."

"Who, then?"

"No one you know, or knew," Lea said.

An intuition hit me. "My mother. That's who you're talking about."

Lea left her hand extended. She smiled, but only said, "Perhaps."

I regarded her hand quietly for a moment, then said, "I'm not sure I can believe that you're really going to protect me."

"But I already have."

I folded my arms. "When?"

"If you will remember that night in the boneyard, I healed a wound to your head that may well have killed you."

"You only did it to sucker me into getting you the sword!"

Lea's tone became wounded. "Not *only* for that. And if you consider further, I also freed you of a crippling binding and rescued you from a blazing inferno not twenty-four hours later."

"You charged my girlfriend all her memories of me to do it! And you only saved me from the fire so that you could put me in a doghouse."

"That does not change the fact that I was, after all, protecting you."

I stared at her in frustration for a minute and then scowled. "What have you done for me lately?"

Lea closed her eyes for a moment, then opened her mouth and spoke. Her voice came out aged and querulous. "What's all that racket! I have already called the police, I have! You fruits get out of our hall or they'll lock you away!"

I blinked. "Reuel's apartment. That was you?"

"Obviously, child. And at the market, earlier this eve." She lifted her hand in the air, made an intricate motion with long, pale fingers, and opened her mouth again, as if singing a note of music. Instead, the sound of police sirens emerged, somewhat muted and indistinguishable from the real thing.

I shook my head. "I don't get it."

She moved her fingers again, and the sirens blended into another silver-sweet laugh, her expression amused, almost fond. "I am sure you do not, poppet." She offered her hand again. "Come. Time is pressing."

She had that part right at least. And I knew she was telling me the truth. Her words had left her little room for evasion. I'd never gotten anything but burned when making deals with the faeries, and if Lea was offering to help me for free, there had to be a catch somewhere.

Lea's expression told me that she either knew what I'd been thinking or knew me well enough to guess, and she laughed again. "Harry, Harry," she said. "If it is of any consequence to you, remember that our bargain is still in effect. I am bound to do you no harm for several weeks more."

I'd forgotten about that. Of course, I couldn't fully trust that, either. Even if she had sworn to do me no harm, if I asked her to take me somewhere she could drop me off in a forest full of Unseelie nasties without breaking her word. She'd done something very similar to me last year.

Thunder rumbled again, and the light flared even more brightly in the clouds. Tick, tick, tick, the clock was running, and I wasn't going to get anything done standing here waffling. Either I trusted myself to my godmother or I went back home and waited for something to come along and squash me.

Going with Lea wasn't the best way to get what I wanted—it was just the only way. I took a breath and took her hand. Her skin felt like cool silk, untouched by the rain. "All right. And after them, I need to see the Mothers."

Lea gave me an oblique glance and said, "Survive the

flood before hurling yourself into the fire, child. Close your eyes."

"Why?"

Annoyance flickered over her eyebrows. "Child, stop wasting time with questions. You have given me your hand. Close your eyes."

I muttered a curse to myself and did it. My godmother spoke something, a string of liquid syllables in a tongue I could not understand—but it made my knees turn rubbery and my fingers suddenly feel weak. A wave of disorientation, dizzying but not unpleasantly so, scrambled my sense of direction. I felt a breeze on my face, a sense of movement, but I couldn't have said whether I was falling or rising or moving forward.

The movement stopped, and the whirling sensations passed. Thunder rumbled again, very loudly, and the surface I stood on shook with it. Light played against my closed eyelids.

"We are here," Lea said, her voice hushed.

I opened my eyes.

I stood on a solid surface among grey and drifting mist. The mist covered whatever ground I was on, and though I poked at it with my foot, I couldn't tell if it was earth, wood, or concrete. The landscape around me rolled in hills and shallow valleys, all of it covered in ground fog. I frowned up at the skies. They were clear. Stars glittered impossibly bright against the velvet curtain of night, sparkling in dozens of colors, instead of in the usual pale silver, jewels against the blackness of the void. Thunder rumbled again, and the ground shook beneath the mist. Lightning flashed along with it, and the ground all around us lit with a sudden angry blue fire that slowly faded away.

The truth dawned on me slowly. I pushed my foot at the ground again, and then in a circle around me. "We're . . ." I choked. "We're on . . . we're on . . ."

"The clouds," my godmother said, nodding. "Or so it would seem to you. We are no longer in the mortal world."

"The Nevernever, then. Faerie?"

She shook her head and spoke, her voice still hushed, almost reverent. "No. This is the world between, the sometimes place. Where Chicago and Faerie meet, overlap. Chicago-Over-Chicago, if you will. This is the place the Queens call forth when the Sidhe desire to spill blood."

"They call it forth?" I asked in a quiet voice. "They create it?"

"Even so," Lea said, her voice similarly low. "They prepare for war."

I turned slowly, taking it in. We stood on a rise of ground in a broad, shallow valley. I could make out what looked like a mist-shrouded lake shore not far away. A river cut through the cloudscape.

"Wait a minute," I said. "This is . . . familiar." Chicago-Over-Chicago, she had said. I started adding in mental images of buildings, streets, lights, cars, people. "This *is* Chicago. The land."

"A model of it," Lea agreed. "Crafted from clouds and mist."

I kept turning and found behind me a stone, grey and ominous and enormous, startlingly solid amid all the drifting white. I took a step back from it and saw the shape of it—a table, made of a massive slab of rock, the legs made of more stones as thick as the pillars at Stonehenge. Writing writhed across the surface of the stone, runes that looked a little familiar. Norse, maybe? Some of them looked more like Egyptian. They seemed to take something from several different sources, leaving them unreadable. Lightning flashed again through the ground, and a wave of blue-white light flooded over the table, through the runes, lighting them like Las Vegas neon for a moment.

"I've heard of this," I said after a moment. "A long time ago. Ebenezar called it the Stone Table."

"Yes," my godmother whispered. "Blood is power, child. Blood spilled upon that stone forever becomes a part of who holds it."

"Who holds it?"

She nodded, her green eyes luminous. "For half of the year, the Table lies within Winter. For half, within Summer."

"It changes hands," I said, understanding. "Midsummer and Midwinter."

"Yes. Summer holds the Table now. But not for much longer."

I stepped toward the Table and extended a hand. The air around it literally shook, pressing against my fingers, making my skin ripple visibly as though against a strong wind—but I felt nothing. I touched the surface of the Table itself, and could feel the power in it, buzzing through the flowing runes like electricity through high-voltage cables. The sensation engulfed my hand with sudden heat and violence, and I jerked my fingers back. They were numb, and the nails of the two that had touched the Table were blackened at the edges. Wisps of smoke rose from them.

I shook my fingers and looked at my godmother. "Let me get this straight. Blood spilled onto the Table turns into power for whoever holds it. Summer now. But Winter, after tomorrow night."

Lea inclined her head, silent.

"I don't understand what makes that so important."

She frowned at the Table, then began pacing around it, slowly, clockwise, her eyes never leaving me. "The Table is not merely a repository for energy, child. It is a conduit. Blood spilled upon its surface takes more than merely life with it."

"Power," I said. I frowned and folded my arms, watching her. "So if, for instance, a wizard's blood spilled there . . ."

She smiled. "Great power would come of it. Mortal life, mortal magic, drawn into the hands of whichever Queen ruled the Table."

I swallowed and took a step back. "Oh."

Lea completed her circuit of the Table and stopped beside me. She glanced furtively around her, then looked me in the eyes and said, her voice barely audible, "Child. Should you survive this conflict, do not let Mab bring you here. Never."

A chill crawled down my spine. "Yeah. Okay." I shook my head. "Godmother, I still don't get what you're trying to tell me. Why is the Table so important?"

She gestured, left and right, toward a pair of hilltops

facing each other across the broad valley. I looked at one, squinting at a sudden blur in my vision. I tried looking at the other, and the same thing happened. "I can't see," I said. "It's a veil or something."

"You must see if you are to understand."

I drew in a slow breath. Wizards can see things most people can't. It's called the Sight, the Third Eye, a lot of other names. If a wizard uses his Sight, he can see the forces of magic themselves at work, spells like braids of neon lights, veils pierced like projections on a screen. A wizard's Sight shows things as they truly are, and it's always an unsettling experience, one way or the other. What you see with the Sight stays with you. Good or bad, it's always just as fresh in your mind as if you'd just seen it. I'd looked on a little tree-spirit being with my Sight when I'd been about fourteen, the first time it had happened to me, and I still had a perfect picture of it in my head, as though I was *still* looking at it, a little cartoonish being that was part lawn gnome and part squirrel.

I'd seen worse since. Much worse. Demons. Mangled souls. Tormented spirits. All of that was still there too. But I'd also seen better. One or two glimpses of beings of such beauty and purity and light that it could make me weep. But each time it got a little harder to live with, a little harder to bear, a cumulative weight.

I gritted my teeth, closed my eyes, and with careful deliberation unlocked my Sight.

Opening my eyes again made me stagger as I was hit with a sudden rush of impressions. The cloudy landscape absolutely seethed with magical energies. From the southern hilltop, wild green and golden light spilled, falling over the landscape like a translucent garden, vines of green, golden flowers, flashes of other colors spread through them, clawing at the gentle ground, anchored here and there at points of light so vibrant and bright that I couldn't look directly at them.

From the other side, cold blue and purple and greenish power spread like crystals of ice, with the slow and relentless power of a glacier, pressing ahead in some places, melted back in others, especially strong around the valley's winding rivers.

The conflict of energies both wound back to the hilltops themselves, to points of light as bright as small suns. I could, just barely, see the shadow of solid beings within those lights, and even the shadow of each was an overwhelming presence upon my senses. One was a sense of warmth, choking heat, so much that I couldn't breathe, that it pressed into me and set me aflame. The other was of cold, horrible and absolute, winding cold limbs around me, stealing away my strength. Those presences flooded through me, sudden beauty, power so terrifying and exhilarating and awesome that I fell to my knees and sobbed.

Those powers played against one another—I could sense that, though not the exact nature of their conflict. Energies wound about one another, subtle pressures of darkness and light, leaving the landscape vaguely lit in squares of cold and warm color. Fields of red and gold and bright green stood against empty, dead blocks of blue, purple, pale white. A pattern had formed in them, a structure to the conflict that was not wholly complete.

Most of a chessboard. Only at the center, at the Table, was the pattern broken, a solid area of Summer's power in green and gold around the Stone Table, while Winter's dark, crystalline ice slowly pressed closer, somehow in time with the almost undetectable motion of the stars overhead.

So I saw it. I got a look at what I was up against, at the naked strength of the two Queens of Faerie, and it was bigger than me. Every ounce of strength I could have summoned would have been no more than a flickering spark beside either of those blazing fountains of light and magic. It was power that had existed since the dawn of life, and would until its end. It was power that had cowed mortals into abject worship and terror before—and I finally understood why. I wasn't a pawn of that kind of strength. I was an insect beside giants, a blade of grass before towering trees.

And there was a dreadful attraction in seeing that power, something in it that called to the magic in me, like to like, made me want to hurl myself into those flames, into that endless, icy cold. Moths look at bug zappers like I looked at the Queens of Faerie.

I tore my eyes away by hiding my face in my arms. I fell to my side on the ground and curled up, trying to shut the Sight, to force those images to stop flooding over me. I shook and tried to say something. I'm not sure what. It came out as stuttering, gibbering sounds. After that, I don't remember much until cold rain started slapping me on the cheek.

I opened my eyes and found myself lying on the cold, wet ground on the shores of Lake Michigan, where I'd first called out to my godmother. My head was on something soft that turned out to be her lap. I sat up and away from her quickly. My head hurt, and the images the Sight had showed me made me feel particularly small and vulnerable. I sat shivering in the rain for a minute before I glanced back at my godmother.

"You should have warned me."

Her face showed no remorse, and little concern. "It would have changed nothing. You needed to see." She paused and then added, "I regret that it was the only way. Do you yet understand?"

"The war," I said. "They'll fight for control of the area around the Table. If Summer holds the space, it won't matter if it's Winter's time or not. Mab won't be able to reach the Table, spill blood on it, and add the power of the Summer Knight to Winter." I took a breath. "There was a sense to what they were doing. As though it was a ritual. Something they'd done before."

"Of course," Lea said. "They exist in opposition. Each wields vast power, wizard—power to rival the archangels and lesser gods. But they cancel each other flawlessly. And in the end, the board will be evenly divided. The lesser pieces will emerge and do battle to decide the balance."

"The Ladies," I said. "The Knights."

"And," Lea added, lifting a finger, "the Emissaries."

"Like hell. I'm not fighting in some kind of fucked-up faerie battle in the clouds."

"Perhaps. Perhaps not."

I snorted. "But you didn't help me. I needed to speak to them. Find out if one of them was responsible."

"And so you did. More truly than if you'd exchanged words."

I frowned at her and thought through what I knew, and what I'd learned on my trip to the Stone Table. "Mab shouldn't be in any hurry. If Summer is missing her Knight, Winter has the edge if they wait. There's no need to take the Table."

"Yes."

"But Summer is moving to protect the Table. That means Titania thinks someone in Winter did it. But if Mab is responding instead of waiting, it means . . ." I frowned. "It means she isn't sure why Summer is moving. She's just checking Titania's advance. And *that* means that she isn't sure whodunit, either."

"Simplistic," Lea said. "But accurate enough reasoning, poppet. Such are the thoughts of the Queens of the Sidhe." She looked out across the lake. "Your sun will rise in some little time. When once again it sets, the war will begin. In a balanced Court, it would mean, perhaps, little of great consequence to the mortal world. But that balance is gone. If it is not restored, child, imagine what might happen."

I did. I mean, I'd had an idea what might go wrong before, but now I *knew* the scale of the forces involved. The powers of Winter and Summer weren't simply a bunch of electricity in a battery. They were like vast coiled springs, pressing against each other. As long as that pressure was equal, the energies were held in control. But an imbalance in one side or the other could cause them to slip, and the release of energies from either side would be vast and violent, and sure to inflict horrible consequences on anything nearby—in this case, Chicago, North America, and probably a good chunk of the rest of the world with it.

"I need to see the Mothers. Get me to them."

Lea rose, all grace and opaque expression, impossible to read. "That, too, is beyond me, child."

"I *need* to speak to the Mothers."

"I agree," Lea said. "But I cannot take you to them. The power is not mine. Perhaps Mab or Titania could, but they are otherwise occupied now. Committed."

"Great," I muttered. "How do I get to them?"

"One does not get to the Mothers, child. One can only answer an invitation." She frowned faintly. "I can do no more to help you. The lesser powers must take their places with the Queens, and I am needed shortly."

"You're going?"

She nodded, stepped forward, and kissed my brow. It was just a kiss, a press of soft lips against my skin. Then she stepped back, one hand on the hilt of the knife at her belt. "Be careful, child. And be swift. Remember—sundown." She paused and looked at me askance. "And consider a haircut. You look like a dandelion."

And with that, she stepped out onto the lake, and her form melted into water that fell back into the storm-tossed waters with a splash.

"Great," I muttered. I kicked a rock into the water. "Just great. Sundown. I know nothing. And the people I need to talk to screen all of their calls." I picked up another rock and threw it as hard as I could over the lake. The sound of rain swallowed up the splash.

I turned and trudged back toward the Beetle through

the thunder and the rain. I could see the shapes of the trees a bit better now. Dawn must be coming on, somewhere behind the clouds.

I sat down behind the wheel of the trusty Beetle, put the key in, and started the car.

The battered old Volkswagen wheezed once, lurched without being put into gear, and then started to fill with smoke. I choked and scrambled out of the car. I hit the release on the engine cover and opened it. Black smoke billowed out, and I could dimly see fire behind it, chewing up some part of the engine. I went back to the front storage compartment, got out the fire extinguisher, and put out the fire. Then I stood there in the rain, tired and aching and staring at my burnt engine.

Dawn. At Midsummer, that meant I had maybe fifteen hours to figure out how to get to the Mothers. Somehow, I doubted that their number was listed. Even if it had been, my visit to the battleground around the Stone Table had shown me that the Queens possessed far more power than I could have believed. Their sheer presence had nearly blown the top off my head from a mile away—and the Mothers were an order of magnitude above even Mab and Titania.

I had fifteen hours to find the killer and restore the Summer Knight's mantle to the Summer Court. And *then* to stop a war happening in some wild nether-place between here and the spirit world that I had no idea how to reach.

And my car had died. Again.

"Over your head," I muttered. "Harry, this is too big for you to handle alone."

The Council. I should contact Ebenezar, tell him what was happening. The situation was too big, too volatile, to risk screwing it up over a matter of Council protocol. Maybe I'd get lucky and the Council would A, believe me, and B, decide to help.

Yeah. And maybe if I glued enough feathers to my arms, I'd be able to fly.

Chapter

Twenty-four

I examined my car for a few minutes more, took a couple of things off it, and walked to the nearest gas station. I called a wrecker, then got a cab back to my apartment, paying for everything with Meryl's advance.

Once there, I got a Coke out of the icebox, put out fresh food and water for Mister, and changed his kitty litter. It wasn't until I had dug around under the kitchen sink, gotten out the bottle of dishwashing soap, and blown the dust off of it that I realized I was stalling.

I glowered at the phone and told myself, "Pride goeth before a fall, Harry. Pride can be bad. It can make you do stupid things."

I took a deep breath and shotgunned the Coke. Then I picked up the phone and dialed the number Morgan had left me.

It barely rang once before someone picked up and a male voice said, "Who is calling, please?"

"Dresden. I need to speak to Ebenezar McCoy."

"One moment." Sound cut off, and I figured whoever answered must have put their hand over the mouthpiece. Then there was a rustle as the phone changed hands.

"You've failed, then, Dresden," Morgan stated. His tone gave me a good mental picture of the smile on his smug face. "Stay where you are until the Wardens arrive to escort you to the Senior Council for judgment."

I bit down on a creative expletive. "I haven't failed, Morgan. But I've turned up some information that the Senior Council should have." Pride goeth, Harry. "And I need help. This is getting too hot for one person to handle. I need some information and some backup if I'm going to sort this out."

"It's always all about you, isn't it?" Morgan said, his voice bitter. "You're the exception to every rule. You can break the Laws and mock the Council, you can ignore the trial set for you because you are too important to abide by their authority."

"It's got nothing to do with that," I said. "Hell's bells, Morgan, pull your head out of your ass. The faeries' power structure has become unstable, and it looks like it might hit critical mass if something isn't done. That's bigger than me, and a hell of a lot more important than Council protocol."

Morgan screamed at me, his voice so vicious that it made me flinch. "Who are *you* to judge that? You are no one, Dresden! You are nothing!" He took a seething breath. "For too long you have flouted the Council's rule. No more. No more exceptions, no more delays, no more second chances."

"Morgan," I began, "I just need to speak to Ebenezar. Let him decide if—"

"No," Morgan said.

"What?"

"No. You won't evade justice this time, snake. This is your Trial. You will see it through without attempting to influence the Senior Council's judgment."

"Morgan, this is insane—"

"No. The insanity was in letting you live when you were a boy. DuMorne's murderous apprentice. Insanity was pulling you from that burning house two years ago." His voice dropped to an even more quiet register, the contrast to his previous tone unsettling. "Someone I dearly cared for was at Archangel, Dresden. And this time your lies aren't going to get you out of what's coming to you."

Then he hung up the phone.

I stared at the receiver for a second before snarling with rage and slamming it down on the end table, over and over, until the plastic broke in my hands. It hurt. I picked up the phone and threw it against the stone of the fireplace. It shattered, its bell chiming drunkenly. I kicked at the heaped mess of my living room, scattering old boxes, empty cans of Coke, books, papers, and startled cockroaches. After a few minutes of that, I was panting, and some of the blind, frustrated anger had begun to recede.

"Bastard," I growled. "That pigheaded, bigoted, self-righteous bastard."

I needed to cool off, and the shower seemed as good a place as any. I got under the cold water and tried to wash off the sweat and fear of the past day. I half expected the water to burst into steam on contact with my skin, but instead I was able to let the anger slip away while focusing on the old shower routine—water, soap, rinse, shampoo, rinse. By the time I finished and stepped out shivering, I felt almost completely nonpsychotic.

I had no idea how to contact Ebenezar. If he was under Warden security, and I'm sure he and the rest of the Senior Council were, there would be no easy way. The best magical countermeasures in the world would create a maze of misleading results for any spell or supernatural being that tried to find him.

For a moment, I debated asking Murphy for help. The Council tended to overlook any method that didn't involve the use of one kind of spell or another. Murphy's contacts in the force might be able to find them by purely old-fashioned methods. I decided against it. Even if Murphy traced the phone number down, Ebenezar might not be at it, and if I showed up there trying to get past the Wardens to get to him, it would be just the excuse Morgan needed to chop my head off.

I mussed up my hair with the towel and threw it on my narrow bed. Fine. I would do it without the Council's help.

I dressed again, putting on a pair of jeans and a white dress shirt still hanging in my closet. I rolled the sleeves up over my elbows. My sneakers were covered in muck, so I dragged my cowboy boots out of the closet and put them on. What the hell. Putting on the boots. Maybe it would do some good.

I got out my big sports bag, the kind you haul hockey gear around in. Into it went my blasting rod, my staff, and my sword cane, along with a backpack stocked with some candles, matches, a cup, a knife, a cardboard cylinder of salt, a canteen of blessed water, and various other bits of magical equipment I could use as needed. I threw in a box of old iron nails and a solid-steel Craftsman claw hammer with a black rubber grip, and put a couple of pieces of chalk in my pocket.

Then I slid the bag over my shoulder, went into the living room, and wrought the spell that would lead me to one of the very few people who might help.

Half an hour later, I paid the cabbie and walked into one of the hotels surrounding O'Hare International Airport. The subtle tug of the spell led me to the hotel's restaurant, open for breakfast and half full of mostly business types. I found Elaine at a corner table, a couple of buffet plates scattered with the remains of her breakfast. Her rich brown hair had been pulled back into a tight braid and coiled at the base of her neck. Her face looked pale, tired, with deep circles under her eyes. She was sipping coffee and reading a paperback novel. She wore a different pair of jeans, these a lot looser, and a billowy white shirt open over a dark tank top. She stiffened a beat after my eyes landed on her, and looked up warily.

I walked to her table, pulled out the chair next to her, and sat down. "Morning."

She watched me, her expression opaque. "Harry. How did you find me?"

"I got to thinking that same thing last night," I said. "How did you find me, that is. And I realized that you hadn't found me—you'd found my car. You were inside it and nearly unconscious when I got back to it. So I looked around the car." I pulled the cap to a tire's air valve out of my pocket and showed it to her. "And I found that one of these was missing. I figured you were probably the one who took it, and used it to home in on the Blue Beetle. So I took one of its mates from the other tires and used it to home in on the missing one."

"You named your car after a superhero on the *Electric Company*?" Elaine reached into a brown leather purse on the chair beside her and drew out an identical valve cap. "Clever."

I looked at the purse. What looked like airline tickets was sticking out of it. "You're running."

"You are a veritable wizard of the obvious, Harry." She started to shrug, and her face became ashen, her expression twisting with pain. She took a slow breath and then resumed the motion with her unwounded shoulder. "I feel well motivated to run."

"Do you really think a plane ticket will get you away from the Queens?"

"It will get me away from ground zero. That's enough. There's no way to find out who did it in time—and I don't feel like running up against another assassin. I barely got away from the first one."

I shook my head. "We're close," I said. "We have to be. They took a shot at me last night too. And I think I know who did both."

She looked up at me, sharply. "You do?"

I picked up a crust of toast she'd discarded, mopped it through some leftover eggs, and ate it. "Yeah. But you probably have to catch a flight."

Elaine rolled her eyes. "Tell you what. You stay here and feel smug. I'll get another plate and be back when you're done." She got up, rather stiffly, and walked over to the buffet. She loaded her plate up with eggs and bacon and sausage mixed in with some French toast, and came back to the table. My mouth watered.

She pushed the plate at me. "Eat."

I did, but between bites I asked, "Can you tell me what happened to you?"

She shook her head. "Not much to tell. I spoke with Mab and then with Maeve. I was on my way back to my hotel and someone jumped me in the parking lot. I was able to slip most of his first strike and called up enough fire to drive him away. Then I found your car."

"Why did you come to me?" I asked.

"Because I didn't know who did it, Harry. And I don't trust anyone else in this town."

My throat got a little tight. I borrowed her coffee to wash down the bacon. "It was Lloyd Slate."

Elaine's eyes widened. "The Winter Knight. How do you know?"

"While I was with Maeve, he came in carrying a knife in a box, and he'd been burned. It was coated in dried blood. Maeve was pretty furious that it wasn't any good to her."

Lines appeared between her eyebrows. "Slate . . . he was fetching my blood for her so that she could work a spell on me." She tried to cover it, but I saw her shiver. "He probably tailed me out of that party. Thank the stars I used fire."

I nodded. "Yeah. Dried out the blood, made it useless for whatever she wanted." I shoveled down some more food. "Then last night I got jumped by a hired gun and a couple of faerie beasties." I gave her the summary of the attack at Wal-Mart, leaving Murphy out of it.

"Maeve," Elaine said.

"It's about all I've got," I said. "It doesn't fit her very well, but—"

"Of course it fits her," Elaine said absently. "Don't tell me you fell for that psychotic dilettante nymphomaniac act she put on."

I blinked and then said through a mouthful of French toast, "No. 'Course not."

"She's smart, Harry. She's playing on your expectations."

I chewed the next bite more slowly. "It's a good theory. But that's all it is. We need to know more."

Elaine frowned at me. "You mean you want to talk to the Mothers."

I nodded. "I figure they might let a few things slip about how things work. But I don't know how to get there. I thought you might be able to ask someone in Summer."

She closed her paperback. "No."

"No, they won't help?"

"No, I'm not going to see the Mothers. Harry, it's insane. They're too strong. They could kill you—worse than kill you—with a stray thought."

"At this point I'm already in over my head. It doesn't matter how deep the water gets from here." I grimaced. "Besides, I don't really have a choice."

"You're wrong," she said with quiet emphasis. "You don't have to stay here. You don't have to play their game. Leave."

"Like you are?"

"Like I am," Elaine said. "You can't stop what's been

set in motion, Harry, but you can kill yourself trying. It's probably what Mab wanted to begin with."

"No. I can stop it."

She gave me a small smile. "Because you're in the right? Harry, it doesn't work like that."

"Don't I know it. But that's not why I think so."

"Then why?"

"You don't try to kill someone who isn't a threat to you. They took shots at both of us. They must think we can stop them."

"They, them," Elaine said. "Even if we are close, we don't know who 'they' is."

"That's why we talk to the Mothers," I told her. "They're the strongest of the Queens. They know the most. If we're smart, and lucky, we can get information from them."

Elaine reached up to tug at her braid, her expression uncertain. "Harry, look. I'm not . . . I don't want to . . ." She closed her eyes for a moment and then said in a voice, pained, "Please, don't ask me to do this."

"You don't have to go," I said. "Just find me the way to them. Just try."

"You don't understand the kind of trouble you're asking for," she said.

I looked down at my empty plate and said quietly, "Yeah. I do. I hate it, Elaine, and I'm afraid, and I must be half insane not to just dig myself a hole and pull it in after me. But I understand." I reached across the table and put my hand over hers. Her skin was soft, warm, and she shivered at the touch. "Please."

Her hand turned up, fingers curling briefly against

mine. My turn to shiver. Elaine sighed. "You're an imbecile, Harry. You're such a fool."

"I guess some things don't change."

She let out a subdued laugh before withdrawing her hand and standing. "I've got a favor left to me. I'll call it in. Wait here."

Five minutes later, she was back. "All right. Outside."

I stood. "Thank you, Elaine. You going to make your plane?"

She opened her purse and tossed the airline tickets onto the table along with a pair of twenties. "I guess not." Then she took a couple of other items out of the purse: a slave-ring of ivory carved in the shape of a ring of oak leaves and attached to a similar bracelet by a silver chain. An earring fashioned of what might have been copper and a teardrop-shaped black stone. Then an anklet dangling with bangles shaped like bird wings. She put them all on, then looked at my gym bag. "Still going with the phallic foci, eh? Staff and rod?"

"They make me feel all manly."

Her mouth twitched, and she started for the exit. I followed her and found myself opening doors for her out of habit. She didn't seem to be too horribly upset by it.

Outside, cars pulled up into a circle drive at the front of the hotel, airport shuttles disgorging and swallowing travelers, taxis picking up men and women in business suits. Elaine slipped the strap of her purse over her good shoulder and stood there quietly.

Maybe thirty seconds later, I heard the clopping of hooves on blacktop. A carriage rolled into sight, drawn by a pair of horses. One of them was the blue-white color of a drowned corpse, and its breath steamed in the air. The other was grass-green, its mane sown with wildflowers. The carriage itself looked like something from Victorian London, all dark wood and brass filigree—and no one was driving it. The horses came to a halt directly before us and stood there, stamping their feet and tossing their manes. The door to the carriage swung open in silence. No one was inside.

I took a surreptitious look around me. None of the straights seemed to have noticed the carriage or the unworldly horses pulling it. A taxi heading for the space the carriage occupied abruptly veered to one side and found another spot. I made an effort and could sense the whisper of enchantment around the carriage, subtle and strong, probably encouraging the straights not to notice it.

"I guess this is our ride," I said.

"You think?" Elaine flipped her braid back over one shoulder and climbed in. "This will take us there, but we won't have any protection on the other side. Just remember, Harry, I told you this was a bad idea."

"Preemptive I-told-you-sos," I said. "Now I've seen everything."

Chapter

Twenty-five

The carriage took off so smoothly that I almost didn't feel it. I leaned over the window and twitched the shade aside. We pulled away from the hotel and into traffic with no one the wiser, cars giving us a wide berth even while not noting us. That was one hell of a veil. The carriage didn't jounce at all, and after about a minute wisps of mist began to brush up against the windows. Not long after, the mists blocked out the view of the city entirely. The street sounds faded, and all that was left was silver-grey mist and the clop of horse hooves.

The carriage stopped perhaps five minutes later, and the door swung open. I opened my gym bag and took out my rod and staff. I slipped the sword cane through my belt and drew out my amulet to lie openly on my chest. Elaine did the same with hers. Then we got out of the carriage.

I took a slow look at my surroundings. We stood on some kind of spongy grass, on a low, rolling hill surrounded by other low, rolling hills. The mist lay over the land like a crippled storm cloud, sluggish and thick in some places, thinner in others. The landscape was dotted with the occasional tree, boles thick and twisted, branches scrawny and long. A tattered-looking raven crouched on a nearby branch, its bead-black eyes gleaming.

"Cheery," Elaine said.

"Yeah. Very Baskerville." The carriage started up again, and I looked back to see it vanishing into the mist. "Okay. Where to now?"

At my words the raven let out a croaking caw. It shook itself, bits of moldy feather drifting down, and then beat its wings a few times and settled on another branch, almost out of sight.

"Harry," Elaine said.

"Yeah?"

"If you make any corny joke using the word 'nevermore,' I'm going to punch you. Do you understand me?"

"Never more," I confirmed. Elaine rolled her eyes. Then we both started off after the raven.

It led us through the cloudy landscape, flitting silently from tree to tree. We trudged behind it until more trees began to rise in the mist ahead of us, thickening. The ground grew softer, the air more wet, cloying. The raven let out another caw, then vanished into the trees and out of sight.

I peered after it and said, "Do you see a light back there in the trees?"

"Yes. This must be the place."

"Fine." I started forward. Elaine caught my wrist and said in a sharp and warning tone, "Harry."

She nodded toward a thick patch of shadows where two trees had fallen against one another. I had just begun to pick out a shape when it moved and came forward, close enough that I could make it out clearly.

The unicorn looked like a Budweiser horse, one of the huge draft beasts used for heavy labor. It had to have been eighteen hands high, maybe more. It had a broad chest, four heavy hooves, forward-pricked ears, and a long equine face.

That was where its resemblance to a Clydesdale ended.

It didn't have a coat. It just had a smooth and slick-looking carapace, all chitinous scales and plates, mixing colors of dark green and midnight black. Its hooves were cloven and stained with old blood. One spiraling horn rose from its forehead, at least three feet long and wickedly pointed. The spirals were serrated on the edges, some of them covered with rust-brown stains. A pair of curling horns, like those of a bighorn sheep, curved around the sides of its head from the base of the horn. It didn't have any eyes—just smooth, leathery chitin where they should have been. It tossed its head, and a mane of rotted cobwebs danced around its neck and forelegs, long and tattered as a burial shroud.

A large moth fluttered through the mist near the unicorn. The beast whirled, impossibly nimble, and lunged. Its spiral skewered the moth, and with a savage shake of its head, the unicorn threw the moth to the earth and pulverized the ground it landed on with sledgehammer blows of the blades of its hooves. It snorted after that, and then turned to pace silently back into the mist-covered trees.

Elaine's eyes widened and she looked at me.

I glanced at her. "Unicorns," I said. "Very dangerous. You go first."

She arched an eyebrow.

"Maybe not," I relented. "A guardian?"

"Obviously," Elaine said. "How do we get past it?"

"Blow it up?"

"Tempting," Elaine said. "But I don't think it will make much of an impression on the Mothers if we kill their watchdog. A veil?"

I shook my head. "I don't think unicorns rely on the normal senses. If I remember right, they sense thoughts."

"In that case it shouldn't notice you."

"Hah," I said in a monotone. "Hah-hah, ho-ho, oh my ribs. I have a better plan. I go through while you distract it."

"With what? I'm fresh out of virginity. And that thing doesn't look much like the unicorns I saw in Summer. It's a lot less . . . prancy."

"With thoughts," I said. "They sense thoughts, and they're attracted to purity. Your concentration was always better than mine. Theoretically, if you can keep an image in your head, it should focus on it and not you."

"Think of a wonderful thought. Great plan, Peter Pan."

"You have a better one?"

Elaine shook her head. "Okay. I'll try to lead him down there." She gestured down the line of trees. "Once I do, get moving."

I nodded, and Elaine closed her eyes for a moment before her features smoothed over into relaxation. She started forward and into the trees, walking at a slow and measured pace.

The unicorn appeared again, ten feet in front of Elaine. The beast snorted and pawed at the earth and reared up on its hind legs, tossing its mane. Then it started forward at a slow and cautious walk.

Elaine held out her hand to it. It let out a gurgling whicker and nuzzled her palm. Still moving with dreamlike slowness, Elaine turned and began walking down the length of the lines of trees. The unicorn followed a pace or two behind her, the tip of its horn bobbing several inches above Elaine's right shoulder.

They'd gone several paces before I saw that the plan wasn't working. The unicorn's body language changed. Its ears flattened back to its skull, and its feet shifted restlessly before it finally rose up on its hind hooves, preparing to lunge, with the deadly horn centered on Elaine's back.

There wasn't time to shout a warning. I lifted my blasting rod in my right hand, summoned the force of my will, and pushed it through the focus with a shout of *"Fuego!"*

Fire erupted from the tip of the rod, a scarlet ribbon of heat and flame and force that lanced out toward the unicorn. After having seen how spectacularly useful my magic wasn't on the Ogre Grum, I didn't want to chance another faerie beast shrugging it off. So I wasn't shooting for the unicorn itself—but for the ground at its feet.

The blast ripped a three-foot trench in the earth, and the unicorn screamed and thrashed its head, trying to keep its balance. A normal horse would have toppled, but the unicorn somehow managed to get a couple of feet onto solid ground and hurled itself away in a forty-foot standing leap. It landed on its feet, already running, body sweeping in a circle to bring it charging toward me.

I ran for the nearest tree. The unicorn was faster, but I didn't have far to go, and I put the trunk between us.

It didn't slow down. Its horn slammed into the trunk of the dead tree and came through it as though it hadn't been there. I flinched away, but not fast enough to avoid catching several flying splinters in the chest and belly, and not fast enough to avoid a nasty cut on my left arm where one of those serrated edges of the horn ripped through my shirt. The pain of the injuries registered, but only as background data. I stepped around the bole of the tree, taking my staff in both hands, and swung it as hard as I could at the delicate bones of the unicorn's rear ankle.

Well, on a horse they're delicate. Evidently on unicorns, they're just a bit tender. The faerie beast let out a furious scream and twisted its body, tearing through the tree, shredding it as it whipped its horn free and whirled to orient on me. It lunged, the horn spearing toward me. I swept my staff up, a simple parry *quatre*, and shoved the tip out past my body while darting a pair of steps to my right, avoiding the beast's oncoming weight. I kept going, ducking a beat before the unicorn planted its forequarters, lifted its hind, and twisted, lashing out toward my head with both rear hooves. I rolled, came up running, and ducked behind the next tree. The unicorn turned and began stalking toward me, circling the tree, foam pattering from its open mouth.

Elaine cried out, and I whipped my head around to

see her lifting her right hand, the ring on it releasing a cloud of glowing motes that burst around her in a swarm. The little lights streaked toward the unicorn and gathered around it, swirling and flashing in a dazzling cloud. One of them brushed against me, and my senses abruptly went into whiteout, overwhelmed with a simple image of walking down a sidewalk in worn shoes, the sun bright overhead, a purse bumping on my hip, stomach twinging with pleasant hunger pangs, the scent of hot asphalt in my nose, children laughing and splashing somewhere nearby. A memory, something from Elaine. I staggered and pushed it away from me, regaining my senses.

The motes crowded around the unicorn, darting in to brush against it one at a time, and at each touch the faerie beast went wild. It spun and kicked and screamed and lashed out with its horn, lunging at insubstantial adversaries in wild frenzy, but all to no avail.

I looked past them to see Elaine standing in place, her hand extended, her face set in an expression of concentration and strain. "Harry," she shouted. "Go. I'll hold it."

I rose, heart pounding. "You got it?"

"For a little while. Just get to the Mothers," Elaine responded. *"Hurry!"*

"I don't want to leave you alone."

A bead of sweat trickled down the side of her face. "You won't be. When it gets loose, I'm not waiting around for it to skewer me."

I gritted my teeth. I didn't want to leave Elaine, but to be fair, she'd done better than I had. She stood against the unicorn still, only a dozen long strides away, her hand extended, the creature as contained as if she'd wrapped it in a net. My slender and straight and beautiful Elaine.

Memories, images washed through me, dozens of little things I'd forgotten coming back to me all at once; her laugh, quiet and wicked in the darkness; the feeling of her slender fingers slipping through mine; her face, asleep on the pillow beside me, gentle and peaceful in the morning sun.

There were many more, but I pushed them away. That had been a long time ago, and they wouldn't mean a thing if neither of us survived the next few minutes and hours.

I turned my back on her, left her struggling against the strength of that nightmarish unicorn, and ran toward the lights in the mist.

Chapter

Twenty-six

The Nevernever is a big place. In fact, it's the biggest place. The Nevernever is what the wizards call the entirety of the realm of spirit. It isn't a physical place, with geography and weather patterns and so on. It's a shadow world, a magical realm, and its substance is as mutable as thought. It has a lot of names, like the Other Side and the Next World, and it contains within it just about any kind of spirit realm you can imagine, somewhere. Heaven, Hell, Olympus, Elysium, Tartarus, Gehenna—you name it, and it's in the Nevernever somewhere. In theory, at any rate.

The parts of the Nevernever closest to the mortal world are almost completely controlled by the Sidhe. This part of the spirit realm is called Faerie, and has close ties with our own natural world. As a result, Faerie resembles the real world in a lot of ways. It is fairly permanent and unchanging, for example, and has several versions of weather. But make no mistake—it isn't Earth. The rules of reality don't apply as tightly as they do in our world, so Faerie can be viciously treacherous. Most who go into it never come back.

And I had a gut feeling that I was running through the heart of Faerie.

The ground sloped down and grew wetter, softer. The mist swallowed sound quickly behind me, until all I could hear was my own labored breathing. The run made my heart pound, and my wounded hand throbbed painfully. There was a certain amount of exhilaration to the movement, my limbs and muscles stretching and feeling alive after several months of disuse. I couldn't have kept up the pace for long, but luckily I didn't have far to go.

The lights turned out to be a pair of lit windows in a cottage that stood by itself on a slight rise of ground. Stone obelisks the size of coffins, some fallen and cracked and others still upright, stood scattered in loose rings around the mound. The raven rested on one of them, its beady eyes gleaming. It let out another croaking sound and flew through an open window of the cottage.

I stood there panting for a minute, trying to get my breath, before I walked up to the door. My flesh began to crawl with a shivering sensation. I took a step back and looked at the house. Stone walls. A thatch roof. I could smell mildew beneath an odor of fresh-baked bread. The door was made of some kind of heavy, weathered wood, and the snowflake symbol I'd seen before had been carved into it. Mother Winter, then. If she was anything like Mab, she would have the kind of power that would give any wizard the creeps. It would just hang in the air around her, like body warmth. Except that it would take a lot of body to feel its warmth through stone walls and a heavy door. Gulp.

I lifted my hand to knock, and the door swung open

of its own accord, complete with a melodramatic Hammer Films whimper of rusting hinges.

A voice, little more than a creaking whisper, said, "Come in, boy. We have been expecting you."

Double gulp. I wiped my palms on my jeans and made sure I had a good grip on both staff and rod before I stepped across the threshold and into the dim cottage.

The place was all one room. The floor was wooden, though the boards looked weathered and dry. Shelves stood against the stone walls. A loom rested in the far corner, near the fireplace, a spinning wheel beside it. Before the fireplace sat a rocking chair, occupied, squeaking as it moved. A figure sat in it, shrouded in a shawl, a hood, as though someone had animated a bundle of blankets and cloth. On the hearth above the fireplace sat several sets of teeth, more or less human-sized. One looked simple enough, all white and even. The next was rotted-looking, with chipped incisors and a broken molar. The next set had all pointed teeth, stained with bits of rusty brown and what looked like rotten bits of flesh stuck between them. The last was made out of some kind of silvery metal, shining like a sword.

"Interesting," came the creaking voice from the creaking chair. "Most interesting. Can you feel it?"

"Uh," I said.

From the other side of the cottage, a brisk voice tsked, and I spun to face the newcomer. Another woman, stooped with age, blew dust from a shelf and ran a cloth over it before replacing the bottles and jars. She turned and eyed me with glittering green eyes from within a weathered but rosy face. "Of course I do. The poor child. He's walked a thorny path." The elderly lady came to me and put her hands firmly on either side of my head, peering at either eye. "Scars here, some. Stick out your tongue, boy."

I blinked. "Uh?"

"Stick out your tongue," she repeated in a crisp tone. I did. She peered at my tongue and my throat and said, "Strength, though. And he can be clever, at times. It would seem your daughter chose ably."

I closed my mouth and she released my head. "Mother Summer, I presume?"

She beamed up at me. "Yes, dear. And this is Mother Winter." She gestured vaguely at the chair by the fire. "Don't be offended if she doesn't get up. It's the wrong season, you know. Hand me that broom."

I blinked, then reached over to pick up the ramshackle old broom with a gnarled handle and passed it to Mother Summer. The old lady took it and immediately began sweeping the dusty floor of the old cottage.

"Bah," whispered Mother Winter. "The dust is just going to come back."

"It's the principle of the thing," Summer said. "Isn't that right, boy?"

I sneezed and mumbled something noncommittal. "Uh, pardon me, ladies. But I wondered if you could answer a few questions for me."

Winter's head seemed to turn slightly toward me from within her hood. Mother Summer stopped and eyed me, her grass-green eyes sparkling. "You wish answers?"

"Yes," I said.

"How can you expect to get them," Winter wheezed, "when you do not yet know the proper questions?"

"Uh," I said again. Brilliance incarnate, that's me.

Summer shook her head and said, "An exchange, then," she said. "We will ask you a question. And for your answer, we will each give you an answer to what you seek."

"No offense, but I didn't come here so that you could ask me questions."

"Are you sure?" Mother Summer asked. She swept a pile of dust past me and out the door. "How do you know you didn't?"

Mother Winter's rasping whisper came to me, disgusted. "She'll prattle on all day. Answer us the questions, boy. Or get out."

I took a deep breath. "All right," I said. "Ask."

Mother Winter turned back to face the fire. "Simply tell us, boy. Which is more important. The body—"

"—or the soul," Mother Summer picked up. They both fell silent, and I felt their focus on me like the tip of a knife resting against my skin.

"I suppose that would depend on who was asking whom," I said, finally.

"We ask," Winter whispered.

Summer nodded. "And we ask *you*."

I thought about my words for a moment before I spoke.

I know, it shocked me too.

"Then I would say that were I old, sick, and dying, I would believe that the soul is more important. And if

I was a man about to be burned at the stake in order to preserve his soul, I would believe that the body is more important."

The words fell on a long moment of silence. I found myself shifting my feet restlessly.

"Fairly said," Mother Winter rasped at last.

"Wise enough," Summer agreed. "Why did you give that answer, boy?"

"Because it's a stupid question. The answer isn't as simple as one or the other."

"Precisely," Summer said. She walked to the fire and withdrew a baking sheet on a long handle. A roundish loaf of bread was on it. She set it on a rack to cool. "This child sees what she does not."

"It is not in her nature," Winter murmured. "She is what she is."

Mother Summer sighed and nodded. "These are strange times."

"Hold on," I said. "What are you talking about, here? It's Maeve, isn't it?"

Mother Winter made a quiet wheezing sound that might have been a laugh.

"I answered your questions," I said. "So pay up."

"Patience, boy," Mother Summer said. She took a kettle from a hook by the fireplace and poured tea into a pair of cups. She dipped what looked like honey into each, then cream, and gave one to Mother Winter.

I waited until each of them had sipped before I said, "Right, patience expired. I can't afford to wait. Tonight is Midsummer. Tonight the balance begins to tilt back to

Winter, and Maeve is going to try to use the Stone Table to steal the Summer Knight's mantle for keeps."

"Indeed. Something to be prevented at all costs." Mother Summer arched an eyebrow. "Then what is your question?"

"Who killed the Summer Knight? Who stole his mantle?"

Mother Summer gave me a disappointed glance and sipped her tea.

Mother Winter lifted her tea to her hood. I still couldn't see her face—but her hand looked withered, the fingers tinged with blue. She lowered her cup and said, "You ask a foolish question, boy. You are more clever than this."

I folded my arms. "What is that supposed to mean?"

Mother Summer frowned at Winter, but said, "It means that who is not as important as *why*."

"And *how*," Mother Winter added.

"Think, boy," Summer said. "What has the theft of the mantle accomplished?"

I frowned. War between the Courts, for one. Odd activity in the magical and natural world alike. But mostly the coming war, Winter and Summer gathering to battle at the Stone Table.

"Exactly," Winter whispered. The skin on the back of my neck rippled with a cold and unpleasant sensation. Hell's bells, she'd heard me *thinking*. "But think, wizard. How was it done? Theft is theft, whether the prize is food, or riches, or beauty or power."

Since it didn't seem to matter either way, I did my

thinking out loud. "When something is stolen a couple of things can happen to it. It can be carried away where it cannot be reached."

"Hoarded," Summer put in. "Such as the dragons do."

"Yeah, okay. Uh, it can be destroyed."

"No, it can't," Mother Winter said. "Your own sage tells you that. The German fellow with the wild hair."

"Einstein," I muttered. "Okay, then, but it can be rendered valueless. Or it can be sold to someone else."

Mother Summer nodded. "Both of which are *change*."

I held up a hand. "Hold it, hold it. Look, as I understand it, this power of the Summer Knight, his mantle, it can't just exist on its own. It has to be inside a vessel."

"Yes," Winter murmured. "Within one of the Queens, or within the Knight."

"And it isn't with one of the Queens."

"True," Summer said. "We would sense it, were it so."

"So it's already in another Knight," I said. "But if that was true, there'd be no imbalance." I scratched at my head, and as I did it slowly dawned on me. "Unless it had been changed. Unless the new Knight had been changed. Transformed into something else. Something that left the power trapped, inert, useless."

Both of them regarded me steadily, silently.

"All right," I said. "I have my question."

"Ask it," they said together.

"How does the mantle pass on from one Knight to the next?"

Mother Summer smiled, but the expression was a

grim one. "It returns to the nearest reflection of itself. To the nearest vessel of Summer. She, in turn, chooses the next Knight."

That meant that only one of the Queens of Summer could be behind it. Titania was out already—she had begun the war against Mab because she didn't know where the mantle was. Mother Summer would not have been telling me this information if she'd been the one to do it. That left only one person.

"Stars and stones," I muttered. "Aurora."

The two Mothers set down their teacups together. "Time presses," Summer said.

"That which must not be may be," Winter continued.

"You, we judge, are the one who may set things aright once more—"

"—if you are strong enough."

"Brave enough."

"Whoa, hold your horses," I said. "Can't I just bring this out to Mab and Titania?"

"Beyond talk now," Mother Winter said. "They go to war."

"Stop them," I said. "You two have to be stronger than Mab and Titania. Make them shut up and listen to you."

"Not that simple," Winter said.

Summer nodded. "We have power, but bound within certain limits. We cannot interfere with the Queens or Ladies. Not even on a matter so dire as this."

"What *can* you do?"

"I?" Summer said. "Nothing."

I frowned and looked from her to Mother Winter.

One aged, cracked hand lifted and beckoned me. "Come closer, boy."

I started to say no. But my feet moved without asking the rest of me, and I knelt in front of Mother Winter's rocking chair. I couldn't see her, even from here. Even her feet were covered by layers of dark cloth. But on her lap rested a pair of knitting needles, and a simple square of cloth, trailing thick threads of grey, undyed wool. Mother Winter reached down with her withered hands, and took up a pair of rusted shears. She cut the trailing threads and passed me the cloth.

I took it, again without thinking. It felt soft, cold as if it had been in a refrigerator, and it tingled with a subtle, dangerous energy.

"It isn't tied off," I said quietly.

"Nor should it be," Winter said. "It is an Unraveling."

"A what?"

"An unmaking, boy. I am the unmaker, the destroyer. It is what I am. Bound within those threads is the power to undo any enchantment done. Touch the cloth to that which must be undone. Unravel the threads. It will be so."

I stared at the square cloth for a moment, then asked quietly, "*Any* enchantment? Any transformation?"

"Any."

My hands started shaking. "You mean . . . I could use this to undo what the vampires did to Susan. Just wipe it away. Make her mortal again."

"You could, Emissary." Mother Winter's tone held a bone-dry amusement.

I swallowed and rose, folding up the cloth. I slipped it into my pocket, careful not to let any threads trail out. "Is this a gift?"

"No," Winter rasped. "But a necessity."

"What am I supposed to do with it?"

Mother Summer shook her head. "It is yours now, and yours to employ. We have reached the limits of how we may act. The rest is yours."

"Make haste," Winter whispered.

Mother Summer nodded. "No time remains. Be swift and wise, mortal child. Go with our blessings."

Winter withdrew her frail hands into the sleeves of her robe. "Do not fail, boy."

"Hell's bells, no pressure," I muttered. I gave each of them a short bow and turned for the door. I stepped over the threshold of the cottage and said, "Oh, by the way. I apologize if we did any harm to your unicorn on the way in."

I looked back to see Mother Summer arch a brow. Winter's head shifted, and I could see the gleam of light on yellow teeth. Her voice rasped, "What unicorn?"

The door shut, again of its own accord. I glowered at the wood for a moment and then muttered, "Freaking weirdo faerie biddies." I turned and started back the way I had come. The Unraveling was a cool weight in my pocket, and promised to get uncomfortably chilly if I left it there too long.

The thought of the Unraveling made me walk faster, excitement skipping through me. If what the Mothers said was true, I'd be able to use the cloth to help Susan, which was something just this side of divine intervention. All I had to do was to finish up this case, and then I could go find her.

Of course, I thought sourly, finishing up this case was likely to kill me. The Mothers may have given me some insight, and a magic doily, but they sure as hell hadn't given me a freaking clue as to how to resolve this—and, I realized, they hadn't really *said*, "Aurora did it." I knew they had to speak the truth to me, and their statements had led me to that conclusion—but how much of it was this mysterious prohibition from direct involvement and how much of it had been another fistful of faerie trickery?

"Make haste," I rasped, trying to impersonate Winter's voice. "We have reached the limits," I said, mimicking Summer. I quickened my pace, and frowned over that last little comment Winter had made. She had taken an almost palpable glee in making it, as though it had given her an opening she wouldn't otherwise have had.

What unicorn?

I gnawed over the question. If it was indeed a statement of importance, not just a passing mutter, then it had to mean something.

I frowned. It meant that there hadn't *been* a guardian around the little cottage. Or at least not one Mother Winter had put there.

So who had?

The answer hit me low in the gut, a sensation of physical sickness coming along with the realization. I stopped and clawed for my Sight.

I didn't get to it before Grum came out from under a veil, Elaine standing close behind him. He caught me flat-footed. The ogre drove a sledgehammer fist toward my face. There was a flash of impact, a sensation of falling, and cool earth beneath my cheek.

Then the scent of Elaine's subtle perfume.

Then blackness.

Chapter
Twenty-seven

I came to on the ground of that dark Nevernever wood. Spirit realm or not, I felt cold and started shivering uncontrollably. That made playing possum pretty much impossible, so I sat up and tried to take stock.

I didn't feel any new bruises or breaks, so I hadn't been pounded while I was out. It probably hadn't been long. Mother Winter's Unraveling was no longer in my pocket. My bag was gone, as was my ring and my bracelet. My staff and rod, needless to say, had been taken as well. I could still feel my mother's pentacle amulet against my chest, though, which came as something of a surprise. My hand throbbed, where Mab had driven the freaking letter opener through it.

Other than that, I felt more or less whole. Huzzah.

I squinted at my surroundings next and found a ring of toadstools grown up around me. They weren't huge, tentacular, horribly fanged toadstools or anything, but it put a little chill in me all the same. I lifted my hand and reached out for them tentatively, extending my wizard's senses along with the gesture. I hit a wall. I couldn't think of another way to describe it. Where the ring began, my ability to reach, move, and perceive with my supernatural senses simply ended.

Trapped. Double huzzah.

Only after I'd gotten an idea of my predicament did I stand up and face my captors.

There were five of them, which seemed less than fair. I recognized the nearest right away—Aurora, the Summer Lady, now dressed in what I could only describe as a battle gown, made out of some kind of silver mail as fine and light as cloth. It clung closely to her, from the top of her throat down to her wrists and ankles, and shone with its own dim radiance in the forest's gloom. She wore a sword at her hip, and upon her pale hair rested a garland of living leaves. She turned green eyes to me, heartbreakingly lovely, and regarded me with an expression both sad and resolved.

"Wizard," Aurora said, "I regret that it has come to this. But you have come too close to interfering. Once you had served your purpose, I could not allow you to continue your involvement."

I grimaced and looked past her, at the ogre Grum, huge and scarlet-skinned and silent, and the horrific unicorn that had apparently been guarding the way to Mother Winter's cottage.

"What do you intend to do with me?"

"Kill you," Aurora said, her voice gentle. "I regret the necessity. But you're too dangerous to be allowed to live."

I squinted at her. "Then why haven't you?"

"Good question," said the fourth person present—Lloyd Slate, the Winter Knight. He still wore his biker leathers, but he'd added bits of mail and a few metal plates to the ensemble. He wore a sword at his hip, another on his back, and bore a heavy pistol on his belt. The gaunt, tense hunger of his expression hadn't changed. He looked nervous and angry. "If it had been up to me, I'd have cut your throat when Grum first dropped you."

"Why call him Grum?" I said, scowling at the ogre. "You might as well drop the glamour, Lord Marshal. There's not much point to it now."

The ogre's face twisted with surprise.

I glared spitefully at the dark unicorn and spat, "You too, Korrick."

Both ogre and unicorn glanced at Aurora. The Faerie Queen never took her eyes off me, but nodded. The ogre's form blurred and twisted, and resolved itself into the form of Talos, the Sidhe lord from Aurora's penthouse at the Rothchild. His pale hair had been drawn back into a fighting braid, and he wore close-fit mail of some glittering black metal that made him look rail-thin and deadly.

At the same time the unicorn shook itself and rose up into the hulking form of Korrick, the centaur, also dressed in mail and bearing weapons of faerie make. He stamped one huge hoof and said nothing.

Aurora walked in a circle around me, frowning. "How long have you known, wizard?"

I shrugged. "Not long. I started getting it on the way out of Mother Winter's cottage. Once I knew where to start, it wasn't hard to start adding up the numbers."

"We don't have time for this," Slate said and spat on the ground to one side.

"If he puzzled it out, others may have as well," Aurora said, her voice patient. "We should know if any other opposition is coming. Tell me, wizard. How did you piece it together?"

"Go to hell," I snapped.

Aurora turned to the last person there and asked, "Can he be reasoned with?"

Elaine stood a little apart from the others, her back to them. My bag rested on the ground near her feet, and my rod and staff lay there too. She'd added a cloak of emerald green to her outfit, somehow making it look natural. She glanced at Aurora and then at me. She averted her eyes quickly, "You've already told him you're going to kill him. He won't cooperate."

Aurora shook her head. "More sacrifices. I am sorry you pushed me to this, wizard."

Her hand moved. Some unseen force jerked my chin up, my eyes to hers. They flashed, a ripple of colors, and I felt the force of her mind, her will, glide past my defenses and into me. I lost my balance and staggered, leaning helplessly against the invisible solidity of the circle she'd imprisoned me in. I tried to fight it, but it was like trying to push water up a hill—nothing for me to strain against, nothing for me to focus upon. I was on her turf, trapped in a circle of her power. She flowed into me, down through my eyes, and all I could do was watch the pretty colors.

"Now," she said, and her voice was the gentlest,

sweetest thing I'd ever heard. "What did you learn of the Summer Knight's death?"

"You were behind it," I heard myself saying, my voice slow and heavy. "You had him killed."

"How?"

"Lloyd Slate. He hates Maeve. You recruited him to help you. Elaine took him inside Reuel's building, through the Nevernever. He fought Reuel. That's why there was ooze on the stairs. The water on Reuel's arms and legs was where Summer fire met Winter ice. Slate threw him down the stairs and broke his neck."

"And his mantle of power?"

"Redirected," I mumbled. "You gathered it in and placed it into another person."

"Who?"

"The changeling girl," I said. "Lily. You gave her the mantle and then you turned her to stone. That statue in your garden. It was right in front of me."

"Very good," Aurora said, and the gentle praise rippled through me. I fought to regain my senses, to escape the glittering green prison of her eyes. "What else?"

"You hired the ghoul. The Tigress. You sent her after me before Mab even spoke to me."

"I do not know this ghoul. You are incorrect, wizard. I do not hire killers. Continue."

"You set me up before I came to interview you."

"In what way?" Aurora pressed.

"Maeve must have ordered Slate to take Elaine out. He made it look like he tried and missed, but Elaine played it for more. You helped her fake the injury."

"Why did I do that?"

"To keep me upset, worried, so that when I spoke to you I wouldn't have the presence of mind to corner you with a question. That's why you attacked me, too. Telling me what a monster I'd become. To keep me off balance, keep me from asking the right questions."

"Yes," Aurora said. "And after that?"

"You decided to take me out. You sent Talos, Elaine, and Slate to kill me. And you created that construct in the garden center."

Slate stepped closer. "Spooky," he said. "He doesn't *look* all that smart."

"Yet he used only reason. Plus knowledge doubtless gained from the Queens and Mothers. He put it together for himself, rather than being told." At that, her gaze slanted past me, to Elaine. I tried to pull away and couldn't.

"Great," Slate said. "No one squealed. Can we kill the great Kreskin now?"

Aurora held up a hand to Slate, and asked me, "Do you know my next objective?"

"You knew that if you bound up the Summer Knight's mantle, Mother Winter would provide an Unraveling to free it and restore the balance. You waited for her to give it to me. Now you're going to take it and the statue of Lily. You're going to take her to the Stone Table during the battle. You'll use the Unraveling, free Lily from being stone, and kill her on the table after midnight. The Summer Knight's power will go to Winter permanently. You want to destroy the balance of power in Faerie. I don't know why."

Aurora's eyes flashed dangerously. She removed her gaze from mine, and it was like suddenly falling back *up* a flight of stairs. I staggered back, tearing my eyes from her and focusing on the ground.

"*Why?* It should be obvious to you why, wizard. You of all people." She spun in a glitter of silvery mail, pacing restlessly back and forth. "The cycle must be broken. Summer and Winter, constantly chasing each other, wounding what the other heals and healing what the other wounds. Our war, our senseless contest, waged for no reason other than that it has always been so—and mortals trapped between us, crushed by the struggle, made pawns and toys." She took a shuddering, angry breath. "It must end. And I will end it."

I ground my teeth, shivering. "You'll end it by sending the natural world into chaos?"

"I did not set the price," Aurora hissed. I caught sight of her eyes out of the corner of my vision and started tracking up to her face. I forced my gaze down again, barely in time. She continued speaking, in a low, impassioned voice. "I hate it. I hate every moment of the things I've had to do to accomplish this—but it should have been done long since, wizard. Delay is just as deadly. How many have died or been tormented to madness by Maeve, and those like her? You yourself have been tortured, abused, nearly enslaved by them. I do what *must* be done."

I swallowed and said, "Harming and endangering mortal kind in order to help them. That's insane."

"Perhaps," Aurora said. "But it is the only way." She

faced me again and asked, her voice cold, "Does the White Council know what you have discovered?"

"Bite me, faerie fruitcake."

Slate stifled a laugh, hiding it under a cough. I felt more than saw Aurora's sudden surge of rage, sparked by the Winter Knight but directed at me. A flare of light erupted from her, and I felt a sudden heat against the side of my body nearest her. The hairs on my arm rose straight up. Her voice rang out, hot and violent and strong. "What did you say, ape?"

"They don't," Elaine said, her voice tense. She put herself between me and Aurora, her back to me. "He told me before we left for the Mothers'. The Council doesn't realize the depth of what's happening. By the time they do, it will be too late for them to act."

"Fine," Slate said. "He's the last loose end, then. Kill him and let's get on with it."

"Dammit, Slate," I said. "Use your head, man. What do you think you're going to get out of helping her like this?"

Slate gave me a cold smile. "That old bastard Reuel's power, for one thing. I'll be twice the Knight I was before—and then I'm going to settle some accounts with that little bitch Maeve." He licked his lips. "After that, Aurora and I will decide what to do next."

I let out a harsh bray of laughter. "I hope you got that in writing, dimwit. Do you really think she would let a man, and a mortal at that, have that much power over her?" Slate's eyes became wary, and I pressed him. "Think about it. Has she ever given it to you straight, a statement, not a question or a dodge, or something she's led you to assume?"

Suspicion grew in his gaze, but Aurora laid a hand on his shoulder. Slate's eyes grew a little cloudy at her touch, and he closed them. "Peace, my Knight," the Summer Lady murmured. "The wizard is a trickster, and desperate. He would say anything he thought might save him. Nothing has changed between us."

I ground my teeth at the meaningless words, but Aurora had Slate's number, whatever it was. Maybe all that time in Maeve's company had softened him, the drugs and pleasures she fed him making him more open to suggestion. Maybe Aurora had just found a hole in his psychology. Either way, he wasn't going to listen to me.

I looked around, but Korrick and Talos ignored me. Aurora kept on whispering to Slate. That left only one person to talk to, and the thought of it felt like someone driving nails into my chest. "Elaine," I said. "This is crazy. Why are you doing this?"

She didn't look up at me. "Survival, Harry. I promised to help Aurora or to give up my own life as forfeit in payment for all the years she protected me. I didn't know when I made the promise that you were going to be involved." She fell quiet for a moment, then swallowed before she said, her voice forced a little louder, "I didn't know."

"If Aurora isn't stopped, someone is going to get hurt."

"Someone gets hurt every day," Elaine answered.

"When you get right down to it, does it matter who? How? Or why?"

"People are going to *die*, Elaine."

That stung her, and she looked up at me, sharp anger warring with a sheen of tears in her grey eyes. "Better them than me."

I faced her, without looking away. "Better me than you, too, huh?"

She broke first, turning to regard Aurora and Slate. "Looks that way."

I folded my arms and leaned against the back of my toadstool cell. I went over my options, but they were awfully limited. If Aurora wanted me dead, she would be able to see to it quite handily, and unless the cavalry came riding over the hill, there wasn't diddly I could do about it.

Call me a pessimist, but my life has been marked with a notable lack of cavalry. Checkmate.

Which left me with one last spell to throw. I closed my eyes for a moment, reaching inside, gathering up the magic, the life force within me. Any wizard has a reservoir of power inherent in him, power drawn from the core of his self rather than from his surroundings. Aurora's circle could cut me off from drawing upon ambient magic to fuel a spell—but it couldn't stop me from using the energy within me.

Granted, once used, there wouldn't be anything left to keep me breathing, my heart pumping, and electricity going through my brain. But then, that's why they call it a death curse, isn't it?

It was only a moment later that I opened my eyes, to see Aurora draw back from Lloyd Slate. The Winter Knight focused his eyes on me, scary eyes empty of anything like reason, and drew the sword from his belt.

"A grim business," Aurora said. "Good-bye, Mister Dresden."

Chapter

Twenty-eight

I faced Slate head-on. I figured as long as I was going to take one of those swords, it might as well have a shot of killing me pretty quick. No sense in dragging it out. But I left my eyes on Aurora and held whatever power I had gathered up and ready.

"I am sorry, wizard," Aurora said.

"You're about to be," I muttered.

Slate drew back his blade, an Oriental job without enough class to be an actual katana, and tensed, preparing to strike. The blade glittered and looked really, really sharp.

Elaine caught Slate's wrist and said, "Wait."

Aurora gave Elaine a sharp and angry look. "What are you doing?"

"Protecting you," Elaine said. "If you let Slate kill him, he'll break the circle around Dresden."

Aurora looked from Elaine to me and back. "And?"

"Elaine!" I snarled.

She regarded me with flat eyes. "And you'll leave yourself open to his death curse. He'll take you with him. Or make you wish he had."

Aurora lifted her chin. "He isn't that strong."

"Don't be so sure," Elaine said. "He's the strongest wizard I've ever met. Strong enough to make the White Council nervous. Why take a pointless risk so close to the end?"

"You treacherous bitch," I said. "God damn you, Elaine."

Aurora frowned at me and then gestured to Slate. He lowered the sword and put it away. "Yet he is too dangerous to leave alive."

"Yes," Elaine agreed.

"What would you suggest?"

"We're in the Nevernever," Elaine said. "Arrange his death and leave. Once you are back in mortal lands, he won't be able to reach you. Let him spend his curse on Mab if he wishes, or on his godmother. But it won't be on you."

"But when I leave, my power will go with me. He won't be held by the circle. What do you suggest?"

Elaine regarded me passionlessly. "Drown him," she said finally. "Call water and let the earth drink him. I'll lock him into place with a binding of my own. Mortal magic will last, even after I've left."

Aurora nodded. "Are you capable of holding him?"

"I know his defenses," Elaine responded. "I'll hold him as long as necessary."

Aurora regarded me in silence for a moment. "So much rage," she said. "Very well, Elaine. Hold him."

It didn't take her long. Elaine had always been smoother at magic than me, more graceful. She murmured something in the language she'd chosen for her magic, some variant on Old Egyptian, adding a roll of her wrist, a graceful ripple of her fingers, and I felt her spell lock around me like a full-body straitjacket, paralyzing me from chin to toes, wrapping me in silent, unseen force. It pressed against my clothes, flattening them, and made it hard to take a deep breath.

At the same time, Aurora closed her eyes, her hands spread at her side. Then she leveled her palms and slowly raised them. From within the circle, I couldn't sense what she was doing, but there wasn't anything wrong with my eyes and ears. The ground gurgled, and there was a sudden scent of rotten eggs. I felt the earth beneath me shift and sag, and then a slow "bloop bloop" of earth settling as water began rising up beneath me. It took maybe five seconds for the ground to become so soft that my feet sank into the warm mud, up to my ankles. Hell's bells.

"Mortal time is racing," Aurora said, and opened her eyes. "The day grows short. Come."

Without so much as glancing at me, she swept away into the mist. Slate fell into place at her heels, and Talos followed several paces behind, slim and dangerous in his dark armor. Korrick the centaur spared me a sneer and a satisfied snort before he gripped a short, heavy spear in his broad fist and turned to follow the Summer Lady, hooves striking down in decisive clops.

That left Elaine. She came forward until she stood almost close enough to touch me. Slender and pretty, she regarded me steadily while she took a band from her jeans pocket, and bound her hair back into a tail.

"Why, Elaine?" I asked. I struggled furiously against

the spell, but it was stronger than me. "Why the hell did you stop her?"

"You're an idiot, Harry," she said. "A melodramatic fool. You always were."

I kept sinking into the earth and came level with her eyes. "I could have stopped her."

"I couldn't be sure you wouldn't have thrown the curse at me, too." She looked over her shoulder. Aurora had paused, a dim shape in the mist, and was waiting.

The watery earth kept drawing me down, and I looked up at her now, at the soft skin on the underside of her chin. She looked down at me and said, "Goodbye, Harry." She turned and walked after Aurora. Then she paused, one leg bent, and turned enough so that I could see her profile. She said in that same casually neutral tone, "It's just like old times."

After that, they left me there to die.

It's hard not to panic in that kind of situation. I mean, I've been in trouble before, but not in that kind of tick-tock-here-it-comes way. The problem in front of me was simple, steady, and inescapable. The ground kept getting softer and I kept on sliding down into it. The sensation of it was warm and not entirely unpleasant. I mean, people pay money for hot mud baths. But mine would be lethal if I didn't find a way out of it, and the mud was already creeping up over my thighs.

I closed my eyes and tried to focus. I reached out to feel the fabric of Elaine's spell around me, and pushed, trying to break through it. I didn't have enough strength. Once Aurora's circle dropped, I would be able to reach out for more power, but I'd be running short on time—and even so, brute strength wasn't the answer. If I just randomly hammered at the spell around me, it would be like trying to escape from a set of shackles using dynamite. I would tear myself apart along with the binding.

Still, that dangerous option seemed to be my only hope. I tried to hang on, to stay calm and focused, and to wait for Aurora's circle to give out. I got the giggles. Don't ask me why, but under the pressure of the moment, it seemed damned funny. I tried not to, but I cackled and chortled as the warm mud slid up over my hips, my belly, my chest.

"Just like old times," I wheezed. "Yeah, just like old times, Elaine. You backbiting, poisonous, treacherous . . ."

And then a thought hit me. Just like old times.

". . . deceitful, wicked, *clever* girl. If this works I'll buy you a pony."

I put the studied indifference of her words together with her whole bloodless attitude. That wasn't the Elaine I remembered. I could buy that she would murder me in a fit of rage, poison me out of flaming jealousy, or bomb my car out of sheer, stubborn pique. But she would never do it and feel *nothing*.

The mud covered my chest, and still Aurora's circle hadn't faded. My heart pounded wildly, but I struggled to remain calm. I started hyperventilating. I might need every spare second I could get. The mud covered my throat and slid up over my chin. I wasn't fighting it any more. I got a good, deep breath just before my nose went under.

Then darkness pressed over my eyes, and I was left floating in thick, gooey warmth, the only sound the beating of my own heart thudding in my ears. I waited, and my lungs began to burn. I waited, not moving, fire spreading over my chest. I kept everything as relaxed as I could and counted the heartbeats.

Somewhere between seventy-four and seventy-five, Aurora's circle vanished. I reached out for power, gathering it in, shaping it in my mind. I didn't want to rush it, but it was hard not to. I took all the time I could without panicking, before I reached out again for the fabric of Elaine's spell.

I'd been right. It was the same binding she'd used when we were kids, when she'd been holding me down while my old master, Justin DuMorne, prepared to enthrall me. I'd found the way out as a kid, because Elaine and I had shared a certain impatience for our magical studies. Besides schoolwork, we'd been forced to pursue an entirely different regimen of spells and mental disciplines as well. Some nights, we would have homework until dinner, then head right for the magical stuff until well after midnight, working out spells and formulae until our eyes ached.

Toward the end, that got to be rough when all we really wanted was to be in bed, doing things much less scholarly and much more hormonal, until other parts ached. Ahem. To that end, we'd split the work. One of us would work out the spell while the other did the homework, then a quick round of copying and straight to . . . bed.

I'd been the one who worked out that binding. And it sucked.

It sucked because it had no flexibility to it, no subtlety, no class. It dropped a cocoon of hardened air around the target and locked it there, period. End of story. As teenagers, we had thought it impressively effective and simple. As a desperate man about to die, I realized that it was a brittle spell, like a diamond that was simultaneously the hardest substance on earth and easily fractured if struck at the correct angle.

Now that I knew what I was doing, I found the clumsy center of the spell, where I'd located it all those years ago, tying all the strands of energy together at the small of the back like a Christmas bow. There in the mud and darkness, I focused on the weak spot of the spell, gathered my will, and muttered, with my mouth clenched closed, "Tappitytaptap." It came out, "Mmphitymmphmph," but that didn't make any difference on the practical side. The spell was clear in my head. A spike of energy lashed into the binding, and I felt it loosen.

My heart pounded with excitement and I reached out with the spell again. The third time I tried it, the binding slipped, and I flexed my arms and legs, pulling them slowly free.

I'd done it. I'd escaped the binding.

Now I was merely drowning in what amounted to quicksand.

The clock was running against me as I started to

feel dizzy, as my lungs struggled against my will, trying to force out what little air remained and suck in a deep breath of nice, cleansing muck. I reached for more power, gathered it in, and hoped I hadn't spun around without noticing. I pushed my palms toward my feet, just as my lungs forced me to exhale, and shouted with it, *"Forzare!"*

Naked force lashed out toward my feet, bruising one leg as it swept past. Even in magic, you can't totally ignore physics, and my action of exerting force down against the earth had the predictable equal and opposite reaction. The earth exerted force up toward me, and I flew out of the mud, muck and water flying up with me in a cloud of spray. I had a wild impression of mist and dreary ground and then a tree, and then it was replaced with a teeth-rattling impact.

By the time I'd coughed out a mouthful of mud and choked air back into my lungs, I had the presence of mind to wipe mud out of my eyes. I found myself twenty feet off the ground, dangling from the branches of one of the skeletal trees. My arms and legs hung loosely beneath me, and my jeans felt tight at the waist. I tried to see how I'd gotten hung up that way, but I couldn't. I could possibly get a hand and a foot on different branches, but I could barely wiggle, and I couldn't get loose.

"You foil a Faerie Queen," I panted to myself. "Survive your own execution. Get away from certain death. And get stuck up a freaking tree." I struggled some more, just as uselessly. One mud-covered boot fell off and hit the ground with a soggy plop. "God, I hope no one sees you like this."

The sound of footsteps drifted out of the mist, coming closer.

I pushed the heel of my hand against my right eyebrow. Some days you just can't win.

I folded my arms and had them sternly crossed over my chest when a tall, shrouded form emerged from the mist below. Dark robes swirled, a deep hood concealed, and a gloved hand gripped a wooden staff.

The Gatekeeper turned his head toward me and became still for a moment. Then he reached his other gloved hand into his hood. He made a strangled, muffled sound.

"Hi," I said. King of wit, that's me.

The Gatekeeper sounded as though he had to swallow half a gallon of laughter as he responded, "Greetings, Wizard Dresden. Am I interrupting anything?"

My other boot fell off and plopped to the ground. I regarded my dangling, muddy sock-feet with pursed lips. "Nothing all that important."

"That is good," he said. He paced around a bit, peering up at me, and then said, "There's a broken branch through your belt. Get your right foot on the branch below you, your left hand on the one above you, and loosen your belt. You should be able to climb down."

I did as he said and got my muddy self down from the tree and to earth. "Thank you," I said. I privately thought to myself that I'd have been a hell of a lot more grateful about five minutes earlier. "What are you doing here?"

"Looking for you," he said.

"You've been watching?"

He shook his head. "Call it listening. But I have had glimpses of you. And matters are worsening in Chicago."

"Stars and stones," I muttered and picked up my boots. "I don't have time to chat."

The Gatekeeper put a gloved hand on my arm. "But you do," he said. "My vision is limited, but I know that you have accomplished your mission for the Winter Queen. She will keep her end of the bargain, grant us safe passage through her realm. So far as the Council is concerned, that will be enough. You would be safe."

I hesitated.

"Wizard Dresden, you could end your involvement in the matter. You could choose to step clear of it, right now. It would end the Trial."

My aching, weary, half-smothered, and dirty self liked that idea. End it. Go home. Get a hot shower. A bunch of hot food. Sleep.

It was impossible, anyway. I was only one tired, beat-up, strung-out guy, wizard or not. The faeries had way too many powers and tricks to deal with on a good day, let alone on this one. I knew what Aurora was up to now, but, hell, she was getting set to charge into the middle of a battlefield. A battlefield, furthermore, that I had no idea how to even *find*, much less survive. The Stone Table had been in some weird pocket of the Nevernever like nothing I'd ever felt before. I had no idea how to reach it.

Impossible. Painful. Way too dangerous. I could call it a day, get some sleep, and hope I did better the next time I came up to the plate.

Meryl's face came to mind, ugly and tired and resolute. I also saw the statue of Lily. And Elaine, trapped by her situation but fighting things in her own way despite the odds against her. I thought of taking the Unraveling from Mother Winter, able to think of nothing but using it for my own goals, for helping Susan. Now it would be used for something else entirely, and as much as I wanted to forget about it and go home, I would bear a measure of the responsibility for the consequences of its use if I did.

I shook my head and looked around until I spotted my bag, jewelry, staff, and rod on the ground several yards away from the muddy bog Aurora had created. I recovered all of them. "No," I said. "It isn't over."

"No?" the Gatekeeper said, surprise in the tone. "Why not?"

"Because I'm an idiot." I sighed. "And there are people in trouble."

"Wizard, no one expects you to stop a war between the Sidhe Courts. The Council would assign no such responsibility to any one person."

"To hell with the Sidhe Courts," I said. "And to hell with the Council too. There are people I know in trouble. And I'm the one who turned some of this loose. I'll clean it up."

"You're sure?" the Gatekeeper said. "You won't step out of the Trial now?"

My mud-crusted fingers fumbled with the clasp of my bracelet. "I won't."

The Gatekeeper regarded me in silence for a moment and said, "Then I will not vote against you."

A little chill went through me. "Oh. You would have?"

"Had you walked away, I would kill you myself."

I stared at him for a second and then asked, "Why?"

His voice came out soft and resolute, but not unkind. "Because voting against you would have been the same thing in any case. It seems meet to me that I should take full responsibility for that choice rather than hiding behind Council protocol."

I got the bracelet on, then shoved my feet back into my boots. "Well, thanks for not killing me, then. If you'll excuse me, I've got somewhere to be."

"Yes," the Gatekeeper said. He held out his hand, a small velvet bag in it. "Take these. You may find a use for them."

I frowned at him and took the bag. Inside, I found a little glass jar of some kind of brownish gel and a chip of greyish stone on a piece of fine, silvery thread. "What's this?"

"An ointment for the eyes," he said. His tone became somewhat dry. "Easier on the nerves than using the Sight to see through the veils and glamours of the Sidhe."

I lifted my eyebrows. Bits of drying mud fell into my eyes and made me blink. "Okay. And this rock?"

"A piece from the Stone Table," he said. "It will show you the way to get there."

I blinked some more, this time in surprise. "You're helping me?"

"That would constitute interfering in the Trial," he corrected me. "So far as anyone else is concerned, I am merely seeing to it that the Trial can reach its full conclusion."

I frowned at him. "If you'd just given me the rock, maybe," I said. "The ointment is something else. You're interfering. The Council would have a fit."

The Gatekeeper sighed. "Wizard Dresden, this is something I have never said before and do not anticipate saying again." He leaned closer to me, and I could see the shadows of his features, gaunt and vague, inside his hood. One dark eye sparkled with something like humor as he offered his hand and whispered, "Sometimes what the Council does not know does not hurt it."

I found myself grinning. I shook his hand.

He nodded. "Hurry. The Council dare not interfere with internal affairs of the Sidhe, but we will do what we can." He stretched out his staff and drew it in a circle in the air. With barely a whisper of disturbance, he opened the fabric between the Nevernever and the mortal world, as though his staff had simply drawn a circle of Chicago to step into—the street outside my basement apartment, specifically. "Allah and good fortune go with you."

I nodded to him, encouraged. Then I turned to the portal and stepped through it, from that dark moor in Faerie to my usual parking space at home. Hot summer air hit my face, steamy and crackling with tension. Rain sleeted down, and thunder shook the ground. The light was already fading and dark was coming on.

I ignored them all and headed for my apartment. The mud, substance of the Nevernever, melted into a viscous goo that began evaporating at once, assisted by the driving, cleansing rain.

I had calls to make, and I wanted to change into non-slimy clothes. My fashion sense is somewhat stunted, but I still had to wonder.

What do you wear to a war?

Chapter Twenty-nine

I went with basic black.

I made my calls, set an old doctor's valise outside the front door, got a quick shower, and dressed in black. A pair of old black military-style boots, black jeans (mostly clean), a black T-shirt, black ball cap with a scarlet Coca-Cola emblem on it, and on top of everything my leather duster. Susan had given me the coat a while back, complete with a mantle that falls to my elbows and an extra large portion of billow. The weather was stormy enough, both figuratively and literally, to make me want the reassurance of the heavy coat.

I loaded up on the gear, too—everything I'd brought with me that morning plus the Gatekeeper's gifts and my home-defense cannon, a heavy-caliber, long-barreled, Dirty Harry Magnum. I debated carrying the gun on me and decided against it. I'd have to go through Chicago to get to whatever point would lead me to the Stone Table, and I didn't need to get arrested for a concealed carry. I popped the gun, case and all, into my bag, and hoped I wouldn't have to get to it in a hurry.

Billy and the werewolves arrived maybe ten minutes later, the minivan pulling up outside and beeping the horn. I checked the doctor bag, closed it, and went out to the van, my gym bag bumping against my side. The side door rolled open, and I stepped up to toss my gear in.

I hesitated upon seeing the van, packed shoulder to shoulder with young people. There were ten or eleven of them in there.

Billy leaned over from the driver's seat and asked, "Problem?"

"I said only volunteers," I said. "I don't know how much trouble we're going into."

"Right," Billy said. "I told them that."

The kids in the van murmured their agreement.

I blew out my breath. "Okay, people. Same rules as last time. I'm calling the shots, and if I give you an order, you take it, no arguments. Deal?"

There was a round of solemn nods. I nodded in reply and peered to the back of the dim van, at a head of dull green hair. "Meryl? Is that you?"

The changeling girl gave me a solemn nod. "I want to help. So does Fix."

I caught a flash of white hair and dark, nervous eyes from beside Meryl. The little man lifted a hand and gave me a twitching wave.

"If you go along," I said, "same rules as everyone else. Otherwise you stay here."

"All right," Meryl said with a laconic nod.

"Yeah," Fix said. "Okay."

I looked around at all of them and grimaced. They

looked so damned *young*. Or maybe it was just me feeling old. I reminded myself that Billy and the Alphas had already had their baptism by fire, and they'd had almost two years to hone their skills against some of the low-intensity riffraff of the Chicago underground scene. But I knew that they were getting in way over their heads on this one.

I needed them, and they'd volunteered. The trick was to make sure that I didn't lead them to a horrible death.

"Okay," I said. "Let's go."

Billy pushed open the passenger door, and Georgia moved back to the crowded rear seats. I got in beside Billy and asked, "Did you get them?"

Billy passed me a plastic bag from Wal-Mart. "Yeah, that's why it took so long to get here. There was police tape all over and cops standing around."

"Thanks," I said. I tore open a package of orange plastic box knives and put them into the doctor's valise, then snapped it closed again. Then I took the grey stone from my pocket, wrapped the thread it hung by around my hand, and held my hand out in front of me, palm down and level with my eyes. "Let's go."

"Okay," Billy said, giving me a skeptical look. "Go where?"

The grey stone quivered and twitched. Then it swung very definitely to the east, drawing the string with it, so that it hung at a slight angle rather than straight down.

I pointed the way the stone leaned and said, "That-away. Toward the lake."

"Got it," Billy said. He pulled the van onto the street. "So where are we heading?"

I grunted and stuck an index finger up.

"Up," Billy said, his voice skeptical. "We're going up."

I watched the stone. It wobbled, and I focused on it as I might on my own amulet. It stabilized and leaned toward the lake without wavering or swaying on its string. "Up there," I clarified.

"Where up there?"

Lightning flashed and I pointed toward it. "There—up there."

Billy glanced at someone in the back and pursed his lips thoughtfully. "I hope you know a couple of streets I don't, then." He drove for a while more, with me telling him to bear right or left. At a stoplight, the rain still pounding on the windshield, wipers flicking steadily, he asked, "So what's the score?"

"Well-Intentioned But Dangerously Insane Bad Guys are ahead coming down the stretch," I said. "The Faerie Courts are duking it out up there, and it's probably going to be very hairy. The Summer Lady is our baddie, and the Winter Knight is her bitch. She has a magic hankie. She's going to use it to change a statue into a girl and kill her on a big Flintstones table at midnight."

There were a couple of grunts as Meryl pushed her way toward the front of the van. "A girl? Lily?"

I glanced from the stone back to her and nodded. "We have to find Aurora and stop her. Save the girl."

"Or what happens?" Billy asked.

"Badness."

"Kaboom badness?"

I shook my head. "Mostly longer term than that."

"Like what?"

"How do you feel about ice ages?"

Billy whistled. "Uh. Do you mind if I ask a few questions?"

I kept my eyes on the chip of stone. "Go ahead."

"Right," Billy said. "As I understand it, Aurora is trying to tear apart *both* of the Faerie Courts, right?"

"Yeah."

"Why? I mean, why not shoot for just Winter so her side wins?"

"Because she can't," I said. "She's limited in her power. She knows she doesn't have the strength it would take to force things on her own. The Queens and the Mothers could stop her easily. So she's using the only method she has open to her."

"Screwing up the balance of power," Billy said. "But she's doing it by giving a bunch of mojo to Winter?"

"Limits," I said. "She can't move Winter's power around at all, the way she can Summer's. That's why she had to kill her own Knight. She knew she could pour his power out into a vessel of her choosing."

"Lily," growled Meryl.

I glanced over my shoulder at her and nodded. "Someone who would trust her. Who wouldn't be able to protect herself against Aurora's enchantment."

"So why'd she turn the girl to stone?" Billy asked.

"It was her cover," I said. "The Queens could have found an active Knight. But once Lily was turned to stone, the Knight's mantle was stuck in limbo. Aurora knew that everyone would suspect Mab of doing something clever and that Titania would be forced to prepare to fight. Mab would have to move in response, and the pair of them would create the battleground around the Stone Table."

"What's the Table for?"

"Pouring power into one of the Courts," I said. "It belongs to Summer until midnight tonight. After that, any power that gets poured in goes to Winter."

"Which is where we're going now," Billy said.

"Uh-huh," I said. "Turn left at that light."

Billy nodded. "So Aurora steals the power and hides it, which forces the Queens to bring out the battleground with the big table."

"Right. Now Aurora plans to take Lily there and use the Unraveling to free her of the stone curse she's under. Then she kills her and touches off Faerie-geddon. She's got to get to the table after midnight, but before Mab's forces actually take the ground around it. That means she's only got a small window of opportunity, and we need to stop her from using it."

"I still don't get it," Billy said. "What the hell is she hoping to accomplish?"

"Probably she thinks she can ride out the big war. Then she'll put it all together again from the ashes just the way she wants it."

"Thank God she's not too arrogant or anything," Billy muttered. "It seems to me that Mab is going to be handed a huge advantage in this. Why didn't Aurora just work together with Mab?"

"It probably never occurred to her to try it that way. She's Summer. Mab is Winter. The two don't work together."

"Small favors," Billy said. "So what do we do to help?"

"I'm going to have to move around through a battleground. I need muscle to do it. I don't want to stop to fight. We just keep moving until I can get to the Stone Table and stop Aurora. And I want all of you changed before we go up there. Faeries are vindictive as hell and you're going to piss some of them off. Better if they never get to see your faces."

"Right," Billy said. "How many faeries are we talking about?"

I squinted up at a particularly violent burst of lightning. "All of them."

The stone the Gatekeeper had given me led us to the waterfront along Burnham Harbor. Billy parked the van on the street outside the wharves that had once been the lifeblood of the city and that still received an enormous amount of shipping every year. Halogen floodlights every couple of hundred feet made the docks into a silent still life behind a grid of chain-link fence.

I turned to the Alphas and said, "All right, folks. Before we go up, I've got to put some ointment on your eyes. It stinks, but it will keep you from being taken in by most faerie glamours."

"Me first," Billy said at once. I opened the little jar and smeared the dark ointment on under his eyes, little half-moons of dark, greasy brown. He checked his eyes in the mirror and said, "And I used to sneer at the football team."

"Get your game face on," I said. Billy slipped out of

the car and pitched his sweats and T-shirt back in. I got out of the van and opened the side door. Billy, in his wolf-shape, came trotting around the side of the van and sat nearby as I smeared the greasy ointment on the eyes of all the Alphas.

It was a little unnerving, to me anyway. They were all naked as I did it, shimmering into wolf-form as soon as I had finished, and joining Billy outside. One of the girls, a redhead who had been daintily plump, now looked like something from a men's magazine. She gave me a somewhat satisfied smile as I noticed, and the next, a petite girl with mousy brown hair and a long scar on her shoulder, held her dress against her front and confided, "She's been impossible this year," as I smeared ointment on her.

Half a dozen young men and another half a dozen young women, all told, made for a lot of wolf. They waited patiently as I slapped the ointment on Fix, then Meryl, and finally myself. I used the very last of it, and blew out a deep breath. I put on my gun, on a hip rig instead of a shoulder holster, and hoped that the rain and my duster would conceal it from any passing observation. Then I drew my pentacle out to lie on my shirt, gathered up my staff and rod, slipping the latter through the straps on the doctor's bag, and picked it up. I juggled things around for a moment, until I could get the grey stone on its thread out and into my hand, and thought that maybe Elaine had the right idea when it came to going with smaller magical foci.

I had just gotten out into the rain when the wolves all looked out into the night at once. One of them, I think

Billy, let out a bark and they scattered, leaving me and Meryl and Fix standing there alone in the rain.

"W-what?" Fix stammered. "What happened? Where did they go?"

Meryl said, "They must have heard something." She reached back into the minivan and came out with a machete and a wood axe. Then she pulled out a heavy denim jacket that had been festooned in layers of what looked like silverware. It rattled as she put it on.

"No chain mail?" I asked.

Fix fussed with a fork that was sticking out too far and said in an apologetic tone, "Best I could do on short notice. It's steel, though. So, you know, it will be harder for anything to bite her." He hopped back into the minivan and came out with a bulky toolbox that looked heavy as hell. The little guy lifted it to his shoulder as though he did it all the time and licked his lips. "What do we do?"

I checked the stone, which still pointed at the lake. "We move forward. If there's something out there, Billy will let us know."

Fix gulped, his frizzy white hair slowly being plastered to his head by the rain. "Are you sure?"

"Stay close to me, Fix," Meryl said. "How are we going to go that way, Dresden? There's a fence. Harbor security, too."

I had no idea, but I didn't want to say that. I headed for the nearest gate instead. "Come on."

We got to the gate and found it open. A broken chain dangled from one edge. Part of the shattered link lay on the ground nearby. The ends had been twisted, not cut, and steam curled up from them in a little hissing cloud where raindrops touched.

"Broken," I said. "And not long ago. This rain would cool the metal down fast."

"Not by a faerie, either," Meryl said quietly. "They don't like to come close to a fence like this."

"Silly," Fix sniffed. "A cheap set of bolt cutters would have been better than just breaking a perfectly good chain."

"Yeah, nasties can be irrational that way," I said. The stone continued to lean out toward the end of one of the long wharves thrusting into the lake. "Out that way."

We went through the gate and had gone maybe twenty feet before the halogen floodlights went out, leaving us in storm-drenched blackness.

I fumbled for my amulet with cold fingers, but Fix and Meryl both beat me to it. Fix's toolbox thunked down, and a moment later he stood up with a heavy-duty flashlight. At almost the same time, there was a crackle of plastic, and Meryl shook the tube of a chemical light into eerie green luminescence.

A gunshot barked, sharp and loud, and Meryl jerked and staggered to one side. She looked down at blood spreading over her jeans, her expression one of startled shock.

"Down!" I said, and hit her at the waist, bearing her to the ground as the gun barked again. I grabbed at the glow stick and shoved it into my coat. "Put out those lights!"

Fix fumbled with the flashlight as another shot rang out, sending a sputter of sparks from his toolbox. Fix yelped and dropped the light. It rolled over to one side, slewing a cone of illumination out behind us.

The light spilled over the form of the Tigress, the ghoul assassin, not even bothering to try a human shape now. In her natural form, she was a hunch-shouldered, grey-skinned fiend, something blending the worst features of mankind, hyena, and baboon. Short, wiry red hairs prickled over her whole body. Her legs were stunted and strong, her arms too long, and her hands tipped in spurs of bone that replaced nails. Her hair hung about her head in a soggy, matted lump, and her eyes, furious as she came running forward, glared with malice. Pink and grey scars stood out against her skin, swollen areas where she'd healed all the damage Murphy had inflicted on her the night before. She flew toward us over the ground, running with all four limbs, mouth gaping wide.

She didn't see the Alphas closing in behind her.

The first wolf, black grease still in half-circles under its eyes, hit her right leg, a quick snapping, jerking motion of its jaws. The ghoul shrieked in surprise and fell, tumbling. She regained her feet quickly and struck out at the wolf who had bloodied her, but the big grey beast rolled aside as a taller, tawnier wolf leapt over him. The second wolf took the ghoul's other leg, bounding away when the ghoul turned on it, while a third wolf darted in at the Tigress's back.

The ghoul screamed and tried to run again. The wolves didn't let her. I watched as another wolf slammed into her, knocking her down. She rolled to her front, but she'd been hamstrung, and her legs were now useless weight. Claws flashed out and drew flecks of blood, but the wolf she'd hit scrambled onto her back, jaws closing in on the back of the ghoul's neck. She let out a last frantic, gurgling scream.

Then the werewolves buried her in a tide of fur and flashing fangs. When they drew away half a minute later, I couldn't have recognized the remains for what they were. My stomach curled up on itself, and I forced myself to look away before I started throwing up.

I grabbed Meryl underneath her arms and started tugging her toward the nearest warehouse. I snarled, "Help me," at Fix, and he pitched in, surprisingly strong.

"Oh, God," Fix whimpered. "Oh, God, Meryl, oh, God."

"It's not bad," Meryl panted, as we dragged her around a corner of the building. "It isn't too bad, Fix."

I got out the glow stick and checked. Her jeans were stained with blood, black in the green light, but not as badly as they should have been. I found a long tear along the fabric of one leg, and whistled. "Lucky," I said. "Grazed you. Doesn't look like it's bleeding too bad." I poked at her leg. "Can you feel that?"

She winced.

"Good," I said. "Stay here. Fix, stay with her."

I left my bag there and unlimbered my gun. I kept it pointed at the ground and made sure my shield bracelet was ready to go, gathering energy into it in order to shield myself from any more rifle shots. I didn't raise the gun to level. I didn't want it to go off accidentally and bounce a bullet off my own shield and into my head.

As I stepped around the corner, I heard a short scream and then a series of sharp barks. One of the wolves appeared in the cone of Fix's fallen light, picked it up in his mouth, and trotted toward me.

"All clear?" I asked.

The wolf ducked his head in a couple of quick nods and dropped the flashlight on my foot. I picked it up. The wolf barked again and started off toward the wharf. I frowned at him and said, "You want me to follow you?"

He rolled his eyes and nodded again.

I started off after him. "If it turns out that Timmy's stuck down the well, I'm going home."

The wolf led me to the wharf the stone had pointed to, and there I found a young man in dark slacks and a white jacket on the ground in a circle of wolves. He held one bleeding hand against his belly and was panting. A rifle lay on the ground nearby, next to a broken pair of sunglasses. He looked up at me and grimaced, his face pale behind his goatee.

"Ace," I said. I shook my head. "You were the one who hired the ghoul."

"I don't know what you're talking about," he lied. "Get these things away from me, Dresden. Let me go."

"I'm running late, Ace, or I'd have the patience for more chitchat." I nodded at the nearest wolf and said, "Tear his nose off."

Ace screamed and fell back, covering his face with both arms. I winked at the wolf and stepped forward to stand over the changeling. "Or maybe his ears. Or toes. What do you think, Ace? What's going to make you talk fastest? Or should I just try them all one at a time?"

"Go to hell," Ace gasped. "You can do whatever you want, but I'm not talking. Go to hell, Dresden."

Footsteps came up behind us. Meryl limped close enough to see Ace, and then just stood there for a minute, staring at him. Fix followed her, staring.

"Ace," Fix said. "You? You shot Meryl?"

The bearded changeling swallowed and lowered his arms, looking at Meryl and Fix. "I'm sorry. Meryl, it was an accident. I wasn't aiming at you."

The green-haired changeling stared at Ace and said, "You were trying to kill Dresden. The only one besides Ron who has ever taken a step out of his way to help us. The only one who can help Lily."

"I didn't *want* to. But that was their price."

"Whose price?" Meryl asked in a monotone.

Ace licked his lips, eyes flicking around nervously. "I can't tell you. They'll kill me."

Meryl stepped forward and kicked him in the belly. Hard. Ace doubled over and threw up, gasping and twitching and sobbing. He couldn't get enough breath to cry out.

"Whose price?" Meryl asked again. When Ace didn't speak, she shifted her weight as though to repeat the kick and he cried out.

"Wait," he whimpered. "Wait."

"I'm done waiting," Meryl said.

"God, I'll tell you, I'll tell you, Meryl. It was the vampires. The Reds. I was trying to get protection from

Slate, from that bitch Maeve. They said if I got rid of the wizard, they'd fix it."

"Bastards," I muttered. "So you hired the Tigress."

"I didn't have a choice," Ace whined. "If I hadn't done it, they'd have taken me themselves."

"You had a choice, Ace," Fix said quietly.

I shook my head. "How did you know we'd be coming here?"

"The Reds," Ace said. "They told me where you'd show up. They didn't say you wouldn't be alone. Meryl, please. I'm sorry."

She faced him without expression. "Shut up, Ace."

"Look," he said. "Look, let's get out of here. All right? The three of us, we can get clear of this. We need to before we can't help it anymore."

"I don't know what you're talking about," Meryl said.

"You do," Ace said, leaning up toward Meryl, his eyes intent. "You feel it. You hear her Calling us. You feel it just like I do. The Queen Calls us. All of Winter's blood."

"She Calls," Meryl said. "But I'm not answering."

"If you don't want to run, then we should think about what we're going to do. After this battle is over, Maeve and Slate are just going to come for us again. But if we declare a loyalty, if we Choose—"

Meryl kicked Ace in the stomach again. "You worthless trash. All you ever think of is yourself. Get out of my sight before I kill you."

Ace gagged and tried to protest. "But—"

Meryl snarled, "Now!"

The force of the word made Ace flinch away, and he turned it into a scramble before rising to run. The wolves all looked at me, but I shook my head. "Let him go."

Meryl shrugged her shoulders and lifted her face to the rain.

"You okay?" Fix asked her.

"Have to be," she said. Maybe it was just me, but her voice sounded a little lower, rougher. Trollier. Gulp. "Let's move, wizard."

"Yeah," I said. "Uh, yeah." I lifted the Gatekeeper's stone and followed it down the wharf to the last pier, then down to the end of the last pier, empty of any ships or boats. A dozen wolves and two changelings followed me. Nothing but the cold waters of Lake Michigan and a rolling thunderstorm surrounded me at the end of the pier, and the stone twitched, swinging almost to the horizontal on its pale thread.

"No kidding," I muttered. "I know it's up." I reached out a hand and felt something, a tingle of energy, dancing and swirling in front of me. I reached a bit farther, and it became more tangible, solid. I drew up a little of my will and sent it out, toward that force, a gentle surge of energy.

Brilliant light flickering through opalescent shades rose up in front of me, as bright as the full moon and as solid as ice. The light resolved itself into the starry outline of stairs, stairs that began at the end of the pier and climbed into the storm above. I stepped forward and put one foot on the lowest step. It bore my weight, leaving me standing on a block of translucent moonlight over the wind-tossed waters of Lake Michigan.

"Wow," Fix breathed.

"We go up that?" Meryl asked.

"Woof," said Billy the Werewolf.

"While we're young," I said, and took the next step. "Come on."

Chapter Thirty

Sometimes the most remarkable things seem commonplace. I mean, when you think about it, jet travel is pretty freaking remarkable. You get in a plane, it defies the gravity of an entire planet by exploiting a loophole with air pressure, and it flies across distances that would take months or years to cross by any means of travel that has been significant for more than a century or three. You hurtle above the earth at enough speed to kill you instantly should you bump into something, and you can only breathe because someone built you a really good tin can that has seams tight enough to hold in a decent amount of air. Hundreds of millions of man-hours of work and struggle and research, blood, sweat, tears, and lives have gone into the history of air travel, and it has totally revolutionized the face of our planet and societies.

But get on any flight in the country, and I absolutely promise you that you will find someone who, in the face of all that incredible achievement, will be willing to complain about the drinks.

The *drinks*, people.

That was me on the staircase to Chicago-Over-Chicago. Yes, I was standing on nothing but congealed starlight. Yes, I was walking up through a savage storm, the wind threatening to tear me off and throw me into the freezing waters of Lake Michigan far below. Yes, I was using a legendary and enchanted means of travel to transcend the border between one dimension and the next, and on my way to an epic struggle between ancient and elemental forces.

But all I could think to say, between panting breaths, was, "Yeah. Sure. They couldn't possibly have made this an *escalator*."

Long story short: we climbed about a mile of stairs and came out in the land my godmother had shown me before, standing on the storm clouds over Chicago.

But it didn't look like it had before the opening curtain.

What had once been rolling and silent terrain sculpted of cloud, smooth and naked as a dressing dummy, had now been filled with sound, color, and violence. The storm below that battlefield was a pale reflection of the one raging upon it.

We emerged on one of the hills looking down into the valley of the Stone Table, and the hillside around us, lit with flashes of lightning in the clouds beneath, was covered in faeries of all sizes and descriptions. Sounds rang through the air—the crackling snap of lightning and the roar of thunder following. Trumpets, high and sweet, deep and brassy. Drums beat to a dozen different cadences that both clashed and rumbled in time with one another. Shouts and cries rang out in time with those drums, shrieks that might have come from human throats, together with bellows and roars that couldn't have. Taken as a whole, it was its own wild storm of music, huge, teeth-rattling, overwhelming, and charged with adrenaline. Wagner wished he could have had it so good.

Not twenty feet away stood a crowd of short, brown-skinned, white-haired little guys, their hands and feet twice as large as they should have been, bulbous noses the size of lightbulbs behind helmets made out of what looked like some kind of bone. They wore bone armor, and bore shields and weaponry, and stood in rank and file. Their eyes widened as I came up out of the clouds in my billowing black duster, leather slick with rain. Billy and the werewolves surrounded me in a loose ring as they emerged, and Fix and Meryl pressed up close behind me.

On the other side of us stood a troll a good eight feet tall, its skin upholstered in knobby, hairy warts, lank hair hanging greasily past its massive shoulders, tiny red eyes glaring from beneath its single craggy brow. Its nostrils flared out and it turned toward me, drool dribbling from its lips, but the wolves crouched down around me, snarling. The troll blinked at them for a long moment while it processed a thought, and then turned away as though disinterested. More creatures stood within a long stone's throw, including a group of Sidhe knights, completely encased in faerie armor and mounted on long-legged warhorses of deep blue, violet, and black. A wounded sylph crouched nearby and would have looked like a lovely, winged girl from fifty yards away—but from there

I could see her bloodied claws and the glittering razor edge of her wings.

I couldn't see the whole of the valley below. Some kind of mist or haze lay over it, and only gave me the occasional glimpse of whirling masses of troops and beings, ranks of somewhat human things massed together against one another, while other beings, some of which could only be called "monsters," rose up above the rest, slamming together in titanic conflicts that crushed those around them as mere circumstantial casualties.

More important, I couldn't see the Stone Table, and I couldn't even make a decent guess as to where I was standing in relation to where it should have been. The stone the Gatekeeper had given me leaned steadily in one direction, but that led straight down into the madness below us.

"What next?" Meryl yelled at me. She had to shout, though she was only a few feet away—and we were standing above the real fury of the battle below.

I shook my head and started to answer, but Fix tugged on my sleeve and piped something that got swallowed by the sounds of battle. I looked to where he was pointing, and saw one of the mounted Sidhe knights leave the others and come riding toward us.

He raised the visor of his helmet, an oddly decorated piece that somehow seemed insectoid. Pale faerie skin and golden cat-eyes regarded us from atop the steed for a moment, before he inclined his head to me and lifted a hand. The sounds of battle immediately cut off, boom, like someone had turned off a radio, and the silence threatened to put me off balance.

"Emissary," the Sidhe knight said. "I greet thee and thy companions."

"Greetings, warrior," I said in response. "I needs must speak with Queen Mab posthaste."

He nodded and said, "I will guide thee. Follow. And bid thy companions put away their weapons ere we approach her Majesty."

I nodded and said to those with me, "Put the teeth and cutlery away, folks. We need to play nice a while longer."

We followed the knight up the slope of the hill to its top, where the air grew cold enough to sting. I gathered my coat a little closer around me and could almost see the crystals of ice forming on my eyelashes. I just had to hope that my hair wouldn't freeze and break off.

Mab sat upon a white horse at the top of the hill, her hair down, rolling in silken waves to blend in with the mane and tail of her horse. She was clothed in a gown of white silk, the sleeves and trains falling in gentle sweeps to brush the cloudy ground at her steed's feet. Her lips and eyelashes were blue, her eyes as white as moonlit clouds. The sheer, cold, cruel beauty of her made my heart falter and my stomach flutter nervously. The air around her vibrated with power and shone with cold white and blue light.

"Oh, my God," Fix whispered.

I glanced back. The werewolves were simply staring at Mab, much as Fix was. Meryl regarded her from behind a forced mask of neutrality, but her eyes were alight with something wild and eager. "Steady, folks," I said, and stepped forward.

The Faerie Queen turned her regard to me and murmured, "My Emissary. You have found the thief?"

I inclined my head to her. "Yes, Queen Mab. The Summer Lady, Aurora."

Mab's eyes widened, enough that I got the impression that she understood the whole of the matter from that one fact. "Indeed. And can you bring proof of this to us?"

"If I move swiftly," I said. "I must reach the Stone Table before midnight."

Mab's empty eyes flickered to the stars above, and I thought I saw a hint of worry in them. "They move swiftly this night, wizard." She paused and then breathed out, almost to herself, "Time himself runs against thee."

"What can be done to get me there?"

Mab shook her head and regarded the field below us again. One entire swath of the battlefield flooded with a sudden golden radiance. Mab lifted her hand, and the aura around her flashed with a cerulean fire, the air thickening. That flame lashed out against the gold, and the two clashed in a shower of emerald energy, canceling one another out. Mab lowered her hand and turned to look at me again. Her eyes fell on the chip of stone on its pale thread and widened again. "Rashid. What is his interest in this matter?"

"Uh," I said. "Certainly he isn't, uh, you know, it isn't like he's representing the Council and they're interfering."

Mab took her eyes from the battle long enough to give me a look that said, quite clearly, that I was an idiot. "I know that. And your ointment. It's his recipe. I recognize the smell."

"He helped me find this place, yes."

Mab's lips twitched at the corners. "So. What does the old desert fox have in mind this time?" She shook her head and said, "No matter. The stone cannot lead you to the Table. The direct route would place you in the path of battle enough to destroy any mortal. You must go another way."

"I'm listening."

She looked up and said, "Queen of the Air I may be, but these skies are still contested. Titania is at the height of her powers and I at the ebb of mine. Not that way." She pointed to the field, all weirdly lighted mist in gold and blue, green mist swirling with violence where they met. "And Summer gains ground despite all. Our Knight has not taken the field with us. He has been seduced, I presume."

"Yes," I said. "He's with Aurora."

Mab murmured, "That's the last time I let Maeve hire the help. I indulge her too much." She lifted her hand, evidently a signal, and scores of bats the size of hang gliders swarmed up from somewhere behind her, launching themselves in a web-winged cloud into the skies above. "We yet hold the river, wizard, though we lose ground on both sides now. Thy godmother and my daughter have concentrated upon it. But reach the river, and it will take thee through the battle to the hill of the Stone Table."

"Get to the river," I said. "Right. I can do that."

"Those who are mine know of thee, wizard," Mab said. "Give them no cause and they will not hamper thee." She turned away from me, her attention back upon the battle, and the sound of it came crashing back in like a pent-up tide.

I turned from her and went back to the werewolves and the changelings. "We get to the river," I shouted to them. "Try to stay in the blue mist, and don't start a fight with anything."

I started downhill, which as far as I know is the easiest way to find water. We passed through hundreds more troops, most of them units evidently recovering from the first shock of battle: scarlet- and blue-skinned ogres in faerie mail towered over me, their blood almost dull compared to their skin and armor. Another unit of brown-skinned gnomes tended to their wounded with bandages of some kind of moss. A group of sylphs crouched over a mound of bloody, stinking carrion, squabbling like vultures, blood all over their faces, breasts, and dragonfly wings. Another troop of battered, lantern-jawed, burly humanoids with wide, batlike ears, goblins, dragged their dead and some of their wounded over to the sylphs, tossing them onto the carrion pile with businesslike efficiency despite their fellows' feeble screeches and yowls.

My stomach heaved. I fought down both fear and revulsion, and struggled to block out the images of nightmarish carnage around me.

I kept moving ahead, driving my steps with a sense of purpose I didn't wholly feel, and kept the werewolves moving. I could only imagine that it all was worse for Billy and Georgia and the rest—whatever I saw and heard and smelled, they were getting it a lot worse, through their enhanced senses. I called encouragement to them, though I had no idea if they could hear me through the din, and no idea if it did them any good, but it seemed like something I should do, since I'd dragged them here with me. I tried to walk on one side of Fix, screen out some of the worst sights around me. Meryl gave me a grateful nod.

Ahead of us, the bluish mists began to give way to murky shades of green, faerie steel chimed and rasped on faerie steel, and the shrieks and cries of battle grew even louder. More important, amid the screams and shouts I could hear water splashing. We were near the river.

"Okay, folks!" I shouted. "We run forward and get to the river! Don't stop to slug it out with anyone! Don't stop until you're standing in the water!"

Or, I thought, *until some faerie soldier rips your legs off*.

And I ran forward into the proverbial fray.

Chapter
Thirty-one

An angry buzzing sound arose from the musical din of battle ahead of us, and grew louder as we moved forward. I saw another group of goblin soldiers crouched in a ragged square formation. The goblins on the outside of the square tried to hold up shields against whistling arrows that came flickering through the mist over the water, while those within wielded spears against the source of the buzzing sound—about fifty bumblebees as big as park benches, hovering and darting. I could see a dozen goblins on the ground, wracked with the spasms of poison or simply dead, white- and green-feathered arrows protruding from throats and eyes.

A dozen of the jumbo bees peeled off from the goblins and came toward us, wings singing like a shop class of band saws.

"Holy moly!" Fix shouted.

Billy the Werewolf let out a shocked "Woof?"

"Get behind me!" I shouted and dropped everything but my staff and rod. The bees oriented on me and came zipping toward me, the wind stirred up by their wings tearing at the misty ground like the downblast of a helicopter.

I held my staff out in front of me, gathering my will and pushing it into the focus. I hardened my will into a shield, sending it through the staff, focusing on building a wall of naked force to repel the oncoming bees. I held the strike until they were close enough to see the facets of their eyes, swept my staff from right to left, and cried, *"Forzare!"*

A curtain of blazing scarlet energy whirled into place in front of me, and it slammed into the oncoming bees like a giant windshield. They went bouncing off of it with heavy thuds of impact. Several of the bees crash-landed and lay on the ground stunned, but two or three veered off at the last second, circling for another attack.

I lifted my blasting rod, tracking the nearest. I gathered up more of my will and snarled, *"Fuego!"* A lance of crimson energy, white at the core, leapt out from the tip of the blasting rod and scythed across the giant bee's path. My fire caught it across the wings and burned them to vapor. The bee dropped, part of one wing making it spin in a fluttering spiral that slammed into the ground on the bank of the river. The other two retreated, and their fellows attacking the goblins followed suit. The green tones faded from the mist at the edge of the river, which deepened to blue. The goblins let out a rasping, snarling cheer.

I looked around me and found Fix and Meryl staring at me with wide eyes. Fix swallowed, and I saw his mouth form the word "Wow."

I all but tore my hair out in frustration. "Go!" I

shouted and started running for the water, pushing and tugging at them to get them moving. "Go, go, go!"

We were ten feet from shore when I heard hoofbeats sweeping toward the river from the far side. I looked up to see horses sailing through the mist—not flying horses but long-legged faerie steeds, coats and manes shining golden and green, that had simply leapt from the far side of the river, bearing their riders with them.

On the lead horse, the first whose hooves touched the ground on our side of the river, was the Winter Knight. Lloyd Slate was spattered in liquids of various colors that could only be blood. He bore a sword in one hand, the reins to his mount in the other, and he was laughing. Even as he landed, the nearby goblins mounted a charge.

Slate turned toward them, sword whirling and gathering with it a howl of freezing winds, its blade riming with ice. He met the first goblin's sword with his own, and the squat faerie soldier's blade shattered. Slate shifted his shoulders and sent his horse leaping a few feet to one side. Behind him, the goblin's head toppled from its shoulders, which spouted greenish blood for a few seconds before the body fell beside the head on the misty ground. The remaining goblins retreated, and Slate whirled his steed around to face me.

"Wizard!" he shouted, laughing. "Still alive!"

More faerie steeds leapt the river, Summer Sidhe warriors touching down behind Slate in helmets and mail in a riot of wildflower colors. One of them was Talos, in his dark mail, also stained with blood and bearing a slender sword spattered in so many colors of liquid that it looked as if it had cut the throat of a baby rainbow.

Aurora landed as well, her battlegown shining, and a moment later there was a thunder of bigger hooves and a grunt of effort, and Korrick landed on our side of the river, his hooves driving deep into the ground.

Strapped onto the centaur's shoulders, both human and equine, was the stone statue of the kneeling girl—Lily, now the Summer Knight.

Aurora drew up short and her eyes widened. Her horse must have sensed her disturbance, because it half-reared and danced nervously left and right. The Summer Lady lifted her hand, and once more the roar of battle abruptly ceased.

"You," she half whispered.

"Give me the Unraveling and let the girl go, Aurora. It's over."

The Summer Lady's eyes glittered, green and too bright. She looked up at the stars and then back to me, with that same, too-intense pressure to her gaze, and I began to understand. Bad enough that she was one of the Sidhe, already alien to mortal kind. Bad enough that she was a Faerie Queen, driven by goals I didn't fully understand, following rules I could only just begin to grasp.

She was also mad. Loopy as a crochet convention.

"The hour is here, wizard," she hissed. "Winter's rebirth—and the end of this pointless cycle. Over, indeed!"

"Mab knows, Aurora," I said. "Titania will soon know. There's no point to this anymore. They won't let you do it."

Aurora let her head fall back as she laughed, the sound

piercingly sweet. It set my nerves to jangling, and I had to push it back from my thoughts with an effort of will. The werewolves and the changelings didn't do so well. The wolves flinched back with high-pitched whimpers and frightened growls, and Fix and Meryl actually fell to their knees, clutching at their ears.

"They cannot stop me, wizard," Aurora said, that mad laughter still bubbling through her words. "And neither can you." Her eyes blazed, and she pointed her finger at me. "Korrick, with me. The rest of you. Kill Harry Dresden. Kill them all."

She turned and started down the river, golden light burning through the blue mist in a twenty-foot circle around her, and the centaur followed, leaving the battle roar, the horns and the drums, the screams and the shrieks, the music and the terror to come thundering back over us. The Sidhe warriors, a score of them, focused on me and drew swords or lifted long spears in their hands. Talos, in his spell-repelling mail that had enabled him to impersonate an ogre, shook colors from his blade and focused on me with deadly feline intensity. Slate let out another laugh, spinning his sword arrogantly in his hand.

Around me, I heard the werewolves crouch down, growls bubbling up in their throats. Meryl gathered herself to her feet, blood running from her ears, and took her axe in one big hand, drawing her machete into the other. Fix, his ears bleeding, his face pale and resolved, opened his toolbox with shaking hands and drew out a great big old grease-stained monkey wrench.

I gripped my staff and blasting rod and planted my

feet. I called my power to me, lifted my staff, and smote it against the ground. Power crackled along its length and rumbled like thunder through the ground, frightening the faerie mounts into restlessness.

Slate leveled his sword at me and let out a cry, taking the panicked animal from a frightened rear to a full frontal charge. Around him, the warriors of the Summer Court followed, the light of stars and moon glittering on their swords and armor, horses screaming, surging toward us like a deadly, bejeweled tide.

The werewolves let out a full-throated howl, eerie and savage. Meryl screamed, wild and loud, and even Fix let out a tinny battle shriek.

The noise was deafening, and no one could have heard me anyway as I let out my own battle cry, which I figured was worth a shot. What the hell.

"I don't believe in faeries!"

Chapter

Thirty-two

Cavalry charges are all about momentum. You get a ton of furious horses and warriors going in one direction and flattening everything in your way. As the Sidhe cavalry came thundering toward us along the banks of the river, and as my heart pounded in my chest and my legs started shaking in naked fear, I knew that if I wanted to survive the next few seconds, I had to find a way to steal that momentum and use it for myself.

I dropped my blasting rod to grip my staff in both hands and extend it before me. The moment I did, Sidhe riders began making swift warding gestures, accompanied by staccato bursts of magical pressure, separate protective charms rising up before each of them to block whatever magic I was about to throw.

The horses, however, didn't do any such thing.

I raised a shield, but not in a wall in front of me. Such a warding would have brought the faerie nobles into contact with it, and no one wizard could hold a spell against the wills of a score of faerie lords. I brought up a shield only a couple of feet high, and stretched it in a ribbon across the ground at the feet of Slate's mount.

The Winter Knight's steed, a giant grey-green beast, never knew what hit it. The low wall I'd called up clipped it at the knees, and it came crashing down to the misty earth with a scream, dragging Slate down with it. Talos, on Slate's right, could not react in time to stop his mount or to avoid the wall, but he threw himself clear as his horse went down, dropped into a roll as nimble and precise as any martial arts movie aficionado could desire, and came up on his feet. He spun, a dancelike step somehow in time with the vast song of the battlefield, and his sword came whipping at my head.

Dimly, I heard other horses screaming, tripping not only on my wall but on one another now, but I had no idea how well the spell had worked on the rest of the Sidhe warriors. I was too busy ducking Talos's first swing and backing out of range of the next.

Meryl stepped between us and caught Talos's sword in the X formed by her axe and machete. She strained against Summer's Lord Marshal, leaning her whole body into the effort, muscles quivering. I'd felt exactly how strong the changeling girl was, but Talos simply pressed against that strength, his face composed, slowly overcoming her.

"Why do you do this, changeling child?" Talos called. "You who have struggled against Winter so long. It is useless. Stand aside. I wish no harm to thee."

"Like you wish no harm to Lily?" Meryl shouted. "How can you do that to her?"

"It does not please me, child, but it is not for me to decide," Talos answered. "She is my Queen."

"She's not mine," Meryl snarled, and drove her forehead forward, into Talos's nose. She struck him hard enough that I heard the impact, and it drove the faerie lord back several staggered paces.

She didn't see Slate come up from the ground a few feet away and make a quick, squatting lunge at her flank.

"Meryl!" I shouted into the tumult. "Look out!"

She didn't hear me. The Winter Knight's sword bit into her just below her lowest rib, and she took more than a foot of frost-covered steel, thrusting up and back. Slate's sword tore through her and came out through her jacket and the flatware coating it, emerging like some bloody blade of grass. She faltered, her mouth opening in a gasp. Both axe and machete fell from her hands.

"Meryl!" Fix screamed nearby.

Slate laughed and said something I couldn't hear. Then he twisted the blade with a wrenching pop and whipped it back out. Meryl stared at him and reached out a hand. Slate slapped it contemptuously aside and turned his back on her. She fell limply down.

I felt the rage rising and climbed back to my feet, gripping my staff in both hands. Slate reached down and dragged Talos up from the ground with one hand.

"Slate!" I shouted. "Slate, you murdering bastard!"

The Winter Knight's head whipped around toward me. His sword came up to guard. Talos's eyes widened, and his fingers made a series of swift warding gestures.

I gathered my rage together and reached down into the ground beneath me, found the fury of the storm within it that matched my own. I thrust the end of my staff down into the misty cloud-ground as if I'd been driving a hole through a frozen lake, then extended my right hand toward the Winter Knight. *"Ventas!"* I shouted. *"Ventas fulmino!"*

The fury of the storm beneath us reared up through the wood of my staff, electricity rising in a buzzing roar of light and energy coming up from the ground and spiraling around the staff and across my body. It whirled down my extended right arm, a serpent of blue-white lightning, hesitated for a second, and then lashed across the space between me and the tip of Lloyd Slate's sword, fastening onto the blade, and bathing Slate in a writhing coruscation of azure sparks.

Slate's body jerked, his back arching violently. Thunder tore the air apart as the bolt of lightning struck home, throwing Slate into the air and hurling him violently to the ground. The shock wave of the thunder knocked me down, together with everyone else in the immediate area.

Everyone except Talos.

The Lord Marshal of Summer braced himself against the concussion, lifting one hand before his eyes as if it had been a stiff breeze. Then, in the deafening silence that came after, he lifted his sword and came straight toward me.

I reached for my blasting rod, on the ground not far away, lifted it, and threw a quick lash of fire at Talos. The Sidhe lord didn't even bother to gesture it aside. It splashed against him and away, and with a sweep of his sword he sent my blasting rod spinning from my grasp. I lifted my staff as a feeble shield with my left hand, and he struck that away as well.

Some of my hearing returned, enough for me to hear him say, "And so it ends."

"You're damned right," I muttered. "Look down."

He did.

I'd drawn my .357 in my right hand while he'd knocked the staff out of my left. I braced my right elbow against the ground and pulled the trigger.

A second roar of thunder, sharper than the first, blossomed out from the end of the gun. I don't think the bullet penetrated the dark faerie mail, because it didn't tear through Talos like it should have. It hit him like a sledgehammer instead, driving him back and toppling him to the ground. He lay there for a moment, stunned.

It was cheap, but I was in a freaking war and I was more than a little angry. I kicked him in the face with the heel of my boot, and then I leaned down and clubbed him with the heavy barrel of the .357 until his stunned attempts to defend himself ceased and he lay still, the skin of his face burned and blistered where the steel of the gun's barrel struck him.

I looked up in time to see Lloyd Slate, his right arm dangling uselessly, swing the broken haft of a spear at my head. There was a flash of light and pain, and I fell back on the ground, too stunned to know how badly I'd been hit. I tried to bring the gun to bear again, but Slate took it from my hand, spun it around a finger, and lowered the barrel toward my head, already thumbing the hammer back. I saw the gun coming down and saw as well that Slate wasn't going to pause for dramatic dialogue. The second I saw the dark circle of the barrel, I threw myself to one side, lifting my arms. The gun roared, and I waited for a light at the end of what I was pretty sure would be a downward sloping tunnel.

Slate missed. A ferocious, high-pitched shriek of fury made him whip his head to one side as a new attacker entered the fray.

Fix brought his monkey wrench down in a two-handed swing that ended at Lloyd Slate's wrist. There was a crunch of impact, of the delicate bones there snapping, and my gun went flying into the water. Slate let out a snarl and swung his broken arm at Fix, but the little guy was quick. He met the blow with the monkey wrench held in both hands, and it was Slate who screamed and reeled from the blow.

"You hurt her!" Fix screamed. His next swing hit Slate in the side of his left kneecap, and dropped the Winter Knight to the ground. "You hurt Meryl!"

Slate tried to roll away, but Fix rained two-handed blows of the monkey wrench down on his back. Evidently, whatever power it was that let Slate shrug off a bolt of lightning had been expended, or else it couldn't stand up to the cold steel of Fix's weapon. The little changeling pounded on Slate's back, screaming at him, until one of the blows landed on the back of his neck. The Winter Knight went limp and lay utterly still.

Fix came over to me and helped me up. As he did, wolves surrounded us, several of them bloodied, all of them with teeth bared. I looked blearily over them, to see the Sidhe warriors regrouping, dragging a couple of wounded. One horse lay on the ground screaming, the others had scattered, and only one warrior was still mounted, another slender Sidhe in green armor and a masked helm. Weapons still in hand, the Sidhe prepared to charge us again.

"Help me," Fix pleaded, hauling desperately at Meryl's shoulder. I stepped up on wobbly legs, but someone brushed past me. Billy, naked and stained with bright faerie blood, took Meryl under the shoulders, and dragged her back behind what protection the pack of werewolves offered.

"This is going to be bad," he said. "We had an edge—their horses were terrified of us. On foot, I don't know how well we'll do. Almost everyone's hurt. How's Harry?"

"Dammit," Meryl growled thickly. "Let me go. It isn't all that bad. See to the wizard. If he goes down none of us are going home."

"Meryl!" Fix said. "I thought you were hurt bad."

The changeling girl sat up, her face pale, her clothing drenched in blood. "Most of it isn't mine," she said, and I knew she was lying. "How is he?"

Billy had sat me down on the ground at some point, and I felt him poking at my head. I flinched when it got painful. Sitting down helped, and I started to put things together again.

"His skull isn't broken," Billy said. "Maybe a concussion, I don't know."

"Give me a minute," I said. "I'll make it."

Billy gripped my shoulder, relief in the gesture. "Right. We're going to have to run for it, Harry. There's more fight coming toward us."

Billy was right. I could hear the sounds of more horses, somewhere nearby in the mist, and the hammering of hundreds of goblin boots striking the ground in step.

"We can't run," Meryl said. "Aurora still has Lily."

Billy said, "Talk later. Here they come!" He blurred and dropped to all fours, taking his wolf-form again as we looked up and saw the Sidhe warriors coming toward us.

The waters behind them abruptly erupted, the still surface of the river boiling up, and cavalry, all dark blue, sea green, deep purple, rose up from under the waves. The riders were more Sidhe warriors, clad in warped-looking armor decorated in stylized snowflakes. There were only a dozen of them to the Summer warriors' score, but they were mounted and attacking from behind. They cut into the ranks of the Summer warriors, blades flickering, led by a warrior in mail of purest white, bearing a pale and cold-looking blade. The Summer warriors turned to fight, but they'd been taken off guard and they knew it.

The leader of the Winter attack cut down one warrior, then turned to another, hand spinning through a series of gestures. Cold power surged around that gesture, and one of the Summer warriors simply stopped moving, the crackling in the air around him growing louder as crystals of ice seemed simply to erupt from the surface of his body and armor, frozen from the inside out. In seconds, he was nothing but a slowly growing block of ice around a gold-and-green figure inside, and the pale rider almost negligently nudged the horse into a solid kick.

The ice shattered into pieces and fell to the ground in a jumbled pile.

The pale rider took off her helmet and flashed me a brilliant, girlish smile. It was Maeve, the Winter Lady, her green eyes bright with bloodlust, dreadlocks bound close to her head. She almost idly licked blood from her sword, as another Summer warrior fell to one knee, his back to the water, sword raised desperately against the riders confronting him.

The waters surged again, and pale, lovely arms reached out, wrapping around his throat from behind. I caught a glimpse of golden eyes and a green-toothed smile, and then the warrior's scream was cut off as he was dragged under the surface. The Summer warriors retreated, swift and in concert. The rest of the mounted Winter warriors set out in pursuit.

"Your godmother sends her greetings," Maeve called to me. "I'd have acted sooner, but it would have been a fair fight, and I avoid them."

"I need to get to the Table," I called to her.

"So I have been told," Maeve said. She rode her horse over to Lloyd Slate's unmoving form, and her lovely young face opened into another brilliant smile. "My riders are attacking farther down the river, drawing Summer forces that way. You should be able to run upstream." She leaned down and purred, "Hello, Lloyd. We should have a talk."

"Come on, then," grunted Meryl. "Can you walk, wizard?"

In answer, I pushed myself to my feet. Meryl stood too, though I saw her face twist with pain as she did. Fix hefted his bloodied monkey wrench. I recovered my staff, but my blasting rod was nowhere to be seen. The black doctor bag lay nearby, and I recovered it, taking time to check its contents before closing it again. "All right, people, let's go."

We started along the stream at a jog. I didn't know

how far we had to go. Everything around us was chaos and confusion. Once a cloud of pixies flew past us, and I found another stretch over the river where spiders as big as footballs had spun webs, trapping dozens of pixies in their strands. A group of faerie hounds, green and grey and savage, went past hot on the heels of a long pantherlike being headed for the water. Arrows whistled past, and everywhere lay the faerie dead and dying.

Finally, I felt the ground begin to rise, and looked up to see the hill of the Stone Table before us. I could even see Korrick's hulking form at the top, as the centaur backed away from the stone figure of Lily, evidently just set upon the table. Aurora, dismounted, was a slender, gleaming form, looking down upon us with anger.

"Lily!" Meryl called, though her voice had gone thready. Fix whirled to look at her, his eyes alarmed, and Meryl dropped to one knee, her ugly, honest face twisting in pain. "Get her, Fix. Save her and get her home." She looked around, focusing on me. "You'll help him?"

"You paid for it," I said. "Stay here. Stay down. You've done enough."

She shook her head and said, "One thing more." But she settled down on the ground, hand pressed to her wounded side, panting.

Aurora said something sharp to Korrick. The centaur bowed his head to her and, spear gripped in his hand, came down the hill toward us.

"Crap," I said. "Billy, this guy is a heavy hitter. Don't close with him. See if you can keep him distracted."

Billy barked in acknowledgment, and the werewolves

shot forward as the centaur descended, fanning out around him and harrying his flanks and rear while their companions dodged his hooves and spear.

"Stay with Meryl," I told Fix, and scooted around the werewolves' flanks, heading up the hill toward the Stone Table.

I got close enough to the top to see Aurora standing over the statue of Lily. She held Mother Winter's Unraveling in her fingers, pressed against the statue, and she was tugging sharply at the strands, beginning to pull it to pieces. I felt something as she did, a kind of dark gravity that jerked at my wizard's senses with sharp, raking fingers. The Unraveling began to come apart, strand by strand and line by line, under Aurora's slender hands.

I stretched out my hand, adrenaline and pain giving me plenty of fuel for the magic, and called, *"Ventas servitas!"* Wind leapt out in a sudden spurt, seizing the Unraveling and tearing it from Aurora's fingers, sending it spinning through the air toward me. I caught it, stuck my tongue out at Aurora, yelled, "Meep, meep!" and ran like hell.

"Damn thee, wizard!" screamed Aurora, and the sound raked at me with jagged talons. She lifted her hands and shouted something else, and the ground itself shook, throwing me off my feet. I landed and rolled as best I could down the hill until I reached the bottom. It took me a second to drag in a breath, then I rolled to my back to sit up.

Sudden wind slashed at me, slamming me back down to the earth, and tore the Unraveling from my hands. I looked up to see Aurora take the bit of cloth from the air with casual contempt, and start back up the hill. I struggled to sit up and follow, but the wind kept me pinned there, unable to rise from the ground.

"No more interruptions," Aurora spat, and gestured with one hand.

The ground screamed. From it, writhing up with whipping, ferocious motion, came a thick hedge of thorns as long as my hand. It rose into place in a ring around the waist of the hill, so dense that I couldn't see Aurora behind it.

I fought against Aurora's spell, but couldn't overcome it physically, and I didn't even bother to try to rip it to shreds with sheer main magical strength. I stopped struggling and closed my eyes to begin to feel my way through it, to take it apart from the inside. But even as I did, Fix started screaming, "Harry? Harry! Help!"

One of the werewolves let loose a high-pitched scream of agony, and then another. My concentration wavered, and I struggled to regain it. Those people were here because of me, and I would be damned if I would let anything more happen to them. I tried to hang on to the focus, the detachment I would need to concentrate, to unravel Aurora's spell, but my fear and my anger and my worry made it all but impossible. They would have lent strength to a spell, but this was delicate work, and now my emotions, so often a source of strength, only got in the way.

Then hooves galloped up, striking the ground near me. I looked up to see the warrior in green armor, the only rider of those original Sidhe cavalry to stay mounted, standing over me, horse stamping, spear leveled at my head.

"Don't!" I said. "Wait!"

But the rider ignored me, lifted the spear, its tip gleaming in the silver light, and drove it down at my unprotected throat.

Chapter Thirty-three

The spear drove into the earth beside my neck, and the rider hissed in an impatient female voice, "Hold still."

She swung down from the faerie steed, reached up, and took off the masked helm. Elaine's wheat-brown hair spilled down, escaping from the bun it had been tied in, and she jerked it all the way down irritably. "Hold still. I'll get that off you."

"Elaine," I said. I went through a bunch of heated emotions, and I didn't have time for any of them. "I'd say I was glad to see you, but I'm not sure."

"That's because you always were a little dense, Harry," she said, her voice tart. Then she smoothed her features over, her eyes falling half closed, and spread her gloved hands over my chest. She muttered something to herself and then said, "Here. *Samanyana*."

There was a surge of gentle power, and the wind pinning me to the ground abruptly vanished. I pushed myself back to my feet.

"All right," she said. "Let's get out of here."

"No," I said. "I'm not done." I recovered my valise and my staff. "I need to get through those thorns."

"You can't," Elaine said. "Harry, I know this spell. Those thorns aren't just pointy, they're poisonous. If one of them scratches you, you'll be paralyzed in a couple of minutes. Two or three will kill you."

I scowled at the barrier and settled my grip on my staff.

"And they won't burn, either," Elaine added.

"Oh." I ground my teeth. "I'll just force them aside, then."

"That'll be like holding open a screen door, Harry. They'll just fall back into place when your concentration wavers."

"Then it won't waver."

"You can't do it, Harry," Elaine said. "If you start pushing through, Aurora will sense it and she'll tear you apart. If you're holding the thorns off you, you won't be able to defend yourself."

I lowered my staff and looked from the thorns back to Elaine. "All right," I said. "Then you'll have to hold them off me."

Elaine's eyes widened. "What?"

"You hold the thorns back. I'll go through."

"You're going to go up against Aurora? *Alone?*"

"And you're going to help me," I said.

Elaine bit her lip, looking away from me.

"Come on, Elaine," I said. "You've already betrayed her. And I am going through those thorns, with your help or without it."

"I don't know."

"Yeah, you do," I said. "If you were going to kill me, you've already had your chance. And if Aurora finishes what she's doing, I'm dead anyway."

"You don't understand—"

"I know I don't," I snapped. "I don't understand why you're helping her. I don't understand how you can stand by and let her do the things she's done. I don't understand how you can stand here and let that girl die." I let that sink in for a second before I added, quietly, "And I don't understand how you could betray me like that. Again."

"For all you know," Elaine said, "it will happen a third time. I'll let those thorns close on you halfway through and kill you for her."

"Maybe so," I said. "But I don't want to believe that, Elaine. We loved each other once upon a time. I know you aren't a coward and you aren't a killer. I want to believe that what we had really meant something, even now. That I can trust you with my life the way you can trust me with yours."

She let out a bitter little laugh and said, "You don't know what I am anymore, Harry." She looked at me. "But I believe you. I know I can trust you."

"Then help me."

She nodded and said, "You'll have to run. I'm not as strong as you, and this is brute work. I won't be able to lift it for long."

I nodded at her. Doubt nagged at me as I did. What if she did it again? Elaine hadn't exactly been sterling in the up-front-honesty department. I watched as she focused, her lovely face going blank, and felt her draw in her power, folding her arms over her chest, palms over either shoulder like an Egyptian sarcophagus.

Hell, I had ten million ways to die all around me. What was one over another? At least this way, if I went out, I'd go out doing something worthwhile. I turned and crouched, bag and staff in hand.

Elaine murmured something, and a wind stirred around her, lifting her hair around her head. She opened her eyes, though they remained distant, unfocused, and spread both hands to her sides.

Wind lashed out in a column five feet around and drove into the wall of thorns. The thorns shuddered and then began to give, bending away from Elaine's spell.

"Go!" she gasped. "Go, hurry!"

I ran.

The wind almost blinded me, and I had to run crouched down, hoping that none of my exposed skin would brush against any thorns. I felt one sharp tug along my jacket, but it didn't pierce the leather. Elaine didn't let me down. After a few seconds, I burst through the wall and came out in the clear on top of the hill of the Stone Table.

The Table stood where it had been before, but the runes and sigils scrawled over its surface now blazed with golden light. Aurora stood at the Table, fingers flying over the Unraveling, its threads pressed against the head of the statue of the kneeling girl, still upon the table. I circled a bit to one side to stay out of her peripheral vision and ran toward her.

When I was only a few feet away, the Unraveling suddenly exploded in a wash of cold white light. The light washed over the statue in a wave, and as it passed, cold white marble warmed into flesh, her stone waves of hair becoming emerald-green tresses. Lily opened her eyes and let out a gasp, looking around dazedly.

Aurora took Lily by the throat, drove the changeling down to the surface of the Stone Table with her hand, and drew the knife from her belt.

It wasn't all that gentlemanly, but I slugged the Summer Lady in the back with a two-handed swing of my staff.

As I did, the stars evidently reached the right position, and we reached midnight, the end of the height of summer, and the glowing runes on the Table flared from golden light to cold, cold blue.

The blow jarred the knife from Aurora's hand, and it fell to the surface of the Table. Lily let out a scream and got out from under Aurora's hand, rolling across the Table's surface and away from her.

Aurora turned to me, as fast as any of the other Sidhe, leaning back on the Table and planting both feet against my chest. She kicked hard and drove me back, and before I was done rolling she had called a gout of fire and sent it roaring toward me. I got to my knees and lifted my staff, calling together my will in time to parry the strike, deflecting the flame into the misty sky.

The red light of it fell on a green faerie steed leaping in the air above the thorns. It didn't make it over the wall but fell twenty feet short, screaming horribly as it landed on the poisoned thorns. Its rider didn't go down with it, though. Talos, his face bloodied, leapt off the horse's back, did a neat flip in the air, and came down inside the circle of thorns unscathed.

Aurora let out a wild laugh and said, "Kill him, Lord Marshal!"

Talos drew his sword and came for me. I thought the first blow was a thrust for my belly, but he'd suckered me, and the sword darted to one side to send my staff spinning off into the thorns. As he stalked me, I gripped my valise and backed away, looking around me for a weapon, for something to buy me a few seconds, for options.

Then a basso bellow shook the hilltop and froze even Aurora for a second. The wall of thorns shook and quivered, and something massive bellowed again and tore through it, into the open. The troll was huge, and green, and hideous, and strong. It wielded an axe in one hand like a plastic picnic knife and was covered in swelling welts, poisoned wounds, and its own dark-green blood. It had a horrible wound in its side, ichor flowing openly from it. It was dragging itself along despite the wounds, but it was dying.

And it was Meryl. She'd Chosen.

I could only stare as I recognized her features, inside the insane fury of the troll's face. It reached for Talos, and the Lord Marshal of Summer whirled, his bright sword taking off one of the troll's hands. She got the other on his leg, though, and dragged him beneath her even as she fell, the weight of her pinning him down, crushing him to the ground with a choked, gurgling cry of rage and triumph.

I looked back, to see Aurora catch Lily by her green hair, and drag her back toward the Table. I ran to it, and beat her to the knife, a curved number of chipped stone, dragging it across the Table and to me.

"Fool," Aurora hissed. "I will tear out her throat with my bare hands."

I threw the knife away and said, "No, you won't."

Aurora laughed and asked, eyes mad and enticing, "And why not?"

I undid the clasp of the valise. "Because I know something you don't."

"What?" she laughed. "What could you possibly know that matters now?"

I gave her a cold smile and said, "The phone number to Pizza Spress." I opened the bag and snarled, "Get her, Toot!"

There was a shrill, piping blast from inside the valise and Toot-toot sailed up out of it, leaving a trail of crimson sparkles in his wake. The little faerie still wore his makeshift armor, but his weapons had been replaced with what I'd had Billy pick up from Wal-Mart—an orange plastic box knife, its slender blade extended from its handle.

Aurora let out another laugh, uglier, and said, "And what can this little thing do?"

Toot blew another little blast on his trumpet and shouted, voice shrill, "In the name of the Pizza Lord! Charge!"

And the valise exploded in a cloud of crimson sparkles as a swarm of pixies, all armed with cold steel blades sheathed in orange plastic, rose up and streaked toward Aurora in a cloud of red sparkles and glinting knives.

She met my eyes as the pixies came for her, and I saw

the sudden fear, the recognition of what was coming for her. She lifted a hand, golden power gathering there, but one of the pixies reached her, box knife flashing, and ripped across her hand with its blade. She screamed, blood flowing, and the golden light dimmed.

"No!" she howled. "No! Not now!"

The pixies swarmed her, and it wasn't pretty. The bright faerie mail of her gown gave her no protection against the steel blades, and they sheared through it like cardboard. From all directions, in a whirling cloud around her, Toot-toot and his companions struck dozens of times in only a few seconds, the bright steel splashing scarlet blood into the air.

I saw her eyes open, burning brightly, even as zipping, darting death opened up more cuts, flaying her pale skin. She hauled herself toward the Table.

If she died there, bled to death on the table, she would accomplish her goal. She would hurl vast power to the Winter Courts and destroy the balance between the faerie Courts. I threw myself up onto the Table and into her, bearing her back down and to the ground.

She screamed in frustration and struggled against me—but she didn't have any strength. We rolled down the hill a few times, and then wound up on the ground, me pinning her down, holding her there.

Aurora looked up at me, green eyes faded of color, unfocused. "Wait," she said, her voice weak and somehow very young. She didn't look like a mad faerie sorceress now. She looked like a frightened girl. "Wait. You don't understand. I just wanted it to stop. Wanted the hurting to stop."

I smoothed a bloodied lock of hair from her eyes and felt very tired as I said, "The only people who never hurt are dead."

The light died out of her eyes, her breath slowing. She whispered, barely audible, "I don't understand."

I answered, "I don't either."

A tear slid from her eye and mixed with the blood. Then she died.

Chapter Thirty-four

I'd done it. I'd saved the girl, stopped the thief, proved Mab's innocence, and won her support for the White Council, thereby saving my own ass.

Huzzah.

I lay there with Aurora's empty body, too tired to move. The Queens found me maybe a quarter of an hour later. I was only dimly aware of them, of radiant light of gold and blue meeting over me. Gold light gathered over the body for a moment and then flowed away, taking the dead flesh with it. I was left cold and tired on the ground.

The gold light's departure left only cold blue. A moment later, I felt Mab's fingers touch my head, and she murmured, "Wizard. I am well pleased with thee."

"Go away, Mab," I said, my voice tired.

She laughed and said, "Nay, mortal. It is you who must now depart. You and your companions."

"What about Toot-toot?" I asked.

"It is unusual for a mortal to be able to Call any of Faerie, even the lowest, into service, but it has been done before. Fear not for your little warriors. They were your weapon, and the only one accountable for their actions will be you. Take their steel with you, and it will be enough."

I looked up at her and said, "You're going to live up to your side of the bargain?"

"Of course. The wizards will have safe passport."

"Not that bargain. Ours."

Mab's lovely, dangerous mouth curled up in a smile. "First, let me make you an offer."

She gestured, and the thorns parted. Maeve stood there in her white armor, and Mother Winter stood behind her, all shrouded in black cloth. Before them on the ground knelt Lloyd Slate, broken, obviously in pain, his hands manacled to a collar around his throat, the whole made of something that looked like cloudy ice.

"We have a traitor among us," Mab purred. "And he will be dealt with accordingly. After which there will be an opening for a new Knight." She watched me and said, "I would have someone worthy of more trust as his successor. Accept that power and all debts between us are canceled."

"Not just no," I muttered. "Hell, no."

Mab's smile widened. "Very well, then. I'm sure we can find some way to amuse ourselves with this one until time enough has passed to offer again."

Slate looked up, blearily, his voice slurred and panicky. "No. No, Dresden. Dresden, don't let them. Don't let them take me. Take it, please, don't let them keep me waiting."

Mab touched my head again and said, "Only twice more, then, and you will be free of me."

And they left.

Lloyd Slate's screams lingered behind them.

I sat there, too tired to move, until the lights began to dim. I vaguely remember feeling Ebenezar heft me off the ground and get my arm across his shoulders. The Gatekeeper murmured something, and Billy answered him.

I woke up back at my place, in bed.

Billy, who had been dozing in a chair next to the bed, woke up with a snort and said, "Hey, there you are. You thirsty?"

I nodded, throat too dry to speak, and he handed me a glass of cool water.

"What happened?" I asked, when I could speak.

He shook his head. "Meryl died. She told me to tell you that she'd made her Choice and didn't regret it. Then she just changed. We found her on the ground near you."

I closed my eyes and nodded.

"Ebenezar said to tell you that you'd made a lot of people see red, but that you shouldn't worry about them for a while."

"Heh," I said. "The Alphas?"

"Banged up," Billy said, a hint of pride in his voice. "One hundred and fifty-five stitches all together, but we all came out of it more or less in one piece. Pizza party and gaming at my place tonight."

My stomach growled at the word "pizza."

I took a shower, dried off, and dressed in clean clothes. That made me blink. I looked around the bathroom, then peeked out at my bedroom, and said to Billy, "You cleaned up? Did laundry?"

He shook his head. "Not me." There was a knock at the door and he said, "Just a minute." I heard him go out and say something through the door before he came back in. "Visitors."

I put some socks on, then my sneakers. "Who is it?"

"The new Summer Lady and Knight," Billy said.

"They looking for trouble?"

Billy grinned and said, "Just come talk to them."

I glowered at him and followed him out to the main room. It was spotless. My furniture is mostly secondhand, sturdy old stuff with a lot of wood and a lot of textured fabrics. It all looked clean too, and there were no stains in it. My rugs, everything from something that could have flown in the skies of mythic Araby to tourist-trap faux Navajo, had also been cleaned and aired out. I checked the floor underneath the rugs. Mopped and scoured clean. The hod had fresh wood in it, and the fireplace had been not only emptied out but swept clean to boot.

My staff and blasting rod were in the corner, gleaming as if they'd been polished, and my gun hung in its holster, freshly oiled. The gun had been polished too.

I went over to the alcove with the stove, sink, and icebox. The icebox was an old-fashioned one that stocked actual ice, given my problems with electricity. It had been cleaned, and new ice put in it. It was packed with neat rows of food—fresh fruits and veggies, juice, Cokes—and there was ice cream in the freezer. My pantry was full of dry foods, canned foods, pasta, sauces. And Mister had a new litterbox, made of wood, lined with plastic, and full of fresh litter. He had a carved wooden bowl as well, and a mate for water, and he had emptied it of food. Mister himself sprawled on the floor, batting idly at a cloth sack of catnip hanging from a string on the pantry door.

"I died," I said. "I died and someone made a clerical error and this is heaven."

I looked around to find Billy grinning at me like a fool. He hooked a thumb at the door. "Visiting dignitaries?"

I went to the door and opened it warily, peeking around it.

Fix stood there in a set of mechanic's coveralls. His frizzy white hair floated around his head and complemented his smile. He had grease on his hands and face, and his old toolbox sat on the ground next to him. Beside him stood Lily, shapely figure showing off simple dark slacks and a green blouse. Her hair had been pulled back into a ponytail.

And it had turned snow white.

"Harry," Fix said. "How you doing?"

I blinked at them and said, "You? The new Summer Lady?"

Lily flushed prettily and nodded. "I know. I didn't want it, but when—when Aurora died, her power flowed into the nearest Summer vessel. Usually it would be one of the other Queens, but I had the Knight's power and it just sort of . . . plopped in there."

I lifted my eyebrows and said, "Are you okay?"

She frowned. "I'm not sure. It's a lot to think about. And it's the first time this kind of power has fallen to a mortal."

"You mean you're not, uh. You haven't?"

"Chosen?" Lily asked. She shook her head. "It's just

me. I don't know what I'm going to do, but Titania said she'd teach me."

I glanced aside. "And you chose Fix as your Knight, huh."

She smiled at Fix. "I trust him."

"Suits me," I said. "Fix kicked the Winter Knight's ass once already."

Lily blinked and looked at Fix. The little guy flushed, and I swear to God, he dragged one foot over the ground.

Lily smiled and offered me her hand. "I wanted to meet you. And to thank you, Mister Dresden. I owe you my life."

I shook her hand but said, "You don't owe me anything. I'm apparently saving damsels on reflex now." My smile faded and I said, "Besides. I was just the hired help. Thank Meryl."

Lily frowned and said, "Don't blame yourself for what happened. You did what you did because you have a good heart, Mister Dresden. Just like Meryl. I can't repay a kindness like that, and it's going to be years before I can make much use of my . . . my . . ." she fumbled for a word.

"Power?"

"Okay, power. But if you need help, or a safe place, you can come to me. Whatever I can do, I will."

"She had some brownies come clean up your place for you, Harry," Fix said. "And I just finished up with your car, so it should run for you now. I hope you don't mind."

I had to blink my eyes a few times, before I said, "I don't mind. Come on in, I'll get you a drink."

We had a nice visit. They seemed like decent kids.

After everyone left, it was dark, and there was another knock at the door. I answered it, and Elaine stood there, in a T-shirt and jeans shorts that showed off her pretty legs. She had her hair up under a Cubs baseball hat, and she said without preamble, "I wanted to see you before I left."

I leaned against the doorway close to her. "You got out okay, I guess."

"So did you. Did Mab pay up?"

I nodded. "Yeah. What about you? Are you still beholden to Summer?"

Elaine shrugged. "I owed everything to Aurora. Even if she'd wanted to quibble about whether or not I'd paid her back in full, it's a moot point now."

"Where are you going?"

She shrugged. "I don't know. Somewhere with a lot of people. Maybe go to school for a while." She took a deep breath and then said, "Harry, I'm sorry things went like that. I was afraid to tell you about Aurora. I guess I should have known better. I'm glad you came through it all right. Really glad."

I had a lot of answers to that, but the one I picked was, "She thought she was doing something good. I guess I can see how you'd . . . Look, it's done."

She nodded. Then she said, "I saw the pictures on your mantel. Of Susan. Those letters. And that engagement ring."

I glanced back at the mantel and felt bad in all kinds of ways. "Yeah."

"You love her," Elaine said.

I nodded.

She let out a breath and looked down, so that the bill of her hat hid her eyes. "Then can I give you some advice?"

"Why not."

She looked up and said, "Stop feeling sorry for yourself, Harry."

I blinked and said, "What?"

She gestured at my apartment. "You were living in a sewer, Harry. I understand that there's something you're blaming yourself for. I'm just guessing at the details, but it's pretty clear you were driving yourself into the ground because of it. Get over it. You aren't going to do her any good as a living mildew collection. Stop thinking about how bad you feel—because if she cares about you at all, it would tear her up to see you like I saw you a few days ago."

I stared at her for a moment and then said, "Romantic advice. From you."

She flashed me half of a smile and said, "Yeah. The irony. I'll see you around."

I nodded and said, "Good-bye, Elaine."

She leaned up and kissed my cheek again, then turned and left. I watched her go. And illegal mind fog or not, I never mentioned her to the Council.

Later that night I showed up at Billy's apartment. Laughter drifted out under the door, along with music and the smell of delivered pizza. I knocked and Billy answered the door. Conversation ceased inside.

I came into the apartment. A dozen wounded, bruised, cut, and happy werewolves watched me from around a long table scattered with drinks, Pizza Spress boxes, dice, pencils, pads of paper, and little inch-tall models on a big sheet of graph paper.

"Billy," I said. "And the rest of you guys. I just wanted to say that you really handled yourselves up there. A lot better than I expected or hoped. I should have given you more credit. Thank you."

Billy nodded and said, "It was worth it. Right?"

There was a murmur of agreement from the room.

I nodded. "Okay, then. Someone get me a pizza and a Coke and some dice, but I want it understood that I'm going to need thews."

Billy blinked at me. "What?"

"Thews," I said. "I want big, bulging thews, and I don't want to have to think too much."

His face split in a grin. "Georgia, do we have a barbarian character sheet left?"

"Sure," Georgia said, and went to a file cabinet.

I took a seat at the table and got handed pizza and Coke, and listened to the voices and chatter start up again, and thought to myself that it was a whole hell of a lot better than spending another night crucifying myself in the lab.

"You know what disappoints me?" Billy asked me after a while.

"No, what?"

"All of those faeries and duels and mad queens and so on, and no one quoted old Billy Shakespeare. Not even once."

I stared at Billy for a minute and started to laugh. My own aches and bruises and cuts and wounds pained me, but it was an honest, stretchy pain, something that was healing. I got myself some dice and some paper and some pencils and settled down with friends to pretend to be Thorg the Barbarian, to eat, drink, and be merry.

Lord, what fools these mortals be.

Author's Note

When I was seven years old, I got a bad case of strep throat and was out of school for a whole week. During that time, my sisters bought me my first fantasy and sci-fi novels: the boxed set of *Lord of the Rings* and the boxed set of Han Solo adventure novels by Brian Daley. I devoured them all during that week.

From that point on, I was pretty much doomed to join SF&F fandom. From there, it was only one more step to decide I wanted to be a writer of my favorite fiction material, and here we are.

I blame my sisters.

My first love as a fan is swords-and-horses fantasy. After Tolkien I went after C. S. Lewis. After Lewis, it was Lloyd Alexander. After them came Fritz Leiber, Roger Zelazny, Robert Howard, John Norman, Poul Anderson, David Eddings, Weis and Hickman, Terry Brooks, Elizabeth Moon, Glen Cook, and before I knew it, I was a dual citizen of the United States and Lankhmar, Narnia, Gor, Cimmeria, Krynn, Amber—you get the picture.

AUTHOR'S NOTE

When I set out to become a writer, I spent years writing swords-and-horses fantasy novels—and seemed to have little innate talent for it. But I worked at my writing, branching out into other areas as experiments, including SF, mystery, and contemporary fantasy. That's how the Dresden Files initially came about—as a happy accident while trying to accomplish something else. Sort of like penicillin.

But I never forgot my first love, and to my immense delight and excitement, one day I got a call from my agent and found out that I was going to get to share my newest swords-and-horses fantasy novel with other fans.

The Codex Alera is a fantasy series set within the savage world of Carna, where spirits of the elements, known as furies, lurk in every facet of life, and where many intelligent races vie for security and survival. The realm of Alera is the monolithic civilization of humanity, and its unique ability to harness and command the furies is all that enables its survival in the face of the enormous, sometimes hostile elemental powers of Carna, and against savage creatures who would lay Alera in waste and ruin.

Yet even a realm as powerful as Alera is not immune to destruction from within, and the death of the heir apparent to the Crown has triggered a frenzy of ambitious political maneuvering and infighting amongst the High Lords, those who wield the most powerful furies known to man. Plots are afoot, traitors and spies abound, and a civil war seems inevitable—all while the enemies of the realm watch, ready to strike at the first sign of weakness.

Tavi is a young man living on the frontier of Aleran civilization—because let's face it, swords-and-horses fantasies start there. Born a freak, unable to utilize any powers of furycrafting whatsoever, Tavi has grown up relying on his own wits, speed, and courage to survive. When an ambitious plot to discredit the Crown lays Tavi's home, the Calderon Valley, naked and defenseless before a horde of the barbarian Marat, the boy and his family find themselves directly in harm's way.

There are no titanic High Lords to protect them, no Legions, no Knights with their mighty furies to take the field. Tavi and the free frontiersmen of the Calderon Valley must find some way to uncover the plot and to defend their homes against the merciless horde of the Marat and their beasts.

It is a desperate hour, when the fate of all Alera hangs in the balance, when a handful of ordinary steadholders must find the courage and strength to defy an overwhelming foe, and when the courage and intelligence of one young man will save the Realm—or destroy it.

Thank you, readers and fellow fans, for all of your support and kindness. I hope that you enjoy reading the books of the Codex Alera as much as I enjoyed creating them for you.

—Jim

Furies of Calderon, Academ's Fury, Cursor's Fury, Captain's Fury, Princeps' Fury and *First Lord's Fury* are available from Ace Books.

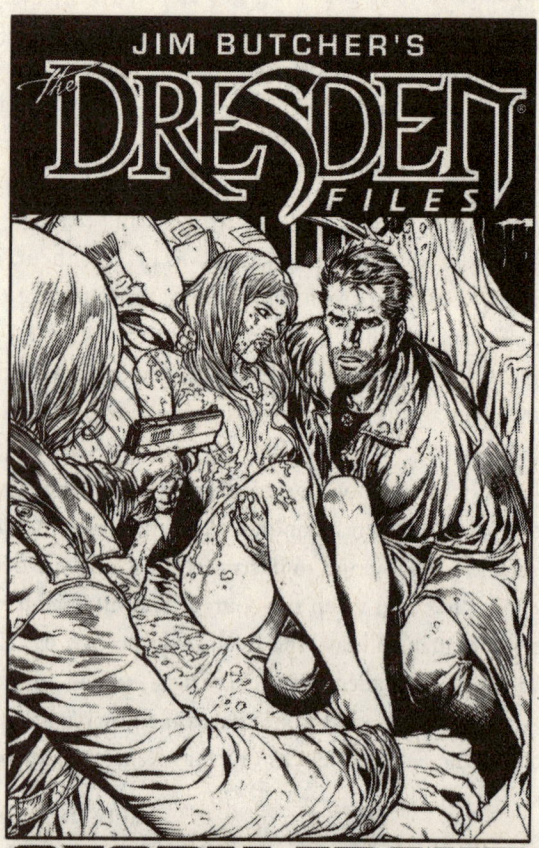

JIM BUTCHER'S
The DRESDEN FILES

STORM FRONT
volume two

HARRY DRESDEN RETURNS!
by Jim Butcher, Mark Powers & Ardian Syaf
Monthly from Dynamite Entertainment!

DYNAMITE ENTERTAINMENT WWW.DYNAMITEENTERTAINMENT.COM

Jim Butcher's The Dresden Files ® and © 2010 Jim Bitcher. All rights reserved. Dynamite, Dynamite Entertainment and the Dynamite Entertainment colophon are ® and © 2010 DFI.

THE DRESDEN FILES
ROLEPLAYING GAME

THE DRESDEN FILES ROLEPLAYING GAME
VOLUME ONE
YOUR STORY

978-0-9771534-7-3 EHP3001

978-0-9771534-8-0 EHP3002

VOLUME TWO
OUR WORLD

on sale July 2010 from your friendly
local game or bookstore — or find them
online at **www.dresdenfilesrpg.com**

ROC

THE DRESDEN FILES

The #1 *New York Times* bestselling series

by Jim Butcher

"Think *Buffy the Vampire Slayer* starring Philip Marlowe." —*Entertainment Weekly*

STORM FRONT

FOOL MOON

GRAVE PERIL

SUMMER KNIGHT

DEATH MASKS

BLOOD RITES

DEAD BEAT

PROVEN GUILTY

WHITE NIGHT

SMALL FAVOR

TURN COAT

CHANGES

Available wherever books are sold or at penguin.com

R0037

ROC

NEW IN HARDCOVER

CHANGES

A Novel of the Dresden Files

By Jim Butcher

Long ago, Susan Rodriguez was Harry Dresden's lover—until she was attacked by his enemies, leaving her torn between her own humanity and the bloodlust of the vampiric Red Court. Susan then disappeared to South America, where she could fight both her savage gift and those who cursed her with it.

Now Arianna Ortega, Duchess of the Red Court, has discovered a secret Susan has long kept, and she plans to use it—against Harry. To prevail this time, he may have no choice but to embrace the raging fury of his own untapped dark power. Because this time Harry's not just fighting to save the world...

Available wherever books are sold or at penguin.com

AVAILABLE NOW

An anthology of all-new novellas of dark nights, cruel cities, and paranormal P.I.s—from four of today's hottest authors.

MEAN STREETS

Includes brand-new stories by

JIM BUTCHER
FEATURING HARRY DRESDEN

KAT RICHARDSON
FEATURING HARPER BLAINE

SIMON R. GREEN
FEATURING JOHN TAYLOR

THOMAS E. SNIEGOSKI
FEATURING REMY CHANDLER

The best paranormal private investigators have been brought together in a single volume—and cases don't come any harder than this.

**Available wherever books are sold or
at penguin.com**